Lesbian Romance:

Loving

the

Heartland

- Lesbian Cowgirl Contemporary Romance Novel

Marjorie Jones

Lesbian Romance:
Loving the Heartland –
Lesbian Cowgirl Contemporary
Romance Novel
A novel by Marjorie Jones
Cover Art by Indie Artist Press
Published by Indie Artist Press
Eagle Mountain, Utah
www.indieartistpress.com
Trade Paperback
copyright © 2014
All rights reserved.
ISBN:978-1-62522-026-4
LARGE PRINT EDITION
February 2015

Look for these other titles by Marjorie Jones
The Jewel and the Sword (Medallion Press)
My Lady's Will (Champagne Books)
The Lighthorseman (Medallion Press)
The Flyer (Medallion Press)
Hope (Indie Artist Press)
Hunting Camion (Indie Artist Press, Writing as Raleigh Kincaid)
Dance in My Heart (Indie Artist Press)
Dawn of Love (Champagne Books, Writing as Starla Childs)
Dawn of Redemption (Champagne Books, Writing as Starla Childs)

To my darling wife and our amazing children...
Honor all families.

If you enjoy this book, please leave a review on Amazon.com!
Indie Artist Press does not receive any percentage of sales from the
works of this independent author. The author earns 100% of the proceeds
from this work of fiction!

One

Bright lights. Big City.

Traffic inched over Las Vegas Boulevard. The slice of Nevada desert glowed bright as day even though the neon-green display on Michelle's dashboard clock read eleven-thirty p.m. Hundreds of tourists meandered along the streets, mingling through the shops and casinos as if time meant nothing. And to them, perhaps it didn't. But to Michelle? Time meant money and she had only fifteen minutes to meet her friend, Lacey Williams, before Lacey had to go back to work.

The great Frank Sinatra, whose indelible imprint still marked Sin City, once said that New York was the city that never slept. Truth be told, Las Vegas ranked a close second in that regard. When she finished her meeting with Lacey, she'd need to race home and put the finishing touches on a project she'd been working on for Brianna Kincaid, one of her biggest clients. She owned the hottest lesbian club in town and was planning to launch a new gay club right next door in the next three weeks.

A gap opened in the lane to her right and she slid her tiny convertible sports car into the slot. Lacey's casino stood on the next corner. She just might make her meeting in time, after all.

Several young men, not one looking older than twenty-two, crossed the street in front of her. The apparent leader of the pack turned in her direction and opened his muscled arms wide, showing off a hard chest beneath a casually-opened dress shirt. "Hey baby," he shouted over her windshield. "You wanna party?"

Oh, yeah. He's toasted.

She gave him her very best I'm-a-local-get-out-of-my-way grin and waited for them to finish crossing the street before she stomped the gas pedal and made for the corner. If they only knew, she thought, shaking her head at the concept that men were all interested in the same thing.

She slipped into the valet parking lane in front of a huge hotel resort and waited for George, the attendant, to claim her car. Gathering her purse, tablet and digital camera, she climbed from behind the wheel.

George, an older guy with a ring of silver hair and a face that would be at home in any mob movie rushed in to take her seat. "Hey there, girly. You lookin' for Lacey?"

"Yup. Is she in her regular pit?" Michelle handed him a ten dollar bill then took the claim ticket.

"Not tonight. She's been workin' the Blackjack table. Pit three, I think."

"Thanks, Georgie. I won't be too long."

More bright lights met her in the lobby. Bells and sirens, laughter and the artificial clank of coins hitting metal trays deafened her as soon as she entered the casino. A slight ache developed in the back of her head.

She dodged a group of elderly ladies making a beeline for the nickel slots and made her way to the Blackjack tables.

Waving to several friends along the way, she skirted the last pit and found a table in the tiny bar on the far side. Less than a minute later, Lacey plopped into the seat across from her.

"I swear, Mike," Lacey declared, using the nickname she'd given to Michelle at their first meeting, "I'm going to have to buy new feet before I ever save enough for next year's tuition." Lacey leaned forward in her chair and rubbed her ankles. They were very nice looking ankles.

Michelle forced her attention back to Lacey's face and smiled. She was a pretty girl, with large, green eyes; perfect skin. Her looks were classic and would fit very well in her chosen career as a television journalist. She was majoring in broadcasting and communication at UNLV. Any station or network would be lucky to have her, someday. "Beats the hell out of working a register or turning burgers for minimum wage, right?"

"True." Lacey leaned back and tugged at the strapless top of her cocktail uniform. The sexy black number barely concealed her ample breasts. "I'll make it quick," she continued. "I know you're busy. I took an early out. Let me run and change, and I'll be right back." Lacey climbed out of the chair and headed toward the employee locker room.

Not for the first time, Michelle admired her friend's

retreat. Naturally blonde and sexy, she exuded confidence and grace. Despite her complaints of sore feet, she moved with an assured sensuality that was purely femme. Michelle was femme, too, but unlike Lacey, these days she could barely walk in low-heeled pumps much less maneuver a casino floor in a strapless mini-dress and four-inch spikes.

She admired Lacey for doing what she had to do in order to finish her education. There was a time when Michelle had done the same thing. Fifteen years earlier, Michelle had been the girl schlepping drinks, hoping for tips big enough to help her make rent. She'd worn the skimpy outfits, put up with men pawing her every chance they got, and sucking up the revulsion. She'd even worn the heels.

Not anymore.

Now she owned her own public relations firm in a city bent on its own self-image. Life was good. With more than a dozen employees, she managed a busy and successful virtual office and produced mobile, internet and print advertising for some of the biggest resorts in a sprawling oasis of decadence and opulence.

Michelle ordered a Long Island Iced Tea and made sure to tip the waitress very well. By the time it arrived, Lacey, looking more comfortable in blue jeans, a UNLV sweatshirt and sensible tennis shoes, reclaimed her seat.

Lacey smiled and waved at the bartender.

"So," Michelle began. "What's so important that it couldn't wait until morning?"

Lacey made an attempt to look coy and relaxed and then, true to her transparent nature, gave up. She preened in her chair and beamed a smile full of even, white teeth. "Okay, I talked to my sister and she thinks it's a great idea. She wants the complete package. Photos. Video. Everything. Oh, and a website. The works."

Michelle choked on her drink. "Are you serious? Miss-I-Have-No-Idea-What-Century-I-Live-In wants a website?"

Lacey's hands fell to her lap and she toyed with her fingernails.

"I knew it. You're lying," Michelle groaned.

"Not entirely. Casey loved the idea and thinks it could only help the ranch!"

"Point in fact. Casey is your brother, not your sister."

"Kendra is practically a man, Michelle; it's not always easy to tell them apart."

Michelle kicked Lacey under the table and gave her a look. They had often discussed how bizarre her family was – five kids, only two girls, and both of them lesbians. "But Casey isn't in charge, is he? Last time we discussed this project, Kendra had no love for anything less than a hundred years old. She wanted no part of your little plan to save the family homestead."

"That's because she's a moron. C'mon, Michelle. Say you'll do it! Please? The ranch has been in our family for over a century – five generations. Once you get there and show Kendra what a great tool the Internet really is, and how powerful the images you're going to produce are, I'm sure she'll come around."

"And in the meantime, I'm doing what? Scurrying about underfoot and making her life miserable? No, thank you."

"You couldn't make anyone miserable if you

tried."

Michelle snorted and took another sip of her drink. "Tell that to my mother."

Lacey rolled her eyes and flopped back in her chair. "So, you'll do it?"

Michelle paused, drilling Lacey with a double-barreled stare. Finally, she sighed. "Yes, I'll do it. But I swear, one of these days, I'm going to learn how to pronounce the word, 'No.'"

"How soon can you leave for Utah?"

"Day after tomorrow, I guess. I only have one project on the wire right now and I'll be finished with the pics tonight. I can turn over the roll-out to Miranda and drive out to your folks place on Wednesday. The rest of the staff manage their own projects and can keep me in the loop on Skype."

"This is going to work. I just know it."

"Don't get your hopes up, Lacey." Michelle's expression fell. "The government has an uncanny way of looking out for itself. If Kendra isn't willing to play their game, the developers might very well take that land for their resort and she'll have to find somewhere else to raise her cows. Money talks, you know?"

"Yeah, I know. But I'm an eternal optimist, remember? The lease doesn't expire for another year, so we have time. We have plenty of time."

Michelle harbored more than a few doubts about this particular project. The first time Lacey had asked her about it, almost six months ago, she had given Michelle all the details surrounding her elder sister. Born a century too late, Kendra Williams seemed the epitome of an old west loner. According to Lacey, she'd raised all four of her siblings, most of them male, alone after her mother and father had been killed in a private plane crash before Lacey had been eight years old. Her descriptions of her sister-turned-guardian fit more readily into the mold of an old western movie than that of a modern ranch owner. She still rode the fences and shoed her own horses. Lacey hadn't watched cable TV while growing up, played video games or anything else a typical American teen should have experienced at the turn of the new century. Of course, Kendra would have been miserable had she actually been born in the old west. Even Calamity Jane had been forced to wear a dress much of the time. Michelle had a feeling that Kendra never would.

Still, Michelle knew how to promote and advertise a business. If she could convince an entire generation of Americans that Las Vegas was the perfect family destination, she could convince anyone of anything. If Kendra remained lost in her dreams of the past, the future would come in and rip out all of those roots she'd so painstakingly protected.

And Michelle's job would be that much harder.

"Screw you, Mac!"

Kendra Williams winced at her brother's lack of respect. Then she slapped him on the back of his head and pulled him away from the Randall County Sheriff, Mac Lawrence. "Settle down, Case. Mind your manners."

"He can't keep us out of that meeting, Kennie."

Kendra dragged her head-strong, younger brother through the lobby of the county courthouse by the breast of his leather biker jacket; past the statue of the coal miner and portraits of twenty Miss Randall Counties, including his twin sister, Lacey. Kendra tossed him toward the double glass doors facing Main Street. "Casey, there is a time and a place for everything, and right now is not the time or the place for your temper. I hate this as much as you do, but we have to live here with these people and pissing of the sheriff isn't going to help our cause."

"That old windbag can't keep us out of a public meeting that has to do with our land!"

"Get your ass in the truck and wait for me."

Casey stood his ground, both an annoying and admirable trait shared by all of the Williams clan. Kendra put her hands low on her hips and released a calming breath. In addition to the stubborn streak, Casey had a knack for dragging trouble with him wherever he went. If he'd just shut up and get in the truck, Kendra could figure out a way to get into that meeting. After a brief moment that felt like ten minutes, Casey turned and strode out of the building.

"He's a pistol, Kennie." The sheriff slid next to her and put his hands in his trouser pockets, his head moving from side to side in forlorn desperation.

Kendra ran a hand through her hair and grimaced, keeping her focus straight ahead. "That he is, Mac. I just wish he'd quit misfiring." She turned to face her old friend. "So, you gonna let me in that meeting?"

"Now, Kendra. The commissioners aren't going to side with some out-of-town developers over you. You know that. What good will it do for you to sit in on a zoning meeting when the request will be denied, anyway? You really didn't even need to come into town for this."

"I lost another forty head last week."

As soon as the words left her mouth, the air in the room changed. Mere tension moved aside for the stirrings of real trouble, sending a finger of electricity over the short hairs on the nape of her neck. Silence stretched for more than a moment before Mac answered.

"Shot?"

"We think so."

Mac released a slow breath and crossed his arms over his chest. Kendra finally looked over at him. She'd known Mac for thirty years. They went to grade school together and then dated briefly in high school before Kendra had grown the balls to tell him she was a lesbian. Not that he'd been much surprised, as she'd found out when he'd breathed a sigh of relief that she wasn't really going to keep faking it. He was the kind of guy who would probably have married her rather than confront her about it.

The high school gym where they'd had this very serious conversation sat about four blocks east of where they stood at that moment. The same school that Mac's daughter, Lenise, attended with Kendra's youngest brother, Brad. Brad and Lenise had been dating for two years and recently attended the junior prom together.

That's what small towns were made of. Families. Generations. Stories.

The Williams' had worked the land and raised beef on a four-hundred acre spread at the Eastern edge of the county for a hundred years. Randall County took its name from her great-grandfather, Colonel John Randall, whose daughter had married a Williams and founded the

Williams Cattle Company. The town hall was named after her uncle, one of the first county commissioners.

No way was a group of dandies from New York City, of all places, going to come in here and take what wasn't theirs.

"Since this whole thing started a year ago, I've lost a grand total of two hundred and twelve cows and three bulls. Now, you want to tell me what I'm supposed to do about that? Who the hell is going to pay for a quarter of a million dollars in stolen and murdered livestock?"

"Damn it, Kennie. This is the twenty first century, you know. What the hell do I know about cattle rustling?' Exasperated, Mac let out another tired breath. He tended to do that when he'd given up the ghost and didn't want anyone to know. Why couldn't he just commit to doing what he needed to do – give her what she wanted? "I'll ask around and see what I can find out."

"You may not know what to do about it, Mac, but I sure as hell do. I have a constitutional right to defend my life and my property. I'm giving you fair warning, if I catch just one of those sons-of-bitches anywhere near my property or my livestock, I'm taking them out."

"Kendra Lorraine Williams, you miserable sonofabitch! This is not the old west. I'll send a deputy out to run your fence lines at least once per shift, but that's about all I can do right now. Don't do anything you're going to regret."

The sheriff's eyes narrowed on her, but she didn't care. For months, her stock had been depleted and if the bastards would steal or kill her cattle, they could just as easily get to her family. In her book, that made them a true threat. If they wanted to play at cattle rustling, she'd give them a game they wouldn't forget. "Go right ahead.

But remember; that's my land for another thirteen months. I have every right to defend it, and my herd."

Two large, wooden doors swung open on the other side of the lobby, drawing her attention to four men wearing fancy suits. She glared at them with five generations of hatred. When they crossed the hard tile floor in her direction, her hands clenched into fists of their own accord.

"Good morning, Miss Williams. Sheriff." The tallest of the men, Harold Mason, nodded his cold greeting with an empty smile. "Have you come to your senses?"

"You're not getting my land, Mason."

"Well, now, Miss Williams, it's not really your land, is it? Some of it is government land and they can lease that land to whomever they see fit."

A flash of fury crashed over Kendra in a wave of heat. In her mind, she lunged for Mason's throat, but in reality, she steeled herself for the real fight.

Mac's familiar gaze fell on her. Quietly he said, "Mr. Mason, I suggest you and your boys head on out before things get ugly around here."

"I'm going to get that land, Miss Williams. It's just a matter of time."

"Yeah, and you'll get my little dog, too, I'm sure. Bring it on, Mason."

Harold Mason grinned like a man who knew something she didn't. "We'll see, little girl. We'll see." The group sauntered out of the courthouse and onto the sidewalk like victorious kings surveying their spoils.

Kendra lifted her Stetson to her head and ran one hand over her jaw. "That bastard is killing my livestock.

He's trying to put me out of business and I swear to God, Mac, I won't let that happen."

After speaking with a member of the zoning commission, she turned and followed the path Casey had taken through the double doors, her cowhide boots echoing on the vintage 1963 tiles.

Damn those citified assholes. She would never allow them to take her land. She had too much invested in it. Blood and sweat. History and honor. All of it wound through the lush pastures and hillsides like a breeze through the trees. She couldn't touch it. No one could walk up and see it. But it was there, as real as the moonlight.

A shining black, extended cab truck rumbled past her as she marched to her own vehicle. The tinted side windows offered no hint to the occupants, but Kendra knew who they were. Mason and his hired band of thieves – also known as lawyers – maneuvered their way through town like they already owned it. If they had their way with the crooked politicians at the state capital, they would own Randall City – the whole damn County – soon enough. The thought made her stomach turn sour.

She pulled open the creaking door of her work truck and threw herself behind the wheel. Casey glared at her. "Did you see that? Those bastards actually smiled at me when they walked by. They smiled, for hell's sake!"

"Now, how the hell could I have seen that? I was in the courthouse until about ten goddamn seconds ago."

"What did the commission tell them?"

Kendra offered Casey a grin. "They said, 'no,' of course. The only way the commission will change the zoning on our land from agricultural to commercial is if we lose the lease and they have no choice but to back that stinking resort. So long as the land has our cattle on it, the commission is on our side."

"And if our cattle aren't on it?"

Kendra turned the key in the ignition and backed out of the parking stall onto Main Street. "Don't matter. Our cattle aren't going anywhere."

"You know you can't fight these guys like it's some kind of range war, right?"

"What would you call it?"

"Times have changed, Sis."

Aw, hell. Here it comes. "I know what you're going to say, Case, and you can save it. I'm not going to hire some person I've never even met to fight my battles for me. Do you have any idea how serious this is?"

"We need the promotion and the publicity, Ken. You can be damn sure those assholes are using every bit of technology they have to make us look like relics."

"I don't care. They brought the fight to me, and I'm fighting them right here. I stood up to the meat companies and the chemical companies, didn't I?"

Kendra made an easy right onto the highway on-ramp and mashed the gas pedal. Black smoke filled her rear view mirror as the diesel engine unwound. She hated this conversation. Last night, Lacey had called from Vegas again, trying to convince her to hire some friend of hers to build a website for the ranch. Kendra had turned the discussion to her studies, her job and her tuition like she always did and Lacey had clammed up tighter than a June bride. Instead, she'd talked to Casey for more than an hour.

Kendra cast her gaze on Casey as she merged onto

the highway behind a double semi-tractor trailer rig hauling coal.

"What, exactly, did you two talk about last night?"

"Nothing. Everything. We're twins, remember? We don't have to talk. We read each other's minds."

Kendra snorted.

Casey stretched his long legs in front of him and grimaced when his motorcycle boots refused to fit beneath the lowest part of the ancient truck's dash. "When are you getting a new truck?"

"Never. Now, what did you two hash out?"

Casey grinned. "She'll be here in about three days."

"I'm going to take a wild guess and say that you don't mean Lace."

"Nope. Her name is Michelle Loving and she's one of the highest paid PR reps and graphic designers in Las Vegas. She's going to build a site for the ranch and develop an entire marketing and promotional campaign for those political folks upstate. Our spread will look so damn good, they'd be crazy to shut us down."

Kendra gripped the steering wheel until her knuckles turned white and threatened to break the weathered skin. What had she done in her previous life to be saddled with a family who ignored her? Left in charge of her younger siblings when she was barely twenty had been hard enough. Now, at thirty-five, half of her brood had turned on her.

The twins had always been her biggest challenge. Single-minded and determined, they tended to get their own way. Casey, more at home on a motorcycle than a horse, had rented a small house in town when he'd returned from his Navy hitch a few months ago. He rarely showed up at the ranch more than a few days a month. Lacey, Casey's elder by twelve minutes, had left home almost three years ago, following a loser named Barry to Vegas. She didn't know that Kendra knew her boyfriend had abandoned her there. To her credit, though, she'd never asked for a handout and had made a life for herself. She found a job and enrolled in school almost right away. In a year, she'll be the first Williams to ever graduate from college.

Kendra sighed. Her brothers and her sister meant more to her than any piece of land. Maybe the fact that the ranch had been their home their entire lives prompted her to fight so hard to keep it.

Hell, she didn't know why she hated change so damn much. Not that it mattered. The world had changed plenty around her and she just plain didn't like it. To Kendra, the world peaked when Armstrong walked on the moon and had careened on a downhill slide ever since. The last thing she needed in her life was some uppity city girl following her around, worried about stepping in something unpleasant for the sole purpose of pulling her into the new millennium. She had enough to worry about just keeping her family and her employees safe. She didn't need some woman underfoot mucking things up even more. "I still don't like it, Casey."

"Can you just trust our judgment, this once? I know you hate the idea, but if we're going to fight these guys on our turf, we have to fight them on theirs, too."

Kendra grunted. She pulled the truck off the main road and onto a small dirt drive. She parked in front of the original homestead, several miles west of the main house her grandfather had built in the forties for her grandmother. The family currently lived there, but they had been fixing up the original house for about three years or so, hammering the nails themselves. Later, they would build another house or two. Eventually, Brent and Brad would get married and have families of their own. Neither of them planned to leave the Heartland, and they'd need places of their own. As serious as Brad and Lenise had become, it wouldn't surprise her if her youngest brother beat the other two down the aisle.

She yanked the manual brake and tossed open her door, which squealed in protest. "I don't like it, but I'll do it." She continued with a bark, "Not that I have a choice! I just don't want her getting in my way, you got it?"

"Aye, Aye, Captain." Casey threw her a mock salute.

"Get out and help me unload the tiles."

Casey slid out of the truck and studied the old Victorian house before joining her at the battered tailgate. Together, they unloaded a dozen cases of ceramic tiles onto the porch. The old wood creaked beneath the weight.

Casey smiled. "It's coming along."

Kendra grinned. "It's livable. I hope your friend doesn't mind a little sawdust."

"You're going to make her stay... here!"

"I hadn't planned on making her stay anywhere, if you'll recall. This is your brainstorm. So, unless you want her to live with you, she can stay here. I don't want to change my life any more than I absolutely have to. Hell, I don't even want her to come here, at all."

"So much for being hospitable and courteous, right? You're going to relegate a guest to living in a half-built relic instead of the perfectly empty room in the main house? Does this place even have running water, yet?"

"Yes, it has running water. And electricity. And four finished rooms, including the kitchen, except for the stove which is on order and will be here in a couple of weeks. It's perfectly livable."

"It's banishment, Kennie. You can't just put Michelle in a corner and hope she goes away. We invited her to come here. She's going out of her way to help us because she's our friend. She's not staying in the back forty."

Kendra's blood threatened to boil over and she shoved open the front door just to get away from Casey.

The more she thought about the waste of time the twins had planned, the more she wanted no part of it. Lace and Case had no idea what they were dealing with.

People like Mason didn't care about the law, or about lobbying government agencies and committees to get what they wanted. They put up a good front, and if they got their way it was a bonus. In the end, though, they would stop at nothing in pursuit of their own greed. They proved it every time one of her cows came up missing. When Kendra failed to agree to sell her land to Harold Mason, things got real ugly, real fast. They would only get worse. Why couldn't anyone else see it? And now, against her better judgment, she added a whole new set of problems to the already crowded list.

The simple truth lay in the fact that lives could be lost in this thing. Some folks might think she lived in the past. They shook their heads when she insisted on riding the fence lines on horseback instead of using the ATV her brother bought for her. Even the neighboring ranches told her to join the twenty-first century and hire a helicopter to help during the round-up.

Not this cowgirl. She preferred the solitude found in the mountain passes on cool summer nights, tempered by the heat of a camp-fire. Damn it, she liked riding the fences and sleeping with a saddle under her head and the stars winking down on her. Nothing in the world matched the exhilaration of running down a stray, roping her and bringing her safely home.

The hair on her arms stood up. Something told her – no matter what happened – all of that was about to change.

Two

Michelle stretched her legs, careful not to touch the brake and dislodge the cruise-control. According to the GPS in her dash, the Williams' ranch should come into view any time. She'd been driving for nearly nine hours, including rest stops, and she was ready to call it a day.

Not for the first time, she shook her head at her current situation. Why had she agreed to do this? She'd never met, or even talked to, Kendra Williams, but the image she carried in her mind – based solely on the descriptions from Lacey and Casey – made her want to turn the car around. How was she supposed to create a marketing and promotion package for the ranch when her client wanted no part of it? It was hard enough to please someone who actually had faith in her!

Cooperation on Kendra's part would be a huge benefit; but Michelle decided not to hold her breath. Rumor had it, held long enough; a person could turn blue and die. But Michelle knew nothing of the cattle business, or land leases, or what rules applied or didn't apply. She'd be working closely with Kendra Williams, whether

Kendra liked it or not.

The car drifted easily around a bend in the highway. Glancing over the passenger side door as the convertible traced the curve of a high, rugged canyon wall, she caught her breath. The Heartland Ranch sat in a wide valley, dotted with stands of Russian Olive and Joshua trees. A stream wound from some hidden crevice in the distant, snow-capped mountains and split the valley floor with a silver tongue. The sky seemed to go on forever with only a few puffy, white clouds lazing near the horizon.

From this distance, she couldn't make out any livestock, but if what Lacey had told her held even a shred of truth, thousands of cows lived in this little slice of what she could only describe as Eden.

Her eyes followed a fence line until she found the main compound. Three huge structures, two barns and a house, sat in the center of a ring made from ancient oaks. She could barely make out the roofline of the house through the late spring foliage, but it must be enormous. The barn loomed even taller, at least a full three stories high. When she drove up the main drive, she couldn't help but smile at the whimsical weathervane twisting atop the copula. A dish, holding hands with a spoon, skipped over a full moon that wore a delightfully cheeky grin. A cow formed one end of the crossbar while a laughing dog clenched its belly on the other.

She brought her car to an unintentional skidding halt on the loose gravel beside a black motorcycle covered in chrome that would have been shining flawlessly had it not been covered in a fine sheen of orange dust, obviously collected during the drive up the long, dirt lane that led to the house. Closing her eyes, she inhaled the pungent air of a working ranch. The aroma of manure mixed with the scent of hay, leather and grease enveloped her. Funny how individually, the scents would not be necessarily kind, but together they smelled of freedom, history and honor.

Still, no matter how serene the surroundings, this job wasn't going to be any nursery rhyme.

"Well, look what the cat drug up!"

At the familiar sound of Casey Williams' voice, Michelle turned. Dressed in a white tee-shirt, black leather vest and black jeans covered with black riding leathers, Lacey's twin brother cut a forbidding image. Michelle knew him well enough to know he had more in common with a kitten than a bear, however, and she rushed from behind the wheel to accept his proffered hug. "Hey, stud. How's the world been treating you?"

"You know me – living the dream. How was your drive over, and how many tickets did you get?"

"It was nice," she replied before adding, "Just one."

Casey reached into the back of her car and pulled her largest suitcase free. "Yeah, but you charmed your way out of the rest, I'm sure."

Michelle laughed and followed him toward the wooden steps leading to a wide porch. "Well, you know me…" She paused as the full façade of the house registered to her tired brain. "Wow. This is a great place. How old is it?"

"Our grandfather built it for our grandmother just after World War II. You'll be staying in Grandma's room."

"I thought the ranch was older than that? Lacey

said over a hundred years?"

"There's another house about four miles up the road." Casey nodded to a dirt road leading away from the compound. "It's even older than this place. Kendra actually thought you might want to stay out there, but we're remodeling it. Slowly. It's not really livable yet, no matter what she thinks. Hell, she'd live in a tent full of holes, if she had to. You'll be here for a couple of months, so if we hurry, you may want to move over there for privacy and such."

At the mention of Kendra's name, Michelle remembered her reasons for being at the ranch in the first place. For a moment, she'd allowed herself to think she was on vacation. The surroundings and the atmosphere coupled with the sprawling main house, complete with leather-clad bell-hop, made for a great fantasy getaway.

"I don't want anyone going to any trouble on my account, Casey."

"No trouble." Casey opened the front door and led Michelle through a large foyer. Her sandals clunked on the hardwood floor; real hardwood, not laminate. An antique sideboard sat against one wall, covered in silver-framed photographs and accented with a huge, beveled mirror.

She caught her reflection and noticed her sunglasses still perched on her nose. She pulled them off and tucked them into the pocket of her wrinkled, pink sundress.

"I had no idea I looked so terrible. Gads."

"You look great. Considering," Casey added with a shrug.

She smacked his arm playfully and laughed.

"Thanks a lot."

Kendra waited until the Loving woman and Casey reached the top of the stairs before she moved from the sitting room to the foyer. She scanned the second floor landing as if searching for a sign that the beautiful woman had actually been there.

Lacey had failed to mention that her little friend was closer to Kendra's age than her own. She'd also neglected to mention that the woman was drop-dead gorgeous. Long, golden hair – folded and tied with a pink, fabric-covered elastic tie at the base of her neck – promised to fall more than half-way down her back when set loose. Kendra's fingers itched to try out the theory. Curved hips swayed beneath the modest sundress. Her tanned, shapely legs called to Kendra and more than her fingers responded.

Kendra spun away from the stairs and headed to the kitchen. Trembling fingers met the handle of the old percolator on the stove.

Damn. What the hell was she thinking? She didn't have time for this. Her body argued that fact with spiraling, moist heat and incessant throbbing. She poured a cup of coffee, leaned her backside against the kitchen counter and ran a hand over her short-cropped hair. Shit. The last thing she needed was a straight-girl crush on top of everything else. Sure she did – because straight-girl crushes always ended so fucking well.

Covered with sweat and dirt, Brent – younger than Kendra by five years, entered the kitchen through the back door. The old screened door slammed shut behind him. Lean good looks and a personable disposition made him a favorite with the ladies. A reasonable, level head made him a favorite with the ranch hands. As second-in-command of the Heartland, he proved reliable and dedicated. Kendra hadn't met a better cattleman in a very long time and took some of the credit for teaching him everything he knew about cows, horses and fair play. Of course, the military had given him a sense of honor, too. All of the Williams boys did a turn in the Navy or the Marines when they came of age. It had been a family tradition since World War I. Hell, even Kendra had enlisted after high school, but two years into her U.S. Marine Corps enlistment, a hardship discharge had called an end to what could have been a pretty promising career.

Brent cursed aloud, dragging Kendra away from the not-so-pleasant memories. He slammed his hat on the counter. Taking a seat at the long, wooden kitchen table, he wiped one large hand over his face and scratched his three day's growth of beard. "We lost another fifteen head last night."

The Williams Cattle Company managed a herd of nearly two thousand cows and twenty-five bulls. In the grand scheme of things, the few animals lost to Mason and his boys didn't seem like a lot. But the attacks came more frequently and the numbers killed or missing each night grew higher and more brazen. *Fifteen in one night.* At this rate, they would be out of business by the first snowfall. Kendra pinched the bridge of her nose and closed her eyes in an attempt to stave off the headache threatening to break free any minute. "Did you find the corpses?"

"Nope. Just the blood trails. Hell, I don't know, maybe it was more than fifteen. I found fifteen trails, that's all I know. Let's you and I pay Mr. Mason a visit, shall we?' He stood and stomped out the kitchen door.

Kendra pushed off the counter, grabbed her hat on the way out of the kitchen and stormed through the same door that Brent had exited. "Whoa, Nellie! Just what the hell do you think you're doing?"

"I'm tired of these goddamned games, Kennie. I'm going to see Mason and end this – once and for all."

Tires crunched over the gravel drive, drawing Kendra's attention to the front of the house. She cursed and rounded the corner just as Mason's truck pulled to a stop beside the Loving woman's little convertible. Damn, even her car was sexy.

"Well, looks like the mountain has come to Muhammad, little brother."

Brent bit his tongue to keep from answering. Mason stepped from the front passenger seat of the extended cab and stretched as if he'd just driven cross country instead of a mere thirty miles. Brent moved across the yard like an animal rushing its prey.

When he reached the side of the truck, he grabbed Mason by the front of his suit jacket and pushed him against the side panel. "Get off our land, you sonofabitch."

Kendra pulled her brother back and stood between them. Brent lunged again, but found himself restrained by his sister's efforts. "Cool it, Brent."

Mason straightened his suit coat and smiled. "Now, Miss Williams... Is that any way to treat a guest?"

"You're not a guest, Mason. You're not invited and

you're not goddamned welcome."

"I came to make you another offer on your land. You drive a hard bargain, and I can respect that. But the fact remains that once I get my hands on the government lease and the zoning changes, your measly few acres won't be of any value to you or me. Sell to me now, and you stand to make quite a bit of money."

"You can't get control of the lease unless you get my land first, and you damn well know it. I'm not going anywhere."

"Calm down, little girl. You haven't heard my latest offer. Three million. If I believe what folks have told me, that's more money than you'll ever see in your lifetime or the next."

"You don't have enough money to buy me out, Mason. You know it, and I know it. This ranch is not for sale." Kendra released the hold on her brother's arm and took a much-calmer step in Mason's direction. "Go to hell."

"Your kind is going extinct, Williams!"

"Not on your life, Mason. Thanks to you killing off my herd, I have a few concerns about the world population of cows, but *my kind* is doing just fine." She poked him hard in the chest. "Now hear me. You won't get my land. Not now, not ever. And the next one of your boys I find within fifty miles of my herd had better come ready for a fight."

The front door crashed open. Kendra glanced toward the house long enough to see Casey and Brad jump from the porch. A second later, they flanked her. Casey leveled their father's thirty-aught-six at Mason's chest, while Brad covered the driver with a twelve gauge.

"You've met my brothers, right?"

Kendra pulled her pistol from her holster and spun the chamber slowly, letting the ominous click punctuate her silence for a moment.

Mason eyed the boys, a slight tic of his upper lip the only sign he felt intimidated. Then he laughed, clapping Kendra on the shoulder before climbing back in the truck. "I like your spirit, Miss Williams. You and your brothers. I'll have my attorney draw up the offer. I have a feeling you'll come around sooner or later." The door slammed shut and the truck pulled away.

Casey tossed the barrel of his rifle to his shoulder. "You know, I really don't like that guy."

Kendra snorted and turned toward the house.

An obviously concerned Michelle Loving crossed her arms over her chest at the top of the porch steps. "What the hell was that about?"

"Nothing. Go back inside." Kendra barely recognized her own voice.

The girl's eyes narrowed and she glared at Kendra. "I'm not going back inside until you explain why Casey and Brad found it necessary to greet that man like this was the O.K. Corral."

Casey ducked his head. "Uh-oh. Now you've done it," he mumbled. "Michelle, this is my big sister, Kendra. Kendra, this is Michelle Loving, from Las Vegas."

"I know who she is, Casey."

Michelle descended the steps and approached Kendra. Taller than she'd first thought, the top of her head came to roughly Kendra's nose. She tilted her head back and placed fisted hands on her hips. "I know exactly who you are," she stated firmly. "I want to know who that man was."

Kendra stood her ground, looking down into Michelle's blue eyes. They were mesmerizing. They matched the color of a summer sky near dawn, when the horizon turned into a bright, fiery ring of color but the stars refused to sleep. Her eyes looked like that band of blue between the two worlds, at the precise moment when day met night.

Rational thought abandoned Michelle's mind when Kendra Williams looked at her that way, as though she could see to the bottom of her soul.

She couldn't remember the question she'd just asked; something about... something. Hell, she could barely remember her own name. M... something.

Kendra squinted and took a step backward. "I have work to do."

She strode toward the barn, taut, lean muscles bunched beneath her jeans and chambray shirt. Michelle's gaze was glued to her backside and she lost track of her surroundings until she heard a voice. She looked to her right to find a dusty, unshaven and unkempt cowboy.

"You'll get used to her. And more importantly, she'll get used to you. She's just under a ton of stress right now, that's all. Just remember, her bark is worse than her bite, until you need to be bitten."

The cowboy took off his hat and nodded his head in her direction. "I'm Brent. It's a pleasure to meet you. We'll let you get settled in today, and then tomorrow I'd be happy to show you around the ranch."

"Michelle Loving. Sounds great."

The younger Williams nodded again and followed Kendra's path into the barn.

"I have homework to finish. Ya'll coming inside?" Brad shouldered his shotgun and turned to the house.

"Yeah." Michelle followed Brad up the steps and made her way back upstairs.

That was Kendra Williams? Her heart fluttered in her chest. She should have known she'd be gorgeous. Lacy possessed a rare beauty and her twin brother wasn't hard to look at either, if you were into that sort of thing. But she'd never considered how good looking Kendra might be. Funny, she'd already decided she would have trouble with her before she'd left home, so what she might look like had never entered her mind.

When Kendra had fastened her sharp, green eyes on Michelle, she had actually been able to hear Kendra's heart beating. Or had it been her own?

Once inside her room, she looked out the window. Kendra pushed through the barn door with a coil of rope thrown over her shoulder. Her lips curled in an absent-minded grimace as she looked up at the sun, as though she were judging the time the same way cowboys did in the old days. She shrugged the heavy ropes higher onto her broad shoulder and swaggered to the corral.

Kendra moved like the earth belonged to her; proud and strong. Like nothing in the world could touch her. When she reached the fence, she climbed onto the bottom rung and draped the ropes over the post. Removing her cowboy hat to reveal short-cropped brown hair styled very much like her brother's, Kendra wiped her brow with the back of one sleeve.

She was exactly the rough and butch kind of woman that attracted Michelle Loving almost exclusively. There was something about a good woman in touch with her masculine side that made Michelle swoon like some femme character in a romance novel. The strength and assurance... The capable attitude and dominating presence... it all came together to make Michelle's knees weak and that secret place between her legs melt like a river of sweet butter.

Kendra shoved her hat back on and whistled sharply. A large horse prancing on the other side of the enclosure whipped its head in her direction.

Even the animals seemed to recognize her power...

The horse hurried to stand in front of Kendra. She removed an oversized leather glove and stroked the animal's neck. The horse bobbed its head lower to grant her access, and then nudged her with its muzzle.

Just then, Kendra turned her attention to the window where Michelle stood—watching. Catching her breath, she dropped the curtain and backed away from the window. Had Kendra seen her staring? Tentatively, she peeked around the curtain. Kendra had returned her attention back to the horse, thankfully.

Michelle fell onto the bed. So what if Kendra had seen her staring? She was probably as arrogant as any man and would expect her to ogle, right? Michelle had more important things to think about than the curve of Kendra William's ass in faded denim, or the way her eyes danced when she looked in her direction, or the little muscle in her jaw that had pulsed ferociously as she'd confronted that man in the front yard.

The man in the yard... Who was he? Her forehead creased as she glanced toward the window. She would not look outside, again. She wouldn't. She forced her attention back to the matter at hand. That man had to have something to do with the reason she was here. Perhaps he was Mason, himself? Whoever he was, Kendra and her brothers had no love for him.

Groaning, she pushed herself off the bed.

Enough!

She glanced out the window again. Kendra was gone, and so was the horse.

Well, Michelle-girl. You sure know how to pick 'em. You've landed yourself right in the middle of a war – complete with a denim-covered cowboi to save the day. Good job.

Pushing aside her own self-directed sarcasm, she changed her clothes and finished unpacking. Most of the furnishings she'd seen so far were antique, but the bedroom suite took her breath away as soon as she'd seen it. A huge bed, intricately carved with a full head and foot board carved from a dark, aged wood took up most of the space. A marble topped dresser with an enormous beveled-glass mirror sat against one wall. A pitcher and bowl set, a silver brush and matching comb with a matching picture frame shimmered on the surface. She fingered the frame and smiled at the black-and-white photo of a young woman, probably Lacey's grandmother.

She closed the empty suitcase and carried it to the closet. When she turned around, she met a wall of a man and screamed.

"Easy, babe." Casey laughed as he caught her shoulders to steady her.

"Good Lord, Casey. Make some noise, why don't you?" One hand moved to her chest as if she could return the erratic beats of her heart to normal.

"But your tax dollars worked so hard to make me stealthy!" He released her and sat on the edge of the bed. "You settling in okay?"

"Yup. This is a really nice place, and this room is fabulous."

"It was my grandmother's. She lived here after Grandpa died because she couldn't stand being in the master bedroom without him. Mom and Dad moved into that room. Later, when Grams died, Kendra lived in here."

"Well, it's very nice."

"You want the tour? Brent's making dinner and we have the time before it's ready."

"Sure." She slipped her bare feet into a pair of fuzzy slippers.

"Where's your room, Casey? I can just imagine the flowered wallpaper and lace curtains." She laughed at the expression of agony that crossed over his handsome features.

"Not even. Nah, my room is pretty much like the rest of the place, these days. The day I joined the Navy and shipped out for basic training, Gladys tore down my rock posters and put away my collection of human skull candle holders."

Michelle shook her head. How could he say that with a straight face? "Who's Gladys?"

"She was kind of a cross between a nanny and a housekeeper. Kennie hired her when we were still underfoot. Hell, Brad was only three when the folks died.

Kenny had more than any twenty-year old could handle. Kids to raise, and a ranch to run."

"I'm sorry. I didn't mean to pry."

Casey shrugged. "No problem. Truth is, I barely remember them. Lace and I were seven or eight. This is your bathroom. You'll have to share, but we tried to clean up some before you got here."

Casey pointed to a door to his left then pushed it open.

A rather standard bathroom lay on the other side. Shower, tub, toilet, sink. She could manage.

She followed him further down the hall. "This is Brad's room?"

"Yup. Brent has an apartment over the barn, and Lacey's room is in the attic. As the only girl, she got the private part of the house. And spoiled rotten, but that's a whole-nother story."

"She's not the only girl," Michelle quipped.

"You know what I mean. We think of Kendra more like a mom, you know? Or maybe it's because Kendra never really came off as a girl. And this last door is Kennie's room. Come on. I want you to see something."

He opened the door and pulled Michelle into a large master bedroom. Light filtered through bona-fide lace curtains with partially drawn shades. Not cheap Venetian blinds, but the kind of shades that blocked all of the sunlight and were covered in a simple fabric with small, cute tassels in the center of the bottom edge. The queen-sized bed, covered in a deep purple comforter and a collection of various throw pillows, was not an antique.

A collection of empty picture frames hung over the bed in place of the headboard. A writing desk, an old rocking chair and a bureau with a man's jewelry box and a pair of spurs on top completed the room.

Simple, with a rustic elegance. Simple she understood, but having finally met the rough rancher in person, the elegance surprised her. Maybe she was more feminine than anyone really gave her credit for?

From the descriptions she'd heard from Lacey, and to a certain extent, Casey on his frequent visits to Vegas, Kendra exuded the Old West. According to her brother and sister, Kendra should live in a dime-store novel, riding trails, sleeping under the stars, chasing outlaws. The organized room spoke of a deeper level to her personality.

"In here," Casey called.

Michelle turned and realized she stood alone in the center of the room. Casey waved to her from a door in the corner.

"I think you're going to like this." He pushed the door open to reveal a paradise of personal hygiene.

A huge claw-foot tub sat on a raised platform across from the door, surrounded on two sides by a shelf lined with empty planters and at least a dozen candles. A separate brass and glass shower stood in the corner, and a wall jutting from the end of the double sink counter apparently hid the toilet. Muted colors of dusty rose and beige placed this particular remodeling project in the mid-eighties. Even the marble counter-top had a thread of rose in the striations.

"Nice, right?"

"This is beautiful. A little dated, but not bad at all."

"Dad had it built for Mom right before the plane went down. I think she might have used it once, if at all."

It looked like a magazine layout. Everything was clean and … sterile. She tilted her head and suddenly felt as if she were invading someone's privacy. But not a live someone. The counter stood void of anything to indicate that Kendra used this space as her own. Rose colored towels hung perfectly on the bars, matching fingertip towels on top. Nothing – no toothbrush, no make-up - not that Kendra wore much, if any at all. Not even a hairbrush was visible.

"Kendra doesn't use this room, does she?"

She heard Casey stifle a sigh. "Nope. She doesn't. Lacey did, though. She loved it in here. I thought maybe after dinner, if you like, you can relax in here a bit. Take advantage of that tub? It's not a shrine or anything."

She smiled and left the bathroom. "No. I mean, thanks and all, but it just wouldn't feel right. This is Kendra's room."

Casey rolled his eyes and closed the bathroom door. "Like, she'd give a rat's ass." He cleared his throat and chuckled. "Anyway, the offer's there if you want it. Come on. Let's see if Brent has finished burning dinner."

Three

Full, robust scents trailed up the stairs, meeting Michelle before she reached the landing. Her stomach rumbled. "Do I smell steak?"

"Yep." Casey groaned. "When Brent cooks, we have steak. It's the only thing he knows how to cook."

Brad bounced down the stairs behind them. "That's not true. He's a great cook. Better than you, Casey. You burn water."

"Bite me, kid." Casey shrugged. "Whatever. So long as I don't have to cook it, I'll eat it."

"You mean, so long as you don't have to pay for it, you old cheapskate," replied the youngest Williams.

Michelle admired the friendly banter between the brothers. An only child, she'd never had that kind of relationship with anyone. Well, until she'd met Lacey. Now that she'd met her friend's family, Michelle understood the strength flowing through her. A girl would need a lot of it to hold her own with brothers like these, and a sister as tough as Kendra.

Brent poked his head through the swinging door which must lead to the kitchen. "Soup's on! Everybody head into the dining room."

Michelle followed Brad and Casey as they stampeded through the small living room and then an archway. They each grabbed a chair and trapped themselves beneath a dining room table big enough to seat at least ten people. Almost everything she'd seen so far looked like a scene out of time. Except for Casey's leather, everything in the room, including the people, spoke of a time long passed. Even the portraits hanging in vintage frames held dull photographs of long-dead relatives.

The front door slammed and heavy footsteps rang through the space. The sharp sound muted as the bearer crossed the Oriental rug in the living room and picked up when boots met hardwood again. Michelle looked over her shoulder.

Kendra took off her cowboy hat and slapped it on her thigh. A small burst of dust escaped, but it seemed like more of a habit than a deliberate action. She must have already cleaned off the Stetson before she came into the house. Worn, tanned leather chaps hugged her thighs, framing the juncture between her legs quite nicely. They may cover her jeans, protecting them from the elements and the earth, but they did nothing to hide the inherent tone of her muscles. Kendra hung the dusty hat on a tree in the corner of the dining room and stared at her brothers.

Bending and twisting at the waist, she unbuckled her chaps and then draped them over another branch of the coat tree. She turned to the sideboard without a sound and poured water from a ceramic pitcher adorned with purple and pink flowers into a large matching basin and rinsed her hands. When she finished, drying her hands on a small, linen towel, she turned to glare at her brothers again. Raising one arched brow, she said, "Gentlemen?"

Casey and Brad stared back at her for a moment, and then shifted their gazes to Michelle. Simultaneous expressions of chagrin—mixed with mutual understanding—crossed their features and they both jumped to their feet.

The sudden rush snapped Michelle's attention away from Kendra's slow, graceful movements. Heat crept up her neck and her heart raced. She'd been staring. Again. Biting her lip, she reached for the chair. Casey beat her to it and pulled it out for her. "Sorry, Michelle. Let me get that."

She tilted her head and looked up at him. "Thanks." Had Kendra chastised her brothers on her account? Lacey was right. Kendra seemed about as old fashioned as they came.

She had settled into the high-backed, cushioned chair before any of the Williams boys took a seat. Kendra seated herself at the head of the table, pulled the linen napkin from beneath the silverware next to her china plate, unfolded it and placed it over her lap. Her hands were steady and sure, her fingers calloused. The backs of her knuckles held more than a few scars and Michelle couldn't help but wonder where each had come from.

"Miss Loving. Do you have everything you need?"

Michelle cleared her throat. "Yes. Thank you."

Kendra nodded and turned her attention to Brad,

seated directly across from her. "Did you finish your homework?"

"Almost."

"Almost doesn't cut it. You finish before you work Apache."

"I can finish before I go to bed, but if I wait till later to train her, I'll lose the light."

Kendra reached for an open bottle of wine on the table and poured herself a moderate glass of dark red merlot. "I don't care. Homework first. If you want to work with Apache, maybe you would be better served to do your homework when you get home from school instead of saving your morning chores for after school. Get up earlier."

When she finished speaking, she placed the rim of a crystal wine glass to her lips and sipped.

Oh, dear. Michelle forced herself to swallow as she turned her gaze away from Kendra's full mouth before someone noticed.

Brad groaned the same way Michelle used to when she was in high school. Everything seemed more important than school work to her, too.

"But, Kendra—"

"That's it, Brad. You have responsibilities on the ranch just like the rest of us. Right now, that responsibility is to earn sufficient grades to graduate. Training that filly for your girlfriend is a noble and kind thing. But it doesn't mean you can slack off on your studies."

"Yes, ma'am."

Brent backed through the swinging door carrying a platter of steaks. He placed it in the center of the table then took the seat beside Brad. "Kendra, it's your turn."

The men bowed their heads and folded their hands in front of them, forearms resting on the edge of the table. Kendra did the same, the lines at the corner of her eyes softening just enough to make a difference. Suddenly less than comfortable, Michelle felt like she had intruded again. She imitated the postures surrounding her.

"Father in heaven, we thank you for the life you've given us; now and for eternity. We thank you for the strength to fight our battles with pride and honor. Please, lay your blessings upon the food you have given us and make us worthy to accept it. Amen."

A mumbled chorus finalized the offered grace before the Williams men pulled the lids off of various serving dishes. Steaming potatoes and green beans filled two of the bowls, while a platter at the other end of the table held a dozen bright yellow ears of corn.

Casey picked up Michelle's plate. "Here, let me get you set up, Michelle. What would you like? Steak?"

She nodded. "Yes, please. It looks wonderful."

"Rare? Medium?"

"Rare, please."

Casey dug around the platter until he found the right piece for her and then continued to fill her plate. When he set it back in front of her, it contained a feast she'd never be able to finish.

Once everyone had been served, Michelle said, "You really didn't need to go to all this trouble for me. I mean, the silver and china; this great meal. I don't want to put anyone out."

Kendra shifted in her seat, but did not look up from her plate. "We didn't."

Brent raised a mouthful of steak to his lips, but stopped before speaking. "What she means is, we always eat family meals. This is normal for us."

"You guys eat on china every day?"

"Yep. We're all pretty busy and this is the one time of day when we're all in the same place at the same time. Might as well make the most of it."

"I think that's wonderful. Most people eat on the run these days. I know most of my meals come in Styrofoam boxes."

The meal progressed with easy conversation. Kendra remained silent through it all, but Michelle felt her presence like a distant wild wind; visible on the horizon, but never quite reaching her.

From the corner of her eye, Michelle studied Kendra's movements. Efficient. Determined. The gentle hold she placed on the delicate silverware and the light touch that she used to grasp the crystal stemware contradicted her appearance. She seemed out of place, even in the antique world in which she'd chosen to live. Her clothes and gruff attitude belied her gentle manners and stoic silence.

"What is it you do exactly, Miss Loving?"

Kendra's voice sounded firm. Not unfriendly, but measured and deliberate. It startled Michelle and she dropped her fork, the clank of silver on china echoed the beginning of a short, awkward silence.

She retrieved the fork and sliced another piece of steak. "I'm a public relations consultant. I create marketing campaigns, mostly online. I tell people what to think."

"In my experience, people think what they want to

think."

"To a certain extent, that's true. Individuals have the ability to think for themselves and make decisions based on what is best for them, but conformity is also a human trait. Trends and fads are nothing new, and I help to create those trends and fads."

Kendra scoffed. "Sheep."

"Pardon me?"

"You breed sheep, Miss Loving. You count on the fact that large segments of the population tend to follow the same patterns. Not everyone does."

"I create marketing campaigns that bring certain issues, businesses, and even people, into a better light among the masses."

"Marketing campaigns." Kendra placed her knife and fork together on the plate at the four o'clock position one might use at a fancy restaurant to let the server know the diner had completed her meal. Michelle half-expected a uniformed busboy to come from the kitchen and collect the dishes.

"Yes. Marketing campaigns," she replied, matter-of-factly.

"And how do you apply that to a working cattle ranch?"

"Well," she said, hedging her thoughts. *Here we go.* "Lacey explained a little bit of what has been happening here. You're in danger of losing your range lease and we thought we could build a comprehensive website to increase the value of the ranch to the community, as well as show the people that issued the lease just how valuable you and your community find it. Show them the land is being used for the purpose intended and there's no need to change anything."

"'Increase community value?'" Kendra quoted, turning Michelle's matter-of-fact statement into a question. No, not really a question...

An accusation.

Had she heard anything she'd said? Or did she only hear what she wanted? For Lacey's sake, she smiled through her annoyance. "Yes. We will be increasing the value that the community places on the ranch."

"How do you plan to do that?"

"We would like to have a portion of the site dedicated to education. For instance, students who have no access to this lifestyle can learn about what you do here."

Kendra skidded her chair back a few inches and crossed one ankle over her knee. "And you think showing them the beef raising process will do that. How?"

Michelle sensed Kendra's reluctance like a hammer in her chest. Subtlety was not this woman's forte. Michelle put down her silverware and leaned back in her chair. Crossing her arms, she glared at Kendra. "It will show the global community that this ranch is a valuable asset to our nation's history and culture. And people, especially politicians, *like* community service. And if they can take credit for supporting something along those lines, they will."

"I don't buy it."

"Kennie, why don't you –"

Kendra cut off Brad's comment with one raised finger, but didn't look at him. "Miss Loving –"

Did Kendra just growl at her?

"I appreciate your motives," Kendra continued, "and those of my misguided family, but I don't hold any hope that this little project of yours will do anything but cost me a shit-load of money, not to mention the distraction it will cause when we have more important problems to worry about. I've agreed to let you do this. I've agreed to pay for it. But, you will stay out of my way. You won't cause me any more problems or headaches than I already have. Take your pictures. Write your stories, or lessons, or whatever you're going to do. Just don't think for one minute that I'm going to help you do it."

Kendra grabbed her hat and stomped out of the house. Why did the woman have to smell so damn good? Like honeysuckles and spring rain.

She'd changed her clothes, too. She looked even better in blue jeans than she had in that little dress. Her hair was still tucked up on itself and when she'd come up behind her, before dinner, when her face had turned over her shoulder watching Kendra approach, she'd been oh-so-tempted to pull it free. She wanted to watch it fall over her shoulders and down her back.

Her naked back.

Throwing open the barn door, Kendra stepped inside and waited for her eyes to adjust to the darkness. Apache whinnied and her mother, Navajo, echoed the sound. When she could see clearly, she moved to the third empty stall and lifted her saddle from its perch.

A long ride. That's what she needed. A night on

the range overseeing the herd. She'd bring her fence kit along and make some repairs. Maybe she'd find where Mason's boys were coming through. When she left the barn through the opposite end, she whistled to Preakness, her quarter-horse gelding. The tall Grey trotted from the other side of the corral and nudged her in the cheek with his velvety muzzle.

The sun reflected off the weathervane she'd made for Lacey almost fifteen years ago, sending rays of light onto the dusty ground. She looked behind her as the fireball dipped its bottom edge below the horizon. She'd have to hurry if she planned to make the night-watch camp before it grew too dark to see.

"You were a bit rough on her, weren't you, Sis?"

"I don't have time to chat, Brent. I'm taking the night watch. I'll send Ken Bastian back in the morning."

"Ken is scheduled to be out there for two days. I think he'd prefer to get paid, don't you? He and that little wife of his need every dime they can get—"

"So pay him." Kendra pulled the cinch tight under Preakness' belly, waited a moment for the horse to relax, and then pulled it again.

"So, you're giving the hands paid time off now? I think the guys will appreciate it. Mighty nice of you."

Kendra flipped the stirrup back into place and turned to face her brother. Brent leaned against the fence, one foot on the bottom board, and let his arms hang over the top. He looked exactly like their father when he did that. Her heart skipped a beat and she pushed the longing back where it belonged, too. "What do you want?"

Brent spread his arms wide – just like Dad. "Who

me? Nothin'."

"You think I should apologize."

"Should you?"

Kendra pulled off her hat and ran her other hand through her short hair. Settling the hat back on her head, she replied, "Nope." She turned back to Preakness. After positioning the bit, she took up the reins and lifted one foot in the stirrup. Frozen in time, she closed her eyes.

What if Michelle was in her room right this minute, crying? She winced; she *had* been rough on her. Michelle had agreed to do this for her family out of kindness. According to Lacey, she didn't need the money. Michelle Loving had more than enough clients to keep her firm in the black. In fact, when Lacey had called last night, she'd said Michelle probably shouldn't have taken the job from a business standpoint. To make the website the way she wanted, she'd have to leave her business, her home, for at least a month. As a businesswoman herself, Kendra knew how risky that could be.

And what had she done?

She'd insulted the woman.

Her foot fell back to the loose dirt, but she didn't turn around. "Are you still there?"

"Yup."

"Where is she?"

"In the house. She tried to help Brad with the dishes, but he wouldn't let her. I think she's in her room."

Hell.

She'd have to go apologize now. If there was one thing on this earth she hated as much as Harold Mason, it was apologizing. She wasn't any good at it, first of all, and secondly… she rarely felt the need to. But she'd been out of line with Michelle.

Kendra left Preakness saddled in the corral and returned to the house. Brent walked with her part of the way, before pulling his truck keys from his front pocket and heading to his Ford. "I'm going to town for a bit. Don't wait up."

Kendra climbed the porch steps and paused.

Loud, fast piano music came from the parlor. She walked the length of the porch until she found a partially opened window. The shade rested half-way down and she squatted to peer beneath it.

Brad and Casey stood on either side of her mother's old upright, singing along with an old, fifties rock-and-roll number. Michelle sat on the bench, pounding the keys like a cross between Jerry Lee Lewis and the goddess Venus. Her hair had come loose and danced around her head—wild and full of life. When she turned her face to look at Casey, Kendra could barely breathe. Her smile lit the whole room. Sweet, feminine laughter rang through the house like no sound had in years. She looked like she belonged there, in her mother's parlor, playing her mother's piano. She looked like part of the damn family.

But, she didn't look any worse for wear from Kendra's comments, either. She was hardly crying in her damn pillow.

And Kendra was going to apologize?

No. Not just no, but *hell* no.

If she had any part of her worth anything, it was her honesty. She'd been nothing but honest with the woman, and Michelle Loving obviously didn't give two cents for her thoughts on the matter, anyway.

Kendra stomped back to the corral, jumped on Preak's back and made her way out of the compound. A couple of days away from the house was just what she needed.

"You're really good, Michelle." Brad flopped on the sofa, breathless. His cheeks glowed red from the exertion.

"I used to play all the time. I just don't always have the time these days. Say, don't you have homework to finish?"

Brad groaned. "Not you, too?"

"Go on," she coaxed. "Finish it up and then I want to hear all about this Apache person."

"She's a filly, not a person," he responded with a chuckle and a slow shake of his head. "City folk."

Michelle grinned. "You don't say? And what are you doing with her?"

"I'm breaking her for my girlfriend. She's two."

"You're girlfriend is two?" Casey, sitting on a chair on the other side of the piano, feigned shock.

Michelle smacked him in the arm and laughed.

"Very funny, Case." Brad lifted his long frame from the couch and headed upstairs. "I'll take you out to see her when I'm done. Give me about thirty minutes."

"Okay. It's a date." Michelle waited for Brad to go up the stairs before she took his spot on the sofa. Casey stayed in the overstuffed chair by the window, looking content and relaxed. Pretty much the polar opposite of his older sister. Except in his eyes. They had the same lonely eyes.

"She doesn't like me very much, does she?"

Casey frowned. "Kendra? She doesn't like anyone very much. But, mostly, it's just an act. She cares about this ranch, this family, more than she cares about herself. She'll come around. Don't you worry your pretty little head about it."

Michelle looked past Casey and tried to make out the barn in the failing twilight. "Where did she go?"

Casey shrugged. "I don't know. Probably out to check on the herd. We've lost a ton of stock over the past few weeks."

"What do you mean, 'lost'?"

Casey paused and leaned forward, resting his elbows on his knees as though what he was about to say was the most important statement in the history of mankind. "I mean, someone has been killing off our herd. A few each week. Even more, lately. Upwards of ten every night. We don't have any proof, but we're all pretty sure its Harold Mason. That's why we have to watch over the herd; post guards. It's costing us a fortune, but we don't have much choice. We can't let them graze unattended like we normally would."

"And that's what all the excitement was about this afternoon?"

"Yeah. You know, he's trying to buy the ranch. See, in order for a person to qualify for a range lease, you have to own your own land first. Then you have to agree to use the land for the purpose it was set aside for originally. In this case, grazing.

"But Mason is a powerful man. He thinks he can come in here, buy us out, and then have his friends in high places change the land usage. He wants to put in a resort. You know, the kind where city folk can come in, play cowboy for a couple of weeks and go back to their designer coffee and iPads."

"And you think he's killing your livestock to make you sell out to him." Michelle could hear the doubt in her own voice. "It sounds like something out of an old western movie. People don't really do that, do they?"

"You'd be surprised." Casey reclined and crossed his legs just like his big sister had at dinner.

All the kids, except Lacey – who was totally femme, like her – seemed to share traits, but Kendra owned them. Everything about her, from her walk to her growl, was original. She'd never met anyone like Kendra. Disturbed by her train of thought, Michelle stood, meandered across the parlor, and pretended to study an old oil painting of a tall ship on rough seas. "So, what can you do about it?"

"Fight back. That's why you're here. Kendra would rather handle it on her own, of course. The old way. But it's a new world out there, whether she likes it or not. We'll let her fight her range war. Hell, I'll fight it with her when it comes to that. But, in the meantime, we'll wage a little techno-war and gain as much support as we can."

"I think we need to focus on the contributions this place makes as a part of American heritage. Play up the old west theme and check out having the buildings registered as historical landmarks."

"Already on it. I sent the paperwork in last month."

"Good. That will look great on a website."

A few minutes later, Brad descended the stairs and

Michelle walked with him to the barn. The setting sun created a red and yellow glow over the horizon. The canyon walls in the distance had turned black. The mountaintops welcomed the stars. A horse whinnied far in the distance, drawing her attention. A lone rider topped a rise, the woman and her beast in perfect harmony as they sped over the range.

Michelle stared, knowing it was Kendra Williams.

When she reached the pinnacle, she stopped. The tiny horse pranced on the horizon, spun and then reared on its hind legs.

One minute, she felt like she witnessed something spectacular; rare; even magical.

The next minute, Kendra was gone.

Four

Preakness reared onto his hind legs as if to tell Kendra that he either didn't want to spend the night outside the comfort of his stall or he looked forward to the freedom of a night on the range. Kendra suspected the latter. She pulled the reins, forcing him off balance. She braced for the jolt of the animal's front hooves as they met the hard earth, which followed a moment later. Using her dulled spurs to kick Preak's ribs, she pushed her mount forward.

Darkness fell over the range. In the distance, she spied the glowing yellow lights of several campfires. The night watch settled in for the long, quiet night. At least, Kendra hoped it would be quiet. She suspected differently, however, since Mason had made it a point to take at least ten head of cattle every night for the past month.

Early on, the livestock had simply vanished. She'd suspected mountain lions, at first. Later, blood trails had seemed to confirm her suspicions, but the numbers of missing livestock belied her theory. There were simply too many. She'd begun to suspect foul play. She'd begun to suspect Harold Mason.

The night watch worked in shifts guarding the herd because of the threat, and even though cattle continually vanished, none of the hands had heard any shots. Was he using bows? Sniper rifles from far enough away that they simply didn't hear the shots? Whatever he was doing, Kendra feared the possibility of an increased risk to her family. If Mason could get onto her property and take the herd, he could take something of more value.

"Rider coming!" Carlos Rodriguez shouted, his deep voice carrying over the night air.

Shuffling answered Rodriguez' warning. Kendra walked Preakness into the firelight. The off-duty herdsmen stood in a line in front of the fire, their figures casting an eerie silhouette, six-shooters drawn toward her. "It's me. Holster those damn things."

"Sorry, boss," Carl replied. "We aren't taking any chances."

Kendra dismounted. "It's all right." Better than all right. The time may come when such precautions were more than necessary. In fact, she was rather impressed with the guys' willingness to defend her property.

Carl handed her a tin cup filled with the mud he called coffee. "What are you doing out here?"

"Got bored." The lie tasted even more bitter than the drink. "Everything OK? Any sign of Mason's thugs?"

"Nope. It's been quiet all day. I guess Brent told you about last night?"

Kendra took a sip and grimaced. "Yeah. How many of the boys are posted on the herd?"

"Eight. We're working two shifts tonight instead of three to keep more of the herd covered. That way we'll have four guys awake at a time instead of just two or three. But there's a lot of ground out there. If they slip by the guys, they can still cause problems. We need more men."

"I know." Kendra handed the cup to Carl before turning back to her horse. "I'm going to ride the perimeter. See if I can find anything." She untied a bedroll from the back of her saddle and tossed it to Carl. "Roll that out for me, will ya?"

"Sure thing, boss."

By the time she'd ridden ten minutes, silence surrounded her. It seemed like even the wind stood still. *Waiting.*

The hair on the back of her neck stood up and she rubbed one hand over the tingling sensation. A cow lowed in the distance, telling her she neared the herd. Preakness picked his way through the dark.

How had it come to this? What made one person so damn greedy that he would stop at nothing just to prove he could get what he wanted? Power, she'd heard, could change a man. Make him bent on retaining and expanding his control over others at any cost. That sure as hell described Harold Mason.

The first offer had come in almost a year ago. Half a million dollars for her land and immediate surrender of the range lease. It wasn't the first time someone had asked her to release her lease, but no one had wanted to buy her land before. She'd written back immediately and politely declined the offer. Three more offers, each one increasing in value, followed over the course of several weeks. Then, Mason had come to Randall City in person and planted seeds of doubt in the minds of the Randall County Commission, the mayor and other influential citizens. He told them his friends in the legislature had already agreed to give Mason control of the range lands at the end of the lease term and if the county wanted a slice of the money pie, they'd better get on board quick.

Mason had lied, of course. Her family had been awarded the lease every time they'd applied for it, consistently, for more than one hundred years. The Heartland was the oldest, most established and successful cattle outfit in the county. In three counties. The government wouldn't just stop awarding the lease without a damn good reason.

The commissioners had all listened politely, nodded their heads in silent dismissal of the claims and moved on to other business. Everyone, including Kendra, had thought that would be the end of it. They hadn't expected that Mason would set up shop right on Main Street. He gave large sums of money to local charities. He sponsored three local youth teams: football, baseball and soccer.

It wouldn't surprise her if Harold Mason was the guy that the local priest went to when he needed to confess. The man had invested time and energy in creating a bona-fide persona for himself in the community.

Michelle Loving had talked about community value. She wouldn't have to explain that to *Saint Harold Mason*; not by a long shot.

It wasn't long after Mason had settled in that Lacey had suggested fighting his fire with some of their own. "We need a powerful campaign against Mason's ideas. And we need to make sure the same people Mason is talking to can see it. Let me talk to my friend. She does this sort of thing all the time."

Kendra had said no. She didn't need any help. She never needed help. At barely twenty, she'd gained custody of her orphaned brothers and sister. She'd taken them through school, chicken pox, first dates and broken hearts. Both mother and father, she'd tended to them as if they were her own. If should could do that, raise four decent citizens possessed of honor and courage, she sure as hell could defend herself against some silver-tongued-devil with a fat checkbook. She wasn't entirely without resources.

But in the end, they'd done what they always had. They ganged up on her until she couldn't bear to disappoint them anymore. And if she did stand her ground, they would do what they wanted anyway, more often than not. She really shouldn't be surprised they'd hired Michelle Loving behind her back.

A picture of the shapely Miss Loving passed in front of her. Hair loose, round hips encased in blue denim, Michelle Loving slid next to her. Eyes dark with wanting; lips parted for a kiss. She could feel her heat against her despite the very real chill of the late spring night. She inhaled Michelle Loving's scent in the dry air. The scent of woman.

How long had it been since she'd paid attention to something like that?

If she were completely honest, she couldn't remember. She'd dated a couple of women in the city when the kids were younger, but found the games required of her a waste of time and energy.

One woman she had fallen head-over-heels for had played her for a complete fool. Another gal, here in town, had been more than a little interested, but Kendra had nipped that right in the bud. Dating someone around here had been out of the question, of course. The last thing she needed was to defend her sexuality in a state known for its religious convictions. The kids – her family – were far more important than her happiness. Hell, *they* made her happy, right?

As it was, half the town didn't know she was gay and the other half wallowed in their own plausible deniability. Her mother had known. Her father hadn't. Her mother didn't care. She suspected her father would have. Not that he was a bible-beater or excessively judgmental. But he was old-fashioned and set in his ways. She was lucky, really. He would have had a better time of it with a tough, lesbian daughter working alongside him than an effeminate, gay son, certainly. "There's nothing wrong with being a tomboy, Kennie-girl," he'd said on the one occasion that she'd attempted to bring it up. "You'll grow out of it and find yourself a right nice fella. Don't you worry, none."

When her parents had been killed, her love life got put on the back burner, anyway, so what did it matter? Concerned more with homework, school plays, and keeping the ranch in full operation, she hadn't been on a real date since Brad had been in the second grade. On top of everything else, she'd had to prove to the Good Ol' Boy network that she was as capable as any man. It hadn't been easy, not one little bit, but it had been worth it. All of it.

And if she didn't figure a way out of her current situation, it will have all been for nothing.

Why was all of this bothering her now? When she had so many more important things to worry about? Was she so hard-up that the mere presence of a woman in her home made her remember everything she'd given up for the sake of her family?

Sure. That's must be it. It wasn't Michelle Loving that made her randy as a goat. It was the fact Michelle Loving was a beautiful female. Kendra just needed to get laid.

Pushing the thoughts out of her mind as best she could, she moved her horse toward the first cowboy in a circle of guards.

"That you, Kennie?"

"Yeah." She nodded at Cran Willard. "You staying awake?"

Cran raised a thermos mug of what must be coffee. "You know it. Everything's been quiet so far."

"Keep an eye out. We *haven't heard anything* before."

"Will do. Hey, are you gonna let Brad ride in the Sunny Days Rodeo this summer?"

"I'm thinking about it. We'll see how his geometry final goes."

Cran grinned. "You're too hard on that kid, you know that? What's geometry got to do with keeping your ass on a bull for eight seconds?"

Kendra smiled back at the older man. "Nothing, except when the bull breaks you in half, you might actually have to get a real job, someday. A high school diploma tends to help out in that department."

"You're too hard on that boy."

"He only has to put up with me for one more year of high school, and then he can ride all the bulls he wants to."

Kendra pushed on, completing a full circle around the herd before returning to camp. Her bed roll lay beside the fire. Stars called to her from the heavens, beckoning sleep. She didn't want to listen to them.

She made short work of unsaddling her horse and turned him out to pasture.

So far, so good. The cowboys had seen and heard nothing. But that didn't mean that nothing would happen, or hadn't happened already.

She hated the waiting and the not knowing. A woman of action and few words, she knew herself well enough to know she couldn't sit on her haunches forever. She had to do something and she needed to do it quick.

But what?

Mac was right. This wasn't the old west, as much as she wanted it to be. Times changed around her and the days of rounding up the bad-boys and hanging them from oak limbs had long passed.

She settled on her bed roll, entwined her fingers and rested her head on her hands, staring into the heavens. Somewhere, in the night sky where the angels danced with the wranglers, laid the answer. She just had to open her ears and listen to it.

A meteor streaked across the sky.

Make a wish, Kennie. She heard her mother's voice as clear as day. She was five and had wished for a baby brother. She'd been granted *that* wish with a vengeance. Brent. She smiled.

What should she wish for now? Peace to live her life the way she always had? Happiness for her family? For herself? A debilitating illness for Harold Mason? She smiled. No such luck. Her eyes fell closed and a golden-haired vixen took up residence in her thoughts. Her smile faded.

She would not wish for that.

Not in a million years.

Bright rays of light streamed through the lace curtains in the guest room. Dust floated in the beams. A horse whinnied in the courtyard.

Michelle stretched beneath the soft coverlet and pushed herself up sideways onto one elbow. A silver tray holding a cup of coffee and a Danish rested on the small table beside her bed.

Brent.

The coffee still steamed and she wondered if his presence in her room hadn't been what had awakened her. She looked at the clock and frowned.

Six-thirty?

She groaned aloud. Would the ranch not be here at noon? Who in their right mind wakes up at six-freakin-thirty? Tempted to throw herself back on the pillow, she tossed the coverlet aside instead, dwelling on the fact that lots of people had to get up this early to work and that she was obviously spoiled since most of her clients were available only at night thanks to the Las Vegas night life. She rushed to dress and braid her hair while she swallowed several gulps of cooling coffee. She picked up the Danish and then made her way to the kitchen.

Brent hung up the phone just as the swinging door whispered closed behind her. "Well, good morning, Bright Eyes." He smiled like the cat who ate the proverbial little yellow bird. What was it called? A canary? It was way too early to be awake.

"Morning," she replied around a mouthful of pastry.

"Are you ready to go?"

She nodded and adjusted the black leather backpack which held her camera, collapsible tri-pod and digital recorder. "Thanks for the coffee and this amazing little confection. Yum!"

"No problem. Come one, then. Let's get started."

Michelle followed him outside and stopped short. "What are those?" she asked, nearly choking on her last bite of breakfast.

"Horses."

"Well, I mean, I know that, but what are they doing here?"

Brent tilted his head and grinned. "This *is* a ranch." He was quite handsome when he smiled, she mused. "This big guy right here is Triple Crown. We call him T.C. He's a gelding. That means he's had his—"

"I know what it means," she laughed.

"Anyway, he's mine. I've been riding him since I broke him more than ten years ago. I was just a kid then. We kinda grew up together." Brent moved to a dappled grey horse that was a couple of inches shorter than T.C. "And this little girl is Bethany. She's yours."

"Huh?"

"You're going to ride Bethany."

"Seriously?" She wasn't getting anywhere with Mr. Personality if he thought she was actually going to ride all morning. Her ass already hurt at the thought.

"Don't panic. She's tame and very well-mannered.

Practically has one foot in the grave. But if you want to see the ranch, we'll have to go by horseback. Unless you'd prefer to get a hundred pictures of the fence line, because that's the only place the road really goes."

"I guess not." She bit her lip and took a step forward. "No, I can do this. I mean, how hard can it be, right? I went horseback riding in Hawaii when I was a kid."

The huge beast turned toward her and blew a wicked breath out of its flaring nostrils. It shook its mane and stamped one foot.

Right. Famous last words.

Kendra squatted next to the new blood trail.

At least they'd found the carcass this time. The animal had died more than a few hours ago. Probably just before dawn.

While Kendra had slept.

"What do you want us to do with the carcass, boss?" Carl mounted his horse and crossed his arms over the horn, reins falling over his fingers.

"I'll send one of the guys back with a trailer. I want Mac to see this."

The gun-shot wounds in the animal's flank and one in her neck already festered in what promised to be a scorching sun. And it was only ten in the morning. She pulled her hat off and wiped the sweat on her forehead with the back of one long sleeve.

The sound of hoof beats came from the south and she turned. She didn't have to watch very long to recognize the riders. Brent, she'd know anywhere. The novice next to him, the one gripping the saddle horn for dear life and not doing a very good job of it, could only be Michelle Loving.

She needed her around right now like she needed a shot of turpentine.

They reined in next to Carl. Rather, Brent reined in. The woman practically fell ass-over-applecart right out of the saddle. If it weren't for the dire circumstances, it would have been cute as hell, too.

"Another one?" Brent took off his hat, wiped the sweat from his brow, and put it back on. Damn, he looked just like Dad.

"Another nine."

"Another nine what?" Michelle's voice sounded odd in the landscape usually dominated by men. The hair on Kendra's arms stood up at the sound.

"Another nine of those," answered Carl, indicating the carcass with a coiled rope. He tossed the rope and Kendra caught it with one hand.

Michelle's face paled in the morning light when her eyes fell on the dead cow.

"What happened?"

"She's been shot, Miss Loving." Kendra turned away. If she didn't look at her, she wouldn't have to think on how beautiful she was. She wouldn't see the light dancing off her hair, blinding her. Instead, she tied the rope around the cow's hind legs and double-checked the knot. She would drag the carcass into the shade of a nearby stand of Joshua trees before running home to call Mac.

Michelle appeared at her side, a camera clutched in

her slender fingers.

"What are you doing?"

"I'm going to photograph this."

"What the blazes for?" She tightened the knot.

"If someone shot your cows, don't you have to have a record of it? I mean, that's not legal, is it? This is a crime scene." She focused her camera and snapped a picture of the wounds on the cows flank.

Kendra shook her head. "These should make some pretty awesome images for that website of yours," she mumbled. Taking a deep breath, she continued, "No. It's not legal. And 'someone' didn't shoot them. Harold Mason did, or he hired someone to do it, at least."

Michelle lowered the camera and stared at her with a determined gleam in her eyes. "He's the man who came to the house yesterday."

"One of them."

"Casey filled me in on some of the more gruesome details." She repositioned the camera and took a few more pictures. "I had no idea it was so bad."

"Then we agree. This is more dangerous that my little sister let on, and I can't blame you one bit for heading home, quick fast and in a hurry. This is bigger than anything a little computer file can fix."

Michelle stood straight, turned and fixed her gaze on Kendra's face. "I disagree."

"Excuse me?"

"I disagree." Michelle paused and took a step closer to Kendra. "I believe I can be of great help on the political activism and campaign side of the things. Therefore, I disagree."

Kendra stood motionless for more than a moment,

unable to make her feet move; caught in the uncanny and amazing gaze of this … woman. This obviously straight woman.

Finally, she forced herself away and strung the rope to the back of her saddle. She secured it, trying to ignore that Michelle Loving was hot on her heels, standing just a few inches away. Preakness lurched and then settled again.

She launched herself into the saddle and murmured, "Somehow, I figured you would say that."

Apparently ignoring her comment, Michelle continued. "I've taken some great shots of the herd and the ranch this morning. I have a few ideas about the site and I'll have something for you to review this afternoon. Once you understand the concept better, perhaps you'll be more inclined to support it."

"I'm not available this afternoon."

"Well, when *will* you be available?"

Never.

She stifled the sigh threatening to leave her lungs. Instead, she mounted her horse and used her knees to turn him in the direction of the trees. She didn't have time for this. She urged him forward.

A few minutes later, Michelle rode beside her.

This time, Kendra's sigh escaped without warning.

"When will you have time to look at the site? And we'll need to put together some information on the history of the ranch, you're family, and I'll need to scan some of the photographs I've seen around the house. If you have any shots of old goings-on, that would be great, too."

Now that took things too far. She turned in the

saddle, hoping the expression on her face would tell Michelle exactly how she felt. Kendra leveled her eyes on hers with the same look she gave the big Brahma she kept in the back corral because everyone was so damn afraid of it.

Michelle Loving didn't so much as flinch. "What?"

"You're not putting anything about my family on the Internet."

Her eyes narrowed. "Why not?"

"Because it's nobody's business, that's why. I watch the news. It's not safe."

"I think you're missing the point. I'm not going to publish your bank account numbers, for crying out loud. Just short biographies about your parents and your grandparents. We need to convince everyone that you belong here. That you represent a way of life that isn't so easy to come by, these days."

"A way of life?" Kendra wanted to yell, but years of dealing with her siblings gave her the control she needed to maintain a low tone. "This isn't a 'way of life.' It's not some story that city folks tell around a camp fire in an RV park. This *is* my life, Miss Loving, and I'd appreciate it if you'd stick to business."

Silence hung in the air for a brief second, punctuating her insistence. Michelle's tongue darted from between parted lips and moistened the bottom one. Kendra's body hardened, the blood rushing to her groin making her throb with wanting. Did she do things like that on purpose? Did she know what kind of affect such a gesture had on her? Probably not.

"This is my business, Ms. Williams. I'm only trying to do what you are paying me to do. I've given this a lot of thought, and the fact is that this is a family ranch. Generations have lived and died here to secure it and I personally don't think it's fair for Harold Mason to force you out. Now, the publicity campaign is only a part of an overall plan to save this place. The other part includes using the law. I don't know what your part is, but a little bit of co-operation won't hurt."

"I already told you. Count me out."

"But you're the biggest source of information. Lacey can barely remember anything. I need *your* help."

Kendra saw the pleading in her eyes and suspected that she didn't do it often. She looked away, focusing her attention on a dust devil swaying the desert brush as it moved across the plateau. Destructive and beautiful at the same time, like a small tornado.

"How about this," Michelle offered quietly. "I'll design the site. You help me – when you can," she stressed, "and if you don't like it, I won't publish it."

"And I have final say on what stays and what goes?" She ran a hand over her face and grimaced. Kendra couldn't believe she was about to agree to help her.

"Of course."

Kendra glanced back at Michelle's face as the cheerful tone in her voice washed away a small lingering doubt. She looked like a typical woman who had just won some kind of battle. Except there was nothing typical about the way Kendra's heart raced when she came within ten feet of her, or the way she lost her breath when she so much as thought about her. She felt like a little kid with a crush.

Michelle settled into her saddle. She straddled the

cushioned suede in skin-tight blue jeans that hid... nothing.

Kendra calculated the distance from the ranch and guessed she'd been in the saddle for more than three hours or so. Her citified behind must be plenty sore right about now. She was tough. Kendra had to give her that much.

"Fine. You win this round," she acquiesced. Kendra had other battles to fight right now. And one of them involved keeping her head screwed on straight whenever Michelle Loving so much as breathed in her direction.

Michelle clicked on the image in the upper right corner of the lap-top computer. Rolling hillsides covered in dark green brush and dotted with purple and yellow wild flowers leapt to life, covering most of the screen. This image would become a common theme throughout the site. She'd already modified it once, created a rustic edge treatment and positioned it in the center of what would become the home page.

She glanced at the clock again. She'd been working for five hours and had accomplished far less than she'd hoped. Kendra should be arriving any moment to check her progress, as they'd planned earlier in the day. Michelle wanted to impress her, but had, instead, spent most of the afternoon daydreaming about the domineering cowboi.

For some reason, it mattered to her what Kendra thought of her and her work more so than with other clients. Maybe it was because Michelle and Lacey were so close. Or maybe it was because Kendra represented something mysterious.

She glanced at the snapshots scattered on the surface of the dining room table. One, in particular, caught her attention and she picked it up.

The twins sat double on a reddish colored horse. A younger version of Kendra held a rope hooked beneath the horse's chin. Kendra's eyes stared back at her, full of wanting. She seemed so alone in the photograph, taken just months after her parents had been killed, according to the date scribbled on the back.

Did she regret her decision? She'd obviously sacrificed a lot over the years to keep her family together. No wonder she felt so strongly about not wanting to sell the ranch. A few million dollars was a lot of money to turn down. She could take the money and carry on with her life, but that would mean that her sacrifices would have been for nothing. No, she'd put her entire life into saving everyone and everything around her from certain loss. Michelle traced the lines of Kendra's jaw on the glossy paper and frowned. *Who takes care of her?*

Kendra cleared her throat behind her and Michelle jumped.

"I didn't hear you come in." Michelle slid the photograph behind several others on the table, hoping Kendra wouldn't notice.

"Sorry." Kendra placed her hat on the same hook she'd used last night at dinner and took the seat next to her at the table.

Michelle stared at her, suddenly aware of the harsh lines around her mouth and the deeper sadness in her eyes than even the old snapshot had revealed. "I hope it's okay to use the dining room?"

"Sure, it's fine. So, what have you got so far?"

Aware her mind had wandered, she shook her head. "I have a template ready and a few images for you to approve."

She looked back to the screen and used the mouse to highlight some words.

"Most people want to believe in something bigger than themselves. If I can create an image, a brand, for you and your family that plays on the nation's heartstrings, we can put pressure on the powers that be to leave well enough alone."

"I already told you I don't want our personal lives on display."

"You won't be on display. I'm talking about showing people what a real, working cattle ranch is like. Very general stuff." Her voice cracked.

Kendra didn't answer, but focused her attention on the screen.

She stayed silent for the next ten minutes as Michelle ran through the design elements with her. She nodded once, when Michelle showed her the photograph with the flowers, but otherwise, she might as well have not been in the room.

Except for the constant erratic heart rate she caused and the rise in temperature Michelle experienced as each slow second ticked by.

Michelle glanced at Kendra once or twice and each time, she wanted to smooth the worry lines from her brow. Kendra needed to hear someone say that everything would be alright. Michelle shifted in her chair as she realized suddenly that she wanted to be that person.

The thought made her breath catch. Kendra turned her attention to Michelle's face and she felt the impact of Kendra's eyes to her very core. Spirals of desire formed in her gut, clenching her with a minute taste of what it might feel like to have Kendra's hands on her. She swallowed and Kendra's eyes danced to her throat and then settled on her lips.

Did she feel it, too? Or was it just her fanciful imagination playing tricks on her?

Any woman in her right mind would want the strong, lonesome cattlewoman who sat next to her. The same wasn't true for Michelle. Women didn't lust after Michelle Loving – computer geek, too plain, too smart. She'd heard it all.

But something in Kendra's eyes called her a liar.

A small glimmer of something she couldn't explain shone in the green depths. Something that made her hope.

Five

Damn it.

Kendra wanted to kiss her.

What the hell was the matter with her? The whole world could crash down on her any minute and she was stuck playing school-yard games with some straight girl?

"It looks fine to me." But what did Kendra know about it? Michelle could be terrible at her job and she wouldn't know the difference. All she cared about right now was the way Michelle's long, black lashes framed those impossibly deep blue eyes.

"What?" Michelle's lips trembled as her voice trailed away.

"The website thing. It looks good." Kendra pushed herself away from the table with both hands and rose to her feet. "Show it to Brent tonight and see what he thinks. Or better yet, ask Brad. He's the computer genius in the family."

"Okay."

One word answers. Kendra didn't know her well, but that seemed a little out of character for Miss I-know-what's-good-for-you. Kendra frowned.

"I should have more done after dinner. Maybe we can all sit down together?"

"I'm sleeping out again tonight."

Michelle's scowl deepened. "Because of the herd?"

"Yeah."

"Don't you get scared out there?"

Scared? Hell, yes, she got scared. She worried her family could be in real danger. She worried things would get a whole lot worse before they got any better. Could she handle it? Or would she make some bonehead mistake which could cost her family everything? What would it be like to have someone scared for her? Someone who could ease the stress and pain of the lonely life she'd chosen?

Kendra brushed the thoughts aside. There wasn't anyone to fit that bill within a thousand miles. She doubted anyone existed at all, really. Certainly, not some prissy city girl.

"No," she lied. Or maybe, she didn't. Not really. Michelle was talking about being afraid of the dark, or wild animals; that sort of thing. No, she wasn't afraid of the dark. On the contrary, she preferred the sky to a roof any day of the week. Now, if Michelle were under that roof...

She shoved her Stetson on her head. "We done here?"

She didn't wait for an answer. The urge to run proved too strong. That wasn't true. The only urge she had when in the same room as Michelle Loving had nothing to do with running and everything to do with running her hands all over Michelle's amazing body.

Kendra shook her head and willed her body to calm. The fire in her jeans seemed to have a mind of its own, however and she could only hope she didn't walk funny as she made her way to the barn.

Why had she agreed to work with Michelle directly? Brent knew as much as she did about the ranch and the problems they faced at the moment. He could give Michelle all the information she needed and then some.

But, in the end, she knew she wouldn't back out. Something about the woman called to her and although she'd tried, she couldn't ignore it.

For the first time since Brad had been down with whooping cough when he was four years old, Kendra wished she didn't have to sleep on the range tonight. But she'd promised Carl she'd be there before sundown. She glanced at the horizon and judged the sunset about an hour away.

Kendra allowed her horse to pick its own way down the rocky slope. Tired and dirty, she leaned back in the saddle. Carl's coffee and the plate of second-day stew she'd eaten earlier with the boys sat heavy in her stomach. She needed to check with one last cowboy before she headed back to camp for the night.

Or maybe she'd make another round. The thought of lying about the camp with nothing to occupy her thoughts but Michelle Loving made her tense. And wet.

A single gunshot tore the night's silence. Kendra jerked her head in the direction of the sound even before the report disappeared into the starry, moonlit canopy. The guard she'd just passed sat on his horse a hundred yards to the east, his hand raised above his head holding his pistol. The rider spun his horse, raced in her direction and fired again.

An instant later, the thunder of God rolled over the hillside.

"Stampede!"

The ground shook. Like a single entity, the herd bore down on her. Kendra's focus turned forward and caught sight of Cran, standing beside his horse cleaning a front hoof. The man had enough sense to leap into his saddle and get out of the way. As Kendra passed, Cran fell into line not far behind her.

Kendra spun Preakness hard to the left. The horse lurched into a dead run. She had to keep in front of the herd. Like trying to control a thunder storm with a lasso, she needed to keep the cattle's hell-bent attention on her.

A shot fired and she concentrated her attention on the sound. A second shot revealed a flash of light. She returned the age-old signal and location technique, which told the other riders that she had the lead position. Several more shots followed. Unable to risk turning around again, she counted the blasts. Sixteen shots, not including her own. Two shots each. Eight men. So far, everyone was accounted for.

Nobody stops a stampeding herd. The only thing she and her men could do was to keep up; try to keep the herd from scattering in the dark and let them run themselves out. The dangers lie mostly in the ground. Preakness stretched his head low and ran like the wind. In the dark and at the speed they traveled, a prairie dog borough could land Preakness in the glue factory and

Kendra in a shallow grave.

Horns clashed, cattle screamed and the heavy rumble of hooves on abused earth surrounded her. Focusing her attention on staying in the saddle, she rode ahead of the herd.

Over the course of the next few minutes, the single shots repeated. Eight. Nine. Ten. A pause. Eleven. Twelve. She added her own shots to the din. Thirteen. Fourteen.

She waited for the last two shots.

They never came.

Damn it!

Kendra's heart lurched into her throat.

Finally, the herd slowed behind her. She turned Preakness left, and then right, making a wide zig-zag pattern in front of the herd, slowing the forward momentum by small notches. No longer in the grip of the stampede, the cattle responded, coming to a halt several miles from their starting point.

Kendra sped along the herd's perimeter until she found Cran, breathless and pale in the moonlight.

"Come with me," she ordered.

Kendra fired her pistol twice. Fourteen shots answered her. She rode the perimeter of the herd until she collected the men riding with her that night. She scanned their dirty, sweating faces. Some of them – the younger boys – were pale, having just witnessed their first stampede and finally understanding the awesome power of nature. Others, who had been through the destruction in the past, wore relieved expressions. Carlos made a sign of the cross. Each of them looked carefully at the faces of those around them.

Kennedy Bastion was missing.

Michelle sat at the kitchen table, nursing a cup of hot tea. Her laptop open in front of her, she scanned her e-mail. The chime from her social network account alerted her to an instant message.

So, how's it going?

Michelle smiled at Lacey's unexpected appearance and typed her reply. "Okay. Except your sister doesn't like me very much."

She's a big wuss. Just don't let her bully you.

"I won't. Hey, that Mason guy came to the ranch yesterday. Your family had to run him off."

Oh, I would have loved to have seen that!

"I'll bet. It wasn't funny. Casey and Brad saw him pull up and went straight for their guns. GUNS! Did you forget to tell me something about what's going on? Something about livestock getting killed?"

The window sat idle for a moment.

No. But if things are getting out of control, come back home.

"No. It's okay. I'll stick it out. Besides, I think your brothers are just boys being boys, anyway. It's not like they were going to shoot anybody, right?"

Right. Well, I'm off to bed now. Hey, why aren't you in bed?

"It's only two a.m. I'm still on Vegas time, I guess. LOL."

Get some rest. I'll talk to you soon.

"G'nite."

She closed the window. The last thing she needed now was to get stuck surfing meaningless messages for the next hour. She sipped her tea and leaned back in her chair.

They weren't really going to shoot anyone. Were they? The boys were just playing hero. Right?

The front door opened and closed, followed by footsteps through the foyer. The dark shape moved through the swinging door from the hall, reached out and flipped on the light.

Brent offered her a disarming smile. "What are you still doing up?"

"Playing catch up from being offline all day. It's normal for me. I'm a bit of a night owl. Did you have fun?"

His disarming smile changed to one of Cheshire-cat satisfaction. "Oh, yes. I had a very nice time."

Michelle smiled. Lacey must have been serious when she described Brent as a young Hugh Hefner with boots. "Casey drove back to town and said to tell you he'd be back tomorrow."

"Thanks. But I ran into him at *The Dollar*." Brent poured himself a tall glass of water from a pitcher in the refrigerator. He gulped it down and poured another. "Best hangover cure in the world. Water before you pass out."

"You drove home like this?"

"Hell, no." He wiggled his eyebrows. "She went straight to my place."

"And does *she* have a name?"

"Cynthia."

"Are you sure?"

"Well, yeah. I mean, I think so."

Michelle laughed. "I hope she has a heart of steel, cowboy."

"They all do." Brent finished his second glass of water and placed the empty glass in the sink. "I'm going to bed. You should too. Dawn comes early on a ranch and if we're going to see the rest of spread tomorrow, we'll be leaving at daybreak."

Daybreak? Again? Michelle cringed and looked at the clock in the corner of her computer screen. "Are you serious? Sheesh. I *should* go to bed then."

"Yep." He threw her another charming smile and headed back the way he'd come in. Michelle shut down her computer, unplugged her mobile hotspot and slid it to the center of the table. She stretched and followed Brent to the foyer.

A horse whinnied just as he opened the front door. "Hey, Kennie's back."

Michelle's heart skipped a beat, stealing her breath.

Get a grip on yourself. She's just a girl.

A very lean, very butch, very good-looking girl.

But, she hadn't planned on seeing her again before morning, at least. The prospect of having Kendra see her in her flannel pajamas bottoms, spaghetti strap camisole and fuzzy slippers caused her more chagrin than it should have. She should have brushed her hair.

"What the hell?" Brent's voice carried inside from the porch.

The urgency in the sound made her take several steps forward and she leaned outside the still-open door. She followed the direction of Brent's gaze to find Kendra riding one horse and leading another into the courtyard.

A body draped over the second mount.

When Kendra entered the circle of light cast by the porch light, she reigned in and dismounted. She looked terrible. Covered in dust and dirt, her face bore a haggard, tired expression. She dropped the reins and moved one hand over the length of her horse's neck.

"Brent? You want to call Mac for me?"

"What happened?" Brent asked, seemingly instantly sober.

Kendra climbed the steps and brushed past her as if she weren't even there. Brent followed her inside and they both continued to the kitchen. Michelle looked back at the horses. The second horse shifted and turned, revealing the face of the body it carried.

Eyes wide, the expression looked frozen in shock. Blood smeared his cheeks and his hair appeared matted with it. His neck and one arm were bent at odd angles, indicating breaks even to her untrained eyes.

Her stomach rebelled and she closed her eyes before turning her head away. What happened to him?

She hurried to join the others in the kitchen.

"I don't know what set them off." Kendra leaned against the counter and Brent sat at the table, his fingers poised to dial the old rotary phone.

"What happened?" She asked, wrapping her arms around her stomach in response to the leftover queasiness.

"Stampede," Kendra replied.

"That man was trampled?"

Kendra's eyes shone her direction. *Emerald fire.*

"*That man's* name is Kennedy Bastion. He was

twenty-three years old and he has a wife and a baby. I've known his father my whole life and I have to call him in a couple of minutes to tell him his son is dead. Does it really matter that he was scared out of his mind while a few hundred cows used him as a steppingstone?"

Michelle felt the color drain from her face. "I... I didn't mean anything..." She closed her mouth when her voice failed her. Tears stung the back of her eyes. "I'm sorry."

"Kennie. Lighten up. She was only asking. This isn't her fault."

Kendra glared at her, her eyes narrow and cold. "Did you get Mac, yet?"

"They're putting me through to his house. Hang on."

"Tell them to hurry up. I need to use the phone."

Michelle crossed to the table, picked up her cell phone and turned it on. "Here. You can use this."

Kendra looked at it like she didn't know what it was. "I'll wait."

"I don't mind. Call your friend."

Michelle met Kendra's eyes, which squinted slightly as though she were trying to figure out some unsolvable puzzle. Wrinkles formed in the sun-bronzed flesh at the corners. Wrinkles ingrained from years of worrying and working in nature's harshest elements. Had any of them come from laughter? She doubted it and for some reason that thought made her heart ache for Kendra Williams.

"I said I'll wait."

Kendra pushed off the counter and paced. She found it hard to concentrate with Michelle in the room, yet she suddenly missed having someone to share her pain with. What would happen if she allowed herself to feel for someone. A woman.

She cast the thought aside as guilt washed over her. How could she even think about something like that when Kennedy was dead? He'd never hold his wife again. He wouldn't see his baby son grow up. Little Kenny would never know his father. She closed her eyes and ran her hands over them to stop the tears.

At least Kenny had had it for a little while. He had known what it was like to be loved, and what it was like to love someone back with the power of... she didn't even know what.

Kendra had never felt like that. Not once. In thirty-five years, she'd never been loved by a woman. For thirty-five long, empty years, she'd been completely alone.

She was tired.

"You can use the phone now, Kennie. Mac's on his way."

She cleared her throat. "Thanks."

"I'll be back in a minute." Brent brushed past her and placed a quick, reassuring pat on her shoulder before leaving the house.

Kendra sat at the kitchen table and pulled the phone toward her. Michelle sat at the other end of the table, her hands folded in her lap and her head bent. Her hair, loosened from its earlier knot, spilled over her shoulders and rested on her breasts. She looked like she was trying to be invisible.

Not happening. Kendra would notice her even if she *were* invisible.

Clearing her head of the wasteful notions, she dialed Kyle Bastian's number from memory.

Her old friend answered on the fourth ring.

Kendra couldn't speak. She cleared her throat and tried again, but no sound came out. She couldn't form the words. Her eyes misted and burned. She bent her head.

It was all her fault. If she'd put on more crew, if she'd finished her rounds sooner, maybe she could have prevented the stampede. Kennedy died because Kendra had failed. And now, she wasn't even strong enough to tell the boy's father what happened...

What was happening to her? She wasn't weak. She'd never been weak! She loathed weakness in anything, especially herself. Michelle looked up at her and Kendra read the expression in her eyes.

Pity.

The one thing she hated more than weakness.

Straightening her shoulders, she cleared her throat again. "Kyle? It's... um... it's Kennie Williams."

"What's happened?"

"It's bad, Kyle. I'm sorry."

"Is he dead, then?"

Kendra took a deep breath, gritted her teeth and whispered, "Yeah."

She listened to the mechanized sobs while trying to hold back her own. She failed. The pain laced through the phone lines and hit her like a sledgehammer. She heard mumbling for a moment, and then a woman's scream. Margaret sounded like she was literally dying of heartbreak.

Brent came back into the kitchen, a young woman just a step behind him. Great. Another female. She jumped to her feet and the chair crashed to the floor. Handing the phone to Brent as she passed, she headed for the door.

She had to get some air.

Once outside, she negotiated the steps with the same determination she used for everything else. She wiped her eyes and forced herself to stop crying. Deep breaths. Solid footing. Fists. She would not be bested by simple, unnecessary emotions.

Kennedy's horse shimmied away from her when she reached for the reins, but Kendra grabbed them and steadied the frightened animal. Animals could sense death. They didn't like it any more than humans did.

She dropped the reins and stepped on them while she untied the coarse ropes holding Kennedy's body to the saddle. When the boy fell free, Kendra slipped him into her arms. Why did everything feel heavier when it was dead? She groaned as she half-carried, half-dragged the body to the front yard. Then she laid his remains on the soft, green grass. She hated that Kennedy's mother or young wife would see him like this.

Pulling her neckerchief from around her throat, she walked to the tap around the corner of the house, by the back door. She spun the gauge and soaked the bandana.

When she returned to the front yard, Michelle knelt over Ken's body with a washcloth in her hand. She pulled it over Kennedy's face with tender, deliberate strokes and sniffled.

What was *she* crying for? Kendra grimaced and stepped over to her. "What are you doing?"

"I thought I'd clean him up some," she whispered as she looked up at Kendra. Michelle's eyes were wide and reflected the porch light like a cat's. Wet, spiky lashes framed the deep blue pools. She *had* been crying. "Is that all right?"

No. You're not a part of this. You don't belong here. I don't care how beautiful you are, or how badly I want you to hold me right now. Leave me alone. Go back where you came from. I don't need you. I don't need anyone. "Yeah. That's fine. Thanks."

By the time they finished cleaning Kennedy's face, neck and hands, Mac's police car sped up the driveway. The lights in the grill and dash flashed red and blue as his brakes squealed to a halt. Mac heaved his huge frame from the front passenger seat and rested his eyes on Kennedy's lifeless body. He took a step forward and put his hands in his pockets.

"You called his dad?"

Six

"Yeah. I called him."

Over the next few hours, the yard buzzed with activity. Kendra leaned against the corral and ran a hand over her face. Dawn illuminated the horizon with a halo of pink and yellow, turning what few clouds threatened in the distance a bright gold. She focused her eyes on the mystical band of blue between earth and sky; day and night.

Behind her, the ambulance crew placed Kennedy's body on a gurney and slid him into the back of the county-owned vehicle. Quiet voices trailed toward her on the morning breeze.

Someone leaned against the fence next to her. She looked over to find a deputy named Brian Whitlock. He'd gone to school with the twins. He was a decent enough kid, but still green around the gills.

"We're taking him now. Sorry it took so long to get the coroner here."

"Where was he?"

"With his girlfriend," answered Brian with a sheepish grin. He practically blushed. "When we called his house, his wife said he was working. I could have gone my whole life without having that conversation."

"I'll bet." Kendra turned her eyes forward and watched the sun climb over the hillside. "How're they doing?"

"His dad's hanging in there, but his wife and mom are still pretty messed up. That lady friend of yours staying with you took them inside."

Kendra felt her heart grip in her chest. Lady friend?

She hated to admit it, but Michelle had been a huge help through the whole ordeal. When Margaret Bastian had first arrived and seen her son, lying on the ground, beaten and bloody, she'd lost it. Michelle might as well have been the only female around. Kendra had no idea how to handle a distraught woman. But Michelle did. Michelle had held the older woman as she'd cried out every last tear. When Kenny's wife had shown up a few minutes later, Michelle had done it all over again. Then, she'd left Linda and her mother-in-law alone to console each other, silently slipping away until she was needed again. Kendra couldn't help but notice her, hovering on the outside of everything as if she wanted to be there in case she was needed, but not wanting to intrude if she wasn't.

Graceful.

She reminded Kendra of her grandmother. A true lady.

A mournful squeak, like from an old movie, told Kendra that the front door opened. She glanced over her shoulder and straightened when she saw Margaret and Linda exit the house. She strode toward them, not sure what she could say, or if she should say anything.

Guilt rode hard on her back, and she forced herself to meet their moist eyes.

"Kenny," Margaret whispered, reaching toward her with one unsteady hand. "Thank you."

Thank you? She didn't know how to respond. Instead, she took her friend's mother's hand and helped her down the steps. Then she turned her over to her husband.

Linda sucked in a deep, quivering breath as she passed Kendra, but she suspected that the young woman received very little life from the automatic function. When Kendra's parents had died, she hadn't breathed for a full year. Not really. If it hadn't been for the babies, she might not have ever breathed again.

Another set of footsteps came down the creaking stairs. She didn't have to turn around to know it was Michelle. Her honeysuckle scent enveloped her. She closed her eyes for a moment and let it.

The Bastion family climbed into their pickups and followed the ambulance down the dusty drive. The cops followed. Brent and his date went up to his place over the barn. Brad went back into the house, his expression pale; his eyes red. The kid probably couldn't remember a time that Kennedy hadn't been hanging around. Soon the courtyard stood hollow. Empty. Quiet.

The ranch seemed to hold its breath.

"Are you alright?" Michelle's voice resonated with concern. Kendra could feel Michelle reaching out to her as clear as if she touched her. Kendra's muscles tightened.

"Yeah. I'm fine."

"I don't believe you." Michelle took a step toward her.

Kendra turned to face Michelle in the drive. She'd pulled her hair back again, revealing full cheeks and a determined chin. Michelle shivered and Kendra didn't know if it came from the morning chill or her scrutiny.

"Why? Why don't you believe me?"

"You're human, aren't you? You're a woman. It's been a long, shitty night, and you haven't slept. You've lost someone close to you, on your watch. You can't possibly be alright."

"Then why did you ask?" Kendra couldn't help the small, wan grin that parted her lips.

Michelle shrugged. "It *is* a silly question, I suppose, under the circumstances."

If Kendra wasn't careful, she'd begin to feel again. She braced herself against the temptation to let herself go. She couldn't afford it. Too many people depended on her to be strong; to always be in control. She couldn't let them down.

"Life's a bitch, Miss Loving."

"I don't believe that, either. And I don't believe you believe it. It's okay to—"

"Okay to what? It's okay that I let a boy die? It's okay that I can't even keep my own people safe? Is it okay that some rich son-of-a-bitch is stealing my ranch, my family's home, right out from under me? Is it?"

"You're upset, Kendra." She touched Kendra's arm.

Comfort threatened to steal her defenses.

Michelle's warmth and strength flowed into her and she cringed against the temptation to let her be the strong one. Michelle stepped closer.

Yes, she was upset, all right. Michelle upset her. She made her think of things better left alone. Worse, she made her think of herself. Didn't she deserve some measure of happiness after all these years?

Kendra turned her body into Michelle's. She was right there. Right in front of her. She could take her in her arms and allow herself to feel. Just this once.

Confusion settled in her mind, and she could feel her eyes begin to narrow of their own accord. She'd just met Michelle. Two days ago, she couldn't stand the thought of her being here. Yesterday, her very presence made her angry. Now, Michelle just made her weak. Michelle's strength seemed to outweigh her own; to feed from hers.

Michelle's eyes searched hers and Kendra knew she was trying to reach her – to find some life somewhere deep inside. She shouldn't. She wouldn't like what she found.

A wisp of curly blonde hair rested on Michelle's shoulder.

Lifting one hand, Kendra brushed it away. Michelle trembled. Short, hesitant breaths made Michelle's chest rise and fall beneath her thin cotton top. Kendra's body mimicked hers.

Kiss her.

Michelle's tongue darted from between her lips, moistening them. Kendra's entire body moaned with wanting. She couldn't move. Michelle held her captive with just her eyes and the gentle pressure of her fingers as they stroked her arm.

"It's OK," Michelle whispered. She moved her hand to stroke Kendra's jaw and smiled. "Everything will be fine."

"How?" Kendra choked on the word.

Michelle shrugged and turned away. "Have faith."

With both hands, Kendra gripped Michelle's shoulders and turned her back to face her. "I don't have any more faith."

In the next instant, her lips crushed against Michelle's. Frantic, she drew all of the strength she could from her. Her hands moved to Michelle's back and when Michelle's hands did the same, Kendra nearly burst. Michelle tasted of life and joy. Her hands roamed over Kendra's back, urging her closer. Kendra ignored any lingering doubt and let herself feel.

She ignored the part of herself that would balk and pulled Michelle closer. The peaks of her breasts pushed against her own. Running her tongue over Michelle's lips, she begged entrance. She wanted to consume her. She needed it.

Just this once.

When Michelle parted her soft, full lips, Kendra's mind exploded in a riot of sun-washed color. Michelle moaned and Kendra caught the sound in her throat. Moist heat consumed those places ignored for so long. Her entire being throbbed and pulsed. She wanted to be inside Michelle, wrapped tightly in an embrace that would last forever. She could already feel Michelle around her, giving her so much more than she took.

She barely knew her, but she knew that much.

What did she taste like? There...? What would she

feel like in her most sensitive places? Silky. Smooth. Warm and pulsing...

Wet.

Kendra would never just take from her. Michelle Loving possessed an honest, pure soul. Nothing about her was tainted. She still believed...

She deserved better.

Kendra pushed her away. Breathless, her chest heaved and her heart beat like a jack-hammer. Wide eyes met her gaze. Confusion played over Michelle's parted lips as they moved like she wanted it to say something, but couldn't find the words.

Kendra backed up a step. "I'm sorry. I shouldn't have done that."

Michelle's eyes narrowed for a brief second. She squared her shoulders. "Like I said. You're upset."

"That doesn't excuse my behavior." Kendra brushed one hand through her hair and forced herself to turn away.

"It's OK. Really..."

Her words died in the approaching roar of a half dozen riders.

Crap.

Had they seen?

Michelle stepped back when Kendra's attention focused over her shoulder. She turned to find six men on horseback racing into the compound. They looked like something out of the Wild West. Cowboy hats, leather vests and chaps, even the horses they rode seemed to be made from something untamed. Dust covered them as if they'd ridden hard and their horses were flecked with white lather.

A lanky cowboy with dark hair past his shoulders dismounted a black horse, tossed his reins to one of his five companions and jogged across the courtyard. Michelle recognized him as one of the men she'd met the day before, on her tour of the ranch. Of course, he'd been downright jovial then. He seemed far more serious now. "Kendra? We found something."

"What is it?"

Michelle felt invisible. All of Kendra's energy, focused on her a moment ago, drifted away until she couldn't be sure it had ever existed. Only the tingle left in her lips told her anything had happened.

Kendra had kissed her. Michelle's fingertips touched her lips.

And Michelle had kissed her back. What was wrong with her? She had only just met Kendra. Still, the warmth had surrounded her like a blanket; comforting in its protection. When Kendra held her, nothing could harm her. Her aura exuded trust and determined pride. And lonely confidence.

Kendra's voice carried over the several feet separating them and brought her back to the moment. "This is an arrow, Carl."

"I know that, boss. We found eight of them. Someone shot the herd with these, last night. That stampede was deliberate."

Kendra's neck turned red. Michelle stepped closer, though she didn't know why. She couldn't be of any help. She just needed to be near Kendra.

Kendra held a broken arrow in her strong, tapered fingers. Only the shaft and feathers remained where someone had apparently cut it close to where the tip should have been. The hollow metal crimped in a hard line. The blunt tip held traces of blood.

Michelle ran her hand over Kendra's arm and felt the muscles bunch beneath her fingers. Kendra didn't acknowledge her, but she didn't pull away. The man, Carl, seemed to notice her for the first time. He nodded and tipped the brim of his hat. "Good morning, ma'am. It's a pleasure to see you again."

She smiled and dropped her hand.

"How's your work coming along?" He was being polite. It was obvious in his speech. Were all of the people associated with the ranch trained on how to treat a lady? She felt like a school marm in a western novel.

The concept of using the Internet to fight Harold Mason, however, suddenly seemed naive, at best. She shrugged and folded her arms. "I'm feeling more than a little useless right at the moment. I imagine you and your boys are hungry?"

Carl looked at Kendra in silence. Kendra stared at the arrow shaft, twisting it through her fingers as if it contained the answer to some question only she knew. Then she nodded.

"Yes, ma'am. We could eat."

Michelle almost shook her head. Did Kendra have the final say so about everything on the ranch? When people ate. When people slept. When people worked.

When people kissed.

"All right, then. I'll make some breakfast for

everyone. I hope you like scrambled eggs, because that's pretty much the extent of my culinary expertise."

"That'll be just fine, ma'am."

"Michelle, please. You can call me Michelle."

Carl strode back to where the rest of the cowboys tended the horses. Michelle rocked back on her heels and hugged herself against the sudden tension in the air. She peeked at Kendra, standing beside her with her head still bent over the arrow. Instead of examining it now, she seemed to consume it with her eyes. Her white-knuckled grip almost bent the metal.

"What does all this mean, Kendra?"

"Mason wasn't doing enough damage by just killing my livestock. He spooked the herd last night. Deliberately. He killed Ken Bastian."

"How can you be sure it was him?"

"Who else would it be?" Michelle heard the rage in her voice, felt it in the tightly reined tremble of Kendra's shoulders.

"There's nothing you can do right now. Let's go inside and have something to eat. You need to get some rest and we'll call your friend, the sheriff."

Kendra snorted. "For all the good that will do."

Michelle made her way into the house. Kendra followed behind her, so close that she could feel her warmth and hear her quiet breaths. Her skin tingled in remembered sensation. When they reached the foyer, Kendra touched Michelle's shoulder and she froze.

"Miss Loving. About before…"

Michelle stared straight ahead and then closed her eyes. She couldn't bear to turn around, to look at Kendra. "Yes?"

"I am sorry."

Brad clumped down the stairs, his boots echoing in the small space. "Sorry for what?"

Kendra cleared her throat. "Nothing, kid."

Then she was gone. Michelle turned around just as the front door slammed shut. She sighed. The poor gal couldn't catch a break if her life depended on it.

"Was it something I said?" Brad stared after his sister. No, Kendra would be more like his mother, really.

"No, Hon. She's just still upset about last night. Did you manage to get any sleep?"

"No. Not really. But I have to go to school, anyway."

"Can't you take even one day off?"

"Not really. It's only a week until finals. I have to go."

Michelle walked with Brad into the kitchen and opened the fridge. "I'm making breakfast. Would you like some eggs?"

"Cereal is fine for me. I need to hit the road."

"Did you know Ken Bastian?"

"Oh, yeah. Gosh, he started working here when he was about fourteen or so. I guess I must've been about ten. It's a small town. Pretty much everybody knows everybody, or knows somebody who knows 'em. Believe me. It's not easy keeping a secret around here."

Michelle clutched an egg in one hand and leaned against the counter. "I'm really sorry."

Brad shrugged. She could see a lot of Kendra in her youngest brother. The same attitude carried on strong shoulders; *I can do anything. I don't need anyone.*

Michelle turned her attention to the stove. The ancient appliance looked like something her grandmother would have used and she estimated its installation date around the turn of the last century. She bent low and searched for any sign of how to turn it on.

A match struck behind her. A small, weather-worn hand circled around her, a single wooden match gripped between two fingers. She recognized the slender, tapered fingers instantly. Sweat broke out on her forehead when she remembered the feel of them on her back, in her hair.

Kendra's arm circled her back, trapping her between warm body and cold stove. With the palm of her hand, Kendra twisted the far-right knob and then set the small flame to the front-right burner. It burst to life.

So did Michelle. She placed the pan over the flame and scooped a tablespoon of butter onto the cast-iron surface. A loud hiss cried from the contact. Kendra's body pressed against hers, searing her where they touched. Kendra lifted the match to her lips and blew out the flame. Kendra's hot breath disturbed the tiny hair's on Michelle's neck, sending shivers across her sensitive flesh.

"They kicked me out of the barn," she stated.

Michelle faced her. "Did they?"

Michelle's eyes focused on her lips. Full and sensuous, they called to her like nothing she'd ever experienced. Soft and powerful, she could still taste them.

"Do you need any help?"

Michelle blinked and felt heat suffuse her cheeks. "What?" Oh... um... no. I think I'm okay."

Liar.

Michelle placed a couple of pats of butter in the

bottom of the pan. The butter began to melt immediately, as though it didn't stand a chance between the heat of the stove and the heat radiating off Michelle's body.

"I'm going to take a shower, then."

Michelle swallowed against the lump in her throat. "Okay."

Kendra didn't move. Less than an inch separated their bodies. Michelle didn't move, either.

"Butter's burnin'," said Brad around a mouthful of kid's crunch cereal.

Michelle grabbed the handle of the old-fashioned cast-iron pan and then screamed. "Damn!"

The heavy metal had burned her hand. Hadn't these people ever heard of Teflon?

Tears stung her eyes as she sucked on the tip of three fingers. Kendra's fingers, warm and strong, pulled her hand away from her mouth. She dragged Michelle toward the sink and turned on the faucet. There, she held her fingers and palm beneath a steady stream of cold water and shook her head.

"I hope you're better at designing websites than you are at making eggs." Kendra teased.

It was *her* fault that Michelle had lost track of herself. How long had they been standing there, staring at each other, for the pan to get so damned hot? But she didn't say anything to Kendra, fearing that any suggestive ideas might frighten her away. Of course, Kendra probably had no earthly idea what she was doing to Michelle.

The water offered some relief, but her fingers still throbbed. Small blisters formed on the pads. "No question about it," she managed to reply.

A hint of a smile curved the corners of Kendra's mouth. "Good."

"I can cook. I'm just used to twenty-first century implements. You know, things like pans with handles that don't get hot? Microwaves." Did you know that you don't have a microwave?"

Kendra nodded. "Yep. Don't need one."

"How do you make pop-corn?"

Kendra chuckled. The sound wove through her like a heavy liqueur and made her knees just as weak. "We don't make it very often, but when we do, we use cooking oil and kernels. Simple. You just have to keep shaking the pot."

Michelle wanted to roll her eyes, but the description seemed to fit Kendra so well. Everything about Kendra screamed of the past. Her carriage and her mannerisms, even her build, looked ancient and wise. Masculine and feminine at the same time. Broad shoulders holding up a warm, sensitive heart.

Suddenly, Michelle felt out of her own time and place. She was the one who lived in the wrong century, not Kendra.

Kendra turned off the water and inspected Michelle's fingertips. "I think you'll live. If you don't feel like cooking, don't worry about it. I think Carl was just being polite."

Michelle felt herself frown. "Well, then. Are you hungry? You haven't eaten."

Kendra's eyes fell on Michelle's mouth. "Don't do that."

"What?"

"Be nice to me. Try to take care of me... of us."

Kendra dropped her hand as if the burns were contagious and turned away.

"I'm not. But the eggs are already mixed. Are you hungry, or not?"

"No."

Liar.

She knew only one thing for sure.

She wanted Kendra Williams more than she'd wanted anything or anyone for a very, very long time.

Seven

"Feel like going for a ride?"

Michelle looked up from the computer screen and smiled. Kendra leaned against the archway with her arms crossed over her chest.

"I suppose. Where are we going?"

"I'm going to ride the fences this afternoon. Should take maybe three hours, or so."

"I could get some pictures." She had enough pictures, but the thought of spending several hours alone with Kendra overpowered her work ethic. She looked back at the screen. She'd almost finished formatting the templates she'd use for each page. She could afford to take the afternoon off. "Sure. I'd love to tag along."

"Good." Kendra pushed off the wall with one shoulder and reached toward her. She took Kendra's hand and a shiver of delight raced through her arm. Kendra's calloused fingers tugged at her hand gently and she allowed Kendra to help her to her feet.

Not that she needed help. But Kendra's old fashioned manners and insistence that she be treated like a lady played over her and made her forget she lived in a modern world. Should she be offended when Kendra opened doors for her? Last night, when they had dinner, Kendra had pulled her chair out for her instead of letting one of her brothers do it. Then, like now, Michelle had felt special and demure.

No, she shouldn't be offended. She would enjoy the attention for as long as it lasted. A part of her didn't want to finish the project. She wanted to stay here as long as she possibly could.

"You've never ridden before you came here, have you?"

Michelle smiled. "Does it show?"

"Only a little," Kendra chuckled. "But that's okay. I've saddled that same mare you rode the other day. She's about as gentle as they come."

"You knew I'd agree to come along?"

Kendra opened the front door for her and stood to the side. "I hoped."

Heat stole through her and crept up her neck and cheeks. Unable to meet Kendra's gaze, she passed through the door and down the steps to the horses. Kendra helped her mount then moved to her horse. Large saddlebags bulged from behind Kendra's saddle and she admired the way she mounted around them as if they weren't there. Her legs were covered with the chaps again, but the tight muscles of her backside showed through the faded denim of her work jeans.

Turning the horse with barely perceptible movements of her knees and a light hold on the reins, Kendra urged Preakness forward. Michelle followed.

"What's my horse's name, again?"

"Bethany Lynn."

"She's very tame."

Kendra laughed, slowing down so they rode side by side toward the range. "She's old."

"How old?"

"Oh, I'd have to say she's at least twenty-two."

"And that's old?"

"Yep. For a horse, anyway. She'll probably outlive us all for spite, though."

"She doesn't seem spiteful."

"In her youth, only one person could ride her. But she's mellowed over the years."

"And who was that?"

Kendra fell silent and stared forward for a moment. Had she said something wrong? Kendra seemed to move away from her without actually moving at all.

"She belonged to my mother." Kendra turned her gaze on Michelle and offered a half-grin.

"You miss them a lot, don't you?"

Kendra drew an unsteady breath and Michelle thought she might have winced a little. "Yeah."

"What happened? Lacey's never told me much about it."

Unease settled over the landscape. She wanted to take the question back, but she also wanted to know the answer. Kendra's life had been so hard and so lonely. If she was going to be Kendra's friend, she wanted to know how to help her.

For a moment, she thought Kendra wouldn't answer the question. Then a faraway gaze settled over her face and she squared her shoulders. "My parents had a very special relationship. Did you know my mother was a bona-fide rodeo queen?"

Michelle shook her head and smiled. "No. I didn't know that."

"She was. And she rode like the wind. She could rope and brand and keep up with any cowboy I've ever met, too. A true frontier woman. She didn't look it, though. She was beautiful. Small and fragile, but with the spirit of a man twice her size."

"Kind of like you..."

"Oh, no," Kendra continued. "She was all girl."

Michelle smiled. "So are you."

"Not really. I used to fret over how masculine I am, but in the end, it all paid off."

"Paid off?" Michelle giggled. "I don't understand."

"I was always afraid that nobody – no man – would find me attractive. When I realized that I didn't want a man to find me attractive, and when I wound up taking over a working cattle ranch... well, let's just say that I'm okay with who I am. I don't need to be *pretty*."

There was no denying that Kendra was on the butch side. Michelle had no idea how Kendra might personally identify herself, but the labels boi, dyke, butch all came to mind. But how could she not know how beautiful she was? How incredibly soft and sensitive and *womanly* she was?

"But Mom? Mom was definitely more of a buckle bunny. She wasn't from around here, you know? She grew up in Arizona and Dad met her when he rode the circuit. Rodeoing was part of their blood. That, and ranching."

"What about you? Do you compete?"

"I rode the local circuit when I was a kid, but didn't plan to make rodeo my life the way they did. Besides, the PRCA – that's the Professional Rodeo Cowboys Associ-"

"I know what the PRCA is, "Michelle interrupted with a giggle. "I do live in Vegas, remember?"

"Ah, yes. That's right. Well, they wouldn't let me compete in Saddle Bronc because apparently, if you don't have the right equipment between your legs, you just don't have big enough balls, no pun intended. And well... touring with the lesbian rodeo wasn't an option for me. But sometimes, we'd all go on the road and make a family vacation out of it. We'd spend six or eight weeks driving all over the Western US, chasing those eight seconds. That last time though, I was home on leave and just wanted to relax for a couple of days. I told them I'd watch the kids if they wanted to get away for a little alone-time. Since they competed all summer and fall, they had their own plane to make it easier to get from place to place. They wouldn't be away from the kids so much that way." Kendra pointed over a hill in the distance. "There's a private air strip right over that hill."

"Really? Your own airport?"

"Not an airport, really. Just a private runway. It's pretty overgrown these days. There's nothing else over that way except the old Sutton Gold Mine. It's been closed up for years."

"Wow, it really is like a setting out of an old movie around here. Sorry, you were saying?"

"They took me up on it and hired a driver to take Mom's horse, little Miss Bethany Lynn, here, up to

Wyoming, and Dad's roping horse, too. Then they took off for a couple of days R and R before the show."

"What happened?"

"Bad weather headed them off over the Great Salt Lake and they crashed on Antelope Island. Turns out, the pilot they'd hired was drunk, so we have no idea if the weather killed them or he did. There were no survivors, so I never got a chance to find out."

"I'm so sorry, Kendra." The words seemed empty and feeble in the wake of all that Kendra had lost. Not only her parents, but her youth and her dreams.

"It was a long time ago."

"Still, you must feel it."

Shifting in her saddle again, as though the conversation made her increasingly uncomfortable, Kendra grinned. She looked as though she might want to say something, but that trying to speak would be too risky.

Michelle inhaled a deep breath of warm, clean air. "So, where are we going?"

The change in conversation seemed to lighten the weight from Kendra's shoulders and she smiled. "I've got something I want to show you."

"What? Aren't we mending fences?"

"Not exactly."

The light played in Kendra's eyes like a child with a secret. Nothing about her seemed young, but for that short moment, she could almost find Kendra playful.

"What are you up to?" Michelle asked.

"You'll see."

She narrowed her eyes on Kendra, not sure if she should trust her, and shook her head.

"Look. Over there." Kendra pointed behind her and she turned.

A herd of antelope raced over a hill, turning and moving as a single unit. Their brown and white bodies glistened in the sun as they bounded over the uneven terrain. Tall antlers gave them an almost majestic appearance.

"How beautiful!"

"I'd have to agree."

Something in Kendra's voice made Michelle turn back to face her. Kendra's gaze settled over Michelle's face and stole her breath. Flustered, Michelle gathered her camera and snapped several hasty shots of the herd for the website and then turned the camera back on Kendra.

Kendra chuckled in that disbelieving way that seemed to be a part of her and asked, "You doing okay? How's the backside?"

"Fine, thanks," Michelle responded. "Yours?"

This time, Kendra laughed aloud. It was the first time she seemed to truly let go around Michelle. The sound was infectious. And encouraging.

"Fine. We're almost there."

They rode in silence for another half mile or so before Kendra turned them off the fence line and into a wild stand of trees. Michelle ducked under several low branches, keeping her eyes on Kendra's back. Ever confident, Kendra bent low and pushed through the branches. Before long, she led them to a small clearing. An oblong pool of water sat in the center. A steady breeze rustled the leaves overhead and the wild scent of moss tickled her nose.

Kendra dismounted, took Bethany by the halter and patted her neck before helping Michelle to the ground.

"This is incredible, Kendra. I swear, you'd never know it was here."

"Not many people do. My folks used to come here all the time. I used to swim in the spring, but it's pretty damn cold this time of year."

Kendra opened one of the saddle bags and Michelle peered inside. "A picnic?"

"We got to eat, right?" quipped Kendra in reply.

Michelle's heart fluttered and then skipped at least one beat. No one had ever planned a picnic for her before. She swallowed over the lump in her throat and wiped her eyes. Would Kendra notice they'd misted? God, she hoped not. Finally, she found her voice. "So, what's for lunch?"

You.

Kendra shook off the errant thought.

Light sneaked through the shadows cast along the ground and spilled over Michelle's shoulders. What would she look like in the moonlight, shoulders bare and silvered against the purple, velvet night? She couldn't be any more beautiful than she was right now, but it was worth testing out.

Someday.

Kendra still didn't know why she'd been compelled to bring Michelle to the spring. She rarely came here anymore, but something made her want to share it with Michelle. Something she'd been powerless to ignore. Maybe it was because of Kennedy's death and the fact that she'd been suddenly reminded that life is fleeting. Or maybe, she just wanted to get away from everything for a while. Maybe it was everything happening at the ranch that made her want to share something pure with another person. Whatever it was, it had her squarely at its mercy. If she wasn't careful, she could easily lose herself. Michelle had invited her in, after all, and Kendra seemed powerless to resist anymore.

Kendra dug through the saddlebags and brought out a plastic container of fried chicken and biscuits. A second plastic bowl held potato salad and a third was filled with pickles and a few pieces of celery. She handed Michelle the first one.

"Yum. Did you make it?"

"Er... no."

Michelle smiled at her. She didn't judge or assume Kendra should have. But she also looked like she expected that she could have. No presumptions. No expectations. Just faith.

Maybe that was why she felt so damned comfortable around her. As much as she didn't want to, she did. Of course, for a woman like her, that comfort played like warning sirens in the back of her mind. Still, she couldn't keep herself from enjoying Michelle's company.

Kendra retrieved the hobbles from her saddle pack and knelt to bind Preakness's front legs. He liked to check out the local habitat a little too much. Bethany shouldn't wander; she was more of a homebody in her old age.

Michelle pulled a medium-sized blanket from the

first pack and spread it on the grass, not far from the edge of the spring. A soft breeze lifted her hair beneath the brim of her borrowed cowboy hat. What light filtered through the overhead branches caught the strands and turned them into pure gold.

Kendra licked her lips. The memory of Michelle's mouth beneath hers sent a fire straight to the apex of her thighs.

None of this seemed like a good idea, really. She took off her hat and scrubbed one hand through her hair. This is the last thing she needed – some kind of romance with a hired hand. Great thinking. If she had a brain, she'd turn tail and run as fast as she could.

Part of her still wanted to. And not the part between her legs. That part wanted to explore and caress every inch of Michelle's body, mind, and soul. It was too late to run, now. Nope. She was well and truly hooked.

"You coming?"

"What?" Kendra swallowed hard. *Do not blush. Do not blush.*

"I've made you a plate. Are you coming to eat?"

Dear God. She swallowed hard. "Um, yeah. Of course."

Kendra sat down on the edge of the blanket. Michelle sat only an arm's length away. If Kendra lifted her hand, she could easily stroke her cheek. A shock tingled her fingertips with wanting and she made a fist.

Michelle smiled and bit into a drumstick. "This is really great chicken."

"Brad made it."

"Really?" Michelle examined the morsel and her eyes widened. "Did you teach him to cook?"

Kendra answered with a nod and finished chewing before she spoke. "Yeah. On a ranch, everyone has to pitch in, and the Heartland is no exception. The kids learned that fairly early on. Lacey did most of the cooking, of course, since she's a girl."

Michelle's sculpted brow arched over her red plastic drink cup.

Kendra's heart lurched for a moment. "What did I say?"

The cup poised in mid air, suspended just in front of Michelle's amazing, full, soft lips...

"So are you."

"So am I, what?"

"A girl."

"Yeah. So?"

"So, what's that supposed to mean? Lacey did the *women's* work?"

The censure in Michelle's expression was priceless, and Kendra tried not to laugh. "Well, yeah, because Lacey will be doing that sort of thing when she's married. It just seemed natural that it be her primary household responsibility."

"You mean, *duty*. It's her duty to her family to be a good homemaker. Because she is a girl. Because she *can* get married." Michelle's features formed a confused frown.

"Right. I think." Kendra stumbled. She didn't like stumbling.

"And you have no intention of ever getting married, I suppose." Michelle's voice had a unique mixture of accusation and resignation that Kendra found both confusing and delightful.

"Well, you know, for a long time, that wasn't really a viable option for someone like me."

"Sure it was. I'm sure there are lots of men who would be happy to marry the owner and operator of the Heartland Ranch."

"In case you haven't noticed, babe, I'm gay."

"I know that. That's not the point. The point is that you're placing Lacey into a preconceived gender role, just like all those people who say that two women who love each other have no right to get married and raise a family because their genders aren't 'right.' Who will be the husband and work and wash the car and mow the lawn? Who will be the wife and take care of the kids, wash the dishes, cook the meals and do the laundry? It's the same thing. It's total bullshit."

"Uh huh."

"And then there's the whole having-a-family-at-all thing. Two women and two men can't procreate, so they shouldn't be allowed to get married... Nevermind the gazillion kids who need loving homes or advances in medical science and technology. For crying out loud. I don't need a penis to get pregnant. I need sperm and a turkey baster!" Michelle took a deep breath and paused for a moment. "Sorry. I get a little carried away, I guess."

"You're preaching to the choir, here. I'm all for getting the rights I deserve, but I live in the real world. Right now, since I'm unwilling to marry for anything less than ninety-nine and forty-four one hundredth's percent pure love... I can't get married. See, the odds aren't exactly in my favor in this tiny little corner of Utah, even if it is legal now. And I still don't think there is anything wrong with a woman, or any person, devoting herself to her family. Wasn't that what the women's movement was all about? Giving women the choice to choose a career, or family?"

"Or both," added Michelle.

"Who would want to do both? Seriously. If you have the opportunity to have one full time job, why in God's name would you voluntarily choose two? No, being a homemaker is an honorable and rewarding career choice all by itself."

Michelle snorted. "One my mother never made."

"Your mom wasn't devoted?" Kendra frowned. Her own mother, in spite of her love for the rodeo and the way she helped her father on the ranch, was a dedicated and proud wife and mother. Her family came first. Her husband and her children. The ranch was her husband's job and she helped during the roundups and such, but otherwise... Mom was mom.

"Well, not how you mean. She had plenty of things to keep her busy outside of the house. Things that made her feel... worthwhile."

"Raising children is worthwhile."

Michelle scowled and then sighed. "That's not what I meant."

"I know," Kendra replied, smiling.

"Did you know that Lacey wants to be a reporter? She's already applied for internships at the affiliate stations in Las Vegas and Reno. And she's doing really well in school. She has as much chance of making it as anyone, I think." Michelle's words rushed together as if she were defending the entire female gender. Even on the tail end of a political rant, she looked more charming than ferocious.

"I know that, too." Kendra bit into a pickle.

"You're teasing me now, I think."

"Yep." The deep crease in her forehead smoothed. "Well, it really is good chicken."

A strong gust of wind passed over them. Michelle's plate tumbled out of her hand and landed a few feet away. She gasped and tossed herself after it. "Holy cow! Where did that come from?"

She caught the plate while Kendra grabbed several items that had been tossed by the burst.

Another downdraft made Michelle plant her hand on top of her hat. "What's that sound?"

Kendra listened. Something very much like the thunder of a distant train rushed into their hidden pocket. "It's a microburst. Hang on!"

"A what?"

Kendra could barely hear Michelle over the increasing noise. Before she could answer, the swirling winds of the tornado-like miniature storm broke around them. The air filled with dust, leaves and small branches. She squinted against the grit to find Michelle curled into herself about two paces from her. Kendra fell on her, pulling her as gently as she could to the ground and then shielding her from the torrent. Preakness screamed and Bethany answered as both horses stamped and pawed at the earth. Preakness was unable to move freely, but Bethany didn't have that problem. With a whinny and leap that sent her front hoofs into the air, she broke free and raced out of what she could only perceive as an immediate threat.

All Kendra could do was to wait until the ministorm had passed to settle Preakness and round up Bethany. Right now, her attention was fully on keeping

Michelle safe.

The hot desert wind trapped inside the vortex mixed with dust and razor-like sand to coat the back of Kendra's neck. A second later, the backside of the storm pelted her shoulders with debris. She tightened her hold on Michelle's trembling frame. Even though she could hear nothing over the pandemonium, Michelle's frantic breaths reached her in the rise and fall of her breasts. "Keep your eyes and your mouth closed! It's almost over!"

Michelle nodded and pushed her face further in to Kendra's chest. Kendra's body tensed. It seemed as if all her blood rushed straight to her groin. *God, Michelle felt good when she held her like this.*

As quickly as it had started, the haymaker moved away. Kendra opened her eyes and glanced upward. The yellow-brown windstorm rose a good hundred feet into the blue afternoon sky. Michelle pulled her head back from Kendra's chest as quiet settled over them. Kendra looked down to find Michelle staring up at her with wide, moist eyes. Several streaks of dirt marred her cheek and forehead. Kendra wiped them away with her thumb.

Only a heartbeat separated them. Barely an inch of space kept her lips from claiming Michelle's. Michelle chose that moment to moisten her lips, dried from the hot wind. She made a face reminiscent of a small child's first contact with broccoli. "Ew. Dirt," she choked.

Kendra laughed. "Yeah."

She should let go of her.

She should kiss her.

Dirt on her perfect lips or not, she should...

Michelle pulled away from Kendra and hugged her

knees to her chest. "What the hell was that?"

Kendra, ignoring the heat gathering in her boxers, stood and then helped Michelle to her feet. "It was a microburst. We call them haymakers, or dirt devils, depending on where they show up – in a hayfield, where they can save you a ton of trouble during the harvest, or in the desert, where they do nothing but pick up a ton of dirt."

"Really? Well, we're surrounded by your hay fields, not desert, so why am I such a mess?" Michelle laughed and glanced over her shoulder as Kendra settled Preakness, who was still a little skittish.

If Michelle was a mess, she'd be hard-pressed to find a more beautiful disaster. "The desert isn't that far from here. I've seen some storms like that one spin for miles. They aren't usually that strong, though, or that tall. Are you okay?"

Michelle brushed off her backside and laughed. "Yeah, I'll live."

Preakness released a shrill cry and glared at Kendra with one large, black eye. Kendra whispered under her breath, "Yeah, I know, boy. Dirt or no dirt, I should have kissed her."

Michelle took off her knee-length, cream chiffon skirt covered with light blue flowers and discarded it. Why had she even packed it? Every time she put it on, she hated it. Even if she'd loved it, of course, it would never do. It also represented the very last of the items she'd brought with her. She hadn't planned on needing anything for a funeral.

Services for Kennedy Bastian were set for Monday morning at ten. Margaret had called an hour ago and asked if Michelle would please attend. She thought the request rather odd, but at the same time, she had been there to offer what comfort she could and perhaps this was the older woman's way of acknowledging that fact. Perhaps, at the reception afterwards, Michelle could help in the kitchen and free others from the task of filling endless bowls of potato salad, or as Brad had called them last night over dinner, funeral potatoes.

And Kendra might need her, as well. The last couple of days had been a whirlwind of activity. Kendra was in and out of the house, racing to town one minute to help Kennedy Bastian's family with the funeral plans, running errands for his mother, or putting pressure on the Sheriff to open an investigation into the cause of the stampede.

Michelle had barely spent five minutes with Kendra since their time by the spring. She'd become distant again, it seemed, although in all fairness, Kendra was incredibly busy. It was amazing she'd even had time to go for that ride, now that Michelle thought about it. Why had she done it? Why had Kendra taken an entire afternoon off just to show Michelle that spring? Maybe she was coming around to the idea of a publicity campaign?

Not that it helped her with her current problem on little bit.

She released a sigh and slid on her jeans. She'd have to go shopping.

She hated shopping.

In the kitchen, she found Brent nursing a hangover and Brad frying two eggs, over easy, in the same vile pan that had burned her fingers four days earlier. They still ached and made working on her laptop less enjoyable than it should be. The early Saturday morning sunlight danced outside the window while a hummingbird hovered at a feeder hanging from the eaves.

Everything seemed so at peace, even with the intermittent moan or two from Brent. It was misleading, of course. Nothing was truly peaceful.

"You know, if you would stay home every once in a while, I'll bet your head wouldn't hurt so much," Brad quipped as he flipped his eggs before sliding them onto a plate.

"Forget it, kid. Life's too short."

Michelle smiled as Brent moaned again. "He's right, you know. Why do you do this to yourself? It hardly seems worth it to me."

"It's fun."

"You're green!" Michelle chuckled.

"I'll be fine in a couple of hours." Brent made a great show of sitting up straight. "So, what do you have planned for today?"

"Shopping." Michelle poured herself a cup of coffee and took the chair next to Brent. "I have to pick up something for tomorrow. Any good shops in town?"

"Well, let's see... There's the Pick and Shovel. And the requisite big-box or two. Nothing a fancy lady like yourself would use."

Michelle snorted. "Please. I shop at the big-box all the time. But this time of year, I'm wondering if they'll have anything in black." As soon as the words left her mouth, she tried to bite them back.

Brent must have sensed her discomfort. He reached out and patted the back of her hand. "It's okay."

"I didn't mean it to sound like that. I'm so sorry."

"It's fine." His fingers stroked hers.

The kitchen door creaked open. Brent withdrew his hand and winked at her.

Brad, his plate full of eggs, browns and bacon, sat at the end of the table. "Morning, Kennie. There's some bacon left if you want some."

Michelle turned in her chair to find Kendra standing in the doorway. Her eyes, clear and ever alert, showered heat in Michelle's direction and made her aware of every crevice in her body. Kendra blinked, as if she'd caught herself on some other plane of existence, and made her way to the stove. "Thanks, Brad. Maybe later."

"Hey, Kennie? Are you still going upstate to the horse auction?" Brent asked.

Kendra nodded, leaning against the counter and blowing into her mug before sipping the strong coffee. "Picking up the new horse trailer, too. I'm leaving in about an hour. Why? Want to come?"

"No, not me. But Michelle here needs to find a real clothes store. I thought maybe she'd like to hit the mall."

Michelle's heart leapt in her breast. Nobody knew about the searing kiss she'd shared with their sister. Brent only tried to help. But the chance to spend another day, even another hour, with Kendra made her feel positively twitterpated! Like a school girl with a crush on the quarterback.

Still, she said, "Oh, I don't want to be an

inconvenience to anyone. I'll just run into town."

"Really, it's fine. Kennie's going upstate anyway. It'll be fine. Right, Ken?"

She turned just in time to see Kendra shrug and place her still-full coffee cup in the sink. "Yeah, it's fine."

"Are you sure? I suppose I'd be able to get more images for the website if I tag along."

"Of course. No problem at all. I could use the company, actually. Be ready to leave by nine. It's a long drive."

A long drive? How long? Michelle didn't have time to ask Kendra before she disappeared through the doorway.

"You better get ready to go. If she says she's leaving in an hour, you can set your watch by it," said Brent.

"How long a drive is it?"

Brad shrugged. "About two hours, I guess. The auction starts at noon."

"Are you coming?"

"Nah. I'm working with Apache some this morning, then Lenise and I are catching the matinee in town."

Brad scraped the remains of his breakfast into the compost receptacle and rinsed his dish. Brent succumbed to his throbbing head and decided to take a nap on the living room sofa.

Her heart racing, Michelle stood and pushed her chair back under the table. "Have a great time at the movies, Brad," she offered before turning to leave the kitchen.

"What?" he asked.

"The matinee? You're going to the movies? Have a great time."

"Oh, yeah, right. We will!"

Michelle hurried upstairs to fix her hair.

So far, so good. Kendra had trouble focusing on the winding mountain pass leading them to the city, but she had managed to keep them on the road. If she kept her eyes on the road and her foot on the gas, she could get through the day without making a fool of herself. Simple, right?

She stifled a self-deprecating laugh. It was a losing battle.

Every few seconds, her eyes left the highway and rested on the woman beside her. Michelle had changed into a light skirt and blouse. Her hair hung loose around her shoulders. Hands folded in her lap, eyes fixed out the window – she looked less than comfortable in Kendra's beat-up old truck.

A woman like her should be surrounded by luxury. Soft linens. Fine clothes. Refinement, in general. She didn't need some hick cowboi-dyke who felt more at home on horseback than anywhere else in the world. Hell, was Michelle even gay?

Sure, they'd kissed, but that didn't mean Michelle was gay, right? Kendra had kissed plenty of women in her life, most of them, in fact, not gay. Michelle had kissed her back, though. The memory struck a hot, wet chord between Kendra's legs and she shifted in her seat. Heat radiated through her groin like a hot mist. She shifted again, trying to alleviate some of the moisture in her jeans.

The memory of that kiss rode her like a summer storm, insistent and demanding, every moment. Every time she closed her eyes, she relived it. She shouldn't have done it, but she didn't regret it. Not one little bit. She didn't have time for a woman in her life, and she had too much decency to play with women the way Brent did – especially straight women. But a part of her wanted to make time for the headstrong Miss Loving.

Until she was sure that the gorgeous woman sharing the bench seat was gay, she should be off limits. And even then...

The *what-ifs* wouldn't go away. What if Michelle were gay? What if Kendra let herself feel something good and pure, for once? What if she opened her heart... just a little... and made time to share her world, including her burdens, with someone special.

What if...?

The last couple of days had been crazy for Kendra, but they hadn't erased the warm, horrible, wonderful, awful, awesome, frightening feelings that had developed in the few days before that. That day at the spring had been amazing and provided her with just a tiny bit of hope that maybe, just maybe, she could love again. People got happy endings all the time, right?

But not her. She'd never found one. Not in her entire life. So, the question remained... was any of it worth the risk?

"How far is the mall from the auction?"

Kendra forced herself to swallow before answering. "About twenty minutes or so, depending on the traffic."

BANG!

The truck lurched and spun as a loud crack tore through the cabin. "Hold on!" Kendra growled.

From the corner of her eye, Kendra noticed the dead-white complexion of her companion.

Refocusing her attention on the road and regaining control of the truck, she fought the steering wheel and brought them to a skidding halt on the side of the road. Loose rocks flew from beneath the tires and a cloud of red dust blew over the hood.

"What just happened?" Michelle's breathless voice trembled.

"Blowout, I'm guessing. You'll need to get out, and go stand over by that boulder." Kendra pointed to the far right, off the road about fifteen feet. "We're in the Red Narrows, and it's a dangerous curve here. The oncoming traffic can't really see us."

Michelle nodded and slid out of the truck. *Talk about dangerous curves...* The loose-fitting skirt did nothing to hide the rounded swell of Michelle's hips and bottom. Kendra licked her lips and stifled a quiet moan.

Circling the truck until she found the offending tire, she cursed under her breath.

"Can you fix it?"

Kendra turned around to find Michelle exactly where she'd ask her to wait. Somehow, that truly surprised her. She leaned against the boulder, looking all vixen and seductive with her hair flying loose in the breeze and her gorgeous ankles peeking from beneath her skirt.

"Well, can you?"

"Can I what?"

"Fix the tire, silly."

"Oh. Yeah. It'll just take a minute."

Michelle stood out of the way, forcing herself to be calm instead of shifting nervously. If it wasn't safe for her to stand by the edge of the road, how safe could it possibly be for Kendra to work there?

Kendra took off her worn and faded denim jacket and laid it over the side wall of the pickup truck's bed. She climbed into the back of the truck and looked for something. A moment later, she bent at the waist to reveal the curve of one of the best blue-jean-covered asses Michelle had ever seen.

When Kendra stood upright again, she had located the jack and tire iron. She tossed the tire iron to the earth without a glance. After leaning the heavy, metal jack against the interior truck wall, she placed one booted foot on the truck's railing and launched herself expertly to the ground. With seemingly little effort, she pulled the jack over the side and let it thump onto the dusty, red rock-strewn ground.

Kendra applied the lug wrench to the bolts holding the damaged tire in place and twisted. Grunting, she seemed to be having some trouble.

"You need some help?"

Kendra let go of the wrench and released her breath. "No. I got it."

She tried again to loosen the bolts.

"You sure?"

Kendra growled.

Michelle tried to hold back the laughter threatening to bubble to the surface.

"What?" Kendra called over her shoulder.

Michelle placed a hand over her mouth. Had she laughed out loud? "Nothing!"

The first bolt spun free and Kendra made short work of the rest.

She positioned the jack under the truck near the blown-out tire and began to pump the handle. Muscles made from long hours herding and working cattle flowed like ocean waves beneath the fabric of her white dress shirt. Michelle caught her breath at the sight. There was nothing even remotely funny now.

She remembered the feel of those arms wrapped around her, gentle and feminine, but as hard as coiled steel. Her insides quaked, forcing her to close her eyes. When she opened them again, her heart beat in a solid staccato.

Kendra pulled off the old tire and shoved the spare into place before replacing the nuts and lowering the frame. Still crouching beside the tire, she turned to glance at Michelle over her shoulder. "You laughed at me," she quipped, the smile in her voice evident. Kendra sent Michelle a look meant to tease, one eye squinting against the sun. She turned back to the truck and tightened the lug nuts.

"No. I would never do that..." But Michelle laughed again, anyway.

Kendra snorted and rolled her eyes. "Lord, save me from insincere women." She secured the spare tire in place with the iron and stood back, crossing her arms over her chest.

Michelle had a clear view of her back as her shirt stretched taut over squared shoulders. The laughter died in her throat and she swallowed. Hard.

"Well, it'll get us there. But we'll have to pick up a new tire in the city." Kendra lifted the large jack back into the bed of the truck as though it weighed nothing at all.

Michelle didn't answer.

"Good thing I wasn't pulling that empty horse trailer," she continued. "Could've flipped the whole damn thing."

She still couldn't respond.

Kendra turned to stare at her. Was it possible for someone to spontaneously combust from a simple glance? Michelle vaguely remembered seeing a documentary about people who burst into flames for no reason. They must have been under the watchful scrutiny of Kendra Williams.

Kendra took a step closer. Michelle wiped her palms on her skirt and her stomach trembled.

A person would have to be blind not to see the sparks.

"Miss Loving..." Kendra closed her mouth, as if the words she wanted to say wouldn't come.

"Michelle. My name is Michelle."

Fists clenched at her side, Kendra stopped at least two paces from where Michelle stood. "I don't know what's happening here, but..."

Oh, no. Here it comes. She couldn't bear the thought of hearing those words from her. Not from Kendra. She'd heard them so many times.

Bad timing.

My life is too complicated.

Let's be friends.

I'm straight...

At least she could be almost dove-soap certain *that* wasn't the case here.

"Don't worry about it, Kendra. Really. I mean, it was one little kiss, right? You were upset; things were tense. It was only natural. No harm, no foul."

She forced herself to walk back to the truck. What she really wanted to do was run for the border. As far away from the humiliation and possible heartache as she could get.

Kendra followed her, like Michelle knew she would. Why did she have to bring this up here? Where she had no escape? She threw herself into the front of the truck and tried to pull the door closed.

One of Kendra's weathered hands caught the edge and held it open. "Wait one cotton-pickin' minute!"

"We're going to be late, Kendra."

"What was that all about?"

Michelle shrugged. "What do you mean?"

"I didn't get to finish what I was saying."

Why did she insist on saying it? Why couldn't she just get in the truck and drive? Michelle closed her eyes and bit her lip until she thought it would bleed. She tried to pull her other leg into the cab, but Kendra's body was in the way, positioned between her legs like some primal being. A wave of tangible passion collided with reason and crashed over Michelle's thundering heart.

Kendra leaned forward slowly, her flesh putting off heat to rival the sun. Passion eclipsed reason as Michelle realized she'd jumped to the wrong conclusion. She braced herself for a powerful, searing kiss. Her body yearned for it.

A truck pulled into the open space behind them, drawing their attention away from the moment. Three men climbed out and made their way over to them. One of them wore a dirty, red ball cap, which he pulled off momentarily to wipe his forehead. The second one, the largest of the group, had short-cropped black hair. The third was smaller than the other two. When he grinned against the morning sunlight, his parted lips revealed missing teeth. None of them looked like good Samaritans.

"Ya'll need some help?" Red-hat asked before spitting chewing tobacco on the ground.

Kendra ran a hand through her hair and pushed away from the door of the truck, her head bent at a forward angle. "No thanks, man. We're good." Her voice was deeper than usual, as though she were putting on a show.

Michelle knew why. If these strangers believed her to be male...

Silence followed. The men looked at each other and one of them grinned knowingly. The ruse hadn't worked. Worse, it was fairly apparent that they had interrupted something.

The largest of the three men spoke. "Fellas, I think we may have just stumbled upon a straight-up lezbo porno."

Kendra bristled, raising her head to its normal, confident aspect. "You guys can just drive on. We had a flat tire. I fixed it. We were just leaving."

"Yeah, a big strong *man* like you wouldn't have any trouble fixing a flat, right?" The little guy replied, sarcasm dripping from every pore of his being.

"Fuck you!" Kendra growled.

Michelle had heard that tone of voice before. Kendra's temper was on a tightrope.

"Aw, come on, honey. Don't be like that," the second man cajoled. "We'll just watch."

"Michelle, get in the truck and lock the door."

Michelle's first reaction was to obey, but she didn't follow it until Kendra made a hasty line for her side of the truck around the front end. Michelle reached for the door handle, but Red-hat got to her first. One of her legs was still hanging outside the cab and she instinctively raised her knee. She made hard, immediate contact with the man's groin and he fell to the ground. Screaming.

Kendra yelled from the front of the truck, "Lock the door!"

Michelle scrambled to reach the handle and slammed the door just as the her attacker rolled away, clutching his groin and retching. She reached across the seat to grab her cell phone out of her purse. Why wasn't Kendra in the truck yet? Panic closed her throat and stole her breath. She fumbled in her purse, searching blindly for her phone while scanning the windshield for any sign of Kendra.

Kendra was pinned between the biggest of the three men and the hood of the truck, his outstretched arm holding her at length and his fist balled next to his face. He swung hard, making crushing contact with Kendra's cheek. The force spun her around. Michelle's eyes met Kendra's. She screamed, "No! Stop!"

"Stay in the truck. Lock the fucking doors!" Kendra's voice was strong and forceful and not afraid. "Stay in the truck!"

Red Hat had found his feet. He banged on the

window with his fist only once before circling the front of the truck. He helped Toothless hold Kendra's arms while their friend rubbed his jaw. "I wonder if I kick your ass, if that's really beatin' a woman?" He laughed. "And when we're done with you, we're gonna show your lady friend what it's like to have a real man."

Michelle couldn't take it anymore. A thought struck her – clear, concise and right between the eyes as she stared at the asshole in front of her.

The Williams Clan really liked guns.

She spun onto her knees and reached between the back of the seat and the back of the cab. Her fingers touched cold steel and she grinned. She yanked the shotgun from behind the seat and checked to see if it was loaded. By rights, it shouldn't be.

But it was.

She kicked open the door, raced around the front of the cab and shot once into the air. Then she cocked the five-shot, pump-action Winchester and leveled it at the three men.

There is a very distinctive sound that a pump-action shotgun makes when the shells are chambered. The men dropped their hands. They let go of Kendra, who fell to one knee before steadying herself and standing upright. She spit blood onto the red dirt, wiping her mouth and nose with the sleeve of her shirt. She glared at the blood stains left on the fabric and Michelle heard her thick breaths.

Michelle turned her attention to their attackers. "I am so sick and tired of jerk-offs like you telling me how you would just love to show me what a real man is like. I'm sick to death of people like you spewing hate and violence. I'm gay. She's gay. We're both women. Get the hell over it, and if you don't want to find pieces of your damaged brains all over the goddamned highway, I suggest you get in your truck and drive back to whatever cave you crawled out of.

"Now!" Michelle raised the gun higher and reinforced the stock against her shoulder.

Red-hat picked up his ball cap and headed toward his truck, pulling his keys out of his front pocket. The other two followed, with the little guy limping for his trouble.

Michelle didn't move until they had pulled back onto the road and were well out of sight around the curve. She began to shake, her stomach lurching into her chest. Lowering the gun, she ignored her weakness and rushed to Kendra's side.

Kendra's lip was split and a line of blood smeared across her cheek. Michelle moistened the hem of her skirt and wiped it away.

"Those guys hit like pussies," Kendra managed to whisper with a smile. "They barely broke the skin." The tremble in her voice was unmistakable. Kendra laughed, but it obviously made her ache. She clenched one hand against her side. "You know, you could have just told me you were gay. You didn't have to go to all this trouble."

Tears finally burned the corners of Michelle's eyes as she sucked in a breath. "Are you okay?"

"Hey," Kendra answered, standing up straight. "I've had worse from my mother's old mare. They were pussies, remember?"

In a stand-still moment that lasted the briefest of seconds and the infinity of eternity, tenderness engulfed her, taking Michelle's breath away. Warm lips pressed against hers, bitter with blood and sweet with passion.

Slowly, Michelle felt her muscles relax. First her neck, then her shoulders, until her entire body seemed to float on a summer breeze. Hot and inviting. Strong, soft hands grasped her shoulders and pulled her into a hollow of chambray and woman. A quiet squeak left her throat and she couldn't begin to fathom where it had come from. No air was left in her lungs to form it.

Prompted by pressure from Kendra's lips and tongue, Michelle opened for her. Kendra tasted of coffee and mint and blood, the heady mixture intoxicating as it made its way through Michelle's body like a drug.

How had this happened? For days, Kendra had kept her distance until Michelle thought she would scream. Then that picnic, but no moves... And now? Now, Kendra filled her mind with images of their naked bodies wrapped in the sunlight and nights spent counting the stars.

She didn't know what the powerful ache in her heart meant. She only knew it lessened when Kendra held her like this. When Kendra kissed her, and ran her gentle hands over her back and...

Passion heated her blood as the kiss deepened...

Dear God!

Kendra filled her palm with Michelle's breast as Michelle arched into her touch. Her arms, leaden and heavy, moved around her neck. She became greedy for Kendra's attentions, pulling her lips with her teeth, stroking the short hairs on the nape of Kendra's neck.

Everything about Kendra screamed for her attention. She wanted to feel her next to her. Inside her...

Kendra pulled away, her breasts heaving with shortened breaths. "This is crazy."

Michelle frowned. Would she apologize? Again? Compared to the last kiss, they just made love on the side of the highway. How could she possibly live with herself if Kendra said she was sorry! Tears stung the back of her eyes.

"Now isn't the time or the place for ... this." Kendra pushed away and retrieved her jacket from the back of the truck, escorting Michelle to her side door. "Can you just see the headlines? *Dykes who should have known better run down by semi while making out on the side of road. Film at eleven.*"

Relief swamped Michelle's chest. She wasn't sorry! She was just... practical. Michelle didn't know if that thought made her laugh or if it had been Kendra's joke, but she laughed just the same.

Kendra collected her tools, tossed them into the back and then hurriedly slid behind the wheel and started the engine. Then she shifted her attention back to Michelle, the glow in her eyes completely serious. She lifted one hand and gently palmed Michelle's cheek. "Are you alright?"

Michelle leaned into the warm, fragile touch. "I'm fine, Kendra."

Kendra inhaled a breath and held it for a moment. When she released it, she looked deeply into Michelle's eyes. "What I was going to say before... well, I don't know where any of this is going, but I know that I didn't know what was missing in my life before you got here. Hell, I didn't know *anything* was missing. Things are kind of crazy right now, but I just wanted to say ..." She paused and ran a hand through her hair, exhaling what seemed like frustration. "Hell, I'm no good at this stuff. I'm just glad you're here, that's all."

A ripple of pleasure washed over Michelle, making her skin tingle and burn. She sensed how difficult such an admission must be for a woman like Kendra. Of its own accord, her hand stroked Kendra's smooth, square jaw in a reflection of her hand on her cheek. "Everything will be fine. You'll see."

Michelle couldn't remember a time she'd been so happy. If it weren't for the recent tragedy at the ranch, she wouldn't have been able to keep herself from giggling every time Kendra looked at her. Maybe she'd never had anything to giggle about, until now. She marveled that the stoic, uncompromising cowboi beside her was responsible for the change.

Kendra concentrated on the horses brought to the auction block. She'd bid on two already, having won the first and lost the second. She raised her head in a barely perceptible nod and the auctioneer accepted her latest bid.

A moment or two later, Kendra owned the pretty little mare she'd called a Palomino. She sat back in the bleachers and rested her elbows on the bench behind her. The position put one of her arms around Michelle and she tamped down the urge to lean into Kendra.

What would happen if she did? Would Kendra be uncomfortable with the show of affection? Would she push her away? The burgeoning feeling she was experiencing still seemed too new to allow such an assumption, so she refrained and rested her elbows on her knees instead.

Glancing back at Kendra over her shoulder, she asked, "How many horses are you going to get?"

"I'm shooting for six. That's all I can haul back in the new trailer. But I'll be coming back next week for six more."

"Why so many?"

"I'm putting on another half-dozen or so hands next week. They'll all need something to ride."

Another horse came up for bid, so Michelle fell silent and let Kendra pay attention to the bidding. A commotion ensued to their left. Several cowboys held a young man by the arms as he tried to break free. The cowboy shouted at a man she couldn't see clearly as if he wanted to kill him.

She elbowed Kendra to get her attention. "What's going on over there?"

Kendra shrugged just as the crowd parted and Harold Mason came into view. The air around her rippled with tension and she glanced back at Kendra. A muscle in her jaw worked furiously as she gritted her teeth.

"What's he doing here?" Michelle asked, returning her gaze to Mason and his men.

The cowboy put his head down and raised his hands before shrugging off his friend's hold and marching out of the enormous barn.

"I don't know. But I think I'd like to talk to that guy that just left. I'll be right back."

Kendra rose to her feet and sauntered down the bleachers. Despite the concern thrumming through her mind, Michelle couldn't keep her eyes off the fit of Kendra's jeans and the ease with which she moved. For such a butch woman, she seemed to exude an inherent grace, as if nothing could ever catch her by surprise. Always wary. Always alert. But often underestimated by her slow, natural movements and relaxed manner. Michelle found the contradictions more than a little appealing.

She watched Kendra until she exited through the same door as the earlier cowboy who'd been so upset with Harold Mason. She sighed, shaking her head, as Kendra disappeared.

Moony as a school girl, that's what you are.

She could no longer stifle a giggle before she leaned back on her elbows, closed her eyes and relished her sudden blessings.

The bench to her right sagged under considerable weight.

She turned and found Harold Mason sitting close beside her. Too close. His presence startled her, like when she watched television and blinked just as the scene changed from one to another.

Piercing black eyes fell on her. The lack of emotion behind those eyes stole her smile.

"You know, Miss Loving, a person should carefully consider who they go to bed with."

Anger burst through her chest and her mouth fell open. "Excuse me?"

An oily smile spread Mason's lips, but didn't reach his eyes. "Figuratively speaking, of course."

Something about the man scared her, made her want to run away. She wanted to slide further down the bench seat, but felt any retreat on her part would only fuel the man's ego and make him even more dangerous. "How do you know my name?"

"I make it my business to know everything about what concerns me. You work for Kendra Williams. That concerns me."

Fight fire with fire. If he wanted to play intimidation, she was more than willing. Buffering her spine with false bravado, she called on the hard-won experience of years spent dealing with casino managers and pit bosses. "Concerned, or scared, Mr. Mason?"

He laughed. "Scared? Not in the least, Miss Loving. I just thought I'd give you the opportunity to cut your losses. A successful woman such as yourself shouldn't feel obligated to a project just because of friendship. That pretty little waitress back in Vegas won't hold it against you if you back out. It's just good business."

He knew about Lacey? A shimmer of something bordering on evil crawled through her spine. She swallowed against the sudden lump in her throat. "I know good business, Mr. Mason. Don't worry your pretty little head about me."

The slight angered him, she could tell. Or maybe the tick in his left eye came from the fact that she didn't turn tail and run the minute he'd threatened her. And a threat is exactly what he'd given her. A threat against her and a threat against Lacey. Her pulse ticked the long seconds away like drops of water filling an empty barrel. It seemed an eternity before Mason shoved his hat on his head and rose to his feet.

A sinister grin replaced the twitch in his eye. He strode away without another word.

Her eyes narrowed at the sudden retreat, until Kendra climbed the bleachers and reclaimed her seat.

"What did he want?" Kendra leveled a steady glare at Mason's back.

"Do you think he's dangerous, Kendra? I mean, yeah, he's not very nice to cows, and his irresponsibility cost Kennedy Bastian his life, but do you think he is dangerous enough that he would have hurt Kennedy or anyone else directly? On purpose?"

Kendra spun her head in Michelle's direction, fire heating the green of her eyes until they shone like emeralds. "Did he threaten you?"

With fists clenched and a pulse visible in her temple, Kendra regained her feet.

"Kendra, wait!" Michelle gripped Kendra's arm and pulled her gently back to the bench. The steel cords of muscle beneath her fingers told her only Kendra's decision to wait stopped her from chasing Mason. If she'd wanted to go after him, Michelle's grip wouldn't be able to stop her.

"If he threatened you, I'll kill him."

The brooding cowboi was back. The woman who lived in another time, who hated microwaves and cell phones. The woman who would just as soon hang a rustler from the nearest tall tree as call the cops. Michelle shivered at the sincerity in Kendra's eyes. "Yes. He threatened me, but," she hurried to add. "I'm fine. But he knew things, Kendra. He knew my name, first of all, and he knew I came here because Lacey asked me to. He knew Lacey is a server in Vegas. I'm worried more for her than myself right now. And you and I both know that you're not going to shoot him at twenty paces, so sit down."

Kendra's eyes narrowed into cagey slits and suddenly, Michelle wasn't so sure. Michelle pulled her cell phone from her bag and handed it to Kendra. "Call Lacey. Tell her to come home."

A rough laugh rose above the din of the auction. Kendra turned her head toward the sound and grimaced when her gaze fell on Harold Mason again. Michelle found Lacey's number in her contacts and touched the screen to begin the call. Then she placed the phone in Kendra's palm. She looked at it with a scowl and reluctantly placed it to her ear.

"If he comes near you again, I swear to God I'll take him out," she whispered to Michelle.

Michelle knew she meant it.

Every single word.

Kendra had only managed to buy four new mounts. She'd lost the last two she'd bid on not because of a lack of funds, but because she wasn't about to pay more than they were worth and the bid winners got robbed. She loaded the last of them into the back of her new horse trailer and locked the tailgate. Michelle stood to the side of the truck, which now sported a set of four new tires, and spoke quietly on her cell phone.

While they'd made the trip to buy horses, Kendra did have something even more important to show for it. She had new information about the man she was dealing with in Harold Mason. The cowboy who had all-but attacked Mason had been full of details about how the man operated.

His name was Kevin Cooper and he'd owned a ranch in Panguitch, Utah. His father had left it to him when he'd retired, and his grandfather and great-grandfather had both worked the land. The eldest of the Coopers had cleared the land that family homestead sat on with his own hands. The story was familiar. It was her own.

Three years ago, Harold Mason had become the owner of that ranch in a court battle that had gone on for two years. According to Cooper, Mason had hired hot-shot, five-hundred-dollar-per-hour attorneys and bribed judges who all *relied* on Mason's word over his. He'd hired his own attorney, but it had done little good, in the end. Mason had produced documents, some shady and some outright forged, that made it appear as though Cooper had agreed to sell the land and the house to Mason, and then changed his mind after the deal was done.

The oddest thing about it, and what had Cooper so vehemently angry over the whole thing, even two years later and several hundred thousand dollar *richer*, is that Mason hadn't done anything with the land. He hadn't broken it up into residential lots. He hadn't sold it for a profit. He had sold off the livestock for pennies on the dollar and both the land, and the family home, sat abandoned and disintegrating for lack of use and love.

Everything deserved to be loved. Even land and old houses. And citified public relations experts and ranchers.

Kendra's gut clenched when Michelle tossed her hair over her shoulder and tucked several loose strands behind her ear. Head tilted, she noticed Kendra watching her and smiled. Something made her blush and she ducked her head before turning away and finishing her conversation.

If anything happened to her, Kendra would never forgive herself. How had she become such an important part of her entire being in just a few days? Kendra's eyes narrowed as she studied Michelle's back. She must be losing her mind, that's all. She shoved away the inclination to name the feelings moving over her with the force of a hundred wild Mustangs.

In a month, maybe less, she'd be finished here and heading back to Las Vegas. Back to her glitzy world of rhinestones and lights. And Kendra would be here, fighting to save her family's life's work. Alone.

Like she'd been doing her entire life.

She'd never minded it before. She'd made her decision and stuck by it with pride and conviction. That's who she was. Her rewards were simple. Casey and Brent had grown into good men. Brad would, too. Sooner than she'd like, if she were going to be completely honest. Lacey was as head strong as she was, insisting that she fend for herself and refusing to accept Kendra's offers to pay her tuition. She'd only hoped her parents would be happy with what she'd done.

Then this woman came barreling into her life like a summer storm. She took her breath away each time Kendra looked at her, made her body as hot as a brush fire. Even now, she wanted Michelle. More than anything she'd ever wanted anyone in her very lonely life. What would she feel like wrapped around her? Her smooth skin naked against hers? Kendra's body responded to the thoughts with an insistent throbbing. She closed her eyes against the sweet pain of it.

Yeah. She wanted her, alright.

But what would happen when she left? She'd be alone again. For the first time in her life, that thought bothered her.

"Ready to go?"

Kendra snapped her attention back to the moment. "Yeah."

Once Kendra merged into the heavy, evening traffic, she asked, "Who were you talking to back there?"

"My office. Just checking in."

Kendra nodded. "Did you get enough pictures?"

"Yeah. Tons. Thanks for bringing me along. And for the mall, too. I found a great dress. I know you were bored out of your mind. You didn't have to stay."

Yes, she did.

The thought of leaving Michelle alone for even one second wounded her. Especially after the encounter with Mason this afternoon, and those assholes in the morning.

Lacey, too. Of course, Kendra's younger sister had fought her, at first. Kendra had expected no less. But ultimately, she'd promised to pack up and wait for Casey to come get her. Casey had reluctantly agreed to move back to the ranch for the time being.

It had been a long time since the Heartland Ranch had seen the whole family under one roof. She only wished it was for a happier reason.

A sense of longing mixed with reluctance. Foreboding settled over her like a heavy fog.

Mason had officially declared war, as far as Kendra was concerned. She glanced at Michelle as she settled in for the long drive home. She could design her site, make her phone calls and send her letters to all the bureaucrats she wanted. Who knows, it might even help...

Kendra, in the meantime, would circle the wagons and wait only so long. Then she'd be forced to act. She didn't doubt for one second that Mason was capable of a hell of a lot more than stealing or slaughtering her livestock.

No way in hell would Kendra allow that man to harm her family.

Or the woman who had so easily invaded her heart.

Running into Kendra Williams and her new comrade at the auction had been more than a surprise. Apparently, the best laid plans of mice and men often go astray, regardless of how well those plans are laid out and paid handsomely for.

Kendra Williams was bruised and battered, but very much alive.

When the auction concluded, he climbed into his truck and retrieved his cell phone from his suit-coat pocket. He dialed the first number saved in the recent calls list and waited for the obnoxious ring-back tone to stop.

"Hello?" Charles Lassiter answered almost immediately.

"You want to tell me why I just had a conversation with the Loving woman at the county auction?"

"Um..."

"And do you want to tell me why she was sitting next to Kendra Williams the whole time?"

"Well, see, what happened was-"

"I don't want your goddamn excuses. I want the job done right the first time. You and your boys be at my office at nine tonight, and you better bring my money."

"Yes, sir, Mr. Mason. We'll be there. If there's anything we can do to make it up-"

"You can do your job."

Mason disconnected the call and shoved his phone back into his pocket. He really shouldn't have expected anything. That's what came from hiring lowlifes to conduct real business. Unfortunately, his resources were limited and he'd made a fatal mistake. He'd underestimated Kendra Williams' luck.

And her determination. It didn't surprise him that she wasn't selling out for cash. She had money. But he hadn't realized how much the ranch meant to her. Of course, that was just icing on the cake, when it came right down to it. Taking something from her that meant nothing wouldn't have quite the sweet taste of victory that he was looking for, now would it?

Putting out an order to have her killed had been a move of desperation on his part. A mistake he wouldn't repeat. That order wouldn't go out again until she knew he would have the ranch when it was all said and done. That would be sweet icing, indeed.

Eight

Flowers covered every available surface of the Bastian's living room. Michelle carried a gorgeous, etched-glass vase filled with fresh lilies and struggled to find a place to display them. Kennedy Bastian's family and friends milled about in small groups, talking among themselves in hushed voices. Every so often, someone laughed with a painful tinge to the sound, but more often, someone cried. The new widow sat on a crushed velvet sectional beneath the front windows, her fourteen-month-old son curled in her lap, sleeping. Michelle had offered to take the boy upstairs, but understandably, the young mother hadn't wanted to let him go.

The afternoon wore on until Kendra, her brothers, except for Casey who had gone to Las Vegas to bring Lacey home, and Michelle were the only guests left in the small house. She felt, more than before, that she intruded on their grief. After all, she'd never even met Kennedy.

"You okay?" Brent leaned against the wall next her, where she stood by the door to the kitchen.

"Yeah, I'm fine."

"You don't look fine. You look tired."

She offered him a smile, hoping it hid her agreement. She *was* tired. Unable to sleep last night, she'd stayed awake until four in the morning and nearly finished the website. She stifled a yawn. "I'm fine. Really," she stated, covering her mouth and yawning the words.

"I'll get Kennie. I think it's about time to head home."

Kendra.

Just the mention of her name made Michelle's stomach dance with nervous knots. A flush heated her cheeks and she looked at her feet. She hoped Brent hadn't noticed.

"I don't care what it takes, Kendra. I want that bastard put away!" Kyle Bastian's voice cracked through the dull air, lighting it with determined and obvious pain.

Michelle pushed herself off the wall and followed Brent into the kitchen. Kendra held Kyle against the pantry door with one strong arm across her friend's chest. In her free hand, she held a shotgun, pointed at the ceiling. She had obviously just disarmed him, somehow, and was holding the gun out of his reach.

"I know how you feel, Kyle. God damn it, I do. And we'll get him. But I'm not letting you go off half-cocked. We need proof. And we'll get it. You do this and you're the one who's going to spend the rest of his life locked up. Is that what you want? Is that what Ken would have wanted?"

Kendra's voice sounded hollow, as if she didn't believe a word of what she'd just said. She tried to do the right thing when Michelle knew how badly she wanted to go for Mason herself. A hundred years ago, Kendra and Kyle would be riding for Mason right this minute. Guns blazing. Honor held high like a standard.

But this wasn't the Old West. The new west insisted on civility and due process. Well, maybe not civility, but there were laws that had to be followed. Even her fierce cowgirl had admitted that much.

"Let him go, Kennie," Margaret Bastian whispered. The sight of the tears streaming down the old woman's face made Michelle's eyes sting with tears of her own.

Kendra complied and Kyle seemed to lose all of his strength. He fell into Kendra's arms, weak and barely able to stand. Kendra held him, stroking the back of his head while she passed the shotgun to her brother. Where some might have felt uncomfortable, Kendra seemed to offer her own strength to her friend. She bore their weights as if she'd been born to the task.

Kyle released a sob and buried his face in Kendra's chest. "He was my boy."

Kendra glanced over to Michelle as if she'd just realized she stood there. Unshed tears made her eyes sparkle. When they finally escaped, they trailed down her cheeks like rivers of silver sorrow.

"We'll get him, Kyle. You have my word."

Kendra felt like she'd just been dragged behind her truck. She could handle hours in the saddle, brand a hundred head and work until her fingers bled raw from rope burns, but today had wiped her out. She opened the front door and ushered Michelle ahead of her over the threshold. Brad and Lenise settled in the den to watch a movie. They'd wanted to stay in town and go to the theater, but Kendra wasn't comfortable with that; not right now. Brent had decided to stay in town, a decision she didn't much care for, but had no control over. This left the house almost completely empty.

She closed the door. The click of the latch sounded louder than it should have.

Michelle turned around and stepped up to her, wrapping her arms around Kendra's waist. She leaned her head on Kendra's chest for a second before raising her chin and looking directly into her eyes. "You're tired, Ms. Williams."

Kendra's throat felt dryer than a desert in a drought. She could only nod.

"Are you hungry?"

"No." She cleared her throat. "No, thanks. I had plenty of funeral potatoes and ham at the luncheon."

Kendra still wasn't used to the easy way Michelle moved against her; like she belonged there. And she knew it. Her hands settled on her back and Kendra held her. She'd wanted to do this all day, but a funeral didn't seem like the right place to announce to the community that Kendra Williams finally had someone special, and that someone was a girl. A woman.

So, she'd kept her distance. But she'd ached to hold Michelle all day. Michelle belonged in her arms. Even Kendra knew that much.

"Do you want to lie down?"

Michelle's question shocked her a little and her entire body responded. An image of the two of them – writhing naked on her bed – flashed in her mind.

Somehow, she didn't think that's what Michelle had meant. The thought brought a half-smile to her lips.

Michelle eyed her with more than a little suspicion and a small grin of her own. "What's so funny?"

Kendra shook her head. "Nothing. No, I don't want to lie down."

Sure, I do...

"We could put together a couple of the web pages. The template is finished. We just need to write the text and we're done."

Kendra frowned. When she finished the site, Michelle would go back to Vegas. She should get her out of here as quickly as possible, but the thought made a rock form in her gut. "How long will that take?"

"A couple of weeks, I guess."

"Is that all?"

Michelle moved into the dining room and sat in front of her laptop computer. She moved the mouse-thing and the screen jumped to full-color life. "A few days ago, you couldn't wait to get rid of me."

Kendra joined her in the dining room where she took a seat at the table, as well. With her elbows resting on the surface, Kendra ran a hand through her hair. She was suddenly aware of them... her hands. She didn't know what to do with them. She only knew that the sound of Michelle's voice, with that teasing note, sent warm rivers of heat and passion all the way up her legs. "I've reconsidered."

"Have you, now?" Michelle flirted with her. Kendra found that she liked the way her voice moved over her like a caress; as physical a manifestation as if she'd touched her.

Kendra stood, circling Michelle's chair. She placed her hands on Michelle's shoulders – it was a good place for them – and kneaded the soft muscles. "Yes. I have. I guess you're growing on me."

Michelle moaned under her touch and Kendra's body ached more urgently. "Do you really want to work right now?"

Michelle hissed when Kendra pulled the tip of one finger over the side of her neck and traced her earlobe. Such beautiful ears.

"Not really," she answered, her voice quivering.

"What do you want to do?" Kendra leaned forward and nipped the side of Michelle's neck gently with her teeth, then soothed the sting with her lips.

Michelle's entire body trembled.

Gaining her feet, Michelle turned toward her. She recognized her own passion in the other woman's eyes. A dangerous combination, if her body burned even half as hot as her own. "Are you sure?"

Michelle nodded.

Kendra felt like she'd just roped the wind. Powerful and urgent. Wild and untamed.

Crushing her lips to Michelle's, Kendra kissed her from inside herself. The more she gave to her, the fuller she felt. Her heart burst until she couldn't breathe. Michelle kissed her back, her mouth open as her tongue probed in timeless rhythm. How long they stayed like this, she couldn't even begin to guess. Everything was right when they held each other, when Kendra allowed herself to feel; to cherish Michelle the way she deserved.

Kendra moaned and Michelle echoed the sound, stirring the hollow between her legs to a fever she'd never known. Moving as one, lips searching each other for some indication of surrender, they stepped toward the stairs. She'd never make it. She wanted Michelle now, right now. Right here.

She remembered her younger brother and his girlfriend in the den, only a few feet away and down the hall.

Stealing herself against the pain she knew would come, she stopped and parted her lips from Michelle's greedy grasp. "Wait... wait."

"No, I don't want to," Michelle heaved with ragged breaths. "Can't wait."

Panting, Kendra stared into her eyes. Her breasts rose and fell with labored breaths. She deserved so much more than Kendra could ever give her. A part of her conscience told her to stop this recklessness before it was too late. She didn't listen, but they had to be careful. The kids...

Instead of doing the right thing – sending Michelle to her bedroom alone – Kendra placed one extended finger over her lips and whispered, "Shh."

Then she led Michelle to the top of the stairs, down the hall, and through her own bedroom door. Unable to wait another moment, Kendra reclaimed Michelle's lips, mouth, and body, kicking the door shut with the heel of her boot.

Together, they fell onto the bed.

Better...

The least she could do is make love to her in a bed, when every instinct in her body wanted to take her on the dining room table. She could live with herself after this. She hoped.

Michelle stared up at her, chewing her bottom lip in a mixture of coquettish flirtation and a hint of genuine curiosity. The amazing and beautiful woman reached for Kendra and when her hands made contact, they felt like branding irons on her stomach and hips. If she seared her this much through her shirt, she was a dead woman, for sure.

But what a way to go.

Like a woman possessed of something unknown and unknowable, Kendra stood before stripping her clothes away, piece by piece. Rising to her knees, Michelle matched Kendra's impatient and frenzied movements. With one hand, Michelle was pulling Kendra's shirt free of her waistband, and with the other, she worked the latch on Kendra's belt. Impatient, Kendra sat on the edge of the bed and struggled to pull off her boots. By the time she'd kicked them to the floor and bared her chest, Kendra could no longer stand to not touch Michelle. She turned back to the bed and found Michelle had somehow managed to divest herself of the silky black dress she'd worn to the funeral. She wore only a black lace bra and matching panties. The contrast of her light skin – so light she doubted the sun had ever seen parts of her – and the dark fabric mesmerized Kendra.

Divine.

Nothing short of a goddess could be this beautiful...

Full breasts strained against the cups of black lace. The slight mound of Michelle's belly fell away to rounded hips made for a woman's hands. Her hands. The same one's that she hadn't known what to do with a few moments earlier knew exactly what they wanted to do right now.

Michelle reached behind her back and released the clasps of bra. The black lace fell away.

Torment washed over Kendra in waves until she slid the length of her body next to Michelle's on the soft folds of the comforter. She palmed one breast and reveled in the exquisite weight of it in her palm. Sucking in a breath, she allowed the sensation to travel over her entire body. With awe and a bit of inspiration, Kendra leaned on one elbow and gazed at Michelle's body as she trailed her fingertips lower; over her belly, over one hip, slowly down the outside of one smooth, silky thigh.

Michelle's thighs parted, inviting Kendra to explore the hidden treasures beneath the small band of black lace.

Kendra obliged. Pushing the narrow lace aside, she moaned as her fingers slid over the slick surface beneath. Michelle arched her head back into the pillow, granting her access to her neck. Kendra snuggled closer, turning her body to partially cover Michelle's Rubenesque perfection. She licked and teased the hollow of Michelle's throat. She wanted to lick and tease somewhere else, and the temptation to ignore the merits of foreplay reared in the back and front of her mind.

Michelle's thighs tightened around Kendra's probing fingers.

Hot. Slick.

Wet.

Please, don't stop...

Michelle couldn't make her brain communicate with the rest of her body. Nerve endings sizzled in anticipation of what Kendra might do to her next. Her fingers clenched the bedspread on either side of her writhing body. Kendra trailed humid fire over her neck until her lips settled on the aching peak of one breast. Kendra's strong fingers delved deeply inside her at precisely that moment, relentless in their sweet torture. Her tongue laved over Michelle's swollen breast and Michelle's fingers moved to entwine themselves in Kendra's short-cropped hair.

She'd never believed the stories she'd heard... About how one woman's touch could make her into a lunatic bent on only one goal; total consumption. She wanted more than Kendra inside of her. It wasn't about sex. It was about a melding of spirits in a dance of love so basic and primal that nothing else mattered.

Kendra's mouth moved to Michelle's other breast and she gasped.

More. Stop.

Don't stop.

What would happen if she died right here? Who would find her? Her breaths came in shallow gulps which did nothing to feed her blood. The only thing keeping her alive was Kendra. Kendra's heart was her heart. Kendra's blood was her blood. Kendra's breath was her breath. Passion's pressure built inside of her, filling every crevice of her body with liquid fire.

More heat. More flame.

Until she exploded from within and her juices flowed like a dam had broken from the force of a sudden, raging storm.

Kendra shifted her weight and a moment later, she hovered over Michelle. Leaning on her elbows, she stared down at Michelle with blazing fire in her eyes. Kendra parted Michelle's knees further and slowly slid her body lower...

And lower.

When Kendra's mouth fell onto that hot, wet place, it was all Michelle could do not to release a scream to wake the dead. She covered her mouth and allowed her body to guide her. She rocked her hips, grinding her most secret place against the instrument of torture that was hell-bent on her total destruction. In only a moment, only a few thrusts, the heat gathered in her middle, growing stronger with every movement and every silently whispered promise, until finally, a second explosion raced through her limbs, her belly, and her heart.

Unrelenting and singularly determined, Kendra did not release her. Instead, she continued to caress that one part of Michelle's body that screamed for mercy.

More. More.

More!

Michelle's breath came quickly in shallow bursts until her entire body released with an intensity she'd never experienced before. Kendra backed away, leaning on her haunches as she wiped her fingers over her Cheshire-cat grin.

Michelle smiled, closing her eyes as she caught her breath.

Kendra collapsed on the bed beside Michelle, collected her hand and lifted it to her mouth. She traced Michelle's fingers with the tip of her tongue. "Yes?"

Michelle could only nod.

"Good."

A few moments of silence followed, each of them knowing they didn't need to say anything. They had communicated on a level that surpassed words. When the energy pulsing around her diminished and her limbs began to resuscitate from their little death, Michelle turned onto her hip and gazed into Kendra's eyes.

What was Kendra thinking? Was she happy? Would she regret what they'd done as soon as the pleasure wore off?

"Are you alright?" Kendra continued to place tiny kisses on the tips of Michelle's fingers.

"I'm perfect," Michelle answered, her eyes dancing in the dim light that filtered through the drawn shades. "Better than perfect."

"I didn't hurt you, did I?"

"Of course not," Michelle responded with a confused smile.

"It's just that I've been known to get carried away from time to time, and I have to say, it has been a while. I'm a little out of practice, I guess."

Michelle's perfectly arched brows rose slightly and her eyes widened. "You could have fooled me." She paused. "I suppose, the question we should be asking is, was it good for you?"

Kendra's heart opened like the petals of a flower. None of the very few women she'd ever been with had ever asked her that before. Of course, she was fairly certain that most, perhaps all, of them were straight girls looking for a thrill. To them, she'd been nothing more than a vibrator with a pulse. Her satisfaction had meant less than nothing to them. Michelle's question caught her completely off guard, but she couldn't stop the smile from tugging the corners of her mouth. "I'm good. No worries."

"Good. You're good?" Michelle leaned slightly forward, keeping her eyes locked on Kendra, until her lips barely grazed the flesh of her neck. The contact felt like molten rock and sent an arrow of heat coursing through her blood.

"Well, now that you put it that way..."

Michelle moaned quietly, sliding her naked body closer to Kendra. "Mmm hmm." Her tongue darted from between her full, moist lips, stroking that sensitive place on Kendra's neck where her throat met her collar bone.

Like a crash of thunder that comes from a clear, blue sky, the enormous growl of a motorcycle's highly-tuned engine rumbled through the room. Unable to ignore the implications of the sound, Kendra's body froze.

Michelle's mouth stopped working its erotic magic and she lifted her head. "What's wrong?"

Kendra pushed herself upward until she could peer out the bedroom window. "Nothing, babe. Casey's home."

"Oh. Okay... come back here."

Kendra turned back to Michelle at the sound of a playful smile in her voice. "It's not that simple, my darling."

"What isn't that simple?"

"Lacey's car is already in the driveway, and looks like it has been for more than a couple of minutes, if you know what I mean."

"Lacey's home?"

Kendra's heart began to race again, but not for any promises of illicit or erotic moments stolen from her real life. None of her siblings knew she was gay. None of them knew she had avoided settling down while they were growing up not because she was dedicated to their well-being and their care, but because they gave her an excuse not to date the men in town who had asked. They had been her excuse to hide in her closet on the ranch all these years. She closed her eyes and fell back on the bed.

How long had Lacey been home?

Nine

Michelle didn't know whether she should laugh or cry. Her body still tingled with left-over heat. Every time her mind settled on the memory of Kendra's touch, her stomach clenched and heat seared to her very center. She pulled on her bra, grabbed her panties and threw them on as quickly as she could. Her legs trembled.

Kendra finished buttoning her shirt and pulled on her boots. Like two marathon runners in the last half mile of a Twenty-Five *K*, they raced to dress.

Michelle found a tee shirt and threw it over her head and shoulders, and then grabbed a band for her hair. She made a messy-bun out of the tangled mass before tucking loose strands behind her ears.

"How long do you think she's been here?" Her chest tightened with the beginnings of laughter.

"I don't know. I was otherwise engaged, remember?"

Michelle's body responded with a shock of very well-placed heat and a slight tremor. Oh, yeah. She remembered.

"Try not to blush, okay?" Kendra teased her and Michelle discovered immediately that she liked it.

"I'm not blushing." But she knew she was. She felt positively feverish.

"Yes. You are."

She took a deep breath and headed for the door. "You ready?"

"Yeah. But you go first. I'll come down after a couple of minutes."

Michelle threw open the door and padded down the hall on bare feet. She ducked into her room to throw on a pair of jeans and tugged on a shirt and then rushed down the stairs. She reached the bottom step just as Casey opened the front door.

"Hi, Casey!" Did she talk too loudly? Her heart raced in her ears with so much force the sound was deafening. She couldn't tell if she whispered or screamed.

Casey narrowed his eyes with a curious half-smile. "Hi, Michelle."

"You hungry? I was just going to put something on the stove."

Michelle swung herself around the banister and headed for the kitchen.

"Sure, I could eat. Where's Lace?"

"I'm in here!" Lacey's voice came from behind the swinging door. "And I'm none too happy, either!"

Michelle's pulse felt like a steel-drum band as she entered the kitchen to find Lacey browsing the fridge. "What's wrong?"

Lacey turned and offered a faint smile. Michelle accepted a short hug and then leaned against the counter, one fingernail perched between her teeth.

"Nothing, except I lost my damn job to come here." She turned her attention back to the refrigerator. "And I'm going to miss two finals."

"I told you, Lace. It's for your own safety. Who knows what that son-of-a-bitch is capable of." Casey sat at the table and looked at Michelle, his lop-sided grin never faltering.

The back door squeaked open, drawing Michelle's attention. Kendra slid into the room and Michelle stifled a moan born of memory and the power of lust. She must have gone out through the front door to make it appear as though she'd been anywhere but upstairs.

"Hey, baby-girl," Kendra said, crossing immediately to her little sister.

Lacey turned to face Kendra and burst into laughter. "I can't... I just can't do it for one more second."

Casey joined her in the secret joke; at least, Michelle hoped it was secret. She looked at Kendra for some kind of sign, and then flames seem to steal up both of her cheeks. She lowered her head and pinched her nose, her lips spreading into a wide grin.

Crap. If only the floor would open and swallow her whole.

Kendra cleared her throat. "What's so funny?"

Michelle mumbled into her hand, "Your shirt is buttoned wrong." She glanced under her fingers as Kendra examined the front of her oxford button-down. Looking down again, Michelle noticed the satin tag of her tee shirt.

"Hm," Lacey hummed. "And Michelle, dear, your shirt is on inside-out. And backwards. I *wonder* what's been going on here?"

Kendra narrowed her brows and re-buttoned her shirt. "I have no idea what you're talking about. Nothing is 'going on'."

"Oh, come off it, Sis." Casey leaned back in his chair and laughed again. "You can't be serious."

Michelle shook her head and spoke into the curled palm of her hand. "Lacey? How long have you been home?"

"Oh, about thirty minutes."

Yup. Hole in floor. Now, please.

"Who knew you were a screamer?" Lacey patted Michelle on the shoulder as she strolled by, as if they were talking about something akin to the color of the sky or the weather.

Kendra groaned. "Okay, that's enough. We're all adults here, but you have to keep this quiet. Brad can't know. He wouldn't understand."

"Understand what?" Casey asked.

"You know very well 'what.'" Kendra wrung her hands together and Michelle couldn't help but remember, just for a second, what they felt like on her body.

"No, I don't know 'what.' Enlighten me, please."

"You guys have been around a bit. In the Navy, around the world. Living in Las Vegas, for crying out loud. But Brad hasn't. He doesn't know how... diverse... the world is. He doesn't know anything about lesbians or gays, or much of anything. I don't want him to find out. Not yet. Not like this."

Casey and Lacey exchanged a knowing glance, then refocused their attention on Kendra.

Lacey smiled, tilting her head in that way that could only mean, *You poor dear... you poor innocent little thing...*

Her twin cleared his throat into his hand, then crossed his arms over his massive chest. "Um, Kennie... Brad knows you're gay. We all know you're gay."

Michelle closed the two or three feet separating her from Kendra and slid an arm behind her back. Kendra leaned back into the embrace as though she had lived there her entire life.

"What was that?"

"I said that he already knows. He's known for quite a while, in fact. We all have. It's really no big deal."

"He knows?"

"Of course he does. He was... what, Lacey? About eight or nine when he asked us about it?"

"He did what?!"

Michelle could feel Kendra's body heat rising through the fabric of her shirt. "It's okay, Kendra. It's going to be fine."

"No. No. There's no way that little Brad—"

"'Little Brad' is going on eighteen years old. He's a grown damn man, and he is just as much okay with you being a dyke as every single man on this ranch - and woman too, apparently." Casey winked at Michelle.

"But how did he—"

"He asked and I told him. He asked why you weren't married because you were so pretty and stuff. I told him that you hadn't found anybody worth marrying. He made a couple of suggestions - himself included, mind you—like Harvey Whitehouse from the library, Colton Reeve, and that guy who used to pump the gas at the filling station on Old Farmer's Road."

"Christ! He was like ninety!"

"Yeah, but Brad liked the penny candy he used to slip to him every time you filled up that beater truck you used to drive. Anyway, I finally had to tell him that you hadn't found anyone to marry because you'd want to marry a girl and there weren't very many around who wanted to marry a girl, too."

"Oh, God... you didn't."

"Hell, yeah, I did. And do you know what he said? He said, 'Why would she want to do that? Girls are icky."

The kitchen fell silent for a few short moments, long enough for the words to bounce around from wall to wall and fall into a jumbled heap on the kitchen table.

"Icky?" Kendra repeated.

"Icky. And that was that."

"So, basically, you're telling me that everyone on this ranch knows I'm gay."

"Everyone," Lacey interjected.

"And nobody gives a flying rat's ass," Casey continued.

"How did everyone know? I mean, I never dated anyone... not really."

"Well, that *might* have had a little something to do with it, but come on, Kennie. You really weren't trying to hide it. You're... well... you're just a little... I dunno," Casey stammered. "Butch. You're kinda butch. And not just tough like some of those rodeo cowgirls or the gals who help at roundup with their husbands. I mean... you're *really* butch."

"Okay, okay," Kendra chuckled, rubbing her fingers into her forehead as though she tried to keep the top of her head pinned into place. "I get it. I'm butch."

Michelle's eyes began to swell with moisture and

heat. There really wasn't anything to tear up about, right? But she couldn't help it. It felt as though a huge weight had been lifted off of Kendra's shoulders, and the fact that Michelle felt that weight lift meant something. It meant that she truly cared for this strong, independent woman who seemed so relieved that she didn't have to hide anymore. The feelings had grown so subtly over the course of the days she'd been on the Heartland Ranch that she hadn't even noticed it, really. Of course, she'd noticed the flutter in her stomach and the heat that made its way through all of her most intimate parts routinely, whenever Kendra entered a room. But she hadn't noticed the deeper, more connected feelings that swept across her now.

She hadn't noticed...

Lacey popped the top of a soda can, the aluminum sound snaring her attention. Lacey giggled and propped her feet on an empty chair. "So, that's settled right? Ya'll are being big ol' lesbians together."

Kendra growled. "That's enough. We're all adults here."

"I guess that's a good thing," Lacey laughed.

Kendra spun in Michelle's outstretched arm so they were facing each other as they leaned against the counter. "You okay? You haven't said much."

Michelle could only nod. She lifted her head and released a sigh.

"Look at her," Casey announced. "She's bright red."

"That's enough, Case. I mean it."

"So, um, how long as this been going on?" Lacey asked.

"How long has what been going on?" Brad led Lenise into the kitchen through the swinging door.

Kendra stood up straight and answered, "Nothing, Brad. Hey, there, Lenise. I thought you were watching a movie?"

"We did."

Michelle looked at the clock and realized she and Kendra must have been *occupied* for much longer than she'd realized. Time flies when you're having fun, right?

"Hey, there's some guys with a van unloading a bunch of stuff in front of the house, by the way." Brad grabbed an apple from the bowl of fruit on the counter and bit into it.

Michelle perked up and headed for the door. "A black van?"

"Yeah," he mumbled around his mouthful of fruit.

"They're here! She dashed out of the kitchen and raced up the stairs to change her shirt.

She'd rather be boiled in a vat of motor oil.

Kendra sat on her horse and watched the activity unfold on the range in front of her with disgust and annoyance as her constant companions. Brent sat next to her, his horse munching on new grass. Casey reclined in the passenger seat of a jeep, one arm flung over his eyes to block the midday sun.

Eyes narrowed against the glare from several windshields, including the black van, Kendra focused her attention on Michelle. She did her best to ignore the eight men and one woman who'd invaded her home last night.

Her success could be measured with a thimble.

"You know, you could be a little more sociable."

She looked at Brent, leveling as icy a glare as she could manage in the growing heat. She suddenly envied Brad who was, at this moment, taking his geometry final at the high school. Turning her attention to the front once more, she watched Michelle dismount Bethany and approach the camera man.

She held her hands in front of her, her fingers pointing up while the tips of her thumbs met in the middle, staring over the rolling hills and the distant mountains. She looked like an old-school filmmaker. She pivoted on one foot, twisting her body until her jeans hugged every curve, every crevice. A breeze caught her unbound hair, lifting the golden strands on a whisper. She shook her head in an attempt to clear her field of vision, then gave up and tucked several locks behind her ear before scanning the horizon again. Fastened to the image, Kendra nearly moaned.

"Okay," Michelle shouted.

The leader of the pack of vagabonds from the black van – what was his name? Vincent? – approached Michelle with a clipboard in one hand and a bottle of water in the other.

Kendra didn't like Vincent. Her eyes narrowed on the younger man's shoulder-blade length black curls and wide back. He seemed a little too familiar with Michelle. The hint of jealously spiking in her nerves made Kendra push Preakness toward the small crowd.

Vincent turned toward her and smiled. Kendra's eyes narrowed a little further. Never trust a man who smiled like that; all teeth and no grit.

"Jus' the woman I wan'ed to see." The lazy British accent felt like ice water poured down the back of Kendra's shirt.

She didn't answer.

"We need ye to ride yer 'orse across that pasture," he instructed, pointing behind him with his thumb, "an' chase a couple of yer beasties toward the camera."

Kendra raised one eyebrow.

Vincent waved a hand through the air. "'Ello! Cowboy, person? Anybody in there?"

Kendra just stared at him. Hey buddy, you want to lose that hand?

"Hang on, Vin." Michelle patted the director on the shoulder and stepped up to Preakness' neck. She stroked the glossy coat with delicate fingers. "Hey, Kendra. You know, this isn't as bad as you're making it out to be." She smiled up at her and Kendra's heart swelled, stealing what little breath she had left when Michelle looked at her.

"I don't like him. If he pats your ass one more time, I'm going to run over him with my horse."

"Is that what's bothering you? Vincent's flirting?"

"He doesn't have to touch you."

"Don't be jealous, sweetheart. He really isn't any competition. You know that, right?"

"Do I?"

Michelle wiggled her finger in Kendra's direction, indicating she should lean down from where she was perched in her saddle. She complied and Michelle lowered her voice to a conspiratorial whisper. "I'm gay. I don't like guys that way."

Kendra sighed and pursed her lips as she sat

upward again. Was she really? What if she was bi, and just didn't want Kendra to know? Hell, she knew women who had claimed they were gay and ended up marrying men, for whatever reason. All signs pointed to Michelle's integrity, but experience was a hard taskmaster. Kendra couldn't help but worry, just a little, about putting her heart out there in stampede territory.

"Come on, Kendra. Don't make this more difficult than it is. You haven't said more than three words to them since they got here."

"Three? That many? And ya'll keep telling me I'm not being sociable."

It was Michelle's turn to sigh and Kendra hated the fact that she felt exasperated because of her. But she hated strangers on her property. She hated the fact that the whole world would know her business. Her eyes shifted back to the wannabe rock star director. And she hated Vincent. She returned her attention to Michelle. She was prettier, anyway.

Michelle chuckled and pushed her sunglasses further up on her nose as she tilted her head to one side. Her hair came untucked and Kendra's fingers itched to replace the strands behind her perfect little ear. "Can you please behave?"

"Why are they here, again?"

"We are making a publicity video. We'll send a disk to anyone who contacts us about it from the website. And all the major news outlets, of course."

"Like that will do any good."

"It will." Michelle stroked her leg and the touch burned through Kendra's chaps and jeans. Fire shot through her insides and moisture followed, forcing her to shift in her saddle.

"Well, I'm not going to drive the cattle toward the camera."

Vincent replied from several feet away. "Why not?"

What was he; a rabbit? Kendra glared at him. "If you must know, hot shot, I don't trust myself not to stampede them right over your citified ass."

Michelle squeezed her thigh. "Behave!"

She groaned. Could this day get any worse? She supposed the sun could fall out of the sky and land in the back of her pickup. Or her head could literally explode.

"Kendra? Do it for me?" Michelle's voice washed over her in a plea made from blue flame.

She closed her eyes and took a breath. She would do anything for Michelle.

Nudging Preakness back toward her brothers, she grumbled under her breath. Somebody would have to ride with her to make sure she didn't kill Vincent, but she'd do what they asked.

She pulled on the reins when she reached Brent. "Let's go."

"Where are we going?"

"We're going to run a couple of cows and let them film us."

"We are?"

Kendra recognized the sarcasm in her brother's voice. *You mean you caved?* it said.

"Don't start in on me, Brent. I mean it."

Her brother laughed. "Me? I wasn't going to say a thing."

Spurring Preakness to a gallop, she made for the herd. Within a few minutes, she and Brent had cut out three cows and drove them back toward the video crew.

She cringed as Vincent screamed into a bull-horn. "That's righ'. Good. Righ' there! Now! You're goin' to push 'em toward me."

"If he spoke any slower, he'd be talking backwards," Brent stated flatly, shaking his head. "Does he think we're idiots?"

"I think so." Kendra looked for Michelle and found her climbing on Bethany's back again. If it weren't for her, she'd never do something this ridiculous.

"... an'... Action!"

Brent leaned back in his saddle. "Does that mean we're supposed to start? I'm not so sure, you know, me being a dumb-ass and all."

"Ha!" Kendra yelled and waved her coiled lasso in the direction of the three cows. They pranced a moment before they started moving forward.

Brent laughed and joined her. Before they'd moved twenty paces, the cows picked up speed. Kendra and her brother chased them. If it weren't for the cameras, she would love this. Hot wind stung her cheeks and, as Preakness moved from a lope to a run, she felt as if she floated over the range.

Scenery rushed past her in a blur of green and blue. Focused on the ride, she let herself ignore the camera crew as they blew past.

Echoes of the bull horn cried in the distance, but she couldn't make out the words. Brent released a rebel yell and raced against her. A smiled formed on Kendra's lips.

"Think they've had enough?" Brent bellowed over the creaking leather and rushing wind.

Kendra looked over her shoulder and pulled on the reins. Preakness slid to a halt.

So did Kendra's heart.

None of the visitors watched them. Even the camera stood unattended on its tripod. Instead, they gathered in a circle. Some of them kneeled, some stood, looking at the ground.

Bethany snorted and stomped the ground nearby.

Riderless.

Michelle squinted against the pain in the back of her skull. She inhaled and winced. Why was everyone staring at her? And how did they get so tall?

"You a'righ', then, love?" Vincent asked.

He knelt beside her and she realized that she was lying on the ground. She'd fallen off her horse? A stream of memory washed through her mind. Bethany had bucked and pranced and Michelle had fallen off.

She moaned. Every part of her body ached now. Had she blacked out? "Yeah. I'm fine, Vin."

"Out of the way." Kendra's voice came from far away, it seemed, further than it should have been. Squinting against the sunlight, she watched as Kendra pushed her way to Michelle's side through the circle of people. She shoved her way past Vincent and fell to her knees. "What the hell happened?"

"I dunno, mate. She fell off, I'd imagine." Vincent raised his head to the crowd. "Anybody see wha' happened?"

"It's alright, Kendra. I just hit my head, I think."

"You think?" Kendra looked into her eyes, apparently studying her pupils. Her eyes narrowed. "Did you lose consciousness?"

"Just for a second. Nothing serious."

Kendra growled.

"Really," Michelle continued. "I'm fine. Let's get back to work, okay?"

She tried to sit up, but Kendra eased her shoulders back to the soft grass. "Not so fast, sweetheart," she whispered. Michelle could actually feel the sound to the pit of her stomach; soothing, warming, gentling.

Strong hands moved over her shoulders and neck, then moved to her hips and...

"Ouch!"

Kendra turned back to concentrate on her face. "Where does it hurt?"

She sucked in an breath as Kendra kneaded her right thigh. "Right ... there! Right where you're... ow!"

Kendra sat back on her ankles and rested her hands on narrow hips. "I think you can call it a day."

"We have more work to do."

"No, we don't. Come on. Let's see if you can even walk."

She snorted. *Of course she could walk.* As though she convinced herself, she gritted her teeth and said, "Of course I can walk!"

Kendra helped her to her feet and she put her weight on her injured leg. Wincing, she pulled her foot off the ground again.

"That's it. You're going back to the house. Now."

Something inside Michelle shifted. Something she hadn't felt in a long time, if she ever had. She couldn't tell, the sensations were so foreign. Someone took care of her. Someone concerned herself about her well-being. As much as she knew it couldn't last, she liked the feeling of letting go. She leaned against Kendra's weight and she allowed her to lead her toward the jeep. "I'll drive you back."

"What about Bethany?"

"I'll shoot her in the morning."

"You will do no such thing! God, Kendra, it was just a little fall. You can't—"

Kendra laughed. "Settle down, little warrior. I was only kidding."

Michelle laughed and suddenly realized that her ribs hurt, as well. She must have taken quite a fall. So much for her career as a western horsewoman. The thought brought a smile to her face despite the pain.

Kendra knocked on the hood of the jeep with her free hand and Casey jumped.

"What?" He wiped the side of his mouth with the back of one hand.

"Move," Kendra ordered.

Casey jumped out of the jeep and helped Kendra maneuver Michelle into the passenger seat. "What happened?"

"She got tossed. I'm taking her back to the house and calling Doc Weaver—"

"I do not need a doctor." Michelle winced deeply as Kendra slid Michelle's foot onto the Jeep's rusted floorboard.

Kendra ignored her protests, but immediately apologized for hurting her. "Is that better?" she asked as she helped her adjust to the hard seat.

"Yeah," Michelle replied, breathless and gritting her teeth. "I'm fine. Really."

After making certain Michelle was settled completely and firmly into the seat, and pulling the seat belt across her lap as gingerly as possible around her injured leg, Kendra climbed behind the wheel, turned the key and the engine roared to life. "Casey, you bring Preakness and Bethany back with you."

Michelle couldn't suppress the smile that formed at the incredulous expression on Casey's face.

"I don't ride them damn things." Casey's head shook as if he'd rather be thrown off a cliff.

"Don't give me that crap. You ride as well as any of us, now move it." Kendra sped away, leaving her younger brother in a near state of shock.

"I don't need a doctor, Kendra."

"Yes, you do. You hit your head hard enough to black out. You're seeing the doc."

"But I'm fine, really. I know my name. I know your name. And I know I don't need a doctor. Ow!" she yelped when the Jeep hit a particularly deep hole in the uneven terrain.

"Can you remember how you fell off?"

"Yes! As a matter of fact, I can."

Kendra bit her bottom lip as though she considered her words carefully. "Calling him, anyway. Head injury aside, you could have a broken bone in the shapely leg of yours. He only lives about three miles from here. He'll be over before you know it."

Michelle rolled her eyes. "This wouldn't be an attempt to get out of filming, would it?"

"Nope." The Jeep, regardless of how slowly Kendra drove, bounced over the field until they reached a dusty, dirt road. She swerved onto it and sped up.

"I don't believe you."

"Don't care."

They hit a rut and the Jeep tilted drastically, shoving Michelle's leg against the open door jamb. "Shit!" she cried, the pain apparent in her crisp voice.

Michelle released a tense breath that had nothing to do with exasperation and everything to do with the injury to her leg. That muscle in Kendra's jaw twitched again, and she kept her eyes trained on the road, even though Michelle knew she must have driven it a thousand times.

As they drove the remainder of the way in silence, a throb started at the back of her skull and worked its way into her eye sockets. She'd hit her head harder than she'd thought, apparently, and the pain in her leg had changed from the kind that comes from kicking a table leg in bare feet to a dull, consistent ache. Except when they hit a bump in the road. Then it started all over again.

Kendra's aquiline features held a dark frown until they pulled in front of the house. She threw herself out of the jeep and raced around the hood to reach her. Taking her in her arms, she carried her to the porch.

"Kendra, I can walk. Well, I can limp, anyway. You don't have to carry me."

She shoved the door open and headed for the stairs. "Maybe I want to carry you."

Michelle's cheeks burned, so she hid her face in

Kendra's chest. She smelled of leather and roses with a hint of lavender. She could live in that scent.

Kendra passed her door and took her to Kendra's room. Laying Michelle on top of her bedspread, she took off her hat and tossed it onto the bureau. "Don't go to sleep."

Michelle's brows narrowed when Kendra left the room. "Where are you going?"

She didn't answer.

Michelle laid on the bed for a moment before testing her thigh with her fingertips. She winced. *That's going to leave a mark.*

She unbuttoned her jeans and eased them over her hips. Her breath caught as the stiff fabric brushed her leg. A bruise the size of a baseball glove had already formed on her upper thigh and had begun to wrap around the outside of her leg. She screwed her face into a sneer and leaned back on her elbows.

Wonderful. She wouldn't be wearing short skirts for a while. Not that she ever did, really.

Kendra knocked on the open door and approached the bed. She held a bag of ice in one hand and a glass of iced tea in the other. "Here. I thought you might want something cold."

She felt that twinge again, right near her heart. The one that said, "She cares about you." It warmed her soul and made her think of...

Not the future. She didn't know where any of this was going, but Kendra didn't love her. She knew that much. She accepted it. Right now, she needed her, that's all. And when she didn't need her anymore, Michelle would be nothing more than a fond memory. They were enjoying each other's company and having a good time. Michelle had a life and a business back in Vegas. She would have to go home eventually.

"Thank you," she whispered with a smile.

"The ice is for your head. The doc's on his way."

"You called him?"

"I told you I was going to."

"This isn't fair, Kendra." Her voice lowered an octave and she didn't know why. She cleared her throat when Kendra sat on the edge of the bed, unbuckled her chaps and tossed them aside.

"What's not fair?" Her fingers brushed a loose strand of hair and tucked it behind Michelle's ear.

"You're allowed to take care of me, but I'm not allowed to take care of you."

Her hand dropped to her thighs, covered in dusty, worn denim and she looked away. "I don't need anyone to take care of me."

Kendra stood and crossed to the bureau where she'd tossed her hat. Placing both of her palms on the edge, she leaned into it, her head bent. Why did Michelle find it so necessary to get into her head like this? She'd been fine without her for thirty-five years, right?

So, why did the fact that she might have been seriously hurt make her so bat-shit crazy?

She could have broken her neck. She damn near broke her head. And her leg. She probably separated a rib, at least. She closed her eyes and pushed herself off the dresser.

"I'm sorry," Michelle finally continued. "I didn't mean anything by that."

She turned around to find Michelle leaning her back against the wall under her mother's picture frame collection. Her head was down, and both hands rested in her lap. The bag of ice sat abandoned on the coverlet. She worried her fingers and bit her bottom lip so hard, it looked like she might actually remove it.

Damn.

"No, I'm sorry. I shouldn't have been so defensive. I'm just..." What? Just what? Could she tell Michelle that she'd scared her to near to death? "I'm not used to this, that's all."

Michelle smiled. "I know. It's okay. Really."

No, it really wasn't. She could tell just by looking at Michelle that it wasn't. This was exactly why she didn't want a woman in her life. The high-maintenance of a relationship partnered with all the drama that went along with it. She didn't have time for it. She never had, even before she'd inherited four kids.

Sure, she'd dated a bit, here and there. Even had a bona-fide love affair with a barrel racer when she was a kid, following her folks from rodeo to rodeo. That relationship had lasted even while she'd been in the Navy. That had been the real reason she hadn't gone with her parents that day... But she'd never felt like this before.

Not once.

She should say something, but she had no idea what. The air grew so thick, she could chew it.

"Someone's at the door."

"What?" She felt like she was standing on some other planet.

"Didn't you hear it? The doorbell just rang."

"Oh. Yeah. Wait here. I'll get it."

She thought she heard Michelle chuckle as she stomped down the stairs. She groaned. Of course she'd wait there. She couldn't walk. For Christ's sake, she was losing her goddamned mind.

Doc waited on the opposite side of the door, wire glasses on his nose, gray hair combed to the side and a black bag clutched in his gnarled fingers. "Hey Doc. Thanks for coming over."

The old sawbones smiled and stepped into the foyer. "My pleasure, Kennie. I don't mind, you know. I miss the old house call days. So, what's the emergency?" He practically chomped at the bit and a twinkle of excitement sparkled in his moist eyes.

"Upstairs." Kendra and the old doctor climbed the stairs to the second floor. "I have a houseguest. Michelle. She got thrown off Bethany about half-an-hour or so ago. She blacked out for a second. I just thought you should give the once over."

"That's good thinking, Kennie. But then, you've always been protective of the kids, haven't you. You'd make a great mother someday. Make some young man very happy."

Kendra couldn't help but grin just a little. What the old doc didn't know wouldn't hurt him. But he was right. She had worried over her brothers and sister for a long time. Doc should've really had his own room on the Heartland.

A few minutes of examination and Doc declared Michelle none the worse for wear. His prescription, in addition to a round of powerful pain killers from the local pharmacy, included a good, long soak in a full-to-the-top, hot bath. And rest. She'd be sore a few days, at least. If her ribs started to hurt worse in a few days, there was most likely a separated rib, which can hurt just as badly as a broken one, but would have to heal on its own.

Kendra tried to ignore the relief that surged through her, like someone lifted a loadstone off her shoulders.

She'd just found Michelle. Despite all her reasons why she shouldn't want her, she did. She wanted her more than she wanted to breathe. She needed her more than water. If she'd been seriously hurt, Kendra didn't know what she'd do.

What the hell was the matter with her?

"How's the temp?" Lacey poked her head into the spa-like bathroom, not for the first time since Michelle had managed to climb into the huge tub.

"It's wonderful. Now stop hovering. I'm fine."

"I'm not hovering."

Michelle laughed. "You most certainly are." She released a sigh and smiled. "You might as well come in and keep me company."

Lacey closed the door behind her and sat on the marble counter between the matching sinks. "I'm sorry I wasn't out there today. But I made some progress with Channel Thirteen in Vegas, I think."

"Did you get the internship?" Michelle asked as she ran her hands around the bubbles in the tub to make sure they covered her completely.

Lacey pressed her lips together in a sheepish grin. "I don't know yet, but I'm hopeful. Lord knows, I'm going to need a job when I get home."

Michelle's heart plummeted at the sound of the word. Home. She never wanted to go home. A month ago, the thought of feeling so comfortable on a cattle ranch would have made her laugh. But everything about this placed called to her. Nothing moreso than the owner.

Kendra had insisted she use the big tub to soak. She'd drawn the water, added the bubble bath and made sure everything was perfect. She'd even lighted several candles. Then she'd helped Michelle undress. Her stomach tightened as the memories of Kendra's hands on her suddenly felt real, more than remembered. She tamped away the erotic longings, hoping she didn't look like a fool with some love-sick expression on her face.

And then, silently and without any aplomb whatsoever, Kendra had left.

"What are you thinking about?" Lacey's voice held a note of knowledge, like she already knew the answer to her own question.

Michelle's cheeks burned. "Your sister," she giggled.

"Yeah," Lacey responded with a knowing grin. "What's that about?"

Michelle stretched her leg where the bruised muscles still cramped, despite the moist heat of the bath. "I don't know. I mean, she's a really great girl and well, she makes me feel all... I don't know."

"Are you falling for her?"

Michelle couldn't answer. Was she? Was the feeling that she never wanted to leave this place indicative of lust? Infatuation? Or was it more real? Surreal? She'd never been in love. That would explain how Kendra could make her feel all hot and bothered, swoony even if she wasn't in the room. Would it explain why her body tensed and tingled whenever she even thought of her?

Of course, those reactions could easily be the result of having made love to her... aftershocks. Right?

"No. I don't think so," she finally answered. "I mean, I've only known her a couple of weeks. And I'm not looking for anything serious, right? And neither is she, for that matter."

"If you say so. You're both grownups, so it's fine by me. But, just for the record, she is my sister. She raised me, which makes her kinda like my mom, too. So, just, well, if you're not serious and it looks like maybe she is? Don't hurt her."

Michelle winced, and then held out her hand. Lacey leaned forward and took it in a gentle grip.

"I'm not going to hurt her," Michelle whispered. "I promise."

But what about Kendra? Would she... Could she make the same promise?

A rap on the door broke the tenderness of the moment.

Kendra's voice sounded muffled through the door. "What's going on in there?"

"Nothing," Michelle and Lacey answered in stereo.

"I'm going to finish making dinner." Lacey winked and let herself out of the bathroom.

Kendra stepped in and leaned her backside on the counter that Lacey had just vacated. She wore the same leathery, floral scent that she always did. Michelle couldn't tell if it was cologne, or just her. Her hair looked damp. "You feeling alright?" she asked.

Michelle could only nod.

"How's the leg?"

"Ugly as sin, but I'll live." Michelle's voice cracked and she swallowed.

"I'm really sorry about this. I guess Bethany isn't as mellow as I thought."

"Where did you go? Before?"

"I had to close up the barn. Left to Casey, and every horse we own will be free-ranging come sun up."

Kendra's smooth, rounded breasts rose and fell beneath a clean, crisp white shirt. A half-smile made small wrinkles appear in the corner of one green eye. Weathered and strong, everything about her seemed to scream, "I can handle anything," and whisper, "take care of me," at the same time.

She must be losing her mind. A few minutes ago, she'd thought Kendra had left because she didn't want to be with her, or she was scared of getting too close, and now, she seemed as if she wanted to be nowhere else in the world.

"You ready to get out, yet?" Kendra asked.

"No. I don't ever want to get out. It's amazing in here," Michelle sighed, "but I probably should. I'm going to wrinkle up and float away."

Kendra held open a fluffy desert-rose-colored towel. Balancing on her good leg and using the wall to steady herself, she climbed out of the tub. Kendra wrapped the towel around her and rubbed her shoulders to ward off the slight chill of the evening air. Warm breath settled on her neck. A shiver that had nothing to with her damp skin rippled through her flesh.

"Come on. Let's get you tucked in."

"But, it's still early."

"Doctor's orders. You're to stay off that leg for at least a couple of days. Brad downloaded a couple of movies and everything is set up, so it's dinner in bed and a movie-marathon for you."

Dinner in bed sounded nice, actually. But she doubted Kendra was on the menu. Glancing over her shoulder, she offered Kendra a smile that must have relayed her thoughts. Her eyes smoldered behind hooded lids. Strong hands still held her arms, but now they pulled back ever so slightly, until her back settled into Kendra's chest. Encircling her with the towel and a powerful, yet gentle, embrace, her lips made contact with Michelle's still-wet skin. Nibbling for a moment before she turned her in her arms, Kendra then captured her lips in a kiss meant only to pleasure and tease. Her tongue played along the ridge of her teeth and swept her into a rhythm older than time itself. The towel fell away. Heat flushed Michelle's limbs.

Kendra picked her up as if she weighed nothing and carried her to her bed, settling her in the turned down sheets. The cool cotton did nothing to assuage the fire consuming her.

She knew what to expect and thought it would make a difference. It didn't. She felt as desirable as she had yesterday. The only difference came from the knowledge that Kendra wanted her as much as Michelle wanted Kendra. Her heart swelled.

The setting sun played through the windows,

casting shadows around the room as Kendra slowly removed her shirt. Her breasts, bared in the failing light, were smooth and round. And beautiful. Michelle caught her bottom lip between her teeth. What would she taste like?

A clock ticked from the surface of the bureau, but that sound alone filled the quiet. Wearing only her jeans, Kendra laid down beside her. She coaxed Michelle's legs apart with gentle pressure as she rained kisses on her neck. Nipping her throat, teasing and playing her fingers through her wet hair, she pressed her thigh against her... there.

Denim scraped against her flesh. The heady contrast between Kendra's soft touch, her slow movements and the rough texture of her jeans seemed to weave a spell around Michelle. Every sensation brought her closer to knowing her.

One hand moved to cup Michelle's breast before Kendra's lips followed. She laved sweet attention there, and then moved her hand to the juncture of Michelle's thighs. Her body no longer belonged to her. She pushed against Kendra's hand, wanting more and immediately missing the heavy pressure of the denim. Her hips moved faster of their own accord, terrified that the fire being stoked so furiously might somehow fade away.

She moaned. Kendra caught the sound with her lips and continued the slow, deliberate torture, controlling her without saying a word.

Michelle fumbled between them for the button on Kendra's jeans. She wanted to feel the soft folds of her body, the moist heat of her passion and her slick, tender secret places.

Kendra caught Michelle's roaming hands and

moved them away. Michelle groaned from frustration, wanting and primal need.

With a whisper of breath, Kendra pulled away from her kiss, trailing her lips and tongue over Michelle's throat and then visiting each breast with a nip and suckle before continuing over her tummy. Then, Kendra's mouth replaced her hand among the slick folds of flesh and dark curls, and she probed the depths of Michelle's writhing body.

The room spun, forcing Michelle's eyes to close. Her body arched, sending her head back into the pillow. A remnant of pain from her fall threatened to surface, but she ignored it. Her body swelled and heaved under Kendra's attention and nothing could pull her from the power of her lovemaking.

Kendra's fingers found the one place inside of her that sent her over the edge, while her lips and tongue soothed and tormented at once. The shocks of her climax began low in her belly before spreading like a river though her chest, her arms, her legs.

She bit her lip to keep from screaming, until finally, her muscles fell limp. Numb, but not numb as the aftershocks stole her breath.

Tiny kisses trailed over her stomach. She opened her eyes and found Kendra settling beside her. Long, black lashes framed her closed eyes beneath her relaxed brow. The only evidence of her state of arousal came in the short, shallow breaths she tried to hide.

Michelle couldn't stop herself from capturing Kendra's cheek in her palm. She traced one eyebrow with her thumb.

Kendra smiled. "I must be insane."

Her tone made a chuckle form in Michelle's throat. "Why is that?"

"Because, I'm going to leave you now and get your dinner. And then, we're going to watch a movie."

Michelle slid her hand over the firm muscles and soft flesh of Kendra's shoulder and arm until it came to rest on her hip. She played with the fabric of her jeans for a moment before sliding her hand in the direction of the mound at the apex of Kendra's thighs. Kendra caught her fingers and raised them to her lips. "Not tonight, dear. You have a headache."

She kissed each of her fingers before she pushed herself off the bed.

"But—"

"No buts. I probably shouldn't have even done that." A hint of a frown pulled at the lips that had wrought such pleasure as she pulled the sheets taut over Michelle's exposed body. "But... I just couldn't resist."

"I'm glad."

Laughing quietly, Kendra ran a hand through her hair. "I'm sure you are. Wait here. I'll get our dinner."

When Kendra left the room, Michelle sighed, stretching like a cat in the sunlight. Now that her body had returned to normal, her head did throb a little, and the muscles in her bruised leg rebelled. She sucked in a quick breath and threw the sheets aside.

Black now, with mottled gray throughout, the bruise was just about the ugliest thing she'd ever seen. She made a face and covered it again.

She marveled how she hadn't felt pain at all when Kendra made love to her, as if her touch could somehow heal her.

It couldn't last. The marvel and wonder had to wear off at some point. It had for her parents. She could never remember a time when they'd touched each other. No kind words. No loving gestures.

If, by some miracle, Kendra Williams fell in love with her, would the same thing happen to them?

Ten

"I told you not to overdo it."

Kendra shook her head when Michelle flopped onto the park bench in the town square. She refused to use the crutches Kendra had found for her—choosing an old cane, instead—and more than once she'd caught Michelle hopping from one place to another when she thought nobody was watching.

"I'm fine, really. It's just starting to ache some, that's all."

"How much longer will this take?"

Michelle shook her head this time. "You're not a patient woman, are you?"

Patient? Kendra's eyes narrowed. She must have the patience of a saint. She'd been waiting for Michelle for her entire life.

The thought stunned her and she inhaled a deep breath.

She shook off the hollow memory of her heart before Michelle had filled it. She didn't need anyone. And Michelle wouldn't be here forever, she reminded herself.

"I'm just worried about you," she managed to say. "Do you really need to be here for this stuff?"

Vincent, the wonder director, jogged in their direction. He arrived with a huff of expelled air and sat on the bench next to Michelle. Kendra's spine stiffened and she crossed her arms over her breasts.

"I was thinkin', love, that we need to take several stills, as well. We can use them during the opening credits, in a montage. And then combine them with the footage we shot on the way into town this morning. This place is so bloody quaint, I can't imagine anyone wanting to change a goddamned thing. Although, I suppose I can see the point of making it more of a tourist destination. Everything is so... charming. I mean, look at those two women, there. They must be in their seventies and there they go, walking through town without a care in the world."

Kendra followed the direction Vincent looked to find Mrs. Mullarney and Mrs. Wicks strolling through the Peace Garden.

Michelle said, "Sounds good to me, Vin. Go for it. My camera is in my bag, over there."

"I'll grab it. Wait here and stay off that leg. And then I have a few more questions for you."

Vincent dashed to retrieve Michelle's camera. Kendra had come to terms with the fact that Vincent wasn't a very formidable threat. But the type of person that he was seemed to be more in keeping with what Michelle should have. Someone worldly, accomplished. Excited about visiting new places and capable of finding charm in a small town where there really wasn't any.

Michelle should have someone who could give her everything she ever wanted.

Kendra could take her to Paris, or Milan, or Venice – all the romantic destinations – but it wouldn't be enough. Kendra would more than likely hate every moment of it. Michelle deserved someone to share her life, not watch it happen with a scowl permanently etched in her face.

As though he could read her mind, Vincent urged, "Smile."

Kendra turned to face Vincent the very moment he snapped a photograph.

Ah, hell.

"Don't be such a spoiled-sport, Kendra, love. I just wanted to get a picture of the two love birds."

"Good afternoon, Kendra." Mrs. Wicks put out her hand, trembling with age and palsy. "Did I just hear this young man say that this beautiful girl belongs to you?"

Kendra's entire soul crashed to the ground. Why had Vincent said that so loudly? Here? In the middle of the fucking town square!

She licked her lips, but she still couldn't find a single reply or the ability to form it if she had.

"I'm Michelle Loving. I'm working with Kendra on a project."

"I used to bounce this little girl on my knee. I'm Mrs. Wicks, Kendra's kindergarten teacher. She was such a fine little girl. Always running into something to get her in trouble, keeping up with the boys and beating them at their own game a time or two, to boot."

"It's good to see you, Mrs. Wicks." Kendra wanted to vanish. Terror and hints of judgment and shame simmered just below the surface, making her skin burn. "Thanks for stopping by. Mrs. Mullarney is waiting for you on the corner."

"P'shaw, Kendra. She's waiting for the County senior citizen's van. It'll be along in its own time." The frail, old woman turned her attention back to Michelle. Mrs. Wicks continued her barrage. "So, how long have you been seeing each other, dear?"

Kendra stared at Michelle with a plea she hoped she could see. Michelle winked.

Oh, God. What was she going to do?

"We only just met a couple of weeks ago. Well, I guess it could be three now. I'm friends with Lacey back home in Las Vegas."

Good. Make her talk about Lacey, now. She taught Lacey in kindergarten, too. Find out about the buck teeth and the freckles.

"That's nice. You know, many of us had given up hope of Kendra ever finding a nice girl. She's far too serious, you know, now that she's older. When she was a girl, I used to find her in the oddest of places. Once, she tried to climb the flagpole in front of the school."

Michelle glanced at her over the old woman's shoulder. "Did she?"

"Oh my, yes. And another time, we found her in an air conditioning vent. She wanted to see if she could get out of the building in the event we were attacked by Indians, you see. We had to explain to her that those books she was always reading didn't apply anymore. Times had changed, you see."

"She had quite the imagination."

Mrs. Wicks nodded. "But I'm glad that times

change. They're still changing, although things happen a bit slower in Utah, you know. Why, it took forever for that horrible law to change so two young people like yourselves can get married!"

Kendra choked on her own spit. *What did she just say?*

"I think it's wonderful that the two of you have found each other. I'm no spring chicken and I could tell from all the way across the street, the way you look at Kendra, that you are a wonderful influence for her." She paused and her brow furrowed. "Did you say something, dear?"

"I said that Kendra must have had quite an imagination."

"Oh, that's right. Yes, yes, she did."

Please, don't let her say it.

"Kendra?" Mrs. Wicks turned to face her. "Do you still write stories? You were always so good at making things up and writing them down."

She shook her head, stifling a groan. *She said it.*

"That's a shame. In junior high school, Kendra won a writing award. She wrote a story about a small child who spent her summer living in the old west, even though she was born the same time she was. It was very fascinating. It was a time-travel book. Very well done."

"It sounds like it."

"I think I still have a copy of it somewhere. Mr. Wicks, he's been gone now these past four years, taught English at the junior high and could never bring himself to get rid of it. I'll have to see if I can find it for you."

"I'd love to read it," Michelle answered with a patient grin.

"So, dearie. Do you suppose that you and Kendra will settle down and have children? You'll have to adopt, of course, or perhaps go to one of those banks in the city where they keep the sperm in jars, but there's no reason why you couldn't have a family of your own; the two of you."

"What!" Kendra nearly screamed.

"Oh," Mrs. Wicks stammered, her eyes suddenly crestfallen and tired. "Oh, dear. I must remember to think before I speak. Am I wrong? I just always thought that you were... I mean, I assumed... You never date anyone, and well, I just thought..." It was obvious the woman was near tears; embarrassed and quite forlorn.

"No, no, Mrs. Wicks," Kendra spouted. "No, you're not wrong. I mean, you are a little. Michelle and I aren't, well, we aren't together, like that. Or maybe we... Anyway, you're right about me. I am a lesbian. You haven't hurt my feelings or anything."

Mrs. Wicks' bottom lip quivered and she sniffled like a lost child. "You're sure. I would never want to hurt your feelings. You can't tell anyone else, but you were my very favorite student. My very favorite, and I think it's terrible how people sometimes treat you, or you know, gay people, in general."

"It's okay, Mrs. Wicks. Really."

"I should catch up with Mrs. Mullarney. She's old, you see, and she can't quite climb into the van without my help. It's been lovely talking with you," she continued, her distress vanishing with each word. "And you two children will be certain to send me an invitation when you get married. Don't forget me, now. Mrs. Roger Wicks. I'm in the book."

Thick silence, filled only with the roaring engines of passing cars, filled the small square. Mrs. Wicks joined her friend and Kendra watched the pair cross the street.

They were so... old.

Mrs. Wicks had probably been in her forties when she'd taught Kendra's Kindergarten class close to thirty years earlier. Kendra was thirty-five, and she wasn't getting any younger. She had no desire to be pregnant, get pregnant or carry a child. She never had. And she was far too old, now, anyway, wasn't she? But there had been times over the course of her life where she'd wondered about having her own children; leaving behind a legacy of her own.

Did Michelle want children? Not with her, of course, but someday with someone she loved? Technology had come a long way in recent years, and it was possible for Kendra to parent a biological child and not have to be pregnant. Would Michelle be okay with something like that?

She turned her attention to Michelle. She stared forward, supposedly watching Vincent – who had managed to sneak away and return to work without being noticed – and the others set up the main video camera. Kendra knew better.

Damn it.

Michelle's eyes held that same distant expression as they had that day in the truck beside the road. Wounded. Defensive.

Was Michelle falling in love with her? Her gut gripped and twisted on itself, threatening to send her to her knees. She wanted her to, even though the part of herself that knew Michelle was too good for her argued to let her go. Now. Before it was too late.

She also knew that she wouldn't.

Michelle slid from the truck and hobbled toward the house. She smiled through the pain in her leg and glanced at Kendra. Mrs. Wicks had been enlightening, to say the least. She never would have guessed the surly cowboi had the heart of a poet. What she wouldn't give to see that story; to see into the mind of a fourteen-year-old Kendra Williams.

"What are you grinning about?"

"Oh, nothing. Just thinking about Mrs. Wicks. Does it surprise you that she would be so open minded? I mean, the last person in the world I would expect to be in favor of marriage equality would be an old lady in the high hills of Utah."

"I'm pretty sure she's just an old free-love hippie. I can only imagine what she might have been like during the summer of love, if you know what I mean. But that's not what you were thinking about. I've seen that look in your eyes, before, little missy. You're up to something."

"Nah. Not me!"

Vincent's van pulled into the yard behind Kendra's truck, drawing her attention. An unfamiliar sedan followed them.

Michelle followed her gaze. "Who's that?"

"I don't know."

Leaving her on the porch, Kendra descended the steps to meet the visitor. A short, balding man stepped out of the car and met her in the driveway. He carried an envelope and a clipboard.

Kendra took the envelope and scratched her signature on the board. The stranger left with a friendly wave.

Kendra opened the envelope and slid a sheaf of papers from it. "Goddamnit!"

Michelle groaned. Not good news, apparently. "What is it?"

Kendra crumpled the envelope and its contents and then turned back toward the house. Her long stride spoke of barely contained frustration. Gaining the porch, she threw open the door and held it open, obviously waiting for Michelle to enter the house. Even when she was pissed off, she was still a *gentleman*. Michelle limped inside and settled herself on the sofa. "What is it!?" she repeated.

"It's a contract. A sales contract for my land. That arrogant bastard."

"Mason sent a contract? But you're not selling..."

"He doesn't seem to get that, does he?"

Brent slid into the room and leaned against the piano. "Who was that guy?"

"A messenger." Kendra handed her brother the paperwork.

"It doesn't mean anything, Kendra. So he sent you a contract to look over. Don't sign it. Decline the offer. Simple." Brent shrugged.

"It can't be that simple."

"Why not?"

"Nothing is that simple. Why would he send it without any negotiations or discussion, first? Who does that? Nobody does that! Do you remember that guy that

Mason and his goons were shoving around at the auction?" Kendra focused her gaze on Michelle.

"Yeah."

"This may be what he was talking about. He said that Mason went to the county and the land management board and claimed that he'd been in negotiations with that guy for the purchase of his farm. Mason had damn near convinced everyone in authority that the farmer had reneged on their deal, and that they had a binding verbal contract to sell."

"Send him a certified letter stating that you reject the offer. That way there is a record of you turning it down."

Kendra brushed a hand over her jaw and cursed. "That's what he wants me to do. He wants me to turn it down so that it looks like we're negotiating and that I'm actually interested in selling."

"That guy has some nerve." Brent folded the wrinkled sheets and set them on the coffee table.

"Yeah, he does. I have no idea what is worse, ignoring the offer, or answering it."

"We won't do either one." Michelle adjusted her position to take the weight off her injured leg. She stretched her back slightly to relieve a bit of growing tension in her ribs, as well.

"Are you okay?"

"Yeah, I'm fine, honey. So, here's what we'll do. We'll scan every page of the offer contract and put it on the website. We'll 'answer' it in the public forum with an explanation of how the land is not for sale, and never has been, to anyone, for any price. Then we'll paste the link on every newsfeed and blog within a hundred miles of this place."

"He'll just claim that we're smearing him to get more money."

"Let him. We're posting a challenge for him to make public all previous written offers and details of conversations. When he slips up and says he spoke to you at a certain time and place, we'll provide proof you weren't there."

"It's not slander, or libel, or whatever to post it in public?"

"It's only defamation if it's not true. If you call a one-legged whore a one-legged whore, she hasn't got a leg to stand on."

They sat in thoughtful silence for a moment before Brent asked, "You guys want some lunch?" He moved in the direction of the kitchen.

Michelle shifted position again. "We grabbed a bite in town. Thanks, anyway."

Kendra stood and began to pace. "Yeah, thanks." She paused. "I've got work to do."

Michelle frowned as Kendra headed out the front door. The great disappearing Kendra.

What did she expect? That Kendra would share everything with her? Hell, she wasn't even her girlfriend. According to Kendra, they weren't together at all.

In fact, Michelle didn't even know what they were to each other.

Or maybe she knew exactly what she was to Kendra, as much as it hurt.

Nothing. They were fooling around, at least in Kendra's mind, apparently. Her frown deepened. Kendra's reaction in the town square, when that cute old lady had mentioned settling down and having children, proved it. She'd been shocked. No, not shocked... appalled by the notion.

Of course, it could have been shock at having been outed on Main Street. But either way, Michelle needed to be careful with her heart, now more than ever. If she wasn't, she could very well leave it behind when the time came to go home.

She sucked in a breath. No. She wouldn't let that happen. She would share what she could with Kendra while she worked on the project. Have a little fun, make a little noise. Brent did it all the time, so why couldn't she?

Because you're falling in love with her...

She closed her eyes.

An ache started in the center of her chest.

Someone tapped her on her shoulder and settled on the sofa next to her. She opened her eyes to find Vincent studying her. "You alright, love?"

She nodded. "I'm fine. Just a little sore."

"That's not what I mean, and you know it."

She squared her shoulders. "What are you talking about?"

"That cowgirl of yours. You know, I never pegged you for the buckle bunny type."

She snorted. "I'm not."

"Then, why do you go all moony whenever Kendra's about?"

It really is that obvious, she thought.

She replied, "I don't."

Vincent smiled and shook his head. Standing up, he handed her an SD card. "The stills I took in town. See what you can do with them and tomorrow, we'll work on the opening sequence. The crew and I are heading back to the hotel."

She took the disc and slid it into her computer then followed Vincent to the front door. After a quick hug, she watched him climb into the van and pull away. Her attention shifted to the barn.

A storm threatened overhead. Electricity in the air made the fine hairs on her arms stand up. She rubbed away the sensation, squaring her shoulders. Careful of her injured leg. She grabbed her cane and made her way down the steps and across the courtyard that separated the house from the barn.

The door creaked open on old hinges. Inside, two rows of stalls flanked a wide corridor. The far end widened and instead of stalls, one side held a separate room and the other offered what appeared to be storage. The wide doors at the opposite end stood open, revealing a framed landscape that took her breath away. Rolling hills leading to majestic mountains topped with remnants of the winter storms spread out like a postcard. No wonder Kendra loved it here so much.

She stepped forward and opened her mouth to call Kendra.

A bale of hay landed a few inches in front of her.

She screamed. "Oh, my God!"

Looking up, she found Kendra's worried eyes trained on her. Her brow narrowed. "What are you doing in here? You could've been killed!"

"I was looking for you."

"You found me. Back up."

She did as Kendra instructed and a second bale of

hay landed on the top of the first and then rolled to the barn floor.

"Are you okay?" Michelle raised her voice so Kendra could hear her in the back of the loft. She couldn't see her anymore.

"I'm fine." Another bale.

"You don't seem fine."

"Well, I am." Another bale.

How much hay did she store up there? "Are you coming down soon? I don't want to talk to the floor of the loft."

She sighed when Kendra didn't answer. She listened to the scraping of Kendra's boots on the wood floor over her head, continuing to work as though Michelle weren't even there. It sounded like she was moving something heavy from one end of the barn to the other for several moments. Her neck ached from looking up at the worn, aged boards. Did she think she would see her through the flooring? She shook her head. Exasperated, she continued, "If you want me to leave, I will."

Silence.

No scraping. No movement.

Not even a heartbeat.

She looked at the floor one last moment, and then turned to leave.

"Hang on. I'll be right down."

Kendra's voice startled her, and filled her with unexplainable joy at the same time. The heavy crunch of Kendra's boots traveled the length of the hay loft to the opposite end of the barn, then thudded down a staircase she couldn't see.

She turned into the corridor and stopped. The light from the open barn doors cast her in stunning silhouette, except where it reflected off the sweat on her bare shoulders. She'd taken off the button-down shirt that had come to seem like her uniform and wore only a sleeveless tank top. Tight jeans rested low on her hips, leaving several inches of firm flesh exposed on Kendra's torso. Michelle's insides turned over at the remembered feel of her rippled stomach and soft, pliant breasts. She tightened her grip on the borrowed cane.

"I'm sorry."

"Wh-What?" Michelle stuttered.

"I don't mean to take it out on you." She took a step forward. Slow. Deliberate. Like everything else about her.

Never lazy. Just... determined.

"You didn't. You haven't."

She came closer, until Michelle could make out the subtle shades of her tanned flesh. Darker on her shoulders, lighter on her neck where the wide brim of her cowboy hat protected her from the sun. Non-existent on the little band of her hip revealed as she stalked closer.

Michelle swallowed against a lump forming in her throat. If she wasn't careful, she might swallow her tongue.

Kendra stopped right in front of her. Rain fell against the door. Wind howled through the cracks in the walls. Clean, fresh air mixed with the tangy scent of her sweat and the ever-present hint of leather. Michelle licked her lips.

"What did you want to see me about?"

"What?"

"You needed me for something?"

Oh, yeah. She needed her, alright. Do people really tumble in the hay? She shook off the erotic image. "I... um... I just wanted to make sure you were okay, that's all."

Kendra's head lowered slightly. When she lifted it, her eyes held a hint of passion. But just a hint. Something else resided there as well.

Something she didn't understand.

A strange sensation washed over Kendra with the coming rain. Michelle's eyes roamed over her, touching her as surely as if she did so with soft, delicate hands. Her body reacted with powerful need.

Michelle was trying to figure her out. She could see it in her expression and that little line that appeared on her forehead, between her eyes, when she was confused by a puzzle she couldn't solve. When she solved it, the line went away and her eyes danced, but for now, she was just plain perplexed.

"It's raining," she said.

Kendra grinned at the simplicity of the statement, raising her eyebrows. "You don't say?"

A thunderclap shook the walls of the old barn. Michelle leapt toward her, brushing her breasts against her chest. Shivers barreled through her body, coming to rest with electrical intensity between her legs. A gust of wind blew through the doors facing the house and whipped through the tunnel created by the stalls. Michelle's hair lifted in a wild dance, making her look like a temptress, or some goddess of the elements. Her gut grew tight. Her jeans grew moist.

Ignoring her discomfort, she hurried to the doors, caught them and secured them shut. Drenched by the thick drops, she ran to the far end and peered into the sky. If she didn't know any better, she'd swear it was midnight. Rain falling in gusting sheets already pooled in the corrals. She tugged against the wind and managed to shut and bolt the doors.

"Unless you want to get soaked, I'd say we're stuck out here for the duration." She turned to face Michelle. "Shouldn't be too long."

Was that such a bad thing?

She found a lantern and a book of matches. Once she lit the mantels, she carried it to Michelle. She was gorgeous in this light. Hell, she was gorgeous in any light, but at this moment, her hair practically glowed like a halo around her delicate, feminine features. Kendra had never been feminine. Not even in Mrs. Wicks kindergarten class. Everyone had called her a tomboy and said she'd grow out of it. But she never did. When she was in high school, she'd stare in the mirror for hours, wondering what horrible act she'd perpetrated in a former life to deserve what she'd considered at the time, the wrong body. No curves to speak of. She looked far better in boys' clothes than skirts and dresses. She was attracted to the same giggling girls that the guys were. She loathed the thought of going on a date with a boy, but, at the time, she'd thought it was because they wouldn't like her. She didn't giggle. She didn't want to giggle. She never giggled.

Maybe that's what made it so difficult to believe that Michelle could be so femme, and so gay. She'd never met a lesbian who was so... girlie. Apparently, she was far more sheltered here at the Heartland than she'd ever realized. Hell, even Mrs. Wicks knew she was gay!

When she reached Michelle, standing and shivering like a new leaf, she set the lantern on the ground. Then she heaved the bales of hay against Navajo's stall and sat down. Michelle limped in her direction, and then lowered herself onto the bale next to Kendra.

Smoothing her hair, Michelle smiled. "I don't mind waiting it out. I like storms."

Another thunderclap sounded, but she didn't jump. Kendra wished she would. Right into her arms.

"You know, I was more than a little surprised this afternoon, about the whole writing thing." Michelle leaned back against the weathered wood and lifted her good foot to rest on the edge of the bale.

"Really? That's what surprised you? I was a bit more taken aback by the fact a ninety-year-old woman thinks we should have kids."

"Well, there was that, but I'm used to it. You should meet some of the old folks in Vegas. Most of them don't have any problem with it at all. Now, stop changing the subject. You're a writer."

"I was a writer. A long time ago."

"You don't write anymore, at all?"

She leaned against the stall door and Navajo lowered her head to nudge her. "No time."

She hadn't put pencil to paper in years. It was odd, but since she'd brought it up, she kind of felt like maybe she could take it up again. Michelle made her feel like she could do anything.

"Too bad."

"How's the website coming?" There. Talk about her, instead.

Her smile widened and a small dimple appeared in her cheek. She loved that every time she looked at Michelle, she found some new, endearing quality. How had she missed such an adorable little dimple? It must be the way the golden glow of the lantern made her shimmer in the dim light.

"It's coming along great. Another day or two and we'll be done. Filming is almost done, too. Lenise has been a huge help. She's incredibly creative and artistically intuitive. It would sure be a shame if she never pursues that side of herself." Michelle tilted her head and tucked those errant stands of hair behind her ear. That amazing, tiny, perfect little ear.

Kendra wanted to groan.

"And what's next, after you're finished?"

"We'll start a promotional campaign with school systems all over the country. We'll send a link to school boards, congressmen, state and federal representatives. You run an organic operation, so that'll help. We'll get you certified and promote the website and the video as a learning tool for all of the conservation organizations. Hell, we may even be able to get a grant to hire an attorney. There are a lot of people who will get on board to help a true family farm."

"And that's it? We just tell people."

"It's all about increasing awareness. If we can tug a few heartstrings and try to make people think of the good old days, they'll be more inclined to help."

Increasing awareness? Oh, her awareness was

increasing, alright. The lower half of her body throbbed with wanting. Her entire body screamed to take her. Right here. Right now.

Instead, she traced the path of light across Michelle's face with the tip of her finger. Michelle leaned into the touch, nestling her rounded cheek into the palm of Kendra's hand. "Tell me about you," she asked. "Where did you grow up?"

"There really isn't much to tell, Kendra. I grew up in Las Vegas. I still live there. End of story."

She doubted it. "What about your folks. What did they do?"

Michelle laughed but Kendra couldn't make out any humor in the sound. "They play golf. And they drink Martinis. And they spend money."

"So, they're retired?"

"No."

"Then what?"

Her expression grew hard for a moment, and then softened when she gazed back at Kendra. "Nothing. They're terrific old people."

She didn't want to talk about them, that much was obvious. They couldn't talk about Kendra. She didn't want to talk about herself.

"So, will you be around tomorrow morning to help me put together the pages on Harold Mason's offer for the site?" Michelle asked.

They could talk about Harold Mason. Great. Her least favorite topic in the whole of God's green earth. What would happen if they didn't have good old Harold to talk about anymore? What then?

"Your wish is my command." Kendra softened her

sarcasm with a smile.

"I wish there was some way of knowing what, exactly, he's trying to accomplish. Do you think it's just money and greed?"

"Who knows?" Kendra shrugged. "But in my experience, money and greed are usually enough."

Who cares? All she wanted to do was take Michelle beneath her and wipe out all of her worries. When they were together, nothing could touch her. She felt invincible.

As if she could read her thoughts, Michelle smiled up at her. She let her hand cup Michelle's cheek again before twining her fingers in the soft strands of her hair. It was so soft. Like spun sugar.

Kendra captured Michelle's lips. She tasted of light and air. And rain. She swept through Kendra's defenses like the storm that still raged on the side of the barn walls. Tormenting and teasing. Consuming.

Michelle trembled beneath Kendra's touch. She felt it, too. Whatever it was.

How could this feel so right? She didn't want anyone, or at least, she hadn't before Michelle had invaded her organized and disciplined life. Since Michelle Loving showed up, she'd become a fool for everything about her.

Michelle owned her.

And she liked it.

Eleven

Michelle studied the screen on her open laptop without really seeing it. Rain continued to beat the earth with brutal force making her sore leg throb in the damp air. She rubbed it and winced.

Damn her!

She took a breath meant to calm her nerves and hoped Lenise didn't notice. Seated beside her at the dining room table turned work surface, the teenager organized several piles of photos.

Good thing Lenise wanted to help. Left to her own devices, Michelle would probably never finish this project. Her concentration ranked right up there with a hyperactive child on a diet of red dyes and sugar highs. She sat forward in the chair, placed her elbows on the edge of the table and rubbed her eyes with her fingertips.

Concentrate!

Stop thinking about Kendra. Stop wondering about the future. There is no future!

Worse. Whatever time they did have together grew ominously close to an end. In another fifteen minutes or so, the final edition of the website would be uploaded and an email announcement sent to every school board, government office and news agency in the country. Everyone from Ellen to Oprah to the editor of the local paper was getting a press release and a copy of the video once the final edits were completed.

It was almost time to go home.

She should be thrilled to get back to her normal life. She missed the bright lights of her hometown. Didn't she?

And her business needed her. Granted, she didn't actually have an office, but she kept all of her records and files in her apartment. She lived and worked there. Not here. Her employees called her several times each day from their own virtual offices all of them needing information that she couldn't give them because she didn't have access to it. Not from here.

"Okay. What's next?" Lenise asked, her bright eyes curious and anxious to learn.

Lenise sat on the edge of her seat. At least someone was excited about finishing the site. Michelle forced a smile. "Pick your favorite picture from each pile and we'll scan it. And remember what I told you about what makes a good photo."

"Balance and lighting. Got it."

Lenise set to work choosing several photographs from the stacks of vintage images of the ranch. Restless, Michelle stood up and moved toward the piano in the parlor. She let her fingers brush over the keys, and then flipped through a music book on the stand that looked like it hadn't been touched in a thousand years. The yellowed pages were worn and well-loved, but lonely.

Finding an old favorite that seemed to fit her mood, she settled on the bench. The sad strains fell from her fingertips and she closed her eyes. The music seemed to move her fingers instead of the other way around. She found she didn't need the score, after all.

She never did this sort of thing. She was all business. All the time. So, why did she allow a junior in high school to select images for the final page of a very important website? Why did she sit here, playing the piano, when she had work to do? When, exactly, had she fallen completely in love with Kendra Williams?

She pounded the keys over a crescendo as if the answer lay somewhere in the music. She just had to listen more closely. If she listened closely enough, the notes and strains would provide the answer to every question she'd ever had.

By the time she reached the end of the piece, she still had no answer.

Maybe she never would.

But it didn't matter. She would leave here in the next few days, as soon as she finished the video project, and that would be that.

The end.

It was for the best, anyway.

Wasn't it?

She shook her head as no answer came. The song ended. Her confusion didn't. Sighing, she shook her head at her own folly again.

Hopeless.

"Okay, Michelle. I scanned the pictures and put them into the webpage where you said. I think we're all done."

Lenise hovered over her shoulder.

"Good job. Let's take a look and then send her off to the cyber-gods."

"That was a really pretty song you were playing."

Michelle smiled, slightly embarrassed. She hadn't played since that first night at the Heartland. Had it been a month already? "Thanks. I'm a bit rusty."

"No, really. It was very good."

"So, do you want to do the honors?"

"Really?" The young girl's eyes lit up.

"Sure. Sit down here. You're going to upload through the protocol software, right there," she explained, pointing to the button on the screen. "Just click right here."

"Shouldn't we call Kendra, or something?"

"I'm right here," Kendra replied, her voice soft. She moved behind Michelle and hooked her arms around her waist, pulling Michelle flush against her. She leaned over her shoulder to peer at the screen. Her leathery scent enveloped Michelle and the heat of Kendra's body surrounded her. So close, Michelle could feel the beat of Kendra's heart, every pore of her body was aware of her. "What are we doing?" she asked.

Michelle cleared her throat. There were so many answers to that question that she didn't know where to start. So many replies came crashing into her mind, but none of them were good enough. But Kendra was only talking about the website. Not their entire lives...

"We're uploading the final site," Michelle answered, her voice cracking slightly. She swallowed hard against the lump that formed in her throat. "We're done."

A ripple of muscle moved across her back. "Good."

Kendra's voice sounded clipped. Almost...

Sad?

Would she be sad to see her leave?

As much as she wanted to feel that way, she could only deny the suspicion. She probably couldn't wait for her to get out of her way, as she'd been so inclined to tell her when she'd first arrived.

So much had happened in the time since. Michelle didn't want to leave her, but staying meant sharing parts of herself she wasn't ready to share. Not to mention that Kendra seemed less than willing to share anything with her.

No. Better to leave now and avoid any embarrassing displays of emotion later. If she left now, or soon, she'd only leave half of her heart with Kendra. She'd take the other half home. Half of her heart was better than none.

"What does that mean?" Lenise's voice slipped into her mind with the subtlety of a wedge.

"What?"

"That graphic, there." She pointed to the screen.

Michelle shrugged. "That means you did it right. We're done."

Kendra's heart sank. "Well, not really done, right? Don't you still have to send all those emails? And what about the video?"

"Right. Well, we're done with the website,

anyway."

"So, how much longer will you be here?" Lenise asked. "Will you be here for the rodeo?"

"I'll be here for another day or two. Vincent is wrapping the shoot soon and I'll be heading back with them."

"I don't think so." The muscles in Kendra's arms twitched and she hoped Michelle didn't notice as she lowered them to her sides.

Michelle spun to face her and tucked her hair behind her ears. "Excuse me?"

"You're not going anywhere. It's too dangerous."

"Kendra... I have a business to run in Las Vegas. I never said I'd stay indefinitely." *No matter how much I want to.*

Hands on her hips, she directed her gaze at Lenise, who obviously knew her well enough to know when she wasn't happy. The young girl levitated out of the chair, skirted the table and fled into the kitchen. Michelle followed her movements before returning her attention to Kendra.

"Michelle, don't look at me like that. You know I'm right."

"No. I don't know you're right."

"If it's not safe for Lacey to be in Las Vegas right now, it's not safe for you either. Especially when this site makes the rounds."

"What could possibly happen?"

She didn't even want to think about it. "Probably nothing. But I'm not willing to take that risk."

Kendra reached for her hat on the coat rack but felt Michelle's eyes on her back like so many needles. She paused for a moment, and then grabbed her Stetson and placed it on her head. "What?" she asked, firmly.

When she turned around, Michelle was leaning against the table; her firm ass propped on the edge and her rounded hips calling out an invitation she couldn't possibly ignore. Her crossed arms pushed her breasts upward, accentuating the cleavage visible in the v-neck of her lightweight sweater. Kendra's body responded with sudden, undeniable intensity.

"I don't see how any of this is your decision," she declared.

"Because, you're my responsibility."

She scoffed at her. "Since when?"

Ah, hell!

Did she have to be so damn ornery all the time? She could argue a saint into a bottle of bourbon without batting an eyelash. And Kendra was no saint. "Doesn't matter. You're staying here until this whole thing is over and done with. End of story."

"But that could take months!"

Years. If Kendra was lucky. A lifetime, maybe? "Then, I guess you're stuck here."

"But that's crazy, Kendra. I have a life. I have responsibilities. I need some things from my apartment. My equipment? Hell. I've got clients in Vegas who are expecting me to come home. Soon!"

"They can wait a bit longer. I'm not going to let you go running back someplace where I can't protect you."

"They cannot wait. And you don't 'let' me do anything, Kendra Williams. The last time I checked, you don't have any say in what I can or cannot do."

"This is ridiculous."

"I agree."

"Then you'll stay?"

"No." Michelle paused and took a breath. "Not until you admit that you *want* me to. Danger or no danger, you don't want me to leave."

Kendra couldn't take her eyes off of Michelle's lips. When she pulled her lower lip between her teeth, which she noticed happened when her confidence faltered ever so slightly, Kendra stifled a groan. "Obviously, I want you to. It was my idea. You are safer —"

"No, Kendra. Admit that you don't want me to leave."

"We've established that." Why couldn't she breathe? Her mouth was so dry...

"It has nothing to do with any threats, or anything else. You just don't want me to go."

She took a step away from the table, closing the distance between them. Her eyes glowed with liquid fire. Her arms dropped to her side. No more defenses. No more pretenses. By the time Michelle reached her, Kendra thought she would burst. Such innocence wrapped in a package made to tempt and tease. It wasn't fair. Michelle had her outnumbered in so many ways. She was smarter. Stonger. More trusting. More honest. What was she supposed to do? How could she possibly fight her?

A part of her didn't want to fight it anymore. What was so wrong with letting her inside, letting her take care of her and love her?

Michelle stepped into Kendra's offered embrace and leaned her cheek against her shoulder. Kendra hadn't even realized she'd opened her arms. It was as though she were completely out of control of everything around her... especially those elements she'd never been able to control. Light. Air. Wind. Aching...

"I can't."

Michelle's heartbeat seared a path between them, straight to Kendra's own beating heart. She consumed her with her pulse and the rhythm of her breath.

Her whisper filled the room from corner to corner, floor to ceiling. "Then I have to leave."

She might as well have cold-cocked Kendra with a rifle butt. The pain was the same. She tightened her hold on Michelle. "I don't know what you want."

"Yes, you do."

She was right. But Kendra couldn't say it. Not out loud. Michelle represented a part of her life that was better than anything Kendra had ever experienced. Kendra had drawn her into the white noise of her existence enough, already. She should let her go. But she couldn't.

She should keep her here, forever. But she wouldn't.

Michelle deserved better than her, even if she didn't know it, yet. She'd said she would stay if Kendra admitted to her why she should. So, what if she did? How long would it be before Michelle grew restless for everything she'd left behind? She already wanted to leave, didn't she? Back to her lights. Back to her world. If Kendra really forced her to stay, what then?

All she had to do was say the words that Michelle wanted to hear, and she'd stay with her, at least for the time being.

Emotional blackmail. She deserved it, of course. A

chuckle escaped her throat.

Never argue with a woman...

"Michelle." Kendra eased her shoulders back so she could look into Michelle's eyes.

That was a mistake.

One look into the blue depths and she foundered against the jagged rocks of her own soul. She closed her eyes by way of self-defense and steeled herself against the pain.

"What, Kendra? What can't you do?"

She gulped a breath which did little to feed her lungs. "I can't make you any promises. I can't..."

"I don't want promises. But if you want me to risk everything by staying here, you need to put something on the line, too, damn it."

"You're not risking anything by staying here. If you go back, you're risking your life."

Michelle shook her head. "I doubt that."

"Well, I don't. Harold Mason is perfectly capable of murder. He's already killed once."

"No, he startled the cattle."

"A man died. Same difference. You agreed with me when it was time to bring Lacey home. Nothing has changed."

Michelle huffed and growled. "Quit changing the subject!" She took a deep breath that raised her breasts and sent shockwaves into Kendra's hollow insides. "Listen. Here it is, Kendra. I want to stay. I shouldn't, but I do. And I need to know that what I'm doing isn't a waste of time and energy. I need to know if I mean anything to you. Do I? Is this just some game? Or is it real? Does it have a chance of being real? I'm perfectly capable of walking out right now. If it's not real, if we're just... if... we are only..."

Michelle's voice quivered on the edge of something raw. Kendra could hear it in the strained chords of her voice; in the way the pitch rose and fell as though she was on the crest of an enormous wave.

The world's biggest jerk. That's what Kendra felt like when Michelle looked at her like that. As if she'd just pulled her heart from her chest and stomped on it. "Just what? Using each other?" Her voice cracked, disappearing before she could make all of the sounds that made words.

Michelle nodded.

Kendra shook her head and somehow managed to find her voice. "Please, don't go."

"That's not good enough."

Only a couple of feet separated them. If she stretched her arm, she could touch her; feel that soft, translucent skin beneath her rough fingertips. But it felt like miles. "That's all I can give you right now."

Harold Mason studied the lowlife standing on the opposite side of his desk. Thomas Taylor seemed to be the spokesman for the shabby group, and not that it said much at all, the most intelligent. Behind him, one man shifted nervously and another stood as still as a statue. The smallest of the three, James Johnson, looked like he was going to crawl out of his skin at any moment. His face was marked with sores at various stages of healing, or not healing. His eyes darted around the room as though he expected something horrible to seep out of the woodwork. When he opened his mouth, which wasn't often, what remained of his teeth turned Harold's stomach.

The largest of the men stood easily six inches taller than Harold. He was beefy and obviously spent many hours at the gym lifting weights, although that was probably the only healthy aspect to the man's lifestyle. From earlier conversations, Harold had learned that Rocky Shepherd had taken up the hobby while serving a sentence at the state prison in Draper, Utah. He was good to have in a crisis, so long as he wasn't required to think on his feet.

Thomas asked, "You sure about this?"

"What do you care? I'm paying you. That's all you need to know."

"Whatever," he replied, removing the red cap from his forehead, and then scratching his hairline before replacing it. "Fifteen bills each."

Harold reached into the breast pocket of his sport coat and withdrew three envelopes. He rested them on the edge of the desk. "Cash."

Thomas took all three envelopes and then handed one to each of his companions. They didn't bother to count the contents before they tucked them away into the pockets of their jeans.

He had no doubt the money would be gone in a matter of days. Thomas would likely drink his away. James' share would go into a vein or a pipe. Rocky would spend his on women, liquor and making a larger-than-life impression on whomever was lucky enough to share his time when he did. So long as they earned it, Harold couldn't care less. "I want it done tonight. And follow through this time. Why I'm giving you another chance, I have no idea."

"Don't you worry, Mr. Mason. No more foul-ups. We'll take care of it," Thomas replied as he ushered the smallest man out the door.

Harold stood and crossed to the bar against the far wall. He placed three pieces of ice into a crystal tumbler and then splashed two fingers of bourbon over them. The ice cubes cracked under the warmth of the booze. The report reminded him of how close he was to getting everything he wanted; everything he needed. He lifted the glass to eye level and examined the cracked cubes. Kendra would crack too, under pressure. It was only a matter of time. He tossed half the contents of the glass down his throat and relished the burn of the expensive liquor.

Harold glanced at the picture of his father and frowned.

Soon, he'd cost Kendra Williams and her pathetic little family as much as they'd cost him.

In spades.

Kendra listened to the steady rhythm of Michelle's quiet snore and shifted to her right side to watch her sleep. The early streaks of dawn filtered beneath the shades, casting the curves of her cheeks and eyelids in soft shadow. Her full lips parted a fraction, tempting Kendra to kiss her lover awake.

What was it about Michelle that made her just

plain feel better? No matter what happened. Last night, as she held Michelle in her arms, she felt... powerful. Like she could take on a thousand Harold Mason's and never bat an eye.

Mostly, because Michelle had agreed to stay. Kendra knew she'd won that round. But what about the next time Michelle asked something of her that she couldn't give?

As much as she wanted to commit to her, she knew better. The minute she opened herself up to Michelle, Michelle would hold all the cards. Better she just play it close to the vest for now.

Someone knocked on the bedroom door, waking Michelle with a sudden start. "Kendra? You up yet?"

Michelle's sleepy eyes focused on her and she smiled like a vixen with one thing on her mind.

Oh yeah, she was up alright.

"Go away," Kendra called to Brent, on the other side of the closed door. She leaned closer to Michelle, captured her lips and slid her body next to hers beneath the cool sheets. Michelle wrapped one leg over her hip and pulled her closer. Nothing separated them but the morning.

"I think you're going to want to see this."

Her blood froze in her veins at the tone in her brother's voice. Michelle's brow narrowed and she pulled away from Kendra's kiss. She whispered, "It sounds serious. Maybe you should go check it out?"

"Don't want to," Kendra mumbled.

Michelle's quiet laugh washed over her.

Kendra liked the little cocoon she wrapped her in. But, she was probably right. It did sound serious. "I'll be right back. Don't move."

With a heave and a groan of protest, she left the bed and wrapped a bath towel around her breast. Then she opened the door. "What?"

"Somebody broke into the barn last night."

Kendra squeezed the doorknob until she thought her fingers would break. "Show me."

"I'll meet you downstairs in five minutes."

Brent left and Kendra turned back to the bed. Michelle stretched her arms above her head and the sheet fell below one rounded breast. Hair mussed about her face, lips still swollen from the night before, she looked like the well-loved woman she was. "Come back to bed."

Whatever anger Brent's news had awakened died at the purr in Michelle's voice. She could spend the rest of her life lost in those blue eyes, wrapped in those loving, tender arms.

But, as always, her responsibilities pulled her away from something wonderful. She cursed under her breath and pulled on a pair of faded blue jeans and a black, sleeveless undershirt. "No can do. Something happened last night and I have to check it out."

"What?"

"I'm not sure. Could be nothing. Stay here. Get some rest. Save my place."

"I want to come with you."

She shook her head. "You didn't get much sleep last night, lover. It's barely dawn. Go back to sleep."

Michelle snorted in that way she had that told Kendra something, anything, was her fault. Kendra smiled. Maybe it was her fault she didn't sleep much, but if she weren't such a wanton, Kendra wouldn't have been forced to satisfy her most of the night.

Over and over, again and again...

Michelle rolled to her side and stared up at her from the soft folds of the rumpled bedclothes. "If you insist," she whispered on a sigh.

With only regret for company, Kendra grabbed her boots from beneath the bed and a clean shirt from the closet and headed downstairs.

Brad and Brent were in the kitchen with Casey who spoke to someone on the phone. Kendra sat at the kitchen table and pulled on her boots and shirt. "So? What's going on?"

"Hell, I don't know. Everything was just fine when I got home, about three. Sometime between three and six this morning, somebody tossed the barn. The combine, the tools. Everything is busted up and ripped apart."

"Mason." Kendra snarled.

"Your guess is as good as mine, but I'd have to say I agree with you."

Casey hung up the phone. "Mac is sending somebody out to take a report. He says not to touch anything until his people get here. He's going to dust for prints or something."

Kendra ran a hand through her hair and scratched the nape of her neck. She needed to see a barber. She'd been so preoccupied with everything the past few weeks, the short hairs on the back of neck were starting to itch. She blew out a hard breath. "Like that is going to do a damn bit of good."

"It can't hurt," Casey offered.

"Well, might as well get this over with." The last thing Kendra wanted to do was to see her barn in a wreck of damaged property. Her family had worked for years building this ranch and slowly, but surely, she watched it fall down around her ears. All because of one man with an evil streak so wide, God couldn't see the other side.

The larger barn housed the animals and a few pieces of equipment, but most of the heavy duty tools and supplies were stored in the smaller barn. The door practically fell off its hinges when Brent pulled on it.

Inside, the normally neat rows of feed and tools lay scattered on the ground. Bags, sliced open, spilled their contents into useless piles of grain and oats. The exposed engine of her father's combine had been smashed. All of the wiring had been pulled free or cut from their original positions. Cracks spider-webbed through the safety glass around the operator's seat. They'd been smashed with, apparently, the crow bar that lay on the ground near the front wheel.

"They must've used this." Casey picked up the discarded crow bar with the tips of his thumb and forefinger dropping it back into place beside the remains of Brent's four-wheeler.

"What the hell happened here?"

Kendra turned around when she heard Michelle's voice. She wrapped Kendra's old plaid bathrobe around her like a blanket and stepped inside the barn. "I thought you were in bed?" Kendra asked.

"I couldn't go back to sleep. What happened?"

Brent shrugged. "I'll give you three guesses and the first two don't count."

"Mason?" she asked.

"Mason," he confirmed.

"How do we know?"

Kendra knelt beside the tractor and inspected several gashes in the tires. "This took a lot of effort. It sure as hell wasn't just some freak looking for copper wire, or some kid pulling a prank. These tires are thick and hard. It took determination and strength to puncture them. One helluva long blade, too. And one other thing. A damn good reason to do it."

Lacey brushed several papers onto the floor and groaned. Michelle lifted an old, plastic three-ring binder and glanced through the pages. "What is all this stuff?"

Lacey straightened her back and placed her hands on her hips. "This is what passes for my sister's office. Enter at your own risk."

The small room located on the third floor of the larger barn boasted floor to ceiling shelves along two walls and an antique desk that most dealers would kill to possess, although it was coated in a fine layer of dust. Hundreds of folders, binders, books and stacks of paper littered every available surface. How did anyone work in a mess of this magnitude? "What are you looking for?"

"Insurance papers." Lacey's mouth spread into a wide grin. "Want to help?"

Michelle laughed. "I think you're going to need it," she replied as she set to work on a shelf about shoulder level. A few minutes later, she'd cleared a small work surface on the shelf to help sift through decades of unorganized records.

"Lacey, some of these papers are more than fifty years old. When was the last time anyone worked up here?"

"Probably before mom and dad died. I mean, Kendra comes up here and files away the herd records. Branding and breeding and stuff like that. But most of this crap is totally obsolete."

"She needs a computer."

Lacey laughed and shoved a wooden crate into the center of the floor. She used it as a bench as she pulled open the bent and stubborn drawer of an old steel filing cabinet that reminded Michelle of something she might have seen in an Vietnam war movie. "Yeah, right," she grunted, "I can just see Ms. Nineteenth-Century sitting down in front of a nice little workstation with a mocha-frappe. Please! She'd put a bullet in the damn thing within an hour."

Michelle wasn't so sure. "You know, she really warmed up to the idea of a website and taking a more modern approach to everything, lately."

"Yeah. Whatever you say." Lacey rolled her eyes.

Michelle scoffed in return. "What's that supposed to mean?"

"Come on, Mike. She didn't warm up to the idea. She warmed up to you. Which is quite a feat, in and of itself, if you ask me. But honestly, I can't see her caving so easily if you'd happened to be a balding, forty-year-old guy."

Michelle felt the heat of a blush creep up her neck and cheeks. "Well, I suppose that may have had something to do with it. But just the same, I think I'll head into town later and pick up a starter computer for her." She turned back to the shelves and straightened a row of heavy books with titles like *Cattle Management* and

Breeding Techniques for the New Century along the dusty surface. "Nothing fancy. Just something she can keep her records on."

Curious, she flipped open the worn binding of the second book and discovered that the new century in question was the turn of the twentieth. She shook her head in wonder.

A computer was exactly what Kendra needed. She'd hit the Internet and find a few downloads that could help with the management of the ranch. Certainly, not all ranchers were as stuck in the past as Kendra Williams. There must be some kind of software available to help her manage the herd and the finances. It would make a nice good-bye present when it finally came time for her to go home.

Her heart lurched in her chest. As much as Kendra had convinced her to stay for a while longer, someday, she'd have to go home. The thought pushed a hole right through the center of her chest and made her fingers tremble. She shook them and squeezed her hands into tight fists, but the shudder seemed to come from within and would not be denied or ignored.

"Hey, are you okay?"

Michelle forced a smile. "Of course. I'm fine."

Lacey pushed herself off the crate and moved to stand behind her. Michelle kept her eyes focused on the last shelf to be organized. She wasn't ready to tell anyone how she felt about Kendra, and if she knew Lacey at all, that's exactly what her friend wanted to know.

Michelle refused to turn around. A slight tapping drew her attention to the floor where she caught Lacey's cowboy boot-encased toes thumping a steady cadence on the old boards.

When Lacey cleared her throat, Michelle cringed.

"Oh, girl, you better start talking."

Michelle swallowed, but kept her eyes on the shelf. "Talk about what?"

"How long have we known each other?"

"I don't know."

"Three years. And do you think after three years, I can't tell when something's wrong?"

Michelle didn't answer. Lacey was more like a sister than a friend. Their ability to read each other had been one of the driving forces that made them so compatible; so infinitely close. She sighed and turned to face her friend. She'd never been able to keep her feelings from Lacey. Why did she even try?

The moment she looked into her friend's green eyes, so very much like her sister's, Michelle stiffened her resolve. She couldn't put a voice to her feelings. Not after Kendra had been so vividly clear about her own feelings. She'd convinced Michelle to stay, but had not said those three little words that she so badly wanted to hear.

"I'm fine, Lacey. Really."

"Liar. You're in love."

Kendra felt like she'd been kicked in the gut by a rodeo bull. Some force she couldn't recognize stole every ounce of air from her lungs until she thought her knees would fail to support her weight. She placed one hand on either side of the doorjamb outside the old ranch office and bowed her head.

What the hell did Lacey think she was doing?

Like someone watching a train wreck, she found herself rooted to the floor, unable to pull her attention from the carnage. She had to hear what Michelle would say.

Eyes closed, she waited. Holding her breath, she waited. Fingers white-knuckled against the wood, she waited.

"Of course, I'm not in love." Michelle's voice sounded firm and steady.

No quiver. No hesitation.

Unlike Kendra's stomach. She took a deep breath to ease the queasy butterflies upsetting her normally iron-like constitution. Splinters from the rough wood beneath her fingers embedded her flesh.

Michelle didn't love her.

Thank God, she hadn't admitted her feelings yesterday! Rage replaced uneasiness. She'd been right all along. It was just a dalliance; an affair. A fling.

"You're lying to yourself, and you know it," continued Lacey. "But worse, you're lying to my sister. You promised you wouldn't hurt her."

"Your sister doesn't care about me, Lacey. At least, not like that."

Guilt swamped her. Kendra's conscience screamed to tell Michelle how she really felt, but she just couldn't do it. And she couldn't stand there and listen to any more words about something that would never happen. She would never confess how she felt about Michelle to anyone, least of all Michelle, now that she knew, for certain, exactly how Michelle really felt.

She crept away from the door. When she reached

the staircase, she descended half-way down, and then turned and stomped back up to the landing.

She raised her fist to knock on the door when it flew open. Lacey stood in the doorway, her eyes bright and her cheeks rosy – looking every bit as guilty as the time she'd stayed out all night with her best friend when she was supposed to be at a church sleep-over.

"You gals find anything, yet?" she asked her sister.

"No. How long have you been standing there?"

Kendra forced a chuckle. "What? You been talking behind my back again?"

"How long?"

"I just got here. Why?" She hated how easily the lie fell from her lips.

Lacey grinned and shrugged. "No reason. Nope, we haven't found anything yet."

Michelle held a file in the air. "Got it."

Kendra found Michelle's eyes the instant she looked up.

If she was talking about Kendra's heart, she was absolutely right.

Twelve

James stroked the glistening coat on his horse's neck and sucked in a deep breath of hot summer hair. In less than an hour, the great iron-horse would sound its lonesome cry and leave Dead Rock in a cloud of black smoke. Elizabeth would go with it, never to return to the rough community she so despised. Could he let her go? He should. His horse snickered and tossed its mane as if to disagree. "What do you know?" he whispered to his oldest, most loyal companion. "You're just a dumb animal."

Michelle flipped the page in the old notebook and screamed, "No!"

There has to be more. She flipped another page but only another blank page greeted her. For the last ninety minutes, she'd read the most wonderful story of love and adventure she'd seen in a very, very long time.

Dozens of hand-written sheets that nearly filled an old, spiral three subject notebook had taken her on a journey into the old west and it couldn't end now. Frantic, she picked up the notebook and leafed through the remaining pages. All blank.

"Well, that just sucks!" She tossed the notebook onto the desk and rested her chin in her hands.

According to the cover, Kendra had written that story in the twelfth grade. Well, she'd started to, anyway. Apparently, she'd never finished it. She'd have to wonder for the rest of her life if James ever went after Elizabeth, or if he just let her leave him. Both of them regretting it forever.

She sighed and glanced at the clock. She should get back to work.

Michelle closed the file of information she'd finished entering into the program she'd downloaded for Kendra's new computer. The desk-top system perched on the old desk in the barn office like the Holy Grail in the middle of the Tupperware party.

At least the room was neat and clean. Once she'd boxed up the really ancient records and stored them in the back of an unused closet in Brent's apartment next door, she'd found plenty of space for the old books and more current files. Unable to resist, she'd purchased a small oriental rug and placed it over most of the floor. She'd scrubbed the only window until the glass sparkled and replaced the shade. The room would never be elegant. The rising scent of nature from the ground floor where the animals were housed took care of that. But it held a certain, old-west charm that matched Kendra perfectly.

That's when she'd found Kendra's manuscript,

hidden behind a stack of engine manuals. She'd been unable to keep herself from reading the yellowed pages written in clean, strong strokes. At first, she'd felt guilty, but soon the words had taken her away. She glanced at the notebook again and ran her fingers over the cover. She had talent. Anyone who read her words could see that.

But it wasn't up to her. Kendra must have had a very good reason to have stopped writing. Who was she to mourn the loss?

She arched her back and pulled open the next file.

Taxes. She made a sour face.

Yuck.

She'd discovered that most of the files were labeled correctly and anything older than three years, she'd stored with the other papers. It shouldn't take long to input a few years worth of completed records. A small checkbook and dollar sign icon let her into the correct program.

She picked up the most recent return and scanned through the pages. The more she read, the wider her eyes grew.

She pushed the chair away from the desk and stared out the window. Kendra stood on the bumper of the old truck and worked on the engine. Every time she pulled on something-or-other under the hood, her backside swayed from side to side. Kendra was truly beautiful, and Michelle was fairly certain she didn't have a clue. The whisper of a curse made its way to her position on the third floor, dispelling the romantic notion, but endearing her not one iota less.

Why in the world would Kendra put herself

through all of this? The unreliable truck, the threat of losing the ranch because of Harold Mason's money and influence.

She returned to the desk and found the numbers that had made her so curious. According to the taxes filed by the Heartland Cattle Company and Ranch less than one year ago... Kendra Williams was worth millions.

"You had no right!"

"I was trying to help you!"

Kendra paced from one end of the unfinished kitchen of the old ranch house to the other. She couldn't even bring herself to look at Michelle. Not right now. Her heart hammered in her ribcage and she thought her head might actually explode. Michelle had no business going through her things. She had no right to know that much about her. Cleaning the office was one thing. Insurance records? Fine. But to snoop through her tax records? Not fine.

"Listen," Michelle whispered, and then sucked in a long breath as she stood upright and rubbed her bum leg. She'd been refinishing the original cabinets with lots of elbow grease and a belt-sander. They looked good. They looked really, really good.

"I'm sorry," she continued, bringing Kendra's thoughts back to the matter at hand. "I just wanted to make things easier for you, that's all."

Kendra's shoulders ached. She was so tired. She had been this tired for so long, she couldn't remember the last time she felt strong. Before Michelle came, she'd been able to deal with the pressure. Every morning, she lied to herself. A part of her wished she'd never met Michelle. Then she wouldn't feel so weak. But another part of her didn't know what she'd do without her. That part of her felt stronger with someone to lean on.

Of course, Michelle hadn't meant any harm. Of course, she hadn't meant to pry or assume. Kendra closed her eyes and tilted her head back in an attempt to relieve the ache in her neck.

"Why don't you fight fire with fire? Find out who Mason is paying off. Then you can—"

"Then I can what? Pay them off more? I don't think so."

"Why not?"

Kendra shook her head and pinched the bridge of her nose. Lacey, Case and Brent had been after her to do that very thing for more than a year. She just couldn't do it, and it upset her to think that she'd raised them to think she could. It was wrong. Even if that was exactly what Mason was doing, it was wrong. "I don't know... Honor? Pride?"

Michelle snorted and Kendra opened her eyes. "You sound like some goddamn knight or something. Kendra, *he* isn't fighting fair. Why should you?"

"Because that's how I'm built."

"You always do the right thing?"

"Yes. I always do the right thing."

"And you're always in charge? And you always have all the answers? Is that it?"

"Yes."

"I don't believe you."

"Believe it, sister. That's the way it is." Maybe if

Kendra told Michelle enough times, she could start to believe it herself.

Michelle moved away from the counter to stand by the window, taking Kendra's hand in hers as she passed. She stared out of the glass silently for a moment before slipping her arms around Kendra's waist and pulling her close. It felt good. Normal. Deserved.

Michelle whispered, her face turned up to look into Kendra's eyes deeply. "You don't have to take care of everyone else, you know. Sometimes, you need to take care of yourself."

What was that supposed to mean? She shook her head. "I won't use the money to bribe officials, Michelle. Not even to save this ranch."

"How's he doing?" Michelle stepped onto the bottom rung of the old, clap-board fence that surrounded the shoots at the rodeo grounds. A few feet away, Brad paced in the loose dirt. One gloved hand clenched and unclenched over and over again as he seemingly tried to memorize every speck of dust on the ground.

"He'll be fine. He's just a little nervous. If he makes this ride, he qualifies for his PRCA card." Brent climbed onto the fence beside her. "How're you?"

"I'm fine."

He nudged her shoulder with his. "Liar."

She forced a smile and glanced into the stands. Lacey and Kendra sat about half-way up the center. Kendra had barely spoken to her for three days. She'd even spent the last two nights sleeping on the range with the herd – something she hadn't done for weeks. She sighed and looked at Brent. "I really screwed up."

"No, you didn't. Hell, you would've found out about the money at some point, right? It wasn't even a secret. She'll get over it."

"I don't know, Brent. I've never seen her that angry before. Why doesn't she use the money? I just don't get it."

"It's the settlement money. See, after Mom and Dad died, the state agreed to let her have us kinds. On one condition. That she pursue every possible means to gain compensation for the accident. In other words, they wanted to make sure she'd have the money to raise us, without state assistance."

"That's bullshit!"

"Yeah, well, that was the deal. They figured if she was going to be broke and living off the state, they'd just as soon adopt us out."

"Go on."

"So, she agreed with the terms. It was the only way they'd turn four kids over to a twenty-year-old girl whose only life experience was riding the rodeo circuit and a couple of years in the Navy."

"And?"

"Well, she hired one of the local lawyers and told him to do what he could, but that she didn't care if she got any money or anything. To just go through the motions or get enough to pay himself, right? The lawyer made some calls, and even hired an investigator. That's when we found out the pilot was drunk."

"I thought it was your parent's private plane? Did they know their pilot had a drinking problem?"

"He wasn't their regular pilot. So, no, they didn't know. Anyway, this pilot owned a fairly large charter company. Came highly recommended, for all the good that had done. The whole thing had gone to court eventually. The lawyer cleaned out the estate, since the pilot was killed in the crash along with our folks, and in the end, the case shut down his entire operation. Now, that had really pissed Kendra off. The jury had wanted to make an example out of the company for letting something like this happen. They gave us something like twelve million, after the attorney took his cut."

"And she never touched it?"

"Well, I don't know about never. I mean, we've always had enough to eat. And we've never been without something that we really needed. There's no mortgage on the Heartland, and her truck might be a POS, but it's paid for. Kendra's not a real luxurious kinda girl, you know?"

"Yeah, I know," Michelle mumbled.

Lenise waved at her over Brent's shoulder as she crossed behind him. Michelle smiled and waved back. "They really are a cute couple, aren't they?"

Brent looked over his shoulder and frowned. "Most of the time."

Michelle followed the direction of his gaze. Brad took Lenise by her upper arm and led her further away from the chutes. "What's going on there?" she asked.

"Don't know." Brent pushed off the fence and landed in a dusty cloud. "I'll be right back."

Brad and Lenise were arguing. Michelle glanced toward the stands. Kendra must have seen what was happening. She took the bleacher steps two at a time and made her way toward where Michelle waited.

Shouts brought her attention back to the kids.

"I don't care, Lenise! You'll do it because I said so!"

"No, Brad. I won't!"

A moment later, Lenise rushed past Michelle and left the grounds. Michelle turned back toward Brent and Brad to find them in a heated discussion of their own. Brent put his hand on Brad's shoulder and Brad shrugged it off before heading toward his assigned chute.

"What the hell was that about?" Kendra stood beside her.

"I don't know. A lover's spat, I guess. Brad's nervous about his ride."

"He's never been that nervous. No. Something's very wrong."

Brent reached them and put his thumbs through his belt loops. "That boy has a screw loose."

"What's his problem? He's been meaner than a rattlesnake all week."

"Something about how infernal women don't listen. That's all I could get out of him."

Michelle smiled. "See? Just a little spat. C'mon. Let's watch him ride."

The chute pulled open and eight seconds later Brad jumped to the ground after a near-perfect ride. At least, Michelle thought it looked as perfect as she'd ever seen. The judges agreed and scored ninety-seven points. That put Brad in the lead for the day, as well as giving him his pro status. If that didn't cheer him up, she didn't know what would.

Inside the arena, Brad lifted his hat from the dirt and gave a half-hearted wave to the crowd. The expression on his face, however, seemed less excited that she'd have expected. His brow was furrowed, creating deep lines in a forehead far too young for them.

Kendra watched her little brother through a furrowed brow of her own. They looked so much alike. "You're worried about him, aren't you?"

She didn't answer, but leveled her eyes directly into Michelle's. Heat stabbed her midsection and sent a tremor up her spine. She whispered, "I'm sorry."

"Kendra, I—"

"No. Listen. I over-reacted. Like I always do."

"You're under a lot of stress right now, Kendra. It's okay."

"It won't happen again." She pulled Michelle into her arms, gently, almost tentatively, as though she might balk like a skittish horse.

Eyes closed, Michelle let Kendra hold her. She'd missed her touch and now allowed her warmth to encompass her. "Are we okay, now?"

"Yeah," Kendra answered. "Let's go watch the rest of the show from the stands."

Euphoric. It was the only way to describe how she felt when Kendra looked at her like she did in that moment.

She followed Kendra back to the grandstand, her arm guiding Michelle like a beacon on a dark night, steering ships to safe harbor. By the time they reached the stands, it was as though they'd never fought at all.

The second show proved as exciting as the first. Brad's second go-round for the day earned him a score nearly as high as the first, only because his second bull didn't score as well. His hometown crowd went crazy when he won first place for the day. He was officially the high school rodeo bull riding champion.

Michelle glanced around for any sign of Lenise, but apparently she hadn't come back to watch him ride. Or win.

Kids, she sighed. They'd find their way. She forced her concerns out of her mind and concentrated on having a good time. Relaxing for the first time in far too long, she allowed the festival atmosphere to consume her.

Just as the sun moved behind the grandstand to cast long shadows over the arena, Kendra stood and pulled Michelle up with her. "Well, that's it. You ready to go home?"

Home.

Michelle's heart raced. She wished she were going home. But the old house filled with generations of love wasn't her home, as much as she wanted it to be. A slice of regret cut away at her insides. Would it ever be?

Kendra's arm rested around her waist as she led her toward the parking lot. They both turned to the sound of immense applause.

"That sonofabitch," Kendra muttered under her breath.

Harold Mason stood in the bed of a pickup truck in the center of the arena with the rodeo chairman.

The loudspeaker blared to life. "Ladies and gentlemen, I'd like to introduce you to the man responsible for today's festivities and a great friend of our community. Harold Mason has been more than generous with his time and his wallet over the past year, and tonight is no different."

"Thank you, Mr. Chairman. It is with a great love of Randall County and the wonderful, wholesome and family oriented sport of rodeo that I present the Randall High School Rodeo Club with this check for ten thousand dollars!"

Kendra's muscles tensed against Michelle's back. "Look at him. He's like their damn hero, or something."

"You can fight him, Kendra."

Brent sighed. "I know what you're thinking. Match it. Beat it. She already did. She donated twenty-five thousand at the beginning of the school year; anonymously."

"Shut up, Brent."

"It's true! If you would just take some credit, the whole town would be on your side, and you know it."

"I won't buy people's loyalty."

"Then I hope the website turns out to be the miracle we're all hoping for. 'Cause in another few months, I'll be surprised if we have a ranch left."

The sun set over the western edge of the ranch just as Kendra pulled the truck in front of the house. She glanced at Michelle, sitting in the middle of the bench seat with Brent on her far side. For twenty or so miles Michelle's thigh had rubbed against hers. About five miles back, Michelle's left hand had found its way between Kendra's thighs and she'd been hard pressed to keep quiet, much less stay between the lines on the road.

There must be something very wrong in her brain to have kept herself away from Michelle for days over... nothing, really. Her good heart was one of the things that made Kendra adore her so much, yet she'd held against her something she'd done out of...

Not love.

Kindness, maybe.

Appreciation?

But no. Not love.

Kendra's neck grew rigid as she slipped from beneath Michelle's hand and out of the truck. The gorgeous woman on the bench seat next to her had made it very clear to Lacey that she was not in love, which was rather understandable. There was very little about Kendra to love and she would die before she'd let herself believe anything else. As proven by the fact that she, rather selfishly, made up with Michelle for one reason, and one reason only. Because she couldn't stand not being with her for one more minute.

"Is anyone hungry?" Brent pushed his door open with his shoulder.

"Not me. I'm stuffed. Just how many different kinds of barbeque are there around here?" Michelle replied.

Kendra smiled and helped Michelle to the ground. "Several. And if I'm not mistaken, you tried them all. And the cotton candy. And the corn dogs, and how many trips did you make to the beer wagon?"

Glancing up at her with glazed eyes, Michelle answered, "One too many, I think." She practically hummed.

That would explain the hand.

"Take her on inside, Kendra. I'll check on the stock and be inside shortly," Brent offered.

"Thanks."

"I'm fine. Just a little tipsy, that's all."

"Should I take advantage of the situation?"

She'd meant the words to be a joke. The smile that seemed so at home on Michelle's face faded. Passion flared in her lover's eyes. Michelle's bottom lip quivered just enough to make her take it between her teeth. Then Michelle leaned into her; whether from desire or drink, Kendra couldn't tell. And she didn't care.

She hadn't kissed her, really kissed her, in too many hours to count. A soft breeze touched her but did nothing to cool the fire in her jeans.

No wonder Kendra had been impossible to live with all week. At least, that's what the boys on the range told her last night. Tonight, she would sleep in Michelle's arms. No doubt about it.

Kendra lowered her head and brushed her lips against Michelle's fuller, pouting lips. She sighed and Kendra caught the whisper of a sound on her tongue. Michelle tasted of cotton candy and lite beer.

"Kendra!"

She groaned, unwilling to break off the thrill of growing passion too quickly. She raised one hand and waved Brent away without looking.

"Seriously, Sis. You need to see this."

Kendra grumbled even as she pulled away from Michelle's sweet smile. "Hold that thought," she stated emphatically.

Michelle grinned like a cat might while lying in a sun spot. "What thought? Who can think? I can only feel when you hold me like that."

Kendra grew moist and her insides began to beg for just a few minutes alone with her. Now. Right this minute.

"Kendra. Get your ass in here."

"I'm coming," she yelled toward the barn.

"Soon, dear." Michelle practically purred the words.

She laughed at Michelle's play on words. Yeah, she'd had a few too many at the rodeo. She shook her head, touched the tip of her nose where it suddenly itched and jogged to barn.

Inside, she glared at Brent. "What now?"

"That."

Kendra followed the direction indicated by Brent's nod. Apache's stall stood wide open. Apache lay on the straw-covered, earthen floor.

Dead.

"What the hell happened to him?" Kendra raced into the stall and stepped over the horse's lifeless head to reach the back of the rectangular enclosure.

"I can't find a single mark on him. Poison, maybe? Colic? Twisted gut?"

He was right. Kendra stood up when she couldn't find any signs of injury. Ever careful with feed and care for the livestock, she suspected someone else had had a hand in the gelding's death.

And she knew of only one person who would have any motive to do such a thing. "Mason."

"I don't know about that, Kennie. What would he have to gain? This isn't even really our horse. Lenise is going to be a wreck when she finds out."

"Terror. Fear. Intimidation. All reasons why that asshat would do this. Call Doc Granger. I want a full autopsy. I want to know exactly what was in his stomach, and his blood, and for how long. I want to know what killed him."

The barn door swung open and Brad stepped through. "What the hell happened to my horse?"

Her youngest brother's faced suddenly looked younger than it had in years. He wore the same expression he had when his dog died a few years ago. Helpless. Injured. Pale.

"We don't know yet." Brent took a step toward Brad.

Brad skirted past him and knelt beside his girlfriend's horse. Kendra put a hand on his shoulder, but he shrugged it off.

With what seemed to Kendra like icy deliberation, Brad stood. "It don't matter none. It's just a damn horse."

Kendra glanced at Brent, whose eyebrows narrowed in a confused scowl. She suspected that her own face bore the same expression. "You alright, there, kid? Something you want to talk about?"

"No." Brad stared at the horse for a moment, then adjusted his hat and left the barn.

"What's gotten into him?"

Kendra shook her head. She had no idea, but she was damn sure going to find out.

Michelle ran the brush through her hair with quick strokes and winced when it came into contact with a particularly rough knot. When she finished, she rummaged through her make-up bag and found her soft rose blush and brown mascara. It was all she'd have time for before Kendra found her way into their bedroom. She applied just enough of the make-up to be presentable and then stripped all of her clothes off. Then she slipped into a nightgown she'd picked up in town last week. Light lavender satin, almost white, it set off her eyes and gave a soft blush to her skin. At least, she hoped it did. She turned left, and then right, studying her reflection in the full-length mirror. The hemline caught her mid-thigh. She smiled with confidence.

How many times had she looked at herself like this and despised her reflection? Her thighs were too big. Her breasts had left perky behind ten years ago. Her skin was too pale, and her tummy was far from flat. But none of that mattered. Not anymore.

Her confidence had been born from Kendra's admiring glances and heated touch. The feeling that she was beautiful came so naturally now that she could barely remember having felt *not good enough.*

She hurried to the bed.

Should she lie on her back? Or her side? She bit her lip and tried both positions.

On her back.

With her hair spread over her shoulders and curling over the cleavage revealed by the low-cut neckline of her negligee.

It had been far too long since they'd made love. She giggled as she tried to force herself to relax.

A deep breath.

A sigh.

Another giggle.

The front door slammed downstairs. Michelle took another deep breath and waited for Kendra's boots to stomp up the stairs. A minute later, footsteps raced up the staircase, but they turned into another room and a second door slammed.

Brad?

Something heavy crashed in Brad's room.

Any thoughts Michelle had toward giddy laughter, lovemaking or make-up tips for the about-to-get-laid died. She threw on her bathrobe and rushed into the hall. Another loud bang came from behind Brad's bedroom door.

"Brad, honey, are you okay?"

"Go away."

"What's wrong? Do you want to talk about it?"

"Can't you hear? I said, 'Go away!'"

Kendra joined her in the hallway and her heart sped up when she breathed her deep, leather scent. So much for her grand seduction.

The room fell silent. After a moment, Kendra asked, "Is he even in there?"

Michelle nodded. "Yeah, but he won't talk to me."

Kendra turned the knob only to find the door locked from the inside. "Brad, open the door."

Silence.

"Brad?" Kendra repeated.

From the driveway, the jeep's distinctive roar filled the tense air.

Kendra cursed, racing down the stairs and out the front door.

"What's going on?" Michelle rushed behind Kendra, but stopped at the top of the stairs.

"The little shit went out the window," Kendra called from the porch. "He's gone."

"Do you know where he went? Lenise's maybe?"

Kendra shook her head, stepping back inside the house. "Maybe, but they're on the outs, apparently. Damn that pig-headed kid."

Michelle shifted her weight from one foot to the other at the top of the staircase. "Should we go after him?" Dealing with unruly, angst-ridden teens was certainly not her forte.

Kendra turned and studied her from the bottom of the stairs. She wrapped her arms around herself and her brow furrowed. "No. Whatever's bothering him, he needs to cool off before he can talk about it. There's nothing we can do until he comes home."

Her cowboy hat perched on top of her head made her look like some old-western hero. Tight jeans hugged her hips, thighs and groin before tracing her muscled legs and pooling around the heels of her boots.

But it was the look in her eyes that made Michelle weak in more parts of her body than she could name. They shone bright in her tanned face as they roamed up and down over her. Everywhere they settled burned. Michelle made a concerted effort to keep her own eyes open, or she would let the lids drift closed and collapse into a puddle right there in the hallway at the top of the stairs for all the world to see.

"Come to bed," she suggested.

"I wish I could," Kendra replied.

So that's what a bucket of ice water over one's head feels like. Michelle frowned. "You wish?"

"Someone or something killed Apache while we were at the rodeo. The vet, the sheriff and animal control should be here in about a half hour." She rested one boot on the bottom step and leaned on her upraised knee. "If I come up there now, I won't want to leave when they get here."

"Oh, my God. No wonder he's so upset." Michelle sighed and leaned her shoulder against the wall. "I'll get dressed. Do you want me and Lacey to go look for Brad? Seriously, he shouldn't be alone right now."

Kendra grimaced and pinched her nose like she always did when frustration made her head hurt. She adjusted her hat before standing taller than Michelle had ever seen her. "Nah. He's a good kid. He won't get into too much trouble. If he's not back by morning, Casey and I can go hunt his ass down." She paused and tilted her head coyly to one side and her soft lips spread into a crooked smile. "We can't seem to catch a break, can we?"

Michelle played with the belt on her bathrobe. *Would they ever?*

Thirteen

"What time did Brad get home last night?" Lacey opened the refrigerator and pulled out a new carton of orange juice.

Kendra took a sip of coffee and rested the cup on the counter. "About four."

"And you're going to let him get away with that?"

"Don't you worry about it, Lace."

"You never let me get away with stuff like that. You were all over me."

"You're a girl."

"So?"

"So, it's different with girls."

"Kendra. You're a girl," Lacey huffed, her eyes rolling so far back into her head Kendra thought her baby sister might pass out. If Kendra weren't so worried about their youngest brother, she would laugh at her sister's indignation.

Lacey finished pouring a glass of juice, put the carton away and sat at the kitchen table. "Have you heard back from animal control yet?"

She shook her head. "Not yet. It's still early."

"What do you think killed Apache?"

"Not what. Who. Harold Mason."

"What about Harold Mason?" Michelle asked as she came in through the back door.

"Nothing. You're up early." Lacey offered her a cup of coffee.

"Yeah, I think this up-with-the-sun-stuff is catching. I went for a little ride."

"On a horse?" Lacey laughed.

Michelle made a face that reminded Kendra of a petulant little girl. She made her feel better just by coming into the room.

"Yes, on a horse," she replied. "I just felt like being out there. There's something really great about the open spaces all by yourself."

"You were by yourself?" A tingle electrified Kendra's spine and forced her to push herself away from the counter.

"Yeah. Well, most of the time. I checked on the old house. Brent was there working on the kitchen cabinets. They are looking really great, by the way. Huge upgrade."

Kendra ran a hand over her jaw and shook her head. "I'd rather you not do that again, Michelle. It's just not safe."

"But I stayed close to the houses. What could possibly happen?"

She didn't want to think about it. "Anything. Nothing. Just, do me this favor? Don't go out along again?"

Michelle released an impatient sigh that said she didn't like it, but she would do her best. She didn't want to listen to Kendra. She was used to being her own person. It was part of what she admired about Michelle, but not this time. This time, Kendra needed to get her way.

"Alright. I won't go out alone again."

A horn blared in the driveway.

"That's probably the animal control guy. He was going to come back and check all of the feed bins. I'll be back in a few minutes." Kendra took a step toward the front of the house when a gunshot blasted through the air. Glasses rattled in the cabinets.

Lacey jumped to her feet. "That sure as hell doesn't sound like animal control."

Kendra raced to the front door and peeked through the curtains. Michelle bumped into her and tried to peer through as well. "Who's out there?"

Kendra backed away from the window. "It's the sheriff. And he's armed."

"Well, go see what he wants!" Lacey shoved Kendra.

Kendra opened the door and stepped onto the porch. Mac's face was red. So was his neck. He looked like he hadn't slept a wink since he left the ranch at nearly midnight last night. He wore the same uniform he wore the night before, as well. A large stain on his pants, made from kneeling in the barn, proved it. What the hell had happened to get him so riled up?

A sudden thought, more like a feeling, kicked her in the gut so hard she nearly gagged. "Now, Mac. Why don't you put the gun down and tell me what this is all about?"

"I want to see Brad, and I want to see him right now."

"I don't think that's such a good idea. You're pretty piqued at the moment."

"I'm going to kill your little brother, Kennie. I swear to God I'm going to blow that sonofabitch's legs off and watch him bleed out all over the goddamn lawn. Now, where is he?"

"I can understand that you're upset. I'm not real crazy about it either, if it's what I think is going on."

"You know damn well what's going on, Kennie. Don't play stupid with me, and hand over that little piece of sh—"

"It's Lenise, right? She's, uh... pregnant, I'm guessing?"

Mac's shoulders slumped and the shotgun loosened in his grip. He fell back against the hood of the car. His shoulders heaved, as if he sobbed, but no sound came out.

Kendra hazarded a step off the porch and moved toward her friend. "Mac. Give me the gun."

Instead of handing it to her, Mac let it fall to the ground. "Now, what do you say we head inside and talk this whole thing over?"

A car sped up the driveway and Kendra turned to see who it was. Lenise was sitting behind the wheel and her mother, obviously distraught, was in the passenger seat. Lenise stood on the breaks and the car skidded to a stop on the loose gravel next to her father's cruiser. She leaped from behind the wheel and screamed, "No, Daddy! You can't do this! I love him!"

"It's okay, Lenise. He's not doing anything. You ladies go on inside the house and we'll be in shortly."

The door swung open. Lenise ran toward the house where she met Brad, standing on the front porch, in a solid embrace. She damn near knocked him off his feet, in fact. "I'm sorry, Brad. I'm sorry. I didn't mean it. I didn't." She was full on sobbing, barely able to get the words out. Her breaths came in tangled, gnarled gasps.

Brad kissed her lips, her cheeks, and her eyes, as though he could take away every tear. Kendra braced herself against Mac's chest and held him down on the car. "Let 'em be, Mac. You can't stop it and you know it."

He growled, but seemed to relax a measure. More like... surrendered.

Brad pushed Lenise away gently, one hand on either shoulder, and paused to look directly into her eyes. "So, does this mean that you *will* marry me?"

Kendra levitated off the hood of the car with Mac not far behind. "She'll do what?!"

"Kendra. Stop pacing. You're going to wear a hole in the floor."

Michelle patted the sofa next to her. Maybe, if she could get Kendra to sit still for five minutes, she'd be able to think more clearly.

"I can't sit down. What are they going to do? How are they going to live?"

"You have plenty of money, Kendra. I really don't think they'll starve."

"That's not what that money is for. I'm not just

going to give it to them."

"Well, of course not. But in an emergency, which I'm sure they're going to have their fair share of, at least there is something to keep a roof over their heads, you know? I'm not saying, 'Give them a million bucks and hope for the best.' No, I'm saying that there are people in this situation who are a lot worse off and they make do every day."

Kendra stopped in the middle of the floor. Her boots made a stomping sound as she faced Michelle. "I suppose they're going to do this thing whether we agree to let them or not."

She nodded. "Yup."

"So, I should make the best of it?"

She nodded again.

Kendra sat next to her and rubbed her forehead with the tips of her fingers. "Mac seemed a bit more reasonable when they left."

"It must have come as quite a shock. But honestly, things like this happen. At least you raised Brad to do the honorable thing. A lot of young men these days don't."

"He'd better do the right thing. I'll kill him myself if he doesn't. And by the right thing, I mean, pay his fair share. Raise his child. Be there. But married? They are so young."

She laughed and leaned into Kendra. "You should have seen your face when you heard the word 'marry.' I thought you were going to explode."

Kendra laughed, too. "It *was* the shock, I guess. Come here," she continued. With one delicate tug, she pulled Michelle into her chest and leaned back on the sofa, taking Michelle with her.

"It wasn't the best timing, though. Was it?" Michelle sighed.

As soon as she said the words, she wished she could bring them back. The muscles of Kendra's chest twitched beneath her cheek.

"No, but would there ever be a good time to find out your little brother knocked up his high school sweetheart?"

"What did animal control say?"

"Good, old-fashioned rat poison. He found traces of it in Apache's stall. Apparently, Mason just wanted to send another message. Otherwise, he would have killed all the stock."

"What are you going to do?"

"Hire more hands. Post watches around the compound." Kendra shifted on the soft cushions. "I don't want to talk about this right now."

Kendra's voice changed. The house, empty except for Kendra and Michelle, fell to a deep quiet. Even the clock ticking on the piano didn't make a sound. The kids had decided to go back to Mac's place and work out a few things, including a wedding date, and Kendra was certain that Mac had a few choice words for her little brother. Lacey and Brent were out in his apartment having bedded down the animals. Michelle suspected they had conspired to vacate the premises.

Her hands moved over Michelle's back in a soothing rhythm. Michelle didn't want to talk about anything, either. "Let's go upstairs," she suggested.

A growl escaped from low in Kendra's throat, like the purr of a wild animal on the prowl. "I thought you'd never ask."

Michelle stood and took Kendra's hand. In silence, they made their way to Kendra's room. It had become their shared room over the past few weeks, although Michelle hadn't officially moved in. She kept her clothes and personal items in the spare bedroom, but never slept there. Moving her clothing, her day-to-day items, seemed too final; too committed. At some point, they would have to address what they were doing. What did it mean? Was it going to last? Did they even want it to? But not today. Not right now.

Shadows marked the way as the sun settled in for the night. It was still early, but Michelle had no intention to leave the bedroom until morning.

Once inside the room, Kendra shut the door with a quiet click. "Alone, at last."

Michelle smiled at the cliché.

Whole.

Kendra studied Michelle's face, memorizing every plane. Every twinkle in her eye. Michelle made her whole. No matter what fell into her life, she could deal with it. Just so long as Michelle were still there. Still here. "I want you. More than I want to breathe."

Michelle's perfect lips turned into a perfect smile and a subtle rose hue heightened her cheeks. With both hands, Kendra took Michelle's face into her palms and then moved her fingers through the silky softness of her hair. Honeysuckle filled her nostrils and she inhaled the fragrance deep into her lungs. She'd never suck another honeysuckle the same way again, that was for sure.

With a soft mewl, Michelle's tongue darted from between her lips to moisten them and that's all it took. Kendra dove on what seemed like an engraved invitation to kiss. Hunger burned inside her to a degree she could barely stand. She wanted to consume her. While her lips met Michelle's, her body throbbed and pulsed with the beat of one heart and the power of two.

How had she survived so many years without her? It didn't seem possible. If Michelle hadn't been here this morning when Mac showed up, bent on murder, Kendra might have made matters even worse. Hell, she might have been on Mac's side and shot Brad herself.

Even now, Michelle's kiss calmed her at the same time it fanned the flames of her soul.

As if drawn by some unexplainable magnetic force, they moved toward the bed. One body. One mind. One soul. When Kendra's legs met the mattress, she gently pulled her lips away. Starving for air, but wanting more, it was difficult for her to break the kiss. Michelle's gaze roamed over her neck and breasts before settling on her belt buckle. When she raised her gaze back to Kendra's face, her eyes were filled with what could only be described as passion.

Pure.

Hot.

Michelle's delicate fingers, tipped with short, manicured nails colored a soft, fleshy pink, reached for the buttons on Kendra's shirt. She slowly pushed the first button through the hole and revealed a small amount of skin. Gently, she kissed the exposed flesh. Fire consumed her, sending shockwaves of pleasure to the four corners of her mind and every part of her body at once.

Another button. Another kiss. The third button revealed the small mounds of Kendra's breasts. Michelle paused for only a flicker of a moment before she paid the same warm attention to each one. Pulling away the fabric of Kendra's undershirt, Michelle took one erect nipple into her mouth, first suckling and then gently nipping the tip with her teeth.

Lifting her head and tilting it coyly to one side, Michelle smiled and a truly vixen-like quality appeared in her eyes. Her fingers made quick work of the remaining buttons and brushed across Kendra's stomach as she pulled her shirt free of her jeans. Without words, only the whisper of heated breath, she pushed the shirt off of Kendra's shoulders and let it fall to the floor.

And then she fell to her knees, falling softly, but not without an eagerness that sent those flames licking to places that Kendra had forgotten she had. Or maybe she'd never known she had them in the first place.

Michelle worked Kendra's belt buckle loose, and then unbuttoned her old-school button-fly jeans. A ragged breath filled her lungs and she looked down. Michelle sat on her knees in front of her, her mouth so close to her crotch that she could feel the heat of Michelle's breathe through the denim.

It had been so damned long since any woman...

Kendra bit her lip to keep herself from protesting. She wasn't entirely comfortable, but something in Michelle's very countenance screamed that she needed this as much as Kendra did.

Slowly, almost carefully, Michelle slid Kendra's jeans over her narrow hips, bringing her plaid boxers with them. When they reached her knees, Michelle whispered, "Lie down."

Kendra could do nothing but obey. Rational thought had been melted away as the raging inferno crept from her loins to her brain. She sat on the edge of the bed, supporting herself on one hand and reaching forward to stroke Michelle's gorgeous mane with the other. Michelle slipped Kendra's jeans off and tossed them aside. They landed in a heap in the corner, the sound of their landing on the hard wood louder than it should have been.

"Lie down, Kendra. Let me love you."

"Not yet," she returned, her voice raspy even to her own ears.

Michelle's seductive smile turned to an evil grin and she offered the hint of a shrug, as if to say, "Have it your way."

Tenderly, Michelle urged Kendra's trembling thighs apart. It was as though she were consumed with an earthquake that started from her insides and caused tremors in each of her limbs. She couldn't stop it, and she didn't want to. When Michelle's mouth made the first soft, but not timid, contact with skin that hadn't been touched in more years than Kendra could remember, the earthquake shifted. It was no longer inside her. Instead, she was inside the quake, each earth-moving pulse consuming her until she worried, sincerely, whether she might die. She grasped Michelle's hair between her fingers and held on for her life.

"Oh, God," she breathed between gritted teeth. "Oh, God."

Michelle continued to tease Kendra's clit with circles, wide and small. Heavy and light. First she sucked the tiny nub between her lips and suckled and then, with no hint or warning, she pulled away and teased her with short, hard strokes using the very tip of her tongue. Back and forth, she brought Kendra to the brink and then changed tactics like a general waging a battle.

The weight and pressure that built slowly, deep inside of her collapsed Kendra's arm and she felt backward onto the bed. She grasped the coverlet with both of her fists as her legs spread wider of their own accord. Michelle giggled, like any true vixen who knows full well she had subdued her prey.

Kendra lifted her head in time to see her lover adjust her position, her muscles tensing like a lioness going in for the kill, her body trembling as much as Kendra's. Spreading the folds of skin with the fingers of one hand, Michelle slid one finger, and then two, inside before lowering her mouth to Kendra's clit again. With a rhythm that comes from the most basic of human existence, Kendra rocked her hips against Michelle's mouth and fingers. Heat built like a firestorm, climbing through the seven levels of hell until it reached the edges of heaven.

"Come for me, Kendra," Michelle whispered. "Let me taste you."

Michelle pressed her fingers to that spot where the fire had started. She gently massaged as she continued to suckle Kendra's clit with expert attention, until finally, almost without warning, Kendra's world exploded. Michelle groaned with such obvious pleasure that Kendra couldn't be sure she hadn't come undone as well, but the waves of pleasure stole her voice and the sound served only to enhance them. Michelle continued to stoke the fire, slowly and gently until Kendra's body fell limp, ultimately sliding her hands over the insides of Kendra's thighs; hot, slick and wet.

Wet?

Drenched was more like it.

Like a sunrise kisses the night sky, reality slowly descended over her. Her body returned to some semblance of normal, although she doubted she would ever be normal again.

Michelle slid on top of her, surprisingly naked. "Are you okay?"

Kendra could only nod.

When Michelle pressed her thigh against Kendra's sex, she thought she might come again and shuttered with what could only be described as an aftershock of the original quake that had stolen any measure of sense she had left.

"You think you're in charge, do you?" She finally found her voice, although it was still rough with passion.

Those amazing lips, still glistening with the evidence of Kendra's reactions to her skillful talents, spread into a wide grin. "Of course, I am."

A challenge...

Kendra lifted Michelle as she stood on shaking knees, turned them both around and tossed her lover onto the bed. Kendra fell into place on top, catching the bulk of her weight on her elbows, placed strategically on either side of Michelle's upper arms. The effect trapped Michelle's arms close to her breast. The bonus was two perfectly formed mounds of soft, white flesh just waiting to be caressed and kissed, suckled and stroked until Michelle screamed for release.

Never one to disappoint, at least not in the bedroom, Kendra obliged the waiting orbs. Michelle's throat pulsed as she swallowed and then emitted the soft, purring sounds that Kendra had come to recognize as a very good thing. Satisfied that their little power struggle had been decided, she paid less attention to holding her captive with her body and more attention to repaying her in kind.

Within moments, Michelle panted and convulsed with an orgasm that bore witness to their lovemaking in a way that only true ecstasy can bring. Michelle screamed her release, as Kendra had planned, and she caught the sound between her lips, kissing her until she couldn't breathe.

Unable to stop herself, Kendra positioned herself between Michelle's legs and rocked her hips, pressing her mound against Michelle in a way that joined them together at soul level. Before Michelle's trembling orgasm had time to abandon her, Kendra joined her. They came together, breath mingling, their hearts beating as one, their pulses throbbing in unison.

Panting, Kendra collapsed onto Michelle's breast.

How in the name of God was she supposed to live without her?

Michelle's even breaths merged with the night sounds coming through the partially opened window. Propped on one elbow, Kendra traced the lines of her face, relaxed in sleep, with her gaze. Michelle curled against her so perfectly, she hated to move. But, she was more afraid she'd wake her if she stayed in place. Sleep seemed to elude her and she'd given up trying to force it.

Too many things raced around in her mind.

Michelle. Brad and Lenise. Harold Mason. A couple of years ago, her life had been so simple. Raise the kids. Herd the cows. Eat. Sleep.

Simple.

From the minute Mason had clawed his way into Kendra's life that had all changed. And now? Now, it seemed as if everything would collapse at once.

Except for Michelle. She represented everything good that life had to offer. In her, she found peace and even love. She sighed when she couldn't deny it anymore, not even to herself.

She loved her.

More than anything, she wanted Michelle to stay with her forever. Without her, Kendra couldn't bear the weight of all that had been heaped on her.

With effort, she slipped from beneath the blanket and tucked it beneath Michelle's rounded backside. She bit her lip and shook her head slightly to keep from groaning aloud. What god had she pleased to grant her such a woman?

What would happen if she didn't convince Michelle to stay on with her? To live here, on Heartland Ranch... her wife. Mother to her children?

She frowned as she stood in front of the window and looked over the moonlit range behind the house.

Did Kendra really want children? Did Michelle? Sure, she'd raised the others, but they weren't her kids. As much as she'd done to try and make up for their lack of parents, they weren't her offspring.

She scratched her chin and rubbed the heels of her palms over her eyes. She wasn't getting any younger. She had no desire to carry a child; no maternal internal clocks, or whatever the hell they were, ticked inside of her. Well, maybe technically they did. Her eggs wouldn't last forever, right? She remembered that much from junior high health class. But, what about Michelle? Did she want to have a baby someday?

And if the goddess beneath the blanket next to her did want to have a child of her own, was Kendra up to repeating the challenges she'd already faced? Chicken pox. Broken bones. Broken hearts...

She glanced back at the goddess, still sleeping. She'd curled into the place Kendra had vacated and pulled her legs slightly toward her breasts, one of which was exposed to the filtered moonlight.

She'd give anything, she realized, to see this woman feeding their child from that breast.

What if everything worked out? What if they bested Harold Mason at his own game and Michelle actually agreed to stay here, to be a part of their lives?

And what if they didn't beat Mason? What if Kendra lost everything? They'd still have the money from her parents' settlement. After setting up a trust for Brad and Lenise and their growing family, and dividing the rest between the adults, there would be plenty to take care of Michelle and anyone else who came along.

This wasn't the first time these kinds of thoughts had burned through her: children and family.

The ultimate question was: Did she have it in her to start all over?

Every question that whirled from one side of her head to the other seemed to breed three more, like some kind of cancer.

Who was she kidding? she scoffed silently.

She'd never be the same without the ranch.

She pulled on her jeans and a sleeveless tee, and then stepped out of the room. She didn't know where she was going, just that she needed to be by herself for a little while. Her fingers twitched as she stepped out of the house and into the moonlight.

Someone had left the horses turned out in the small corral. She smiled... that someone would be her, of course. She made her way in that direction and waved to the herdsman she'd positioned on the roof of the barn. The tip of a rifle barrel glistened in the moonlight falling across his lap.

The atmosphere reminded her of some kind of castle in the dark ages. Danger lurking at every corner; enemies at the gate. But it wasn't romantic, and it wasn't a fairy tale. She climbed the exterior steps that led to her grandfather's third-floor ranch office over the barn.

Inside, she settled behind the desk. She pushed the new keyboard Michelle had placed there out of her way and flipped on the desk lamp. A small circle of bright white light brightened the space and she frowned. She liked the old light-bulbs better; the ones with the yellow glow. Or, better yet, a lantern or a candle.

Neat bookshelves held her grandfather's old cattle manuals. She read the titles and was surprised to find that the girls had displayed the most important ones. Maybe she'd done a better job educating Lacey about ranching than she'd thought. Of course, Brent had probably helped Michelle and Lacey pick them out of the clutter.

New curtains on the window and a decent rug on the floor made the often-ignored space downright cozy.

Her eyes fell on a notebook on the corner of the desk. She picked it up and smiled.

She hadn't laid eyes on it since just after high school. One of the many novels she'd started back then and never finished. Running her thumb over the edge of the notebook, she scanned the pages.

Then she started reading. An hour later, she set the book on the desk, open to the first blank page.

With a sigh and a groan, she picked up a pen.

And wrote.

Michelle woke as the dawn spread golden light through the sheers covering the bedroom window, a giant grin plastered on her face that made her cheeks hurt. She almost laughed. The chill morning air failed to reach any further than her cheeks. The rest of her snuggled beneath the blanket and pressed firmly against Kendra's warmth.

She never wanted to move from this spot. Nothing could come through the door uninvited. No Mason. No business crumbling in Las Vegas. Just the two of them for eternity.

Was that so much to ask?

The door crashed open and Kendra woke with a start.

Michelle cringed. So much for *no invitation.*

"Brad's getting married!"

"Morning, Lacey," Kendra grumbled. "Don't you knock?"

Lacey rapped slowly on the door three times. "Better? So, what are we going to do about this? Is Lenise really pregnant?"

"Go downstairs and make coffee. We'll be down in a few minutes."

"We?"

Michelle raised her right hand and waved toward the door, in the rough direction of Lacey's voice.

"Oh. Hi, Michelle. Didn't see you there. Hurry up."

"Get out so we can get up, and we'll hurry." Kendra threw a small, decorator pillow at her sister.

When Lacey left, Michelle pressed her back against Kendra again and pulled her arm over her like a comforter. She really was a comforter. The thought brought a smile back to her lips. "Good morning."

Warm breath followed by Kendra's lips touched her neck. Her mouth moved against her skin as she answered. "Mornin'. Should we get up now?"

Michelle wiggled her backside against the warmth she found at Kendra's core. "No."

Kendra laughed, her mouth still embedded in Michelle's neck as she thrust her hips against her backside. "I think I already am. As always when you're around."

Memories of the previous night's activities made her spine tingle and her stomach clench. "You pretty much proved that already."

She expected a soft kiss any minute and closed her eyes. Strong hands. Slow, deliberate strokes over her...

Kendra threw the covers off and slapped Michelle's naked behind with the flat of one hand. "Rise and shine!"

"Ouch!" Michelle half-laughed and half-screamed

as her teeth set to a steady chatter. "It's cold. I don't want to get out of bed."

In a few seconds, it seemed Kendra stood in front of her where she'd pulled the blankets almost over her head. Fully dressed. "Take your time, sweetness. I'm going to get some coffee and see if I can speak civilly to my little brother. And later, I'm running into town. Want to come?"

Did she ever. But that probably wasn't what Kendra meant. She sighed. "Where are we going?"

"The courthouse. I'm swearing out a restraining order and complaint against Harold Mason."

"That's surprising. You? Taking proactive action against Mason? Do you think it'll do any good?"

"No. But it's a start."

"Sure. I'll tag along."

Kendra leaned down and kissed her cheek. "I'm glad you're here." Then she left the room.

Michelle fell back into the down pillow and stared at the ceiling. Restraining order. Why would she think of something like that? Maybe Mac had suggested it. At least she was taking the offensive. Kendra was right. It was a start.

The bed held little of the allure it had a few moments earlier. She heaved herself from beneath the sheets and headed for the shower.

A few minutes later, she dressed and joined the rest of the family in the kitchen.

"And I was thinking of a pink dress. With lots of lace, maybe tea-length with matching pink cowboy boots? What do you think, Lacey?"

"I think you're completely insane for getting

married, that's what I think. And you just described a spoonful of Pepto Bismol."

Michelle smacked Lacey on the back of the head with just enough force to get her attention. "Don't listen to her, Lenise. It'll be just fine. You and Brad will make it work. Right, Lacey?"

Lacey grumbled but somehow forced a smile. "Right. And I think the pink boots will be precious." Sarcasm dripped from her voice like molasses.

Michelle patted Lenise on the back and then poured herself a cup of coffee. "Where's Kendra?"

"She went to meet with the night watch. Man, is this weird or what? It's like we're living in a fortress or something. It's eerie." Lacey shuttered.

"Yeah, but your sister is just being careful. I'm going to log on and get a little work done."

In the living room, she sat on the sofa and hooked up her laptop. She didn't even want to think of how many emails she might find, having been offline so much lately.

She sipped her coffee and waited for her email program to open. Four hundred and forty-eight emails dumped into her inbox. The start of a groan settled in her throat until she scanned the subject lines.

Request for Information – Heartland Ranch and Cattle Company. They were all copies of the emails sent originally to Vincent for the video orders.

The groan turned into a yelp, and then a scream.

Lacey and Lenise dashed into the room and skidded to a halt, staring at her. "What is it? What's wrong?" Lacey sounded panicked despite her earlier nonchalance about possible threats.

"Nothing! Nothing's wrong, Lacey!" Michelle spun the computer on her lap to show the girls the list. "Look at this! We have schools, government offices – you name it – requesting information about the ranch. They want the video. Almost all of them clicked on the information link. They're all in favor of saving the ranch as a symbol of our American heritage."

"Really?" Lacey leaned forward and then fell to her knees in front of the computer.

Michelle took a deep breath, her cheeks on fire from the size of her grin. "It's working!"

"I have to admit, Michelle. I really didn't think anyone would care." Kendra steered her truck into a parking space in front of the courthouse.

"You should have more faith in people."

Kendra hid a cringe. Faith was something she had trouble with. Sure, she believed in God and had all kinds of faith in the Big Guy, but faith in people was a whole different story.

She'd had faith in her parents, and they up and died on her. She'd had faith in the community, and they'd sided with Mason and fell for his used-car-salesman pitches about the resort and how great it would be for them. She'd once had faith in herself. But that was a long time ago.

And now, she was about to have faith in the legal system that did nothing except punish the innocent.

In another six months, when Brad turned eighteen, she had planned to give all of the settlement money away. Every last ill-gotten dime of it. For fifteen years, she'd raised her brothers and sister with only the money she'd earned. She would have given all the cash away the minute she'd received it if the courts and the state would have let her keep the kids anyway. They thought she'd needed it. But it was blood money and she wanted no part of it.

In the end, she'd proved them all wrong. At least she'd accomplished that much.

Disturbed by the direction of her thoughts, she cleared her throat. "So, when will the video be ready?"

"I talked to Vincent this morning and he can ship them by the end of the week I just approved the final edits and he'll have it mastered and uploaded to the host site by Friday. I've got my staff working on the packets that go with it."

"Great."

"And I'll be copying all of the files for the website to the computer in your office this afternoon. Lenise is fully up to speed on how to make changes and the like. The internet connection is all set and this way we don't have to worry about using the laptop all the time."

Because she'd go home eventually, and Kendra was expected to run things from here. Alone.

"Are you okay?" Michelle's voice held a note of real concern and Kendra glanced at her. She stood, half in and half out of her truck, and focused her eyes on Kendra. Her forehead was wrinkled. Nobody had ever really cared if she were alright.

Everyone just assumed that she was.

"Yeah," she answered. "I'm fine."

"Well, let's go get this done, shall we?"

Together, they filled out the proper paperwork and

submitted it for the judge. In the documents, they included a request for a restraining order against Harold Mason and anyone in his employ.

In the papers, they basically accused Mason of cattle rustling, animal cruelty and outright murder. She'd be more than surprised if they weren't laughed out of court.

"For all the good it will do." Kendra held open the door and guided Michelle through it with her hand on the small of her back.

The contact sent a jolt through her. Would she ever get tired of touching Michelle? Even so innocent a gesture made her hot with wanting. Full of curves, soft and pliable, Michelle stole her concentration as much as she'd stolen her heart. She wanted nothing except to form Michelle to her body and make love to her, again and again. A part of her hoped she would grow tired of it. Letting her go would be so much easier that way. But it wasn't going to happen any time soon. Every time she brushed against her, every time she held her, and every time she kissed her was like some new erotic experience. Most of all, Kendra didn't want to worry about her problems when she touched Michelle.

When Michelle held her back, Kendra didn't *have* to worry.

Fourteen

"It's really getting warm, ain't it?"

Kendra wiped the sweat from her forehead with the back of her long sleeve and replaced her hat before looking up at one of the new hands. She and Brent had hired so many over the past ten days, she still didn't know them all. "Yep. It's a scorcher."

"I don't think we've met yet, boss. I'm Charles, but everyone calls me Chuck. I just wanna thank you for the job."

"No problem." Kendra narrowed her eyes. "You used to run with Kennedy Bastian, right?"

"Yes ma'am. Back in high school, we was like brothers, but the past couple of years, I've been working the mines out Colorado way and just got back to town. Too bad about Ken." Chuck shook his head and clicked his teeth.

Yeah. Too bad.

Did Chuck know it was Kendra's fault?

"So, anyway, your brother has posted me on night watch duty and I just want you to know, ain't nobody getting by me."

"Thanks, Chuck. I'm sure you'll do a fine job of it." Kendra slapped the newcomer on the back in a show of confidence and then carried her saddle into the barn.

Chuck followed her. "You know, the thing is, it's been like more'n a week, and I ain't seen nothing. And the guys tell me that the herd has been fine for even longer'n that."

"Well, the man behind all this has a knack for letting us get comfortable for a while before livening things up. Just keep a close eye out. Don't assume nothing is going to happen just because it's quiet."

"Don't fret, none. I'll do what I'm paid to, and that's a fact."

"Good. If you need anything just let us know."

Kendra left Chuck in the barn and made her way back to the main house. Michelle should have lunch ready and her stomach growled. And not just for food. Her arms ached to hold her. Hell, it'd been almost four hours.

A slight shiver ran over the back of her neck and impulse caused her to sneak a peek back to the barn. The new man stood in the open doors and leaned one shoulder against the jamb, a piece of straw clamped between his teeth, and stared at Kendra.

Something about the man didn't sit right with Kendra. She made a mental note to check on his background a little more closely.

When she reached the kitchen, she washed her hands and put her hat on the rack by the back door. The table boasted several platters full of sandwiches, chips, pickles and potato salad. It looked like a regular family picnic and she smiled.

Michelle breezed through the back door. Her skin glowed with the beginning of a tan from the time she'd spent out of doors over the past weeks. She looked healthy and happy and Kendra would give anything to keep her that way. Not once in the past several days had she mentioned going home.

Neither had Kendra, of course. It was as if they both avoided the subject, talking about anything but that.

Truth was, it seemed as if the restraining order had done the trick. Mason had been served with the papers eleven days ago, and not one cow had disappeared, not one piece of equipment had been tampered with and there had been no sign of trouble anywhere around the Heartland.

She still didn't believe it had worked. But she enjoyed the peace while she could.

Right now, she wanted to enjoy a piece of Michelle. Michelle stole into her arms and kissed her cheek, as though she'd read her mind. Kendra's heart sped up more than a little.

"What have you got there?"

"Flowers. For the table."

"Where did you get them?"

"That little garden behind the shed. It's just overrun with wonderful stuff, perfect for culling."

"Ah. That was Mom's." When Michelle paled and made that tiny "O" with her lips Kendra added, "It's okay, Michelle. It's just some flowers."

"I just didn't..."

"Relax. It's fine." It was more than fine. Over the past days, she'd been so much a part of the ranch and everyday goings-on, it was like she'd always been there. Kendra couldn't remember a time when Michelle wasn't a part of her soul. "Mom would love that somebody's using it. Really."

Like a herd of wild horses, the rest of the family barged through the kitchen door and surrounded the table. Lenise and Brad sat next to each other and Brad filled a plate for his young fiancé. He'd been falling all over her ever since the big news came out. She was only six months along, but Brad treated her like she was a month overdue. Lenise had barely started to show, too, as though the weight of the secret had been a huge belt, sucking in her belly and giving inhuman strength to her abs. Now that the shock had passed, she looked radiant.

Regardless of the reasons, now that the whole family knew what was happening, the couple was perfectly adorable.

Laughter and jokes filled the space when Lacey made some wise crack to Casey while Brent settled himself at the far end of the table.

Leaning against the counter with Michelle pressed against her, she let the warmth of the sun through the window heat her back.

Everything seemed so normal. Happy.

Why couldn't it just stay like this?

A sliver of awareness ran up her spine. It wouldn't stay like this, and if she wasn't careful, she'd let her guard down.

A small ache developed in her temples.

Suddenly, it was too still; too quiet.

Too... happy.

Exactly what was Harold Mason planning next?

"I really like that one, Lennie. It's just like you described." Lacey leaned forward in the small plastic chair in the dressing room of the only wedding shop in town and rested her chin in her hands.

"I have to agree. It's perfect."

"Y'all aren't just saying that because you're sick of me trying on dresses, are you?"

Michelle laughed. Apparently Lacey was growing a little tired of the endless parade of cream and pink colored satin and lace, but the dress Lenise wore now really was ideal. Michelle interjected, "No, of course not. The lines are terrific on your figure and you wanted pink, right? And those boots we saw at the western wear outlet will look fantastic with it."

"Does it hide the baby bump enough? I mean, the wedding is still two weeks away and I could be lots bigger by then. Maybe, we should just do a little courthouse thing?"

"Don't be silly, Len," Lacey admonished. "You're not the first girl in this county to get knocked up and hitched, in that order. You're going to be beautiful and someday, none of the exact circumstances will even matter. Hell, nobody will even remember."

Lenise turned toward the tri-fold mirror and twisted back and forth a few times. She made a face and her shoulders slumped. "I just wish we had more time to choose. Four weeks isn't a lot of time to plan a whole wedding."

Michelle's heart sank. Lenise was right. In less than

two weeks, they had sent invitations, put an ad in the local paper, ordered the food, hired someone to do the ceremony and planned the rehearsal dinner. Everyone was exhausted.

Including Michelle, and she didn't even know why she was involved in the planning. It was like everyone expected her to make decisions. Maybe it was the Vegas thing. She was metropolitan, so maybe they assumed she had her pulse on the fashion and party trends of America. They were wrong. She had two employees for that.

Maybe it was because Lenise's mother wanted no part of it. That must be the reason. The other women looked to her because she was the oldest female, not including Kendra who had suggested that the kids get married at the bowling alley and was immediately removed from all planning responsibilities. Of course, Michelle wasn't an expert on weddings or anything, either.

Now, if it were her own wedding...

Where had that thought come from? Michelle hid the tremble in her hands as she pulled a veil from the stand just outside the dressing room and put it on Lenise.

She'd had dreams of her own wedding for as long as she could remember. Tons of food, family and friends gathered to celebrate the beginning of her life with the perfect... woman. Marrying a woman had been out of the question for so long she'd given up the dream a long time ago.

But now?

She tried not to frown, but it was hard – knowing that her life had begun years ago, without someone to share it with. She had relegated herself to the fact that lesbians could not marry each other in the United States. Just when she'd come to terms with it, marriage laws were changing all over the place, thanks to the courage and determination of others who hadn't been so easily dismissed as she. She could get married in some states. In others, she could get a civil union – how romantic! She frowned.

She sighed as an ache gripped her stomach. She had found the perfect person. She had found a reason to begin her real life. She had found a woman that she would do anything for, that she wanted to spend the rest of her life with, but there would be no wedding. No lavish affair where she and Kendra were the center of attention and everyone knew they were just perfect for each other. As much as she loved her, she would not spend the rest of her life with her. Kendra simply wasn't interested.

At least Brad and Lenise had a chance at happiness. At least they'd found each other before it was too late.

"Am I doing the right thing, Michelle?"

Lenise's plaintive tone brought Michelle back to the tiny dressing area. The young woman's eyes brimmed with unshed tears. "Oh, Lenise. I can't answer that. Only you can know that for sure. But let's look at this rationally. You love Brad. Brad loves you. Not that there is anything rational about love, generally speaking. But you were planning to get married in a few years anyway, right? And now, with the baby coming, you'll be the perfect little family."

"But, I'm taking everything away from him. Everything he ever wanted. He was going to ride the rodeo circuit and be a national champion, like his father. And now, he says he doesn't want to do that anymore. He claims he doesn't want to leave me and the baby. But I know it's just killing him."

Lacey approached and gave Lenise a hug from behind, while Michelle held her from the front in a pregnant-Lenise-sandwich. An official group hug. Michelle sniffed. She'd never had occasional for an official group hug in her entire life. "Don't cry, baby. Brad is a big boy, and you didn't do anything to him or take anything away from him. He will do what's right by you, and the baby, and to some extent, for himself. You know why?"

Lenise lifted her head and wiped her nose. "Why?"

"Because he's just like the rest of his family, that's why. Especially Kendra."

"Yeah, they are a lot alike, huh?"

"And another thing. You didn't make this baby by yourself. Brad is just as much this baby's parent as you are. Let yourself appreciate whatever sacrifices he makes, alright? That way, he's not making them for nothing."

Michelle caught Lacey's gaze as she glanced over Lenise's shoulder and frowned. "What?"

"Are you talking about Brad, or yourself?" Lacey asked.

"Well, Brad, of course."

"I'm just asking, because it sounded an awful lot like you were speaking from experience, or something."

Michelle hoped her face didn't pale as the blood rushed to her feet. "Like how?"

"Like loving my sister."

"I don't know what you're talking about."

Lacey crossed her arms. "No more lying about it. Lenise, why don't you get changed and Michelle and I will let the clerk know this is the one. We'll meet you outside."

Michelle followed Lacey into the main showroom and almost ran into her back when Lacey stopped and turned around.

"You love her, don't you?" It was more of an accusation than a question. "I mean, head-over-heels-happily-ever-after love her. Have you told her that?"

Michelle's voice rested somewhere on the edge of a cliff she couldn't see in the dark. Her vocal cords froze and her blood congealed in her veins. "I..."

"You haven't, have you?" Another accusation.

Michelle shook her head. "I've tried, but—"

"Does she love you?"

"I don't think so."

"How do you know?"

"I've asked."

"You what?" Lacey spun and paced several feet away with her hands on her hips and her designer bag swinging from her wrist.

"Well, not in so many words, but I tried to get her to admit she cared even a little something for me when I agreed to stay until this whole mess is over with. But she wouldn't. And like a fool, I stayed anyway. God, I'm an idiot."

Lacey faced her again. "You are an idiot."

Michelle's mouth fell open. She had expected support; a kind word from her best friend, a hug... something.

"If you think for one second that my sister isn't

busting-a-gut-in-love with you, you're the biggest idiot in the history of the world."

A bee hovered over the clear plastic lid on Michelle's diet pop with lemon. Seated with Lacey and Lenise at a round table outside a small family-owned espresso shop on Randall City's Main Street, she concentrated on the fact that her cheap, plastic lawn chair had one leg shorter than the rest.

She peered beneath the scarred surface of the table. Maybe the sidewalk was uneven. A sigh threatened her lungs and she bit her lip.

Lacey had a lot of nerve. Michelle refused to even look at her now, an hour after she'd made that hurtful comment.

Kendra did not love her. Kendra had made that very clear, and Kendra got whatever Kendra wanted.

It was none of Lacey's business, anyway.

A loud roar drew her attention to the street as a motorcycle pulled to a stop in the slanted parking space directly in front of them. Casey eased his long form off the bike and approached them.

"Ladies," he drawled, smirking in that boyish way that reflected the image of his older sister so closely that Michelle's heart jumped. "And you too, sis."

Lacey threw the crumpled wrapper from her straw in his direction, but it fell several feet short of hitting her twin brother. She elected to flip him off instead.

"Love you, too," he replied. To the entire table, he continued, "Kendra sent me to find you. Says you've been gone too long."

Lenise shrugged and Lacey rolled her eyes. "Go home and tell mother that we're fine. Besides, I think everything is pretty much over with, don't you? Personally, I'm ready to go home and pick up the remnants of my life, thanks."

Michelle didn't miss the fact that Lacey looked directly at her, instead of her twin brother.

"Come on, Michelle. Kendra wanted you to go back with me."

"Excuse me?" Michelle raised an eyebrow in her very best I-can't-believe-you-just-said-that glare.

Casey swallowed. "What I meant to say was, she asked me to give you a ride back to the Heartland."

"I'm not ready to go yet. I'll ride back with the girls."

Who did Kendra think she was? Thoughts of her first impressions of the lonesome cowboi refreshed in her mind's eye. Aloof. Powerful. Determined. Arrogant.

The fact she knew she had a vulnerable side, and the rest of her outward appearance had been born from a need to always do the right thing failed to settle her nerves. Only her hand on her knee kept her heel from pile-driving a hole in the pavement.

Kendra didn't love her. Michelle didn't owe her anything. And she certainly didn't have to do as she was told.

Lacey crossed her arms over her chest and sucked half her bottom lip between her teeth.

Michelle wanted to scream. How had she ended up here? How had her very productive and busy life turned into a battle of wills in the middle of cow country?

This morning, she'd been perfectly content with the prospect of spending whatever time she could with Kendra. She'd been perfectly willing to settle for what Kendra could offer, as temporary as it might be.

Heat moved up the back of her neck and she rubbed the back of head where a sharp pain had suddenly developed.

When had she lost confidence in herself? She wasn't *that* woman. The one who snivels and takes the scrapes her partner, man or woman, throws to her when she feels like it. She would *never* be that woman.

"Are you coming or not?" Casey grabbed the leftover pickle on the edge of her plate and bit into it.

"No."

He shrugged, climbed onto his bike and roared east toward the highway onramp.

Silence overpowered the small town noises around her. Even the cars passing by seemed to be moving through some silent film.

Then Lacey rose to her feet and picked up her purse. "I knew you were only playing with her. I knew it. Go home, Michelle. Kendra is too good for you."

She shouldn't have let them go into town alone. She didn't think she'd be this worried, or this crazy. Ever since the attacks stopped, Kendra had had this weird feeling that something else, something big, was going to happen. Like Mason was just building his strength—back building like a goddamned tornado.

She was losing her mind.

The electrical cord in her left hand sparked and she dropped it like it was an open flame.

"Damn!" She sucked the tip of her finger. "Brad, cut the power again."

Infernal machines. She didn't even know why she bothered installing a new range. The whole house needed to be rewired to support the blasted thing.

Maybe it was because she was a sucker for a good deal and Barry at the appliance store had offered her a great deal when she'd bought all new appliances for the old house. Maybe she was a glutton for punishment and remodeling-slash-rebuilding one house wasn't enough.

Or maybe she would do anything to make Michelle want to stay.

Whatever the reason, the stainless steel, five-burner gas range sat in her kitchen in all of its shining glory.

Mocking her.

The cord sparked again.

"Brad?"

"Yeah?" her brother replied from outside the open kitchen window.

"I said to cut the power."

"Oh, sorry." A moment later, Brad came through the back door. "It's off now."

"Thanks."

It was insane for her to even try to concentrate on anything except Michelle. The woman consumed her without even being in the same room. Kendra could sense her. Feel her. She could even taste her without even trying.

And now she risked electrocution to install an appliance in her own kitchen when Michelle wasn't even going to be here much longer. What was she thinking?

Buy her a stove and she'll stay forever? Install a microwave so she can make popcorn without getting her hands dirty and she'll fall madly in love?

Yup.

Insane as they get.

"Hey, Kendra. Where you at?"

"In the kitchen! Keep Michelle out there with you!"

The door swung open and Kendra glanced over her shoulder as she twisted the final wire.

"No can do. She didn't come back with me."

Kendra's forehead itched and she almost growled aloud. "Did she say why?"

"Nope. Just said she'd come home with the girls. She wasn't too happy, either. Actually, none of them were. Here, this came for you."

Kendra shoved the wires into the wall and handed Brad a screwdriver. "Put that cover back on for me, will you."

She took the envelope from Casey and sat at the table. "It's from the Bureau of Land Management."

"Uh-huh." Casey shucked off his jacket and grabbed an apple. "Open it."

Kendra did and read the contents to herself. "Unbelievable."

"What?"

"It says here that the land office isn't going to renew our lease."

"You're kidding? Just like that?"

"Well, that's that." Kendra crumpled the letter and tossed it on the table. "Looks like we're out of business."

"No way." Casey picked up the letter and smoothed it. "We regret to inform you that as of October twenty-second of this year, we will not renew your public lands lease expiring in September of next year. We have received information concerning ranch operations which has made it necessary to reassign the existing parcels to another landowner." Casey frowned. "That doesn't make any sense. What other landowner?"

"Guess."

"Mason doesn't own any land around here. That's why he's been so hot to buy ours."

Kendra cursed and grabbed her hat from the rack. "That we know of."

"We already checked the records. He doesn't own any land. Period."

"Well, it looks like he bought some."

"Where are you going?"

"To town. I damn near killed myself installing that infernal machine for the woman, and Michelle is damn well going to see it."

"I said to get into the goddamn truck."

"What is the matter with you? You can't come screaming into town and kidnap a person." Michelle wanted to ball her fists and beat something, but she maintained a cool facade despite Kendra's sudden appearance on Main Street.

Kendra jumped out of the truck and circled the hood to meet her toe-to-toe on the wide sidewalk. "Why didn't you come back when Casey came to get you?"

"I wasn't ready to come home. We still had shopping to do."

"Not good enough. When I call you, you come!"

"Whoa, chickie. Back off. I don't know who you think you are, but you're not my jailor or my mother."

"No, I'm the person trying to keep you safe. What if something had happened, huh? What then?"

"Did something happen to make you come after me?"

"Yes. I mean, no. Well, yeah." Kendra growled and leaned back against the fender of the still-running truck.

Michelle stepped forward and brushed Kendra's bangs off her forehead. She needed a trim. Then she ran her finger over the deep crease made deeper when Kendra scowled. "Tell me what happened."

"I was worried about you."

"But nothing has happened in weeks, Kendra. The legal papers must have scared him off, and I don't see what all the alarm is about."

"He didn't get scared off. He went another way."

Michelle shook her head as confusion settled in her brain. "What does that mean?"

"He bought some land, I guess. The state has awarded him the land lease and we're going to have to sell the herd." She shrugged as if she'd known it all along and the whole thing was expected. No big deal.

Her heart must be breaking. Michelle's was, and it wasn't even her land. "But, it's not over, right? I mean, we can still do something. I mean, there must be some kind of appeals process, right?"

Her heart lodged in her throat. If it was over, then it was time for her to leave. She wasn't ready to go home to Las Vegas any more than she'd been ready to go home to the Heartland. Kendra still meant more to her than anything else, and she wanted to share her life for just a little while longer...

Kendra's expression closed and she pushed herself off the fender. "Get in the truck. Please?"

She obviously wasn't going to help Michelle understand. If Kendra loved her, really cared about her, wouldn't she want to share everything? In the past weeks, Kendra had taken Michelle into her confidence on so many occasions; she'd begun to feel like a real part of her life.

Now that she felt the ordeal with Mason and the precarious balance of the ranch had been settled, maybe she just didn't want Michelle anymore. The thought stung and she blinked back tears.

She had known it was coming.

When she got back to the house, she'd pack her bags and return to her real life. The whole thing had been a terrific mistake. A complete waste of time.

Reluctant to feed Kendra's demands with compliance, she climbed into the truck anyway and called Lacey to tell her she was going home with her sister.

At least Lacey would be happy she was leaving. Would they ever be friends like they had been? She had no doubt they would remain close, but how close? Would Michelle think of Kendra every time she saw Lacey? Would Lacey remember the pain she felt Michelle had caused her sister? The woman who had raised her?

So much had changed in such a short time. She wished she'd never come.

No.

That wasn't true.

She wouldn't trade her time with Kendra for anything. Not one touch, not one kiss, not one aching, thunderous orgasm. No-one would ever fill her the way Kendra had.

Do not cry!

They rode the thirty miles back to the ranch in stiff silence. Michelle practically hugged her door, and Kendra kept both hands on the wheel the entire time.

The sun hid behind storm clouds in the west. Dark and swirling, they seemed to say what she couldn't.

It's over.

Fifteen

"I didn't mean to order you around."

Kendra's words ricocheted in the back of her mind as Michelle stood in the kitchen. Kendra had tried to apologize more than once since she'd pulled the truck to a stop on the gravel drive. By the time she'd made it into the house, alone, Michelle thought her heart would explode. Sheer determination on her part had been the only thing to keep the tears at bay. But Michelle had clung to whatever independence she had left and used it like a shield.

Kendra already had her heart. She couldn't afford to lose what was left of her soul.

When Michelle hadn't answered her, Kendra had sighed and that sound resonated through her now, as well. And so did every touch, every glance, every argument and every kiss since they'd met.

"There's a microwave, too." The hollow sound of Kendra's voice shook her.

What had Kendra done? A tear spilled from her eyes and trailed heat over her cheek. She wiped it away and then rubbed both eyes. "I can see that."

"Well, hell, I didn't think you'd get all that emotional over it. I just thought it would make life easier for you while you're here."

A smile spread her lips against her will. Did she have no comprehension of what something this thoughtful might tell a woman? It was like Scrooge sending his girlfriend on a cruise or something.

She had to admit it, though. When Kendra bought something new, she went all the way. Five gas burners, an extra large oven and a mounted microwave. Not cheap.

"Why?"

"I just told you."

"No. I mean, why did you do this? So I can make popcorn? I don't think so."

"You deserve nice things, that's all."

"But, I... I don't live here."

Would she say the words she'd been hoping for for so long?

Ask me to move here. Ask me to stay with you forever.

"It was time for a new range, anyway." She shrugged.

Michelle bit her lip and forced a smile. "Well, I'm glad you installed it. But since I won't be here much longer, I hardly see how it had anything to do with me."

Her voice sounded cold. Calculating. She didn't like it. Nobody on the planet made her feel more confused or could bring out the worst in her... or the best. She wanted to scream.

Mason won.

"I suppose you can go home now, any time you like."

A lump formed in her throat. She swallowed against it, but she doubted it would ever really go away. Her words sounded...

Final.

"Yeah. I guess so. I'm sorry everything was such a waste of time, Kendra."

"It was a nice try."

"But, you knew it wouldn't work the whole time."

"A part of me hoped."

She hated awkward silences. Almost as much as she hated good-byes. "I'll go pack."

"You're leaving now?"

"Why wait?"

Kendra glanced at the floor and pinched her bottom lip between two fingers. The rim of her hat hid most of her face. When she looked up, her face wore a mask. Cold. Indifferent.

Just like how Kendra felt about her.

Michelle's suitcase sat open on the bed. Perhaps if her arms didn't weigh a gazillion pounds each, she could have filled it more than half-way by now. But every time she picked up an article of clothing and placed it inside the case, she had to rest. It was amazing how tired one could become when one had no heart left.

"Can I come in?"

Seated in an old rocking chair in the guest room, Michelle glanced at the door. Brent leaned against the doorframe and smiled. "You're not giving up too, are you?"

"Giving up what?" She released the ironic snort she'd tried to earlier. Sure, now her sarcasm worked.

"The fight. I read that letter the BLM sent. They said they were provided with information that made them change their leasing decision. Did anyone think to ask what that information might be?"

Despite her will otherwise, she leaned forward in the chair. A spark of hope, or maybe it was just curiosity, burned in the back of her mind. "Go on."

"Well, it seems to me that Mason probably sent them a bunch of bogus accusations and supplied them with forged records or something along those lines. Why, after every dirty trick and strong-arm tactic that he's employed to date, are we assuming that he's suddenly on the up-and-up, now? We've managed this land for more than one hundred years. Our family. Why would the feds suddenly switch?"

"Money. Mason bribed someone. It's obvious."

"Not to me. Mason is a fat cat around these parts, and he may have some connections back under whatever rock he crawled out from under. But up at the capitol? No, I don't think so. And sure as hell, not in D.C."

"I don't know, Brent. I'm tired. Have you talked to your sister about this?"

"As a matter of fact, I have. She's going up to the BLM headquarters in Salt Lake City in the morning."

"She is? When did you talk to her about this?"

"About two hours ago."

Two hours ago, Michelle had been buried under her covers, sobbing.

It really was over. Kendra wanted her to leave and that's why she hadn't come to tell Michelle that it wasn't time to give up. Not quite yet.

Or maybe, just maybe, she was too bull-headed to ask her to stay.

Energy surged through her limbs and she threw the shirt she'd been holding into the suitcase.

Fine. If she wanted her gone, she'd make herself gone. And Kendra could fight the good fight, or save the day, or whatever-the-hell else she wanted to do without Michelle Loving.

"Tell your sister I'll send her my bill from Las Vegas."

"Tell her yourself." Kendra pushed the door open and braced herself for what she suspected lay on the other side. An open suitcase and a woman out of her mind with rage if the stiff set of Michelle's jaw meant anything.

Even with the fire in her eyes, Michelle still possessed more beauty in one strand of her hair than any other woman alive.

"What do you want?"

You.

Kendra took a deep breath. "I came to ask if you'll go to the capitol with me in the morning."

She froze, half-bent over a dresser drawer with her arms full of socks and satin panties. "What?"

"I'm not good at this political stuff." She glared at Brent who ducked out of the doorway and headed down the stairs. "Brent didn't need to come up here. I was going to tell you myself. I just had some thinking to do. That's all."

"About what?"

She couldn't tell her. How could Kendra explain how much she loved her? Any other fool would just take the risk and tell her, but not Kendra. She loved Michelle too much to make her choose. Michelle's reaction today proved it to her, at least, even if Kendra had proven nothing to herself. She couldn't change who she was and she didn't want to. If Kendra kept her here, Michelle would only grow to resent her.

So, she'd come up with a way to make her stay for just a little while longer. She was the only reason that Kendra would keep fighting. If Michelle left, Kendra didn't care if the whole place went to hell.

So, she lied. "How to move ahead. And I was thinking that we demand to see whatever it was that changed their minds; maybe we can change it back."

"And you want my help?"

"Yeah."

Michelle slowly placed her under things back into the top drawer and stood to her full height. She looked so damned adorable, Kendra's heart ached.

"Alright, I'll go with you. But..."

She didn't finish her thought and chewed on her bottom lip, instead.

"But what?"

"From now on, it's strictly business."

"Well, that was a waste of a morning," Kendra grumbled as she stalked out of the BLM office.

Michelle wanted to run her fingers over that deep crease in her forehead, smoothing it and taking some of the frustration away with it. The weight of the world was back on Kendra's shoulders and a part of Michelle felt guilty for making her bear the load alone. But she had to keep herself safe, too. She was important, too.

As many times as she reminded herself of that, Michelle still didn't believe it. Not really. A flutter of remembered passion gripped her belly, forcing her eyes closed. It would pass in a few seconds. She took a deep breath, opened her eyes and followed Kendra to the truck.

"Are you alright? You don't look so good," Kendra asked.

A smile pasted on her face, she replied, "I'm fine. And I don't think it was as bad as you think. They did confirm that Harold Mason is the other landowner, and they said he supplied them with the reports. I've said it before. Information is power and we have more information now than we did before."

Kendra grunted and ran a hand through her hair before slapping her hat back on. "Yeah. For all the good it does me. Malpheasance? Mismanagement? Land deprivation? It's all a bunch of bunk, Michelle. And they know it. They are just playing along with Mason because he's promised them something, or paid them off. Or worse, because he's paid off their bosses."

Once they reached the truck, Kendra threw open

Michelle's door and waited for her to climb inside before slamming it. Michelle's stomach shook with the impact. Kendra climbed in the other side and locked her hands on the steering wheel. "Maybe it's time I stopped playing nice."

"Ya think?"

Kendra glared at her.

Michelle grinned in return. "Bravo. So, what are you planning?"

"I'm going to pay a visit to an old friend. If I'm going to fight fire with fire, it's time I called in a few favors of my own."

Michelle felt a tug on the corner of her mouth and tilted her head. Kendra Williams had favors to call in?

"What are you looking at me like that for? I have friends."

"I have no doubt. Lead on, fierce warrior."

Kendra pointed her truck toward the highway. Shoulders squared, gaze focused, she looked far less worried than she did determined.

Michelle wished for the hundredth time that she could slide over on the seat. Her fingers itched to trace the inseam of Kendra's jeans; to feel the hard muscles of her thigh beneath her fingertips.

What had possessed her to put a limit on their relationship? Was it really so bad that they only shared what the other was willing to give? At least then, she'd been able to hold her; to be held in return. If she thought keeping herself physically detached would keep her heart from breaking, she had been wrong. Every time Kendra looked at her, she missed her. And if she ached this much now, how much worse would it be next week when she left for good?

Kendra swerved onto the off ramp that led to downtown. The truck swayed, drawing Michelle's thoughts back to the problem at hand. "Where are we going?"

"There." Kendra pointed toward the gigantic, white building sitting on a rise in the landscape. A dome roof identified it as the Utah State Capitol Building.

"Why are we going there?"

"I told you. I'm going to visit an old friend."

"Your old friend who works in the capitol building?"

Kendra nodded, but didn't say anything more. A few minutes later, Kendra pulled into a parking space beside a tour bus. "You ready?"

"Sure. Who are we going to see?"

"The Lieutenant Governor."

Michelle swallowed. "The Lieutenant Governor is your old friend."

"Yep. We... rodeoed together in the old days. It was a long time ago, but it can't hurt to ask, right?"

"Nope. It can't hurt to ask."

Once inside the rotunda, Michelle glanced upwards. What seemed like miles above her, she found a rounded ceiling painted like a sky. Tiny seagulls winged their way across an expanse of blue and white. Several school children dashed past her to catch up with their guide and several women who looked like a mixture of teachers and parental chaperones. One child bumped into Michelle's legs. Knocked off balance, she righted herself to find a little boy, perhaps six or seven years old. He was a beautiful boy, with a mess of dark hair and green eyes.

Suddenly, Michelle imagined that Kendra's child might look very much like this little boy. Was it stupid to wish that she might be able to carry Kendra's child someday?

Kendra's warm hand took her gently by the upper arm. "Are you okay?"

Small shocks tingled where Kendra touched her, moving straight to her belly where they pooled and pulsed. She could only nod, and when Kendra tipped her head in return, releasing her arm, she wished she hadn't responded at all.

"The office we need is up those steps." Kendra indicated a wide, marble staircase.

"What makes you think we can get in?"

"I don't know if we can, but we're here now. Might as well give it a try."

Kendra took the steps two at a time. Her boot heels echoed on the hard stone. Confidence oozed from every part of her. Her posture spoke of determined pride and even her footsteps commanded attention. If anyone could get in to see the second most powerful man in the state, Kendra could.

Michelle shook her head. Part of her was so proud that Kendra had finally decided to fight back. For real, this time. Not with some half-baked idea over which she had no real control. Another part of her wished time had stood still a month ago. That part of her wanted nothing more than to be with Kendra Williams until the day she died.

"You coming?"

Michelle hurried up the final few steps and met Kendra outside a glass enclosed office that was surprisingly sleek and modern. It had obviously been retrofitted into the original, classic design of the structure in some prior decade. It looked out of place surrounded by Greek-inspired architecture, life-sized oil paintings of the men who had served their state in years past and bronze statues of the state's founding fathers, Brigham Young among them. Behind the glass walls, a modern, comfortable office, complete with over-sized leather armchairs and state-of-the-art electronics teemed with activity.

Kendra held open the door and Michelle passed through first. A young woman greeted them from behind a large, mahogany desk. "As I live and breathe! Kendra Williams!"

"Hey, Susan." Kendra answered with a timid smile. She was so uncomfortable with the recognition that Michelle could almost feel her pain.

"What brings you up the hill? Why, I never thought I'd see you here, that's for sure."

"Is the L.T. in?"

The serious tone of Kendra's voice must have registered with the receptionist. Her expression fell into one of all-business and she scanned the open tablet on her desk. "As it turns out, yes. I'll see if the Lieutenant Governor is available. Just a moment," she finally answered. "Is everything okay? Gosh, it's good to see you."

"Everything's fine. Just a friendly visit, that's all."

Kendra took off her hat and rocked back on her heels. Michelle glanced at her face. Her brow creased again and for a second, she chewed the inside of her cheek. She wasn't determined, anymore. No, she was scared to death.

"The Lieutenant Governor will see you, Kennie."

Michelle thought she might choke on her tongue. Just like that? "Boy, I guess he remembers you."

She thought she heard Kendra groan and the receptionist, Susan, grinned. "She's not from around here, is she?"

Kendra's hand settled on the small of Michelle's back and Michelle couldn't be certain if the groan had come from Kendra or from her. She led Michelle down a short hall until she stopped and knocked on a carved, wooden door.

"Come in," a female voice called from the interior.

Kendra opened the door and stepped through. Michelle followed, nervous knots flying around her belly. Michelle wasn't normally impressed by people based upon their titles or positions, but the Lieutenant Governor of the State of Utah? They'd made it past the outer ring, apparently, to the L.T.'s private secretary. That much did impress her and she didn't want to do anything which might make the man think any less of Kendra and her cause. What were the Lieutenant Governor's views? Was he pro-equality and equal rights, or on the side of homophobia and bigotry? Was he somewhere in the middle? Did he even know Kendra was gay? It was probably a good idea to err on the side of the closet, as much as she hated it. Squaring her posture, she glanced around the room and took a quiet step away from Kendra.

"Kendra Williams." The woman who had called to Kendra took several steps forward with her arms opened wide. She wore a blue pant-suit with silver buttons. Long black hair, swept up and away from her face and neck, was tied in a knot at the back of her head. A pair of thin, wire-framed reading glasses hung from a delicate chain around her neck.

Michelle judged her to be just a few years older than Kendra... maybe forty-five?

"Hello, Helena. It's been a long time." Kendra took the woman in an embrace, and then held her shoulders and smiled. "You look amazing."

"Well, it's not the rodeo, but my job does keep me fit, I'll tell you that much." She smiled and tilted her head over Kendra's shoulder. "And who is your friend?"

Kendra started as if she suddenly remembered Michelle was there. A tight fist seemed to ground into Michelle's gut. Her throat burned. "Oh, sorry, Hel. This is Michelle Loving. We're working together on something and we thought you might be able to help out. Michelle, this is Helena Sanderson, champion barrel-racer, card cheat, former State Senator, and current Lieutenant Governor of Utah."

"I'm pleased to meet you, Ms. Loving. Why don't the two of you sit down and make yourselves comfortable?"

"Michelle?" Kendra placed her hand on Michelle's shoulder when she didn't respond, under the guise of regaining her attention, of course.

Who was she kidding? She touched Michelle because she couldn't stop herself from touching her. She'd been unable to stop herself all morning. Every chance she'd had to brush up against her, she'd taken. She just wanted to feel her.

"What?"

"Let's sit down."

"So, what can I do for you, Kendra?"

Kendra found it difficult to relate her problem to Helena. Twenty years ago, they'd rodeoed together. Fifteen years ago, Kendra had broken off a two-year affair to raise her siblings. She'd asked Helena to stay with her. But her lover had had bigger dreams than working a cattle ranch and raising children who weren't even hers. Based on the fact they now sat in the second most important office in the state, Helena was married to a man, and she had two children of her own, her former lover had achieved everything she'd ever wanted.

Kendra, on the other hand, was still a cowhand with dirt under her fingernails. She'd never change.

Michelle shifted in her chair. She was so quiet, Kendra glanced toward her. What was wrong with her? She looked...

Angry.

She doubted Helena, or anyone else for that matter, would recognize it. But the slim line of her lips and the thick pulse in her neck told Kendra she didn't like being here. Not one little bit.

When she finished explaining her situation to Helena, Helena made a steeple from her fingers and pressed the tips beneath her chin. She stared at Kendra in silence for a long moment.

Finally, she asked, "And you're sure it was this Mason fellow who rustled your cattle?"

"Rustled and outright slaughtered, yes."

"What proof do you have?"

"Not much, Helena. But my gut tells me I'm right."

The lieutenant governor placed her hands, palms flat, on the surface of her desk and stood. "Well, that's good enough for me, Kennie. Let me make some calls and see what I can do."

"I really appreciate it, Helena."

Helena skirted the desk and leaned against it, right in front of her. Vague memories of the older woman sliding against her swirled in her mind. Hot steamy nights spent entwined in the back of her truck, or in Helena's father's motor coach when he wasn't looking. Young hearts beating together in dangerous – so very dangerous – mindless passion.

It did nothing to her now. Her body seemed to live on a whole different planet. Still attractive, Helena simply no longer appealed to her.

What appealed to her was Michelle's soft, round curves and fiery spirit.

"We had some good times, didn't we, Kendra?"

"Yeah, we did."

"Why did you wait so long to ask me for help?" The state official was gone and in her place sat the women Kendra had loved so many years before. The difference was chilling and obvious.

"I didn't want to impose on our friendship. I mean, if it got out that you pulled strings for... well, for a lesbian? The rumors could kill your career. It's Utah, remember?"

"Let me worry about that." She paused. "I really am sorry about how things turned out, Kennie."

"It was a long time ago, babe. I'm over it."

"Are you?" The tone was accusatory and compassionate at the same time.

Kendra's blood heated and her cheeks flamed. She glanced at the chair next her and, for the first time, noticed that Michelle was gone. "Where's Michelle?"

"She left a couple of minutes ago. Didn't you hear her?"

"Crap," she whispered. Kendra hadn't even noticed! Maybe she wasn't as over Helena as she thought she was?

No, that was wrong. She was over it. Completely and fully. No hard feelings. No lingering doubts.

"You haven't answered my question. Are you really *over it*?"

"I'm not pining for you, Hel. It's been almost twenty years."

"It's been thirteen years. It's been thirteen years, five months and three weeks, actually."

Kendra grinned. "And how do you know that?"

"Because I've been counting. It's easy to do if you never lose track in the first place."

"And you think *I'm* not over it?"

"Yeah, that's exactly what I think. Because if I'm not stupid, and I don't believe I am, you're in love with that woman who was just here and for some reason, the tension between the two of you is thicker than horse shit."

"You're crossing a line, Helena." Kendra stood and rubbed the sweat off her palms and onto the thighs of her jeans. "You have no right to judge me or what I'm about. You're the one living a goddamn lie. For crying out loud, you're a Republican!"

Helena gained her feet, standing a full three inches taller than Kendra and obviously not having any problem using that height to her advantage. She closed the distance between them with two long strides. "You think that's easy? You think I am proud of standing behind a closet door so thick that it would take ten Paul Bunyan's to cut through it? I place my constituents and the greater good over myself and, plenty of times, over my own family. I've worked on legislation to feed the hungry, educate our children, fund our schools and our homeless shelters... to provide counseling to those who can't afford it and I've been working to sway the Governor on Obamacare for the past three goddamn years." She took a deep breath and her chest heaved with emotion and passion.

That's the Helena Kendra remembered. Passionate. Determined. Single-minded.

"But you're living a lie," Kendra censured. "Does your husband know you're gay?"

"Actually, my husband *is* gay. We both wear our beards very well. We had children because we had to in order to keep up the illusion, but I'll tell you this much... I wouldn't trade them for the world."

Kendra hadn't expected that Helena could say anything to shock her after all of the years. But that shocked her.

"I'm sorry, Helena. I was out of line."

"No, you're not out of line, Kendra. You're just hurting and you have to let your guard down every now and again. Coming to me for help was the first step. Now, you've got to stop letting the fact that I broke your heart get in the way of falling in love, and letting someone else fall in love with you."

Shifting her weight from one boot to the other,

Kendra grinned. "You're awfully full of yourself, you know that?"

"Yeah. I know that. It's a job requirement in politics. I'll call you in a few days and let you know what I was able to work out."

Sixteen

Michelle had never wanted to disappear as much as she did at this moment. The history between Helena and Kendra was so obvious, a priest could see it. Old friends? She stifled a snort. *Old lovers* was more like it. Only a woman who had slept with someone looked at her with that kind of intense longing in her eyes. Even Michelle knew that.

How long ago was it? Was she just some kind of rebound for Kendra? The possibility that she had played her with her sullen glances full of longing and intense quiet made Michelle's stomach turn over.

What if she had only imagined every part of her relationship with Kendra? What if it wasn't just over, but had never actually existed?

Michelle made a conscious effort to control her steps as she raced down the marble staircase. She had no idea where she was going, only that she had to get away from Kendra and her former lover. What had Kendra been thinking when she brought her here? Did she honestly think that she wouldn't know they'd been together?

The parking lot stretched in front of her, filled to capacity. She dodged a parked car and ran toward Kendra's truck. Out of nowhere, a luxury sedan bore down on her. A scream cut through the air, filled with crying seagulls and the sound of traffic whirring by. Somewhere in the distance, a train blew its whistle.

Kendra's arms encircled her waist and pulled her against the back of the tour bus. "Are you out of your mind?" She held her there, Kendra's body blocking hers from the passing car. "You could have been killed!"

It was as though the world stopped turning. Even the gulls ceased their calls until silence surrounded her. Well, not total silence. She could hear a heartbeat. She just wasn't sure if it was hers or Kendra's. "I--"

She never finished her sentence. With fury and a certain gentleness, Kendra caught her words in a kiss. Her mouth crushed hers and her chest pushed her against the hot metal at her back. Kendra held her so tightly, she couldn't breathe, and she didn't want to. She only wanted to feel. All she wanted was to love her and hope that Kendra might love her back. Someday.

All her convictions to protect her heart flew out of sight as Kendra's lips claimed hers. She didn't care if she lost herself forever...

"No!" She wrenched herself from Kendra's embrace.

"What's wrong?"

"This! This is wrong. Don't you get it?"

Kendra backed up a step and replaced her hat, apparently knocked askew when she'd kissed her. "Get what, Michelle?"

How dense could she be? Or maybe, she wasn't dense. Maybe she was just cruel. She was going to insist that Michelle say it out loud.

The expression on Kendra's face claimed otherwise. Whatever she thought of Kendra Williams, there seemed to be fewer cruel bones in her body than Mother Theresa. Her heart sagged.

"You don't love me, Kendra. I deserve better than that. I don't want to be like Helena. Just some woman you call in a favor to one day."

Kendra glanced at the ground for a moment before she raised her gaze to focus on Michelle. "What are you talking about?" She stabbed Michelle with her piercing, green eyes.

"Don't pretend, Kendra. It's obvious you loved her. Maybe you still do."

"No. That's not true. I mean, I thought I did, at the time, but I know different now."

"You had an affair with her."

She sighed before she answered. "Yes. I can't deny that. But that was a long time ago."

Michelle searched for that hole. The one that should open out of the asphalt beneath her. Only that could prevent her from continuing the one conversation that could make her fall apart. "How long ago?"

"A long, long time ago."

"How long?" Why was she doing this to herself? Why did she need to know this so badly?

To prove that Kendra loves you, too. The whisper flew through her mind so quickly, she wasn't certain she'd really heard it.

"Fifteen, maybe sixteen years ago, now. We broke

up when my folks were killed. We were just kids."

Kendra couldn't have shocked her more than if she'd hit her with a battle-axe.

She'd lost her lover and her parents? At the same time? Was that why she didn't go to Helena for help right away? "You don't love her?"

"Not now. And not then. No matter how much I thought so."

Michelle's knees buckled and she was thankful for the strength of the bus at her back. She believed her. Kendra was telling the truth. She asked, "Are you alright?"

Kendra's lips curled into a sardonic grin. She released a rueful laugh and replied, "No." Then she laughed again. "No, I'm not alright. I'm completely screwed. I don't know how it happened or when it happened, and I sure as hell don't know why it happened, but I love you. I fell in love with you and now, after all these years, I finally know what real love feels like."

Michelle's breath caught like a broken bicycle chain somewhere between her lungs and the outside world. She forced air past the wreckage and squeaked, "Is that so terrible?"

"Yeah. It is. Because I have nothing to offer you, Michelle. It doesn't matter because when this is over I will have absolutely nothing left and that's not fair to anyone. When this is all over, you'll go home. Just like we planned."

Michelle forced herself to concentrate on her work. Dozens of emails needed her attention and the sooner she got Lenise up to speed on the process for verifying the video orders and maintaining the database, the sooner she could go home. She blinked away the sting behind her eyes and focused her attention on the screen.

The only thing saving her now was the fact that Kendra had transformed back into the ancient, untouchable rancher she had been when they'd first met. Gone was the fervent, seductive woman who had taught her about passion and love. She spent all of her time with the herd, in the barn or wrapping up the remodel of the old house so that Brad and Lenise could move in right after the wedding.

She cleared her throat. Business. Just think about business. "Lenise, you need to remember to log out when you're finished working in the bins."

"I do logout."

"The system says you timed out this afternoon."

"That's impossible. I haven't logged on all day."

"Yes, you did. Look, it says so right here."

"Michelle, I swear. I didn't touch it. Yeah, that's my login, but I was with Brad all day. We went to visit my grandmother at the nursing home and then we worked on the house."

"Fine, fine. But, if you weren't online, then who was? Sure wasn't me."

Michelle was grumpy. And grouchy. She was going to become a grumpy, grouchy old maid.

"Maybe one of the boys?"

"They have their own passwords. Why would they use yours?"

Michelle clicked on the first email in her inbox. Her eyes widened as she read the furious tone of the capital letters. It was from a customer from Rhode Island who had ordered a video a couple of weeks ago.

I DON'T KNOW WHAT KIND OF SICK OUTFIT YOU'RE RUNNING OVER THERE, BUT YOU CAN BE SURE I'M GOING TO REPORT YOU TO EVERYONE I CAN THINK OF. YOUR WEBSITE ADVERTISED A FREE EDUCATIONAL VIDEO ABOUT CATTLE RANCHING TARGETED TO CHILDREN. IT DIDN'T SAY ANYTHING ABOUT SLAUGHTERING COWS. YOU BETTER BE HAPPY THAT I REVIEWED THE VIDEO BEFORE SHOWING IT TO MY SECOND-GRADERS. I WOULD HAVE HAD PARENTS BEATING DOWN MY DOOR. I DON'T EVEN WANT TO THINK ABOUT THE NIGHTMARES MOST OF MY CHILDREN WOULD HAVE SUFFERED. YOU SHOULD BE ASHAMED OF YOURSELVES!

~MARCIA LANGDON, ESSEX ELEMENTARY SCHOOL

Michelle sat, open-mouthed, staring at the computer. What was this woman talking about?

Casey pushed open the office door with his shoulder and dumped dozens of DVD-sized parcels on the desk. "These were at the post office. They were returned to the P.O. box we set up for the website. What's going on?"

"I don't know." Michelle glared at the boxes.

"Open one, and let's watch it."

Just as the second-grade teacher from Rhode Island described, the images of slaughtered cattle and men in blood-soaked coveralls wading through ankle-deep blood and guts filled the screen.

"How did this happen?" Michelle's stomach landed somewhere in the region of her feet. Were all of the discs the same? Frantic, she tore into several more packages. They *were* all the same.

Damage control.

She instructed Lenise to draft a letter of apology with a statement of Kendra's dedication to humane processing procedures and healthy products. She made a mental list of the dozens of other tasks she'd need to complete to even begin rectifying this situation. At the top of the list was the simple act of crucifying Vincent.

How many children had seen this massacre? "I've got to call Vincent. I swear, Casey, he's never made a mistake like this before. Never. The wrong file must have been loaded into the POD software."

"Call him." Kendra's deep voice left no room for argument.

Michelle spun toward the voice. Kendra's eyes shot green fire in her direction before landing on the computer screen again.

"Kendra. How long have you been there?"

"Long enough. Is this your idea of positive publicity? What was it you said before? A sense of community, something like that? I'm sure this video has gone a long way to help our little cause. Did the BLM see this shit?"

"Don't be an ass, Kendra," Casey snapped. "It's not

her fault."

"No, Casey. Kendra's right," Michelle interjected. "The damage is done. And I'm ultimately responsible. I hired Vincent and I take full responsibility. If you'll excuse me, I'm going to call him from the kitchen." A wave of nausea collided with a shortness of breath she'd never experienced before.

Kendra had been against this idea from the beginning. More than likely, the only reason she'd finally gotten on board stemmed from the fact they were sleeping together at the time. How had she allowed things to get so screwed up? If she thought for one second she had any chance of a life with Kendra after this whole ordeal was finished, she'd officially blown it. She'd be lucky if Kendra ever spoke to her again.

Once she reached the kitchen, she took a deep breath and picked up the phone. She misdialed three times before she finally got through to Vincent's Video Experiment. After several rings, someone answered.

"Let me talk to Vincent. Now."

"Who's this?"

"Michelle Loving. And you are?"

"Kevin. Michelle Loving?"

"Yes, now where is Vincent?"

"I have a note for you. Something about some videos that never got finished because of the accident."

"What? What are you talking about? What accident? And what do you mean the videos weren't finished? I approved the final cut weeks ago."

"I don't know, lady. I just started here this week. All I know is that the owner was killed a couple of weeks ago, some conglomerate took over and that's when I got hired. Most of the old staff walked out when the new people took over, but one of them said that if you called, I should give you the message."

"What did you say?" she whispered.

"What part of that didn't you understand, lady?"

"Vincent? Vincent's dead?"

"Apparently. Now, you want the rest of the message or not?"

"Yes. Of course I do."

"Call Michael at this number and he'll fill you in. Miss Loving?"

Michelle cleared her throat. "Yeah?"

"I'm really sorry. I don't mean to sound gruff or unsympathetic. I'm just swamped here, you know?"

"Yeah. Sure." Michelle hung up the phone and wrapped her arms around herself. How could Vincent be dead? The guy said he'd been killed? An accident? What did that mean? She took a deep breath and reached for the phone again. A few seconds later, Michael answered.

"God, Michelle. I tried to call you, but the cops wouldn't let me into your apartment, the new owners at Vincent's place wouldn't let me take any records with me, and you're not listed. Jesus, everything is such a mess."

"What happened, Mike? What happened to Vin?"

"He was hit by a car. On the strip. Almost a month ago."

"But how? I mean, I don't understand. I've emailed with him several times in just the past two weeks. He's been personally fulfilling video orders for the ranch."

"That's impossible. We never made the final cuts after that last proof you edited and approved. We sure as hell never got an order from you before he died."

"Well, somebody did, damn it. Every client on the list received some God-awful slaughterhouse video."

"Are you serious?"

"Yup. That's why I was calling Vin in the first place. To read him the riot act about it." She laughed through building tears. "Mike. Who purchased the studio?"

"Some corporation. Laserix Incorporated. I've never heard of them before. If you've been sending orders to Vin's email, then somebody over there must've been confused and sent out the wrong information to the POD platform. The thing is, Vin never made a slaughterhouse video, not even as an undercover sting or anything."

"No. This goes deeper than a misunderstanding. I got replies from Vin's email signed with his name, from his email address. This was deliberate, and if it was deliberate, then..."

"What?"

"I don't know, but I have a hunch that whoever took over his company when he died, did so to sabotage our program here."

"Hang on, Michelle. Are suggesting that Vincent might have been killed on purpose? Like, murdered over this?"

"That's exactly what I'm saying. I'll call you back." Michelle's hand shook as she hung up the receiver.

If Harold Mason owned Laserix Corporation then the probability that Vincent had been murdered jumped considerably. But how could she find out? Corporations could easily hide behind various fronts and conglomerates until the real owners were lost in a mountain of red tape and digital records.

But, nothing else made sense. Not that it made sense, anyway. But, nobody else had anything to gain by sending out those sick pictures to school children. Someone wanted to make the Heartland Ranch, and the entire Williams family, look like a sham of a business and worse. Michelle wouldn't be surprised if CNN were camped out in the front yard by morning.

She ran a hand through her hair and held her bangs in her fist at the top of her head. How could she explain all of this to Kendra? She had so much guilt over Kennedy Bastion's death, already. Michelle not only knew what that felt like now, but she certainly didn't want to put any more weight on Kendra's shoulders. She'd only feel guilty about Vincent, too. She'd blame herself for dragging more innocent people into this mess.

Michelle sure as hell did.

One thing was for sure. Harold Mason was definitely more dangerous than she'd given him credit for, and the monster was alive, and well, and awake.

Twilight shone through the windows casting the kitchen in long shadows when Kendra pushed open the swinging door. Michelle sat hunched over her laptop. Her hair fell in a tangled mass down her back and the set of her shoulders told her she'd all but given up.

She flipped on the light, but Michelle didn't seem to notice.

"I'm sorry about your friend." Kendra wanted to

put her arm over Michelle's shoulder. She didn't.

Michelle remained focused on the screen. "Thanks."

Instead of touching her, consoling her like she wanted to, Kendra handed her a cup of coffee and then sat next to her at the table. Deep bags had formed under her eyes over the past few hours. She'd been searching the Internet all day, looking for something that might link Laserix Incorporated to Harold Mason.

Kendra glanced out the window as the world turned from gold to black.

A chill washed over her. She looked back at Michelle. Better get used to it. She'd be cold for the rest of her life.

Michelle's eyes drifted closed.

"You should call it a day."

"I'll be okay in a few minutes. Just need to get my second wind."

"You've been at this for hours. First emailing all those contacts, and now looking for ghosts in the machine? You need some sleep."

"Really, I'm fine."

Kendra ached to take her into her arms. She missed feeling the comfort Michelle offered; missed offering her comfort. And now, when she needed someone to hold her, she couldn't. It didn't seem fair. She suspected Michelle wouldn't welcome anything more than overtures of friendship.

Michelle rubbed her eyes with the palms of her hands. "I just hope the entire support network hasn't been unraveled. I'm sure the petition would have helped in the media."

"The damage is done, Michelle. I don't see the point."

"The point is, we have to stop this guy. He's not just some overbearing business jerk. He's a murderer."

"I know that, and if I had my way, I'd see to it that he pays for everything. In spades. But like you said, this isn't the old west."

Kendra wished it was. A part of her wanted to ride to town, six shooter strapped to her hip, and call the son-of-a-bitch out. Somehow, she figured Michelle wouldn't see the justice in that.

"Wait a second," she hummed. "I think I found something."

"Like what?"

"A connection. Hang on." She paused to click a few of the tabs along the top of the screen. "Okay. Okay, right here. This is a news report about Laserix Incorporated refusing to go public last year. Several of the high-ranking execs tried to convince the owner it would work, but he fired them all and they sued. They lost."

"Okay, I'm with you."

Michelle clicked a little grey square at the bottom of the screen. "The spokesman for the executives was a man named Carl Wilson. He's mentioned in this article, here, as the executive director for a conglomerate of holdings called Lylewood Industries. They make several products and such, but they also dabble in pharmaceuticals and research and development. There are about twelve companies, all together. One of them is listed here."

She clicked on a few blue lines of text and opened another page. "What about this company, right here?

Isn't this the company that Mason has listed on the contract offer he sent over last month?"

Kendra focused on the black, bold letters on the screen. **Lifestyle and Leisure, LLC**. "Yep. That's the one."

Kendra scanned the page until her eyes fell on the name of another company. Buried inside the text, she found something she hadn't seen in almost ten years.

"Kendra. Are you okay? You look like you've seen a ghost."

"... the now defunct Conner Aviation..." Kendra read aloud.

"What?" Michelle touched her arm, regaining her attention.

Kendra pointed to the screen. "Right there. Conner Aviation."

"What about it?"

"That's the company that supplied the charter pilot to fly my parent's plane."

"Are you sure?"

"I'm positive. What does Harold Mason have to do with Conner Aviation? He's not much older than me, so I doubt he worked there; at least, not for very long before they shut down."

Kendra read the entire article, and then leaned back in her chair. It didn't make any sense. Nothing in the article indicated anything other than the former Conner Aviation had once existed in the same building. But the coincidence could not, would not, be ignored. It sliced through her brain like a duck through water. As soon as the name moved from one side of her mind to the other, the wake disappeared and she was just as baffled as she'd been when she started.

"I can't find anything about Conner Aviation on this site. Let me do a search and see what we can find out."

A few minutes later, Michelle whispered. "Oh, my God. Kendra..."

Kendra sat upright and focused on the screen where Michelle's delicate and beautiful finger pointed. The pilot's picture and obituary occupied the center of the page. "The pilot that killed my parents was Harold Mason's father?"

Seventeen

Michelle set her towel on the counter in the guest bathroom, and then turned on the water in the tub and adjusted the temperature. When it reached a level just below scalding, she flipped the lever and drew her arm back to avoid the shower spray.

After three hours lying awake and staring at the ceiling, maybe a hot shower would help her sleep. The guest bedroom just reminded her of the fact that she'd lost Kendra forever. What had been a beautiful room filled with charming antiques and reminiscent of some luxury bed and breakfast now reminded her more of a dungeon or a prison. She'd had to get out of there.

Not that she'd ever sleep soundly again. She'd be lucky if she ever slept at all. Without Kendra to hold her, make love to her, it hardly seemed worth trying. After discovering her and the way she made her whole body come alive, an empty bed was the last thing she wanted.

Maybe someday she'd find someone to share her life with. Her stomach lurched and her eyes stung.

No. She didn't want anyone else. If she couldn't

have Kendra, she'd be alone for the rest of her life. Alone and pathetic. A ghost of who she'd been before. Independent, yes, but no longer by her own choice. Confident, but faking it. Happy, except when she was alone.

She shoved the depressing thoughts to the back of her mind and took a long shower. When she finished, she toweled off and went back to her room. That room. That empty, lonely, beautiful dungeon.

"I can't do this anymore, Michelle."

She jumped at the sound of Kendra's voice. She flipped on the light beside the door and found Kendra sitting on the edge of the bed in the dark. Still dressed in her work jeans and a long-sleeved white shirt, she looked like she hadn't gone to bed yet. The shirt, unbuttoned down the front to reveal the skin-hugging, sleeveless undershirt she always wore instead of a bra, parted when she shifted her weight. The firm muscles beneath her small breasts bunched when she breathed.

Michelle's mouth went dry and she tried to swallow. "What are you doing here?"

She shook her head. "I don't even know. I don't know much of anything these days, honestly. But I can't take much more of this."

"We'll get him, Kendra. I sent everything I found out to the Las Vegas police. I'm sure they'll investigate Harold Mason once they see the connection between Vincent working for you and Mason sweeping in to buy up the studio so quickly."

"It's not that." Kendra pushed herself off the bed and took two long strides in her direction.

Michelle's fingers fisted in the damp towel. She

held it to her breast over her bathrobe, like a shield for her heart. "What is it, then?"

"It's you, Michelle. I can't stand to be this close to you and not touch you. I can't sleep under the same roof as you and not hold you. It's killing me."

She stood directly in front of her. The earthy scent that was so uniquely Kendra, a combination of woman and nature, consumed her. Kendra was the wind, the sun and the stars all wrapped up in a pair of denim jeans and chambray. Michelle's gut danced in her belly. She was so near. Her body heat touched her and made the shower she'd just left seem like a dip in an icy pond.

"No, Kendra." Michelle backed away a step. Her knees trembled and it was amazing that she could still stand. "I—"

"Don't do this to me. I need you."

Kendra took a step closer until Michelle's back pressed against the wall and Kendra's body blocked any escape. God, she wanted Kendra. But could she risk even more damage to her heart? Kendra only wanted her for a moment. She wanted Kendra forever.

"I need you," Kendra whispered, her voice cracking slightly.

Kendra placed one hand on her shoulder and stroked the column of her throat with her thumb. Wherever she touched burned and sent rivulets of passion through each of her limbs.

Michelle licked her lips cautiously and stared into Kendra's fiery, green eyes. Eyes that bore into her without mercy. Desire. Passion. Need dwelled there, as well. But what about love? She needed more than Kendra could give her.

Didn't she?

Could she allow herself to be one of those women who took what was offered with no pride; no confidence that her lover would be with her in the end?

Kendra dipped her face toward hers. Michelle didn't fight her. She had no fight left. She might not be able to live with herself tomorrow, but she wanted Kendra tonight. Kendra captured her lips, and her heart, in a deep kiss that seemed to meld them in searing connections. She dropped the towel and wrapped her arms around Kendra's neck, pulling her closer.

Selfish.

Demanding.

Michelle returned her kiss and let Kendra lead her to the bed.

She would take what Kendra offered and pretend, for just a moment, that Kendra really belonged to her.

Morning light spilled into Michelle's room. The old rooster in the barn crowed with the coming dawn. Cracking open one eye, Kendra scanned the feminine room. Flowered wallpaper. Lace curtains. The scent of woman.

It hadn't been a dream.

Michelle stirred beneath her arm and mumbled something in her sleep. Careful not to wake her, Kendra pushed herself up to lean against the headboard. She rubbed one eye and pulled Michelle against her.

Kendra held Michelle to her side and listened to her quiet breaths. She loved Michelle more than she ever thought possible. Everything about her spoke of a perfection she didn't deserve. Beauty. Grace. Laughter.

Hope.

Could she ever begin to make herself worthy of such a woman?

Michelle stirred in her arms and pressed herself closer to Kendra's side. Kendra's lips spread into a wide grin. She sure as hell didn't deserve her now. Yet, here she was.

The world had thrown Kendra before. She'd always managed to land on her feet. Over the course of the past fifteen years, she'd raised four kids, managed a world-class cattle ranch and stayed as sane as anyone could.

In a little over six hours, Brad and Lenise would be married. Her job would finally be done.

And she'd survived.

Could she survive Michelle? She frowned. She didn't want to. She wanted to keep Michelle. Why shouldn't she ask Michelle to stay with her forever? Was that so wrong? All she had to do was ask.

Kendra shook her head and allowed her eyes to travel the curves hidden beneath the old quilt. She wanted to believe it was possible. Right now, with morning light golden and full of promise, she could almost trust in love. But, she knew better. It was an illusion.

The sharp clang of Michelle's bedside alarm clock broke her thoughts. Michelle jerked awake and seemed just a little disoriented when one arm shot to the bedside to press the snooze button. Then her eyes focused on Kendra's breasts and she smiled.

Kendra smiled, as well. Michelle looked like some little forest sprite from a fairy tale. Her hair bunched and tangled in charming little knots around her face. Lips, still swollen from Kendra's kisses, tempted her. When her tongue darted from between them for a quick taste, heat pooled between Kendra's legs and she shifted her hips.

"Morning," whispered Michelle.

"Morning." Kendra placed a kiss on top of her head. She hadn't realized until that moment just how much she'd missed her scent in the morning. Something about it made her think everything would be fine, that nothing could interfere with the love they shared.

Nothing except real life. She hid a sigh. She had no misunderstandings in her mind. Someday, sooner or later, she would leave forever.

Michelle cleared her throat, twisted in her arms and sat up beside her on the bed. "We've got to get up. Lenise will be here soon to get dressed. You need to get Brad out of the house before then."

When she yawned, Kendra couldn't suppress a smile. "You're exhausted." Apparently, early mornings still affected her.

She chuckled. "After last night, can you blame me?"

"I didn't mean to keep you up all night."

"I'm not complaining," she responded with a bright, mischievous glow in her eyes.

Too soon, she pulled her hand away. "We don't have time."

"Unfortunately," Kendra replied, tossing the cover aside before climbing out of the bed. "Would you like to shower first?"

A glint appeared in the midnight depths of her eyes. Something between the earlier mischievous and downright naughty. "What do you say we conserve water?"

The entire compound had changed overnight. With the assistance of several new hands and plenty of the old ones, the tidy, efficient inner yard and corral of the Heartland Ranch had been transformed into a quaint wedding spread with bales of hay covered in lilies as a main element.

Lenise and Brad both wanted a country theme, and Michelle had certainly had her doubts about how elegant one could get with hay, straw, and dirt. But in the end, green garlands laced with lilies and white roses turned the barnyard into a slice of paradise.

"Not bad for a couple of gals who don't know a rose from a cactus flower."

Michelle jumped at Lacey's off-handed comment. When she looked at her friend, she saw something in Lacey's eyes that she'd never seen before. Contrition? "I think we managed to pull off a right fine weddin'."

Lacey grinned at Michelle's exaggerated country twang. "I just hope everything goes off without a hitch. I just came from the old house. To say Lenise is a nervous wreck would be the understatement of the decade."

"Yeah, I talked to her earlier." Michelle shifted her weight from one foot to the other and glanced at the ground. She hated those awkward silences that seemed to underscore tense situations. She still stared at the soft earth of the large corral-come-wedding-hall when Lacey touched her arm.

"I'm really sorry, Michelle. I have no earthly idea what came over me the other day. For crying out loud, you're the best friend I've ever had, and I let some petty jealously come between us. It was stupid."

Michelle tilted her head. "Jealousy? Of what?"

"Of you. And Kendra." Lacey dropped her hand and shoved both of her hands into the back pockets of her freshly pressed jeans. "Hell, I don't know. All I really know for sure is you're in love with my sister. And I don't exactly know how to handle it."

Michelle lifted an eyebrow and pinned Lacey with a half-hearted, sardonic stare. "But you were fine when you thought we were just sleeping together? Just using each other?"

"Well, sure. I mean, she would still be the same old Kendra afterwards. But now? Now, she's going to need to survive when it's over. She probably doesn't know this, but I remember the last time. There was this lady who came around for the first few months after our folks were killed. She was nice. I remember, she slept in Kendra's room and they hugged. A lot. Then, she was gone and Kendra was really, really sad. Like, way more sad that she should have been from losing Mom and Dad. It was a different kind of pain, and even I could see it."

Michelle hadn't realized until that moment exactly what Lacey meant. The feeling settled over her like morning dew. "You don't want either of us to get hurt."

"That's part of it, yeah. But at the same time, I hoped you wouldn't end up together. She's mine. She's always been my hero and, I guess, when it comes right down to it, I don't want to share."

"Don't?"

"Didn't. I've been doing a lot of thinking lately. If this whole thing works out, I guess I'm okay with it, now."

Michelle didn't dare hope. Instead, she offered Lacey what she hoped could be counted as a reassuring pat on the arm. What could she say? That she was perfectly content to take whatever time and affection Kendra deemed to grant her and live on it for the rest of her life? That Kendra had made the rules and therefore she wasn't going to have to survive anything? That Michelle was the one who would be forced to remember? And survive.

She couldn't do it. Not even to reassure her best friend in the world that her sister would be just peachy when Michelle finally went home.

Strains of soft country music blared from several speakers on the barn roof. The ceremony would begin any second. Michelle almost laughed out loud at the irony.

Saved by the wedding bells.

Sitting in the front row, like she belonged there, she had a position that allowed her to see the entire audience. There had to be fifty or more people – they had invited over a hundred – in the large corral. Mrs. Wicks and her friend, Mrs. Mullarney, were situated a few rows behind her. Each of them held a delicate, lace handkerchief up to their aged lips. Their eyes glistened with unshed tears in expectation and excitement. Not far from where they stood, Doc leaned against his cane with gnarled fingers that had comforted, healed and brought many of the gathered lives into the world. A large number of the original cowboys who had worked on the ranch, the ones who had carried young Kennedy Bastion to his final resting place, stood together in the back row, their hair combed neatly into single ponytails or parted awkwardly on the side.

These people, the living, breathing entities that formed not only the town of Randall, but the essence of The Heartland Ranch, were like family to one another. She had only been here a few months, but she felt like a part of that family, too.

Just then, Kendra appeared on the threshold of the front door of the house with Brad standing next to her. Both wore black jeans with white, button-down shirts. Their black jackets cut away at the waist, and the long tails added a hint of formality to the setting.

Dashing.

They crossed the yard and entered the corral through the wide gate, flanked by sprays of flowers. Michelle's heart stopped. Her hand pressed against her chest to keep her heart from literally tearing her apart, and then she made a fist to hold it in place. She sucked in a ragged breath, but couldn't breathe. Not really.

In all of the time she had spent with Kendra, this was the first moment that she saw her as the matriarch, hell – the patriarch – of her clan. She had comprised Brad's entire world for sixteen years, and now, Kendra had been forced to give him up before she was ready. Before either of them were ready.

Michelle closed her eyes for a second and opened them as Kendra and Brad passed her and Lacey. Kendra tossed her a wink. She seemed as if nothing could touch her. As always, her confident swagger hid from the rest of the world everything Michelle had learned about her. Kendra, like everyone else, ached. She worried. She pretended. Just like everyone else, she was human.

After Kendra left Brad next to Brent in front of the bales of hay that made up an altar, she made her way back to where Michelle and Lacey sat in the front row. She took her position between them, but slid her arm over Michelle's shoulder. Bending just enough to whisper in her ear, she asked, "What's wrong? You look upset."

Michelle sniffed and did the only thing she could think of. She lied. "I always cry at weddings."

If Kendra suspected she'd found her out, she'd run. She just knew it. Something in the way she made such a point of not divulging her true feelings, to anyone, told her for a fact that Kendra would tear away faster than that freak microburst that had caught them by the spring.

For right now, she'd pretend that being patient would matter.

A deep breath disguised beneath a sigh filled her with more than life-giving air. It filled her with desire and just a little hope. If she could convince Kendra to trust her with her business, she could damn well convince her to trust her with her heart. No way was this cowboi going to ride off alone into the sunset. Not without Michelle riding right beside her.

The music changed to the wedding march. The loud, majestic introduction gripped her attention. Mac walked alongside his daughter, beaming with pride and doing an excellent job of covering his fatherly concerns over the whole ordeal. Lenise looked stunningly beautiful with her hair swept away from her face and her eyes sparkling like diamonds on black velvet. Her gown was perfect. Her pink boots were perfect. Her glow was practically contagious.

Every woman on the planet deserved to look like that.

No, Michelle couldn't give up. Despite all of Lacey's talk of survival, Michelle couldn't *live* without Kendra.

Not anymore.

"I'd like to make a toast." Casey drew his swaying frame upright on a bale of hay placed not far from where Kendra stood with Mac.

"Oh, good Lord. Here it comes." Mac shook his head. "How much has that boy had to drink?"

Kendra laughed and stared up at her brother. "Not enough. He'll be fine."

"On this auspicious occasion, I'd like to wish my little brother and his lovely new wife the very best of everything. The best life, the best children and the best love. Be happy. Be strong. And, for crying out loud, next time? Be careful!"

Kendra laughed along with the fifty or so guests at the reception. Mac grumbled something under his breath about that not being funny, and Kendra slapped him on the back. "Get used to it, old man. She's a married woman, now."

"Yeah, well. I guess I can't do nothing to change it."

Kendra sobered and crossed her arms over her chest. "Lighten up, Mac. They love each other. They're lucky. They have their whole lives ahead of them."

Unlike her. Her entire life had stormed past her like a herd of wild mustangs. She'd never even seen them coming and they'd carried off her dreams in a cloud of dust. That is, until she'd found Michelle.

The more time Kendra spent with her, the more she cursed the fates for bringing them together. How could she ever let her go?

An echo sounded through her soul. *For her own good.* That's how.

She scanned the crowd and found Michelle with Lacey. Both of them were laughing with the bride, who looked incredibly beautiful. Maybe all brides did. All three of the ladies radiated more light and beauty than sunshine. But most of all, Michelle shone with a sophisticated glow. Just about everyone at the reception wore jeans. Even the groom and best man leaned against the corral fence with one boot each propped on the lowest board. But not Michelle. She outshone everyone in a soft skirt and off-the-shoulder sweater. She looked more out of place around here than a cattle-prod in a kitten round-up.

Sure, she'd managed to fool herself over the last couple of days. She'd even talked herself into taking Michelle back into her arms, and her bed. But for what purpose? To have her heart filled to bursting only to explode in some wrecked heap of useless muscle?

You can take the gal out of the city, but you can't take the city out of the gal. Hadn't Helena taught her that?

For two years, she had courted Helena on the circuit. She'd had the best of everything. The best horse. The best trailer. The best schools. And what had Kendra to offer her? Four kids that weren't hers to raise and an old cattle ranch were the good parts. The rest had included complete abandonment by her ultra-conservative, Mormon parents, banishment from her entire family, including her siblings, and precisely zero prospects of making it in politics as an out lesbian in the state of Utah. No wonder Helena had turned her down, flat. She'd had bigger dreams.

Just like Michelle.

"Hey, Kennie!" Brent called as he jogged across the portable dance floor that covered most of the corral.

Kendra stiffened her spine and forced a smile. "What's up?"

Brent shot a glance at Mac before jerking his head toward the barn. "I think you need to see something real quick. You got a sec?"

"Sure. Mac, if you'll excuse me?"

"No problem. I think I'm going to go dance with my married daughter."

Kendra patted Mac on the back as he moved toward Lenise. Then she followed Brent into the barn. Inside, he found Casey learning against a stall chewing on a piece of straw. His cowboy hat, donned specifically and only for the wedding at the insistence of the bride, was tilted far back on his head and made him look far younger than his twenty-two years. When Casey saw Kendra, he pushed off the stall door with one raised boot and crossed his arms. "Did you tell her?"

A tingle rushed up Kendra's spine. "Tell me what?"

Brent mimicked Casey's stance out of sheer genetics. They both looked like their dad. "We heard something from one of the hands."

"And?"

Casey looked at Brent, who nodded toward him.

"Somebody better tell me what the hell is going on."

Casey smiled. "We have a name. Marcus Miller. Apparently, this Marcus character is the one who fired the arrows at the herd and started the stampede. It got all out of hand. They weren't trying to stampede the herd. That was just a bonus, apparently. He also helped out during the vandalism and some of the other stuff around here."

Kendra's hands formed into tight balls at her side. "Can we link this guy to Mason?"

"Well, that's the problem. He skipped town. Nobody has seen him in more than a month."

"I don't care if he crawled under a rock on the moon. Find him."

Both of her brothers grinned like two little boys lost in the women's unmentionable section of the only department store on Main Street. Brent rocked back on his heels. "We were hoping you'd say that. We hear he might be in, of all places, Las Vegas. If it's alright with you, we'd like to duck out of this shindig early and get on the road."

"Go. And when you come back, I want the son-of-a-bitch singing like a church choir on Easter Sunday."

Casey laced his fingers together and popped all of his knuckles at once. "I think we can manage that."

"Brent's driving," she announced before heading back to the reception.

Had it finally come to this? Would Kendra encourage her own brothers, the boys she'd raised to be respectful gentlemen, to beat information from someone if she thought it could save the ranch? Kennedy Bastian's face flashed in front of her mind's eye. The terror in his mother's voice when she'd heard the news echoed in her ears. And it wasn't just Ken Bastian. If this jerk was in Vegas for the past month or so, he could have just as easily been involved in whatever happened to that filmmaker.

A new tremor raced through Kendra's limbs. A feeling she'd not experienced once in her life. Not when her parents were killed. Not when Helena left her. Not even when she'd learned the pilot was drunk.

Hatred.

Yeah. She was tired of playing by the rules.

The boys caught up with her as she reached the edge of the dance floor. Everything seemed so normal. A bride and groom. Family. Friends. Normality.

But nothing was normal.

"Just bring him back here," she stated in a voice that didn't sound like her own. "I want to look him in the eye when he spills his guts. I want to hear that bastard's name from the horse's mouth and then... Mason is all mine."

"Will she recover?" Kendra wanted to scream, but what good would that do? It wouldn't change a damn thing.

"Absolutely. She isn't in any danger. Most of her injuries are superficial. She's very lucky."

Lucky? Lacey had almost died and the doctor

called it luck? Kendra rubbed the back of her neck to soothe the throbbing pain that had developed the second Mac had called her.

Lacey was alive. There had been a terrible accident. The truck was totaled, but Lacey was alive. She had a broken arm, cuts and scrapes. But no severe head trauma. She'd been wearing her seatbelt. She was alive.

"Thanks, doc," Kendra whispered. "Can we go in now?"

"Sure. Just... be prepared. She's looked better."

Kendra took Michelle's hand and thanked God she was with her. The only other time in her life when she'd been this terrified was when her parents had been killed. If she lost one of the kids, she didn't know if she'd survive.

The emergency room smelled of alcohol and Kendra rubbed her nose. Dimly lit, it looked sterile and unfriendly. Lacey lay on the bed. A splint held her arm out at an awkward angle. The surgeon was on his way to set the bones in the operating room, but that was only the beginning of the process. Broken in three places, it would be days before the swelling would go down enough to put on a cast. Her fingertips, stained with blood, were tipped with broken fingernails and twitched when she moaned.

And her face...

Kendra winced, but only because Lacey's eyes were closed. Lacey's face was covered with bandages down the left side, but they did little to hide the blood. It seeped through the gauze and fed her fury.

"Oh, Lacey," Michelle gasped as she rushed to the side of the raised bed and took Lacey's good hand in hers. "How do you feel, honey? Can you hear me?"

"Hurts," she responded, her voice muffled and the words slurred from the swelling and the bandages and the pain killers.

Michelle closed her eyes, whispering what could only be a prayer to herself.

Lacey wrenched her hand from Michelle's grasp and traced the bandages on her face. A tear slid from her exposed eye and what was visible of her face twisted into something unnatural. Filled with pain.

"No, Lacey. Don't touch it," Michelle admonished.

Lacey sobbed. Her lips moved as though she tried to form words, but no words came. Only the wailing of a woman who would never see the same face in the mirror again. For as long as she lived, she would never again recognize her own reflection.

"Lacey," Kendra whispered. "What happened, baby-girl?"

Lacey sniffed, obviously trying to regain some measure of control. "I don't... I don't know. I remember trying to pass a coal truck out from the mine, but there was a truck – an SUV – that wouldn't stop pacing me. Every time I tried to speed up and go around the truck, they'd speed up and take over the passing lane. But they never passed me. They just kept right beside me. And then, after the truck got up to speed, they wouldn't let me around them at all. They slowed me down, and then finally let me get through. I figured they were drunk or falling asleep or something, so I tried to leave them behind."

"Did you get a good look at their faces? I mean, if Mac can track down the SUV, could you identify them?"

"I don't know... maybe. One of them was real ugly, with hardly any teeth. He was in the passenger seat, so I saw him pretty good... oh, God. I just remembered, he was like... smiling at me. Like he was having fun, you know? That's how I noticed his teeth."

Kendra and Michelle exchanged a curious glance, but neither of them said anything aloud. Was Michelle thinking the same thing?

"The other guy was bigger. I didn't see him very well at all. He was wearing a red hat; a baseball cap. Dirty and bent, like he'd been breaking it in forever. He seemed huge compared to the other guy. He had longer hair, too. Kinda shaggy curling under the hat."

"Oh, my God... Kendra?" Michelle breathed, glancing at Kendra again. "You don't think... I mean, it couldn't have been the same guys. Could it?"

"I was just thinking the same thing." Kendra's hands formed fists at her sides.

"What guys? What are you talking about." Lacey's voice hitched as though something horribly frightening had just crept into the room with them.

"Nothing, baby. Just that we had a run in with a couple of guys just like that a couple of months ago up in the Red Narrows. Michelle had to run them off with a shotgun before they beat me to death."

"This wasn't an accident, Kendra. They..." she gasped as if she were in pain for a moment and then began to hyperventilate.

"What is it, Lace?" Michelle held her hand again, looking back at Kendra as if she knew what to do.

A nurse appeared with a syringe which she placed into one of the many intravenous tubes in Lacey's arm.

Michelle made room for the nurse to work as she injected something into the tube.

"They hit the truck. In the tailgate. They hit me on purpose, Kendra. You know, like those pit maneuver things on TV? They made me wreck on purpose!" She forced her hand away from Michelle's grip a second time and placed it gently on the bandage over her cheek. "They did this to me..."

She sobbed, her entire body trembling, and then she fell silent. Her breathing evened a little and she slept.

The nurse removed the syringe. "It's just a painkiller, but a pretty strong one. Does she abuse any type of drugs?"

"Of course not. Why would you even ask such a thing?" Michelle's voice was firm and she sounded truly offended.

"You'd be surprised these days, hon. I don't mean any disrespect, but we have to ask. It makes a difference in what kinds of drugs we can use for her, and her tolerance levels play a part in how effective they are. If she hasn't built up a tolerance, this dose should let her sleep for a few hours. By the time she wakes up, she'll be all finished with surgery and snug as a bug in her room."

Kendra's rage had taken on a new and brilliant color of hate while her sister had been explaining what happened. Her fingers itched to squeeze Harold Mason's neck beneath them. She stormed from the curtained cubicle.

How had she allowed this to happen? At what point should she call herself a first class coward? One, possibly two, dead men. Her own sister maimed and nearly killed. This went far beyond some revenge scheme to take the ranch away from her family.

Mason was insane. He had to be.

No, not insane.

Just evil.

The sharp click of heels on the hard linoleum tiles behind her almost made her stop and turn. Almost.

Michelle's stern voice barely penetrated the angry storm raging in Kendra's head. "Where the hell do you think you're going?"

"Stay with Lacey. I'll come back to get you later."

She pulled on Kendra's arm, but she shrugged her off. "You're going after him, aren't you?"

Kendra continued her forced march out of the emergency room. "You don't want to know where I'm going."

Eighteen

Kendra found Mason at the Randall County Country Club more than an hour later. An hour filled with fury and disgust. Fury fed by the fact that soon, she'd level the playing field. Disgust that it had taken her so long to do it.

The old Jeep's brakes locked up when Kendra stomped on the pedal. She threw the gear shift into first and allowed the engine to stall. Then she threw herself over the door and made her way through the crowded parking lot.

Shiny new cars reflected the moonlight like thousands of earthbound stars. Sitting like a beacon in the stall closest to the huge, carved double doors of the club, a custom luxury truck winked at her.

Mason's truck.

Somewhere inside the sprawling property, Mason laughed and stirred his vodka on the rocks with his pickled finger.

Lacey was scarred for life, languishing in a hospital bed, and Harold Mason was having cocktails.

Just like his father.

Kendra shoved open the doors. Each one slammed into the wall before it ricocheted back in her direction. By the time they closed, she'd made her way half-way through the lobby.

"Excuse me!" An older man with silver hair rushed toward her. "You cannot simply barge in here. You have to be a member."

Kendra almost laughed. Maybe she should. She was half-crazy already. Perhaps a little maniacal laughter would convince Jeeves, here, that she meant business. Instead, she shook her head and moved past him.

The man dashed in front of her and barred a narrow doorway. "I'm sorry, sir. But I really must see your membership card."

Through gritted teeth, she answered, "I'm not a member. But you already know that."

The man's face paled, and Kendra had to hand it to him... He didn't back down. "As I suspected. I'm afraid you'll have to leave."

"Not gonna happen."

"Pardon? Sir, I mean, ma'am, this is really most impertinent and inappropriate."

Kendra shook her head again. "Did they import you or something? Who talks like that?"

"Well, I never—"

"Don't sweat it, Pops. I won't be long."

Again, she moved toward the door. Once more, the irritating guard dog got in the way.

Enough games. "Listen to me very carefully. I'm

going through that door. You can get out of the way, or you can go through those windows over there. I truly don't care which one of those options you choose, but getting out of my way will save me a boat load of time."

A muscle twitched in the man's temple. A few slow seconds ticked by. In what Kendra figured was the best decision of the man's life, he stepped aside. Under normal circumstances, she probably didn't have the physical strength to carry out her threat, but in her current state, anything was possible. She tipped her hat as she passed and said, "Much obliged."

In her entire life, all of it spent in the same house, in the same town, she'd never once set foot inside the country club. And she hadn't missed out on a damn thing. Canned chamber music and the soft clink of silverware on china met her at the arched entrance of the dining room. It only took a moment for her to find Mason among the seventy-or-so diners.

Seated beside a good-looking brunette next to a huge plate-glass window, Mason looked like he was holding court. Like Arthur at the round table, Mason addressed several members of the local government; his knights in shining suits. He leaned back in his chair and grinned while the others laughed and toasted one another.

Kendra took a deep breath and strode through the maze of tables. She recognized a few patrons and when they looked at her, she smiled in return. Mrs. Wicks reached out with one hand as if to stop her. She skirted her outstretched arm. "In a moment, Mrs. Wicks. I'm afraid I'm a bit late for a meeting."

When she reached Mason's table, she considered throwing *him* out the window.

Kendra may have never been inside the club before, but she'd seen it from the highway her entire life. These windows, floor to ceiling monstrosities, overlooked the golf course. Because of the surrounding hills and cliffs, the building had been placed on a small outcropping. Kendra smiled. Those windows sat an easy three, maybe four, stories above the first tee.

Suddenly realizing that his normally rapt audience was staring at something other than him, he turned. The color in his face drained. His eyes grew into saucers for a barely perceptible moment. Kendra realized suddenly why he seemed so... surprised? Shocked? At least for a few seconds before anger shuttered the weaker emotion.

Lacey had been driving Kendra's truck. Nearly killing Lacey had been a complete accident; a mistake. Mason had been trying to kill her, not her sister.

As quickly as Mason's shock had been replaced with anger, an artificial calm surrounded him.

"Well... Kendra Williams. What brings you out here?" The mayor smiled and offered his hand.

Kendra ignored the gesture. The others probably considered the silence awkward. After a moment, the mayor dropped his hand and glanced at his companions.

Mason smiled the same greasy, I-can-get-away-with-murder-grin that he always wore and set down his drink. "Miss Williams. I do believe you're in violation of your very own restraining order."

Then he laughed. Loud and full of the same smug belligerence that always enveloped him.

Kendra's right fist connected with Mason's jaw. His chair tilted backwards and he landed on his back.

It seemed as if the entire room disappeared. The

only thing Kendra could see was Lacey's face. Bruised and bloodied; the salt of her tears making it worse, stinging the huge gash on her cheek.

Kendra dove on Mason and landed at least three more punches before she found herself held by the arms about ten feet away from a bloodied Harold Mason.

"You'll pay for that," he snarled. Mason climbed to his feet with the aid of the mayor and a city councilman. "I swear to you, I'll see to it that you pay dearly."

"No, Mason. I'm done paying. It's your turn. You stay away from my family, or I swear to God, I'll kill you with my bare hands."

Mason looked past Kendra's shoulder and smiled as he wiped the blood from his lips with a white, linen napkin. "Sheriff, I believe you have just witnessed this woman threatening my life."

"Here you go, Ms. Loving." The young-looking Sheriff's deputy handed Michelle her platinum credit card. It was the same deputy who had spoken to her the night Kennedy Bastion died. "It's funny, really. I mean, we get her kid brother, Casey, in here all the time, but this is the first time we've ever had Miss Kendra in the holding cell."

Michelle offered a tight-lipped smile but said nothing in reply. Funny? How wonderful that he found Kendra's borderline nervous breakdown entertaining. She studied the silver name-plate beneath the badge on his chest. "Deputy... Whitlock? How long until she'll be released?"

"Now that you've posted bail, oh, maybe about ten minutes. You can wait around the back of the building in the parking lot. She'll be coming out the back door.

She passed through a dingy room with scuffed tile floors to make her way back to the main doors of the county holding facility. The jail. A thin woman with a small child on her lap occupied one seat. A large man in the seat next to her leered at Michelle with an open, adoring grin. She could count his teeth.

At least Kendra would be pleased to hear that Lacey had been moved to a private room from the ICU. Her surgery had gone well and her arm was pinned in four places. Her face had been stitched, but cosmetic surgery would come later. Right now, they were more concerned with getting her through the dangerous infection period.

While Kendra had been driving around town fuming for her arch enemy like some crazed, cartoon super-hero, Michelle had settled Lacey into bed and waited until she finally woke up.

She glanced at her watch. Almost two in the morning. She took a deep breath and adjusted the bag on her shoulder as she pushed her way through the doors. She jumped back into her car and moved it to the parking lot the deputy had indicated.

Time was running out. Not only for Kendra and the ranch, but for her. She doubted she'd have much business to return to when she finally did go back to Las Vegas. She'd managed to get with some of her clients online and work on their projects from the ranch, but it just wasn't the same thing. Now that the wedding was over, she'd planned to go home on Monday.

Three days. She chewed on one snagged fingernail.

Then she examined the damage.

Lacey wouldn't even be home in three days. Kendra had to run the ranch, the boys had taken off to God-knows-where, and someone would need to take care of Lacey when she came home from the hospital. It would be weeks before she was fully functional again.

And what if Lacey was right and the accident had been a deliberate attempt on her life? What if Harold Mason really had sent someone after her? It made sense, and she wouldn't put it past the old bastard.

Regardless, she couldn't leave now. Threat or no threat, she had to take care of Lacey. The decision to stay rooted in her mind as easily as putting on a pair of comfortable shoes.

Guilt crept through her nerves. Was she only insisting that she stay because Lacey needed her? Or was she using her best friend's condition to make excuses to stay with Kendra?

Did it matter?

She shifted her weight in the driver's seat of the car. Her butt was starting to go numb. Who the hell was she kidding? She couldn't stay here forever. There was no happily-ever-after in her future. In three days, she *should* pack her bags, pick up the pieces of her heart and go home.

Kendra didn't need her anymore. Michelle wasn't in any danger.

She glanced at her watch again. Did that stupid deputy say ten minutes or ten hours? She huffed and folded her arms over her chest.

Just then, the heavy metal door in the back of the building opened. Kendra meandered through it, her hands shoved deep in her front pockets. She didn't look any worse for wear, but Michelle's heart leapt to her throat anyway. Kendra approached the car without a word, and climbed into the passenger seat of Michelle's Mustang.

"You're welcome," she offered with what she hoped was a sarcastic grin on her face.

Kendra still said nothing. Although, she may have released a growl that vibrated the air between them—Michelle couldn't be certain.

Michelle started the engine and pointed the car in the direction of ranch. "I want to go back to the hospital."

"Lacey is sleeping. She told me make sure we went home, to sleep in our own bed, and we can go see her tomorrow."

"Thank you," she whispered, "for bailing me out. You didn't have to do that. I was fine overnight."

"I couldn't let you stay there!" Michelle announced.

"Turn here," Kendra pointed to a side street.

"Why?"

"Just turn," she continued. "It's a long drive back to the ranch. We'll spend as much in gas as it costs for a motel. And yes, I could have stayed there just fine."

Michelle guided her car into the parking lot of a small, businessman's special kind of motel. Once she parked, she turned to face Kendra. "I don't care what you've done, I'm not going to let you spend the night in some bacteria-infested jail. You're too pretty for jail!"

She climbed out of the car to the sound of a reluctant chuckle. Once they checked in and found their room, Michelle sat on the edge of the single, queen-sized bed.

"Sorry, it's not much, is it." Kendra offered. "Kinda cheap."

"Hey, I can camp anywhere for one night."

Kendra went into the bathroom and turned on the shower.

Michelle followed behind her and turned it off. She looked at the faucet long enough for two drops of water to escape before she tilted her head in Michelle's direction. One arched brow shot up and her forehead, already creased with stress, bunched a little more.

Michelle placed one fist on each of her hips in a deliberate attempt to display power and determination. "Are you going to talk to me?"

"About what?"

"Oh, I don't know. How about how I just had to bail you out of jail for attacking Harold Mason while trespassing on private property, in front of witnesses that include the mayor and half the damn city council. Or maybe we could discuss the fact that you have a restraining order against him, which you violated, which will probably be thrown out of court after tonight."

Kendra released a snort and shoved past her into the main room. "Like that was doing a goddamn bit of good. Tell Lacey how effective my little piece of paper was."

"So you just decided that the wheels of justice turn too slowly for the great Kendra Williams, is that it? If you can't get what you deserve, you'll make sure Mason gets his?"

"If that's what it takes, that's what it takes. I'm done sitting on my hands. If you can't handle it, go home."

"Make up your mind! Do you want me to stay or go?"

"What the hell does that matter? You're going to do what you want, anyway. It's not like I have any say or control over you or what you do. Even if I had a right to, you wouldn't listen." Kendra scoffed with a harsh laugh. "You are physically incapable of following directions. If I've learned anything from all of this, I've learned that."

"You're not being fair. First, you treat me like I'm some kind of alien species, then you spend a great deal of time and effort to seduce me, and then you try to run over me like a goddamn *man*, and now, you're telling me that you've had no responsibility in this thing, whatsoever? That's rich, Kendra. That's really rich."

"I don't give a rat's ass what you do, Michelle. Stay, leave. Whatever. If you want to leave, then go!"

"Fine!"

"Fine!"

Silence cascaded over the room like a quilt. Michelle swallowed what felt like her heart. Pain laced through her chest until it fell back into place, bruised and swollen. "Is that really what you want?"

Kendra stood less than five feet from her. Two steps and she could be in her arms. All Kendra had to do was make some indication that she'd welcome it, and that's exactly where Michelle would be. She watched for a sign. A shift of her shoulders; a come-hither gleam in her eyes.

Nothing.

Not so much as a twitch of her fingers.

"No," she sighed. "I don't want you to go."

Kendra's voice sounded almost defeated, as if the fact that she wanted Michelle to stay made her less of a woman, or less of a matriarch for her family. As though admitting that she might need someone else somehow lessened her own ability to lead, or provide, or... something.

"Kendra." Michelle took a tentative step forward. "Why are you making this so hard? Why are you fighting it so damn hard?"

Her head snapped upward. "Fighting what?"

"You know what I'm talking about. You're human. You have feelings. And like tonight pretty much proves beyond a reasonable doubt, you make mistakes on occasion."

"But—"

"No buts. It's okay to screw up every once in a while. I seriously doubt that Mac is going to recommend to the DA that he file charges. This whole thing will blow over. Your sister will recover. She's out of ICU, by the way, and she'll be home as soon as they can put a cast on her arm." Michelle took another step forward. "And you'll keep your ranch. Everything will be just like it was before."

Everything.

Including her lonesome privacy. As much as she wanted the job of providing her stoic rancher with someone to lean on, if Kendra didn't want her, she couldn't stay.

If only Kendra would admit to her feelings. She almost laughed at the thought. Against her better judgment, she closed the remaining space between them. "Make love to me, Kendra." She captured Kendra's lips in a kiss.

God, don't let her turn away. For a second, it seemed like she might.

Then her arms shot around Michelle and crushed her against her chest. Kendra's kiss overpowered her as she took control of the embrace.

Kendra's breath grew ragged and desperate until finally she broke the kiss and stared into Michelle's eyes. The thick muscles in her arms trembled against her shoulders. "What would I ever do without you, Michelle?"

Michelle's heart soared. It was a start.

"Have you heard anything from Casey or Brent?" Michelle poured herself a cup of coffee and joined Kendra at the kitchen table where she sifted through the mail.

"Not yet."

"Have you been able to get in touch with them about Lacey?"

"No. Why? You worried?"

"A little."

"They're big boys. They can take care of themselves."

"I see. So, you limit your worrying to the fairer sex."

Kendra grinned and shifted her gaze from the letter she'd been reading to Michelle. "Are you calling me sexist? I am a woman, you realize."

"That doesn't mean you aren't just a little bit misogynistic."

"I think I'm insulted," she chuckled.

Michelle placed her coffee cup on the kitchen counter. "So, are you just about ready to pick up Lacey?"

"Yeah, in a minute." She'd returned her attention to the mail. She ran her hand over her chin.

She looked tired. She hadn't slept well the night before. In fact, Michelle had woken to find herself alone in Kendra's huge bed. When Kendra finally returned, they'd made love before she'd eventually drifted off. But dark circles threatened her eyes, just the same. Her delicate eyebrows came together in a concerned frown.

"What month is it?"

Michelle giggled. Was she that preoccupied? "Almost October."

"So, should I be surprised that I've just received a notice of a full, three-year audit from the IRS?"

"No, you didn't!" She rushed to the table to read over Kendra's shoulder. "Crap," she muttered. "No, you shouldn't be surprised by the date. But why in the world are you being audited?"

Michelle took the letter and read the contents more carefully. "Discrepancies? Miscalculations? Who does your taxes?"

"I do." Kendra pushed herself away from the table and sauntered to the coffee pot.

"Did you make any mistakes?"

She finished topping off her coffee before she answered. "I seriously doubt it."

"You don't suppose..."

"I'd suppose just about anything where that

bastard is concerned. If he does have something to do with it, it's for no other reason than to keep me busy. To prevent me from fighting for the land."

"Then, it's like a rope-a-dope."

"Exactly." Kendra leaned against the counter and sipped from her mug, the expression on her face indicative of her surprise that Michelle knew what a rope-a-dope was. "I'll tell you, though, I need this right now like I need a hole in the head."

"It says that we can provide records... I mean, you can provide records to back up the old tax filings." Michelle pointed to the line she'd just read. "It just so happens that I computerized all of those records for you, already. A couple of clicks. A little bit of ink. We can have this wrapped up in no time."

"Nothing phases you, does it?"

Some things phased her. Some things knocked her off her feet. A sidelong glance from Kendra when she thought she wasn't looking. One of her kisses. The feel of her naked body sliding against her with nothing between them but sweat and skin... Oh, no, she was hardly a rock. She only wanted to be strong when Kendra needed her.

And right now... Kendra did.

Lacey slid between the sheets of the same bed Kendra had tucked her into a thousand times. Kendra pictured her when she was only four, before their parents' death. Kendra had been young then, too, but Lacey had been so much younger. She'd looked like the smallest angel in heaven. With the biggest heart. An instant later, she'd been fourteen, entirely Kendra's responsibility and completely covered in chicken pox. She'd fussed and fidgeted for weeks, in this very room.

Her gaze drifted over a lifetime of memorabilia. Three cut-glass crowns from various pageants rested in a row on the top shelf of an antique white hutch. Banners and ribbons, horse-show trophies, pictures of her riding Demon, her Arabian-Quarter horse mix, the cheap jewelry box their mother had given to her for Christmas the year before the accident...

A moan emanated from the mass huddled beneath the old quilt on the bed and drew her attention from the past. Her past. The only life she'd ever known. The only life she'd ever wanted.

"Kendra?" Lacey's muffled voice sounded like it came from inside a cavern.

"Yeah, baby-girl?" She sat on the edge of the bed and rested her hand on what should be her sister's shoulder, beneath the mountain of coverlets.

"I'm really sorry about your truck."

Kendra pinched the bridge of her nose and smiled. "I can't believe you just said that, Lace."

"I really am." She rolled toward her and Kendra hid a wince. Her face, still mostly covered with bandages, looked thick and pale. The one eye she could see looked at her with hope and trust, like she could make it all better. Like she used to.

"It's not your fault, Lacey. It's my fault. I'm sorry I let this happen."

"No, Kendra. Don't say that. You're the closest thing to a mother I've got and I love you." She bit her lip and drew a breath that seemed to rattle her entire body.

"I just don't know what I'm going to do now, that's all."

The one thing she'd been unable to stomach in all of the years she'd been caring for her brothers and sister was Lacey's tears. The thought of her sister in pain threatened to send her to her knees. Good thing she was already sitting or she might have just hit the floor.

She gathered Lacey into her arms and let her cry. "Everything will be fine. You'll see. You'll do everything you ever dreamed of, and more."

"How the hell am I supposed to be a TV reporter with some hideous scar on my face? Can you tell me that? I'm going to be so ugly, no one will be able to stand to look at me!"

Michelle appeared in the doorway. Kendra searched her face for some hint of what she should do. What could she say to make Lacey feel even a little better? The doctors had said that she would have a large, jagged scar. They'd done the very best they could, but even with cosmetic surgery, the likelihood that they could repair all of the damage was slim. She wouldn't be ugly. She could never be that. But she was scarred, and Kendra couldn't make it better.

Michelle knelt in front of her and stroked Lacey's back with the flat of one hand. "Lacey, I want you to listen to me. You aren't beautiful because of how you look. You're beautiful because of who you are. And that hasn't changed. A few years ago, you were a dirty little girl curled up on the stoop of my apartment building. Lost. Full of piss, vinegar and pride. Practically homeless because you refused to come back here and face that fact that you'd made a mistake. Now, look at you! You're almost finished with college, for crying out loud. And you've done it all on your own. You have a family who loves you, and friends who adore you. And we don't love and adore you because of your face. It's because you have all of the strengths we wish we had. That's why we love you."

Kendra's mouth went dry as a boll of cotton caught in a dust storm. She could barely breathe. Michelle had just explained exactly why Kendra loved her. Because she possessed all of the strength and determination she wished she'd had all of these years. That's why she worried so much less since she'd arrived. That's why, when she entered a room, power surged through her with the force of a tidal wave. She'd always thought that power came from Michelle, but she'd been wrong. It was her own power; strength she'd had all of these years but never recognized. It had taken a woman's love for her to find the goodness within herself. Her own worth.

When Lacey stopped crying, she crawled back into the bed. Within a few moments, she slept peacefully.

Kendra looked at Michelle, so close that Kendra could feel the swell of her breast against her arm. Her heart crashed. She might be worth a lot of things, but she'd never deserve Michelle.

"We found him." Brent's digitized image beamed in the computer screen.

Kendra leaned against the wall. A rush of air left her lungs. "And?"

"We haven't talked to him yet. Casey tracked him down to a little motel and we followed him most of the day. He spent a few hours at some digital studio place just off the strip."

"Laserix?"

"Yeah, that's the place. How'd you know that?"

"Would you believe me if I told you that Harold Mason owns it?"

"And why wouldn't he? Damn, that boy has a greasy little finger in everything, right? We're going to pay our boy a visit tonight and I have a feeling he'll be more than willing to ride back to Utah with us."

Kendra told Brent about the car accident and Lacey's condition. "We just brought her home this afternoon."

Kendra left out any mention of her arrest for attacking Mason.

"We're going to pick up shit-for-brains and should be home sometime around midnight or one."

"Be careful. I have no idea where Mason's people are. For all I know, he's been watching us all along and you are being tailed."

"Christ, Sis. It's like some bad spy movie." He rubbed his two-day beard and scratched his chin.

"I know. But it's very real. Take it seriously."

"We are. And Case is fairly certain we were followed when we left the ranch. You should have seen that crazy-bitch brother of ours cruise through the Virgin Gorge at about a hundred miles per hour. Christ!"

"Yeah, I don't want to hear about that. Really. Feel free not to share everything."

"I'm just saying that if they were following us, we definitely lost them in the gorge and they haven't been able to tail us here. We parked Lacey's car in long-term at McCarrin and rented a new one.

"Good thinking. Leave her car there and drive the rental back."

"That's the plan. Lacey is going to be pissed." Brent released a short chuckle.

Kendra doubted that. For the past few hours, she couldn't be certain that Lacey felt anything at all. When she woke from her nap, she seemed to have crawled completely inside of herself. It made her want to strangle Mason with her bare hands all over again. As if she had no control, her hands formed into fists in her lap.

"Hey, Sis; the commando kid is ready to rock and roll. I'll call you when we've picked up our guy and with any luck, we'll be home in about twenty-four hours."

"Brent?"

"Yeah?"

"Be careful. Casey is used to this stuff. Do exactly as he says."

"I'm not stupid, Kennie. I'm leaving all the superhero crap to little brother."

Kendra waited until Brent had stood up and turned off his computer before she closed the screen on Michelle's laptop and set it on the counter. She turned to make her way into the living room where Michelle was sitting with Lacey, watching television. It startled her when she found Michelle leaning instead against the doorjamb, watching her.

She stared at Kendra like she'd grown horns and opened her mouth to speak. Nothing came out for more than a few seconds. Damn. How long had she been there?"

"What was that all about?"

Kendra hated the slight tremor in her voice.

Michelle was anything but stupid. Kendra could lie. She could keep up with her story about Brent and Casey meeting with a new transportation company. The look on Michelle's face told her she wouldn't buy it. Not in a million years. "That was Brent."

"I know that was Brent. Where is he?"

"They're in Vegas, like I said."

"Uh-huh."

Kendra shoved her hands into her pockets. "They found the man who has been hired to do most of Mason's dirty work."

"Like what?"

"Like he started the stampede that killed Ken. Like he tore up our equipment. And killed Apache."

"What are they doing in Vegas, besides looking for this guy?"

Kendra stepped toward Michelle. She pulled her hands free and reached for Michelle's hands. She'd folded her arms over her breasts like a suit of armor.

"No," she hissed, backing away a step. "You tell me what they're doing."

"How much do you know about what Casey did in the Navy?"

"He was in operations."

"Yeah. Black operations, maybe? Don't freak out, but Casey and Brent are going to *talk* this guy into coming back here and spilling his guts."

"They're going to talk him into it." Michelle's voice was flat, almost sarcastic, as though she didn't believe a single word she'd just said.

"Convince him it's in his best interest."

"Which probably won't involve talking." An accusation.

"Probably not."

Michelle blanched. "I can't believe this is happening. This is crazy. Things like this do not happen in real life, for God's sake. Your brothers are going to kidnap someone? What are they going to do, throw him in the trunk of their car, bring him home and hide him in the goddamn barn?"

"If we have to, yes."

Michelle had always been so strong. Confident that her world was the only one that existed. Kendra had hoped for too long that Michelle was right about the kind of world they lived in, but that attitude had cost her family too much already.

"Listen to me, Michelle," Kendra whispered. Michelle's head raised and she looked her dead in the eye. The moist droplets in the corners of her eyes tore at Kendra's gut, but she continued. "I trusted you. You have worked your ass off for me and my family. You did everything you could to handle this in a professional and effective way. But we're not dealing with a normal situation, here. This isn't some hostile takeover of a failing corporation. This is a man with one purpose in life; to make me and my family suffer as much as possible in some kind of revenge plot straight out of a Hollywood movie. He's crazy, Michelle. He won't stop until he hurts me as much as he thinks I hurt him. He will stop at nothing and he doesn't care who gets in his way. You should know that by now."

This time, when Kendra reached for Michelle, Michelle allowed Kendra to take her into her arms. She kissed the top of Michelle's head and inhaled the rich honeysuckle scent of her hair. "I'm asking you to trust me now. Can you do that? Please?"

Michelle stood ramrod straight for more than a moment. Kendra didn't breathe. She couldn't.

She couldn't be certain her heart beat.

Until Michelle nodded against her chest and allowed herself to meld into Kendra like they were two sides of the same body.

Nineteen

Cooling water caressed Michelle's breasts as she laid back against Kendra's chest. "We should probably get out of the water before we turn into prunes."

Instead of an answer, she received a nibble on her earlobe, followed by the warm whisper of breath. Small bumps formed on her arms and her nipples hardened into peaks. She could easily spend the rest of the night in the oversized, claw-foot tub.

Kendra finally replied, "I don't want to get out yet. Unless, of course, we can go back to bed."

"Again? Already? My, my, aren't you just the Casanova?"

"Hey, I'm always ready."

Michelle's stomach clenched. She spun in Kendra's arms until her body pressed against hers. Then she captured Kendra's bottom lip between her teeth before sliding her tongue over it to lessen the sting. Kendra groaned in response and deepened the kiss immediately.

A moment later she pulled away and in one fluid movement, lifted Michelle's dripping body. Her eyes clouded with green mist, as if she saw something that no one else could see. She looked into Michelle's eyes for a moment, then turned her gaze over her face, her lips, and then back to her eyes. "Get out of the tub."

Michelle didn't resist. Instead, she climbed from the tub and waited for Kendra to follow. She did; in all of her naked splendor. No matter how many times Michelle saw Kendra's body, she found herself amazed at the perfection. Tight muscles. Narrow waist and curved, flared hips. Long legs.

When clothed, Kendra was rough and tough. She swaggered instead of walked. She had a natural posture that was proud and lean, whether hunched against the wind as she sat strong in her saddle, or bracing the incredible weight of a piece of farm machinery, stacks of lumber, or bales of hay. There was no questioning her masculine side, the traits that made her so good as what she did on the Heartland.

But there was the other side of her; the feminine, beautiful, ghostly side of herself that she never let anyone see. When she stripped off the mostly-male clothing she preferred, she was all woman; with curves and needs and shallows and depths that Michelle felt honored to witness.

Kendra stepped from the tub and wrapped Michelle in a large, cotton towel. She didn't need it. Kendra's arms alone could warm her on the coolest night. If she were lost in a blizzard, she would need only Kendra to survive.

She walked Michelle into the bedroom. In tandem step, they moved together. Her front pressed against Michelle's back, the tips of her breasts in sharp relief on the tender flesh. Kendra's head bent against her neck where she placed tiny bites in that soft spot, right behind Michelle's ear. Her body shivered with promises of more.

Michelle tilted her head, granting Kendra greater access. She could go on like this for hours. A smile spread her lips and her eyes began to drift closed.

Her muscles froze in her arms and she dug her nails into Kendra's arms. Kendra gasped. "Hey, now. You're getting a little rough, aren't you?" Kendra examined Michelle's fingernails and *tsked*, aloud. "You might want to trim those..."

"Kendra?"

"Yeah?" she mumbled a reply as she buried her lips into Michelle's neck again.

Michelle unwound herself from Kendra's embrace and took a single step toward the window. "No, Kendra. Seriously, look. What is that?" She pointed out the window.

Kendra followed her and moved the shade out of the way. The whole room seemed to tremble as orange light glowed brightly from the other side of the hill.

"That... is a fire."

"Where are the damn keys!" Kendra tore through the house, her heart racing somewhere near the back of her throat.

Kendra dashed through the living room and into the foyer. Lacey stood on the bottom step with one hand gripped around the railing. Even so, she swayed on her feet and her skin glowed with a sheen of sweat.

Kendra growled. "Go back to bed, Lacey."

"I heard you. You said Brad's house is on fire?" Her voice cracked either from pain or concern.

Kendra fumed at the fact her confident, do-or-die sister had been reduced to a shell of her former self. Damn Harold Mason. Damn him for everything he'd done to Kendra's family.

Kendra took a step toward her sister and raised one hand to stroke her cheek. Lacey pulled away from her and hid the healing stitches on her right cheek with her hair.

Kendra wanted to break something. Anything. Her eyes narrowed. She wanted to break Harold Mason. Clean in half.

But right now, she didn't have time to spend with Lacey, no matter how much she needed someone to help her feel better. "I want you to go back to bed."

Lacey nodded and turned on the step. She hated seeing her so defeated. A part of her wanted Lacey to fight back, to argue with her about just how weak she really was. The other part was thankful that she acquiesced; Kendra didn't want to have to worry about her, right now, too.

She had to get to Brad and Lenise.

"I called the fire department. They're sending help. There's no answer at Brad's. Neither one of them is picking up their cell phone."

Kendra swallowed. "Find the keys and follow me. I'm taking Preakness."

Kendra saddled her horse in a matter of seconds. She didn't bother to secure the latigo, but held the saddle on Preakness' back by pulling the strap with one hand and holding the reins in the other.

The night air chilled her as it cut into her cheeks. Preakness lurched as if he knew something wasn't quite right, that the spontaneous run over uneven ground held an element of danger.

By the time Kendra reached the house, flames shot through the roof. Bright orange fingers clawed from the windows to the roof. The freshly painted clap boards glowed orange and red before they swelled and bubbled in the intense heat. Kendra leaped from the saddle, letting it fall to the ground as she raced toward the front door with one arm raised to protect her face from the scorching heat.

Damn. It was too hot. She couldn't get any closer to the inferno. She looked up to the flames that danced high into the dark sky. Smoke billowed from the roof and windows, illuminated for a moment by the flames, and then disappeared into the black void.

Kendra had never felt so powerless. Where were Brad and Lenise? Dear God, were they still inside?"

She pushed forward. Her heart thumped against her ribs. The steady beat of flames seemed to match her pulse. The closer she came to the house, the odder the sounds that met her. Crackling fire, the high pitched whine of a house in its final throes of agony. There would be no saving it. She only hoped that her brother and his young wife had managed to get out.

A sudden movement to her left drew her attention. Kendra spun to the figure, hurried over the several feet separating her from it, and fell to her knees. Brad lay in a heap, his face blackened, but not burned. His hands fisted over his chest.

"Brad? Brad, can you hear me?"

Brad sobbed. "No!"

"Brad, listen to me. Where's Lenise?" Somehow, Kendra knew the answer before she'd even asked the question.

"No! They killed her! They killed her!"

"What?"

"I couldn't reach her, Kennie." Brad curled into a ball and pounded the dry earth with the side of his fist. "I just couldn't get to her," he wailed.

"Brad, is she still inside?"

"I tried, Kendra. I tried..."

Kendra jumped to her feet and ran toward the front door. It stood open, sagging on one hinge. Fire lapped at the doorway in a seductive dance, warning her away. Kendra ignored the threat and pushed through the smoke. Once inside, her lungs filled with toxic, heavy air. Worse than the smoke, the heat seared through her. She coughed and held one forearm over her face.

The world inside the inferno was surreal. She couldn't see anything through the smoke, but she could hear the fire sizzling around her. Mere seconds after racing into the midst of hell, she backed out through the door.

Too late. She was too late. "Lenise!" she screamed from the front yard. Maybe she huddled by a window... maybe she could jump. She called for her again.

She ran both hands through her hair and formed fists at the back of her head. She could barely hear her own voice. If Lenise were alive, she certainly couldn't hear her.

A car slid to a stop at the edge of the yard. She turned and found Michelle staring at the flames; at the old homestead completely engulfed. Her mouth hung open and her brow furrowed in deep lines. "Where are they?" she asked, her voice catching on the words.

Where are they...

"Brad's over there," she answered, her own voice scratchy and damaged by the smoke.

Kendra led Michelle to where Brad lay in a tiny ball. When she reached the spot where she'd left her brother, he was gone. Every muscle in her body tensed. "Brad! No!"

Brad climbed the front steps as if he were in a trance. He moved through the front door, one slow step at a time. The heat didn't seem to affect him. The smoke billowed around him like some ancient cloak. Kendra threw herself toward the house and reached Brad just as the ceiling cracked and gave way. Pieces of burning plaster fell to the floor. One of them caught Brad on the shoulder and knocked him to his knees.

Kendra grabbed him from behind and dragged him toward the front door. After a couple of steps, Brad came out of whatever spell has consumed him. He fought like some kind of psychopath, kicking and twisting. "Let me go, Kendra. Just let me burn up with her. No! Let me go!"

Kendra never let go for a second. She tightened her arms around Brad's chest and pulled him to safety. Cool air met her back and she fell to her backside on the hard earth. Brad slumped against her like he'd used to when he was a little boy. Kendra's arms trembled with the force of Brad's sobs.

Michelle knelt beside them and took Brad's hand in her own.

Brad looked at Michelle and his face twisted into a mask of despair. "They're dead. My wife. My baby. They're dead. What the hell am I supposed to do, now?"

Kendra looked at the horizon as more than a dozen riders bore down on the inferno. The herdsmen must have seen the flames.

One object on the horizon didn't exactly look right, however, and Kendra slipped Brad into Michelle's arms before gaining her feet. She stepped away from them and studied the ridge line north of the range. Was that a truck? More than a mile away, Kendra couldn't make out the shape, exactly, but she would swear on a stack of bibles that the shape was that of a pick-up truck. The odd figure seemed to deform for a second, and then bright white lights shone from the front and it sped into the distance.

The house burned. It seemed more than impossible to save it now. Michelle's arms and legs tingled at the same time she couldn't even be sure they were still there. Brad leaned against her. That's the only reason she could tell either of them had any life left.

A couple of fire trucks crunched over the gravel road and the airbrakes whispered beneath the noise of the inferno. Moving as one cohesive movement, the fire fighters hooked up hoses to the second truck and began pumping water onto the flames. One of the firemen approached Michelle and Brad wearing a badge that identified him as the battalion chief. He had kind eyes, but they were sad. It was like he already knew that not everyone had made it out of the house. He glanced at Brad's scorched clothing and called for a medic over his shoulder.

Two EMTs raced across the yard with heavy plastic kits in each of their hands. They took Brad from her and sat him on the ground. He fought them.

Michelle's limbs gave out.

Dear God. Lenise was dead.

Where was Kendra?

Panic threatened to claim what remained of her sanity. She rose and tried to run toward the house, but strong, male arms grabbed her and held her back.

"Where do you think you're going?" The chief's gruff shout somehow managed to penetrate the hailstorm of fire and despair in her head.

"Kendra! Lenise... Lenise was in the house. Kendra. Brad. They tried to get her to her. I don't see her." She stared into the fireman's lined face. "Where is she?"

"I'm here," Kendra called from a few feet away.

Michelle spun toward her voice. Kendra's face, blackened by soot and smoke, hovered in the dark. Closing the distance on shaking legs, Michelle grabbed her and then ran her hands over her shoulders and chest. She was alright. Nothing burned. Nothing broken. A sliver of guilt pierced her when relief washed over her. She looked back to the fire, then to Brad, who lay broken and silent a few feet away.

The chief spoke to Kendra. "The house is a total loss, Kendra. I'm sorry. Once that fire broke through the roof, there really wasn't anything anyone could do."

"It's just a house. But Brad's wife was inside." Kendra nodded toward her little brother. "Lenise."

"Shit." The chief lowered his head for a second. "That's Mac's girl, ain't it?"

Kendra nodded and her chin brushed the top of Michelle's head. "She was pregnant."

"Any ideas how this whole thing started?"

"Yeah. I think you'll find arson may have played a role."

Michelle shot a look at Kendra. Was she serious? Not everything bad that happened in the world was Mason's fault. The house was over one hundred years old. The wiring probably wasn't even close to being up to code. But the muscles working in Kendra's chin indicated she gritted her teeth and screamed her belief that the fire had been deliberately set.

"That's a pretty strong accusation. What makes you say that?"

"I saw a truck up on the ridge. On a hunch, I checked out the back acreage by the old water road, and sure enough, that truck stopped and picked up a couple of guys who did not belong here."

A car Michelle didn't recognize sped into the yard and slid to a halt beside the ambulance. Casey and Brent leapt from the front seats and ran toward them.

"What the hell happened?" Casey shouted as he circled several firefighters who still attempted to put out the massive flames. Michelle wondered why they didn't just let it burn.

Brent stopped short and frowned toward Brad and the EMTs. He swallowed hard, and then looked to Kendra. They always looked to Kendra, like she held the answers to everything. Maybe she did, at least in the minds of her family. She served as the one person in their lives they could rely on; look up to. She tightened her grip around Kendra's waist, offering whatever strength she might wish to borrow. Her arms tightened around her, as well.

"Where's Lenise?" Brent's voice choked as if he already knew the answer.

Kendra shook her head.

Casey sounded as if he were numb. "Lenise was inside?" He asked the question like the answer was unfathomable.

"Yeah. They both were. Brad couldn't reach her, but he got out in time." Kendra kissed the top of Michelle's head, before continuing, "We need to talk. Michelle?"

"Yeah?"

"I need you to stay here with Brad. I'm going back to the main house with Brent and Casey. Go to the hospital with Brad if they need to transport him. Can you do that for me?"

Michelle wasn't certain she could do anything. She wasn't even sure she could take a single step in Brad's direction. What could she possibly say to him? His life had been completely torn apart. She could only imagine how badly he must wish it were him in the burned rubble of the house. But she nodded her assent, anyway. Kendra needed her. For the second time since she'd know this amazing family, Kendra had *asked* for her help. She would not let her down. "Yeah. I can do that."

"Good," she answered with what should have been a reassuring smile, but it didn't quite reach her eyes. She kissed her lips, fast and hard, and released her. To her brothers, she continued, "Come with me. We've got a few things to talk about."

"You're not going anywhere without me."

Michelle's hand rushed to her chest. "Brad? You're hurt—"

"She was my wife, goddamn it. If you're going after Mason, I'm in."

Michelle glanced at his jeans, cut up one side where the EMTs had treated burns on his legs. The skin revealed by the scorched rags was angry and red. "You need to go to the hospital."

"Screw that. I'm fine. Either I go with you, Kendra, or I take him out myself."

Michelle looked to Kendra. Surely, she would insist that Brad go to the hospital. That he rest. Mourn. That he grieve. Whatever someone who has just lost their wife of four days and unborn child is supposed to do. A glint of something she didn't recognize shone in Kendra's eyes. She narrowed them on Brad for almost a full minute.

Then she nodded. "Let's go."

Twenty

Kendra leaned against the barn door, closed against the warm night air and prying eyes. Her blood boiled, heated perhaps by the fire but more likely from the passion and tightly-reined anger that coursed through her veins. Lenise was dead. Her brother was devastated. Her family was in more danger than ever. And the piece of garbage tied to the door of a stall in her barn had the answers. Some of them, at least. He worked for Mason and he had already tried to kill her at least once. For all she knew, that fire was supposed to take out the main house – her entire family – and shit-for-brain's friends had just screwed it up. Again.

Not that it mattered.

Lenise was still dead.

Casey straightened to his full height. He'd spent the last fifteen minutes improvising a kind of table in the center of the barn. Two saw horses held up a wide wooden plank he'd found in the loft. He'd stacked two cinderblocks under one of the horses so the surface of the table was at an incline. Then he'd wrapped a couple of old latigo leather strips around the tabletop. The worn leather was old, but it was strong. Based on the size of their prisoner, that was a good thing.

"*Rocky*, here, is a good, old-fashioned thug, ain't that right, *Rocky*?" Brent stated without really asking the question. "He put up a pretty good fight back in Vegas, but he's more friendly now."

The man, who wasn't one of the assholes from the canyon attack after all, squirmed against the ropes holding him to the stall door and mumbled something incoherent through the bandana shoved in his mouth. Every time he struggled, Kendra's muscles tightened and coiled, ready to strike back should he get loose. Brent had tied him fast and secure apparently, because no matter how many times he pulled on the ropes, the knots didn't budge.

Casey smirked as he leaned his backside against the makeshift table. "Now, Rocky, be nice. Didn't we have this conversation already?" He examined his knuckles which were torn and bruised. "Don't make me go over it again."

"Now," Brent continued, "I'm going to let you speak, and you're going to tell us where Mason is meeting your friends for the payoff. If you scream, we're going to hurt you. There is no point in making a ton of noise because there is nobody around to hear. The firemen are gone. The cops are gone. And, quite frankly, you and your boys just killed the Sheriff's daughter. I'm pretty sure they'll be on our side."

Casey tore the bandana out of Rocky's mouth and let it drop to the ground.

"What the hell is that table for?" he panted. He licked his lips and Kendra couldn't tell if his mouth was dry from fear or simply because he'd had the cloth between his teeth for nearly twenty minutes.

"That's not what you were supposed to say, Rocky," Casey stated before landing a hard right fist in Rocky's ribcage.

"I don't know anything," he coughed. "I ain't even been here! They cut me out of the loop! They don't tell me shit, anyway!"

Kendra's stomach roiled. Under normal circumstances, she couldn't imagine ever standing by and watching something like what was happening right in front of her. On her own property. With her blessing! Even when she was in the military herself, she hadn't believed she could ever do some of the things she'd been trained to, in combat or otherwise. She'd had more than one debate over what constituted torture and how there really couldn't be any excuse for it...

But Lenise was dead.

Her little brother, more like her own son, was devastated.

And this guy had something like... answers.

Where was the compassion for Lenise when this goon's buddies set her grandfather's house on fire with her brother and his wife still inside? They murdered a pregnant woman, and unfortunately for them, that pregnant woman was a member of Casey Williams' family.

Casey smirked. "So, you won't mind giving your friends a call and getting all the new dirt, right, Rocky? You can find out where they're making the drop for us, can't you..."

Casey let his voice trail away as he moved to the opposite side of the table he'd constructed. He bent down and picked up a hose in one hand and an empty gallon milk jug in the other. He placed the jug on the wooden plank. Without a word, he inserted the nozzle of the hose into the jug, reached to the wall behind him and turned on the valve. Slowly, he filled the jug.

Kendra pushed herself away from the doorframe, her arms still crossed over her chest as though they had been cemented there. She made her way to Casey's side and turned her back to Rocky and Brent. She whispered, "You're not really going to do this, are you, Case? I mean, we can't..."

When Casey answered it wasn't in a whisper. He spoke plainly, with a tone of voice that was more controlled than she'd ever heard before. "Speak for yourself, Sis. I can do whatever the fuck I want to. He knows something, or he can find out something. I'm tired of the game. I'm done."

"Nah, no way, man. Your sister's right. You ain't gonna do nothin' to me. Right? What's the water for, man?"

"Oh, the water?" asked Casey. "Come on, Rocky. You're a smart guy. You watch YouTube and CNN, right? You probably know all about water boarding! It's a little game I learned during SERE training with the SEALS. Spent nearly six amazing years of my life with my brothers-in-arms; we traveled the world, met interesting people, shot some, too. But I have to admit it; water boarding was my favorite. I just can't get enough of this shit." He turned off the nozzle and made a show of shaking off the tip on the edge of the jug's small mouth. "That should just about do it. But hey, if you're really good at this game too, don't you worry. I have lots more water."

Brent laughed as he started to untie the knots around Rocky's chest. "Casey, you really can be a jerk, sometimes."

Kendra's stomach turned on itself and she backed away, positioning herself against a stall door. She glanced at the exit, considering the possibility that Michelle might walk through it at any moment. She wouldn't understand. She'd be completely against this particular idea; no two ways about it.

But she was inside, doing her very best to ease Brad's pain in any way that she could. He'd crumbled when they got back to the main house. He'd fallen into a heap on the living room floor and as far as she knew, he hadn't moved. Twenty minutes ago, she'd come out to the barn to find Brent tying Rocky to the stall and Casey frantically building his contraption.

"Let's get this party started, Bro," Casey said to Brent. Together, they manhandled Rocky in the direction of the plank. He fought back as best he could with his arms still tied, but Casey's training came into play again, giving him the upper hand in more ways than one.

"Stop it, now. You can't be serious, right? You're not going to do this!" Rocky bellowed.

"Oh, yes, we are. And when you're ready to talk, you're going to scream the word 'TALK' as loud as you can. If you use that word and then you don't agree to help us out? Well, we're just going to keep right on going," Casey instructed.

"Talk, man," Rocky repeated.

"That's right. 'Talk.'"

"No, man. Seriously. You don't have to do this," Rocky stated flatly, until his voice cracked on the final word. "I'm saying it now. Talk. What the hell do you want me to do?"

The sun peeked over the mountains spilling golden sunlight as far as Kendra could see. Preakness danced beneath her as if he sensed what was about to happen.

On either side of her, Brad and Casey steadied their own mounts. From her position on the ridge, she scanned the wide, green valley below.

"When was he supposed to be here?" Brent asked.

"Anytime, now." Kendra never took her eyes off the black SUV parked at the side of the dirt road, below.

"Are we sure we can trust that guy? How do we know he wasn't full of shit?" Brent continued.

Casey cracked his knuckles. "He told the truth. Trust me."

Brad remained silent. He had barely said anything last night as Kendra, Brent, Casey and Mac laid out the plan in the front room. Kendra wasn't sure what that meant, but for right now, she was pretty sure it meant that Brad was pissed. Pain had riddled him last night and recovery could come later. Right now, *pissed* only helped the situation.

Same thing for Mac.

Right now, he had his mounted patrol, an all-volunteer Sheriff's Posse, which included Brent, on the opposite ridge. Kendra lifted her face and could barely make out the fifteen or so deputies lined up along the opposite side of the valley. Not far from the property entrance, along the main road, Mac waited with fifteen more.

When Mason showed up to pay off the men he'd hired to burn down her grandfather's house and murder her brother's wife, he'd find more than his henchman waiting for him.

Kendra chewed on a piece of straw, hoping that Mason would put up a fight. She wanted this over with. Permanently. Like Casey had said during the planning, if Mason pulled a gun, Kendra was to shoot to kill.

"There he is."

Kendra looked toward the opening of the valley that led from the main highway. Mason's black, extended-cab pickup kicked up a cloud of dust as it progressed over the dirt road.

The radio on her belt chirped. "Everyone, just take it easy," Mac's crackled voice warned. "Let him make the payoff before we move in. Kendra, that means you, too." Kendra didn't answer. She'd wait. She didn't want anything to get in the way of a conviction.

Michelle and Lacey both waited back at the house. Fuming.

Lacey thought they were all insane, but wished she could come along. If she'd been any stronger, Kendra might have let her. Michelle, on the other hand, would probably never speak to her again. She not only considered this half-baked plan crazy, but unethical. She had made no bones about telling Kendra her feelings on the matter, either. Only because she knew, or thought she knew, how badly Kendra wanted the man dead. Not captured. Not tried.

Dead.

But that was only a part of her. The other part, the side of Kendra that held decency and honor above all else, the part of her that had shown up last night, would only seek that end as a last resort.

No. They would try to bring Mason in alive to stand trial for three murders. And his thugs with him.

But if Mason so much as gave any of them a reason...

Well, life was rough sometimes.

The truck stopped and Mason climbed out. Alone. That was rather unusual. He generally had at least two of his thugs with him. Two men exited SUV. She hadn't recognized them last night, but she was fairly certain these were the same guys who had been picked up on her land during the fire. Through the powerful lenses of the binoculars, she made out every detail of their faces. The smaller of the two looked as disheveled as ever. The larger of the pair wore the same red hat she'd seen him in last time. The air around her turned foul as she recalled the putrid scent of his breath as he'd hovered over her, threatening her on the side of the road. Her cheek stung where he'd punched her. She tasted the blood and let it feed her thirst for justice, wiping away the memory and focusing instead on the fact that they'd nearly killed her sister and had taken Lenise's young life.

Red Hat carried a rifle. The second guy had a smaller weapon. A sawed-off shotgun, maybe? Kendra couldn't make it out for certain.

Casey raised a pair of binoculars of his own. "We've got one Remington and what looks like a

Winchester rifle. And let's not forget that Mason keeps a thirty-eight in an ankle holster." He lowered the glasses and smirked. "That nice fellow was just full of helpful information last night, wasn't he?"

"Disappointed you didn't have to go through with it?" asked Brad. "I wish you had."

Kendra's stomach knotted.

"No, little brother. I'm not. If I never have to do that again for as long as I live, I'll be just fine with that. I knew he'd cave. Rocky is just a petty thug." The tone in Casey's voice, bordering on the thin, jagged line between sadness and regret, eased the trepidation in her gut where he was concerned, but it lingered when he caught Brad's scoff.

Brad pulled out his sidearm and checked it over before placing it back into the holster on his hip. Casey mirrored the movements. "Ready."

Kendra picked up her radio. "Mac, they're making the payoff now."

Mac replied. "Move in."

Kendra looked at her brothers, each in turn. Today, they would end it. She lifted her reins in one hand and gently nudged Preakness forward with her booted heels. A sudden shout reached her from the valley floor and she focused her gaze on the group below. "Wait!"

Brad must have seen the same thing she had. Before Kendra could stop him, Brad raced down the steep hill in a dangerous slide of horseflesh and man.

Kendra picked up the radio. "Mac! Brad's halfway down the hill. We're going after him, but be advised. Lenise is with Mason. She's alive. Lenise is with Mason right now! Out!"

"Shit. Brad's going to kill him." Casey kicked his horse forward. Kendra followed and within a few harrowing moments, they reached the valley floor. Brad had a significant lead, but Preakness more than made up for the head start. Kendra crouched low in the saddle and soon drew beside her youngest brother.

Brad didn't even glance at her. He just kept riding. From the other side of the valley, the remaining deputies closed in.

Mason saw them coming. Too far away for Kendra to read his expression, Mason grabbed Lenise around the shoulders and pulled the pistol from his boot. Without preamble, without enough pause to even breathe, he put a bullet in the heads of both of his accomplices. They fell to the ground in a single heap of dead flesh and leather before the sound of the shots had time to cover the distance. He threw Lenise into the back of the truck and changed the clip. Then he leapt behind the wheel and sped further into the hills.

By the time they reached the dead men, Harold Mason was gone.

Brad turned his horse to go after them, but Kendra caught his reins. "Wait, Brad. We know she's alive. He's not going to hurt her now. There is nothing up that road but the old mine. He's trapped, and he knows it. Right now, she is the only card he has left to play."

"She's alive," her brother whispered.

Kendra smiled. "I know, son. I know..."

"Go. I'll be fine." Lacey, struggling with her good

arm, pushed herself higher against the pillows on her bed.

"I can't just leave you here."

"Yes, you can. You have no idea what kind of trouble those guys will get into by themselves. All that testosterone... including my sister!"

Michelle paced from one side of Lacey's bedroom to the other, pushed the curtains out of the way and watched for any sign that Kendra and the others might be coming back. A deputy in a squad car sat in the driveway with strict orders not to let her off the property. But that wouldn't stop her from saddling Bethany and crossing the range. She'd ridden around the property enough in the past few months to know her way around, just fine, thanks. What if Kendra was hurt? What if she needed her?

No. She'd told Kendra she'd stay here and wait for her. "I'm supposed to keep an eye on you."

"Puh-lease. If I could stay on a horse right now, I'd go with you. Now, *you* have to make sure they're okay."

"I don't know, Lace."

"Fine. I'll go." Lacey swung her legs over the edge of the bed. Michelle sprinted to her side and put both hands on her shoulders. "You lie right back down. You're in no condition to go anywhere."

"You are," Lacey returned, flatly.

A sigh from the deepest part of her, where her conscience lived, blew past her lips. "Fine. I'll go. I'll come in from the backside and she'll never know I'm there, right? I'll make sure they're okay and I'll deadhead it right back here."

That should be fine. She'd ride around behind the

old mine and come into the valley through the tree line. Kendra would never even see her. Shouldn't take more than two hours, tops.

"Great idea."

Michelle heard the smile in Lacey's voice and studied her friend for a moment. Her lips twitched into a grin. "Are you going to be okay?"

Lacey brushed her fingertips over the thick bandage on the side of her face. The grin faltered, but didn't fade. She nodded. "Yeah, I'll be okay. Someday."

Michelle suspected she wasn't talking about being alone in the house. Lacey referred to her injury, the permanent disfigurement she'd have to see in the mirror for the rest of her life. But she was tough, and in no immediate danger.

Michelle squared her shoulders and took a deep breath. "Okay, then. I'll do it. You stay in bed."

"Aye, aye, Captain."

Michelle hurried down the hall, caught herself on the doorjamb with one hand and spun into the room she once more shared with Kendra. Once she'd changed out of her nightgown and dressed in her jeans, boots and a thick, cotton tee-shirt, she made for the barn.

Almost there.

She crossed the threshold into the barn and stopped to see if anyone followed her. Several horses stamped in their stalls. If they hoped she would turn them into the pasture for their morning graze, they would be disappointed.

She counted eight men on the property, and none of them knew where Kendra and her brothers had gone. None of them knew that the woman they respected and trusted risked her life to save the ranch and bring a murderer to justice.

Could this really be happening? Was it really just a few months ago that she'd believed her life was boring?

Bethany whinnied a greeting. Michelle stroked her nose before she entered the stall and attached a lead rope to the metal ring at the base of the horse's halter.

Chuck, one of the newer hands, approached from the back of the barn. "You going for a ride?"

Michelle forced a smile. "Yeah. I need to clear my head a little after last night."

"You want some company? Kendra says you're not supposed to go off by yourself, you know."

"I'm a big girl, Chuck. I'm sure I can handle a little trot around the ranch."

He looked at the ground. "I'm real sorry to hear about Brad's little wife. She was a right pretty girl."

"She was a wonderful young woman. Thank you."

His head snapped up and he eyed her with more attention than Michelle understood. After a moment or two, he tipped his hat. "Well, you enjoy your ride. If you need anything, just shout out. I'm sure somebody will be close enough to hear you."

She certainly hoped not.

"I'll do that."

He left the barn the same way he'd come in. Michelle finished dressing Bethany and made a point to leave through the opposite doors.

One slow step after another, Bethany plodded along beside the corrals and then out through the back gate. When she reached the top of the first rise, Michelle looked behind her. No one paid any attention. Each man went about his work as if she weren't there. The deputy stayed in his car. She faced toward the front again, dug her heels into Bethany's ribs and plunged over the hilltop.

The old mine couldn't be more than a thirty-minute ride.

Kendra crept behind the fence line around the Old Sutton Mine. Behind her, her brothers followed. Who would have thought the skills they'd learned from years of deer hunting these mountains would pay off in such a big way? Even if he listened for their footfalls, Mason wouldn't be able to hear them.

A hawk screamed from somewhere overhead. The whole range seemed to wait to see what would happen next. When she reached a fallen log, she crouched behind it and motioned for her brothers to join her.

Mason's truck rested at an odd angle below her, as if he'd stopped in a hurry.

"Look," she whispered, pointing down a steep slope to the mouth of the mine.

"Do you see Lenise?" Brad craned his neck.

"Get down, dumb-shit." Casey grabbed Brad's shoulder and dragged him backward. "Just because we can't see them doesn't mean they can't see us. Stay put." He turned his attention back to Kendra. "Both of you."

Kendra narrowed her gaze. Right. "What are you going to do?"

"Circle around behind and see what I can see. You people make too much noise. Stay. Here," he ordered deliberately.

Casey disappeared behind a boulder and within a few seconds reappeared a short distance up the hill.

"Why does he get to have all the fun?" Brad asked.

"Because he's been trained, I guess. BUD/s training paid off." Kendra caught movement on the far side of the mine. How the hell did Casey make it all the way over there already?

The low branches on the ancient Joshua tree swung as a horse's head poked through the needles. Kendra's heart clenched. It couldn't be her. God, don't let it be her...

It was her.

Michelle pushed Bethany through the branches and pulled her to a stop in plain sight of the truck. And anyone with eyes.

Kendra closed her eyes and swore under her breath.

Brad groaned. "What is she doing here?"

Kendra opened her eyes again and gripped the handle of her pistol. "Being a pain in my ass. What else?"

"Where are you going?"

Kendra crept past her brother. "I'm going to get her out of the damn way. Wait here."

Damn that woman's foolish impertinence. Why couldn't she just sit tight and wait at home for her like a normal woman? Why did she have to come after her like she needed rescuing or something?

She only made it half way back down the hill when a shot erupted from the mine entrance. She spun toward the commotion, and then glanced back to Michelle. She'd heard it, too. So had Bethany, who pranced and crow-hopped too close to the steepest part of the hill for her comfort.

Kendra dashed up the hill. "Get down!"

Bethany snorted and one of her hind legs slid off the embankment. The old mare caught herself and stamped solid ground with anxious, skittish movements. Kendra's heart leapt into her throat. Michelle's bronzed cheeks paled.

"What's going on?" Her voice trembled. White fingers worked the reins and pulled against Bethany's wide-open mouth.

After what seemed like an eternity, Kendra reached Michelle's side. She pulled her from the saddle, lost her balance and landed on her back. Michelle rested on top of her, her breath sweet against Kendra's neck.

If anything happened to her...

She shoved the thoughts aside. Nothing had happened to her. At least, not yet.

Heat stole up the back of her neck. She narrowed her eyes. "I don't have time right now, but when this is over, I want to know just what the hell you were thinking, coming up here. God damn it, woman, can you do nothing you're told to do?"

Michelle pushed herself off Kendra's chest and growled. By the time she reached her feet, Kendra had found hers as well. "Don't you scold me, Kendra Williams, when you're up here getting shot at!"

Kendra grabbed her by the upper arm and dragged her behind the tree line. She took up a position behind a tree and held Michelle behind her with one arm. Where was Casey? Had he made it into the mine? Where had the shot come from?

Across the narrow space, she found her youngest brother. Brad still crouched behind the log, right were Kendra had left him. At least someone could listen to directions.

She leaned her back against the tree and took a deep breath. "Mason didn't exactly give up peacefully. The good news is, Lenise is alive."

She waited for the shock to play across Michelle's features. One second, she beamed, and the next, her brows knotted and she frowned. "What's the bad news?"

Kendra indicated the abandoned mine with a jerk of her head. "She's in there with Mason. As you've probably guessed, he's armed."

"Yeah, I figured that part out all by myself. Where's Mac? Where's Brent? And Casey?"

"Brent stayed with the Posse. They're on the their way, but they were at least a half hour behind by horseback. Mac's on his way, too, I'm sure, but you can't exactly race over these roads. For right now, babe, we're on our own."

"So, what are we going to do?"

She cocked an eyebrow at Michelle. "We?"

"Yeah, we."

"You're going to get back and stay the hell out of the way." She shook her head. "What were you thinking?"

"I was worried about you." A slight blush moved over her cheeks.

Before Kendra realized what she was doing, her fingers traced the line of Michelle's jaw and her thumb brushed over her lips. God, she loved her so much, she could taste it.

Michelle placed one hand over Kendra's and tilted her cheek into her palm. "What are we going to do?" she repeated.

"I'm pretty sure Casey made it inside the mine. We're supposed to wait for him to let us know what's going on, but after those shots, I'm changing the plan." She took her pistol from its holster and checked her ammunition.

Six shots.

And she left her rifle with Brad. Damn.

She had little choice. Wait here and risk the lives of her family, or go in... guns blazing.

Or was there another option?

Michelle wouldn't like it. She studied her expression. Filled with trust and confidence, she gazed up at her with wide eyes. Where did her faith come from? What was it about Kendra that made Michelle love her so much? Nothing about Kendra seemed worthy of it.

She meant only to tease her lips with her own. But once she tasted them, she deepened the kiss until the world disappeared, for just that one reflection in time. She shouldn't be wasting time, but...

But what if it was the last time she ever saw her? What if she didn't come back from what she was planning to do?

Michelle's hands played over her back, working her muscles into knots of desire and wanting. She wanted Michelle with her forever. If she made it through the next fifteen minutes without getting herself killed, she would do anything in the world to keep her.

She'd turn the ranch over to Brent and move to Las Vegas if that's what it took. But the thought of spending even an hour without Michelle hurt too damn much.

A moan escaped Michelle's throat and vibrated against Kendra's cheek. She broke the kiss and took just one more moment to inhale the sweet, soft scent of the only women she could ever love. She committed it to memory and it became a part of her.

Then Kendra turned away.

"What are you going to do?" Michelle took several steps behind Kendra as she headed for the steep embankment above the mine.

"Wait here." Kendra offered a grin, as if she tried to reassure her. "I'll be right back."

Michelle's gut clenched. Something was very wrong here. What exactly did she plan to do? She hugged herself and waited in the tree line, as Kendra had asked.

Kendra half-walked and half-slid down the dirt and rock wall. She disappeared for a few minutes and the only indication she was there came from the clatter of loose stones sliding down the hill. When she reappeared on the old dirt road, she took up position in the center of it.

For the first time, Michelle noticed Brad on the opposite side of the mine. She stared at him and he returned a bewildered expression of his own. Kendra holstered her gun and spread her feet in the dust.

Oh, no!

She wouldn't!

"Mason! If you're even half a man, get your ass out here. I'm the one you want. Leave the girl alone."

The world stopped spinning. Even the trees stopped breathing. Was she completely out of her mind? Michelle's heart raced until she thought it might explode. Tunnel vision narrowed on where Kendra stood her ground. Pride and honor surrounded her like a cloud of protection.

But clouds can't stop a bullet.

"You hear me, Coward! Show yourself."

A shot blasted from the mouth of the cave. The bullet landed within a few inches of Kendra's right boot, but she never even flinched. Instead, she shook her head and continued to taunt Mason. "Is that the best you got? You shoot like a girl. Why don't you come on out here and then maybe you can get close enough to hit something besides trees and dirt."

Mason appeared in the opening. In one hand, he held a pistol. The other formed a fist at his side. There was no sign of Lenise or Casey. One slow step at a time, he moved toward Kendra. Michelle craned her neck to see around the truck. Mason kept moving until he was only a few feet away from Kendra.

They stared at each other for a full minute, ticked away by Michelle's heartbeat.

"So, you think you got the balls to take me in? You ain't the law. You're nothing but a goddamn dyke who thinks she's a man. You plan on taking me down?"

Kendra nodded. "Yup."

"You think you're going to take me alive?"

"Not if I can help it."

Mason's eyes narrowed and the smile faded from his lips. "You're not taking me anywhere."

Faster than she'd ever seen someone move, Mason

raised his gun and fired at Kendra. He missed and Kendra returned the blast, but not before Mason ducked behind the fender of his truck. He fired again and this time, Kendra fell to the ground. Half-crawling, half-dragging one leg, Kendra took cover behind a large rock. Brad opened fire from his perch on the opposite hill. Mason fired back.

Blood dripped to the ground next to Kendra's leg. Michelle bit her lip until she tasted her own blood. Kendra grimaced and tied her red bandana around her thigh.

Shots continued to fill the air and Kendra motioned for Michelle to get down. Michelle fell to her bottom and put her hands over her head. Kendra was hit. Brad was in the line of fire. Her life was in danger and all she could do was to hide behind a tree? Tears burned behind her closed eyelids.

Metallic echoes hung in the air between the rock canyon walls, intensified by the canopy of trees. Then a silence descended over the hillside, deafening and fragile in the emptiness.

"Mason? You 'bout done?" Kendra called into the stillness. Her voice was tense, as though she gritted her teeth.

"Not on your life, you bitch. You're going to pay for everything you ever cost me!"

"What the hell are you talking about, Mason? You brought all this on yourself. Let it end here. Give it up."

"Your family killed my father!" Mason screamed. "Do know what it's like to watch your mother die inside, for weeks on end, and then find her –" Mason's voice cracked again, this time hard enough to make him stop speaking for a moment. "Find her dead? Do you?!" he bellowed.

"I had nothing to do with that. I'm sorry it happened, but you can't keep doing this."

"It was your fault! Your goddamned lawsuit telling all those lies about my father! You left us with nothing! You left me with nothing!"

"What do you want me to do about that?" Kendra returned, glancing to Brad's position in the stand of trees.

"What do I want you to do?" Mason laughed. "I want you to die!"

Mason stood, coming into clear view as though he were invincible. He rushed toward Kendra's hiding place, his gun gripped tightly in his hand, pointed forward.

"Kendra!" Michelle screamed.

Kendra leapt to her feet, wincing at the pain in her injured leg, and leveled her gun at Mason. She pulled the trigger once and Mason stopped short, his eyes wide as a bloom of red soaked through the front of his shirt.

He fell to the ground, twitched and then became still.

It seemed as though the earth stood still. The breeze stopped and the branches of the trees seemed to freeze. A moment later, a soft wind blew through the branches and a hawk called from somewhere in the blue.

Michelle pushed herself up to find Kendra balancing herself with most of her weight on her good leg, limping forward. She moved carefully in the direction of Mason's body. Blood – a lot of blood – pooled in the dirt. It looked black as it formed a layer of thick, macabre mud.

When she reached Mason's body, she picked up Mason's gun and tossed it out of reach. She felt for a pulse and then waved at Michelle to come out of hiding. "He's dead," she confirmed, her voice shaking with a high pitch Michelle had never heard before.

Shrill sirens in the distance sliced the quiet. Michelle rushed down the hill, falling twice before she reached Kendra. Kendra lost her balance when Michelle hit her, arms wide, but steadied when she closed her arms around her. "You fool. You crazy, stubborn fool." She kissed every part of Kendra she could reach.

When she finished, she asked, "Where is Brad?" She turned toward the tree line. "Brad?" she yelled, her voice still as frightened as a child. There was no response.

"He was on the hill, over there," Michelle pointed in the direction of Brad's perch. "Where you left him..."

"Brad?!" Kendra called again.

This time, when there was no answer, Kendra pulled away from Michelle's embrace and limped toward the embankment. She pulled herself slowly up the loose dirt and growth while Michelle found she couldn't move. She couldn't force her legs to take even a single step.

Kendra grunted and hissed as she climbed another step and the pain in those sounds, both physical and emotional, ripped Michelle away from her terrified roots. She hurried to Kendra's side and helped her up the final two excruciating steps.

Sun filtered through the branches of the trees and created a dappled golden light in the underbrush. Brad looked like he might have fallen asleep there, surrounded by moist, fragrant earth. His face wasn't tormented like Ken Bastian's had been. His eyes were closed and his lashes fell like soft fans against his cheeks.

Kendra stood silently for what seemed like minutes but couldn't have been more than a second or two before she fell onto her knees beside her brother. Her cry came like a wounded animal; harsh and guttural. It ripped from her entire body, each pore contributing to the emptiness of the sound. "No!"

Michelle fell to the damp earth beside Kendra, unsure how to hold someone whose entire heart had turned to a vortex of swirling agony. It had been different with Brad last night. She wasn't in love with Brad. As Kendra's heart tore into millions of jagged pieces, so did Michelle's.

The ground on which they knelt was soaked with blood. The realization choked her as her gaze fell on the wound in Brad's side. He'd bled out on the hillside, but he'd never cried out; never called for help.

Kendra picked up her brother's head and shoulders and cradled him in her lap, her own blood soaking into Brad's hair and staining his cheek. Her shoulders shook with each sob she released until she sat in statue-like stillness.

"Breathe, baby," whispered Michelle. "You have to breathe."

"Kendra Williams, I swear to God, one of these days I'm going to kick your ass!" Mac huffed his way to where they sat and bellowed through his trembling, thick jowls. "I don't give a rat's ass if you are a woman. You and your brothers were supposed to wait for us!"

Mac's words vanished in an echo as he apparently noticed his son-in-law's body cradled in Kendra's arms.

"We couldn't risk it, Mac." Kendra seemed to come

out of a trance, placing Brad gently back on the soft ground and then struggling to her feet as she wiped her nose on her sleeve.

The sound of shuffling gravel broke the quiet. Casey stumbled from the mine shaft opening. Blood soaked his shirt and hands, streaming from a gash near his forehead that matted his hair. Brent reached him just in time to catch him before he fell. "Mason..."

Michelle and Mac rushed to his side, Kendra supported between them.

"We got him, Case. Take it easy, now," Kendra said from between gritted teeth as she knelt on her good knee beside him.

Casey gripped Mac's hand until his knuckles shown white through his own blood. His brows narrowed and he stared first at Brent and then at his sister. "Don't let him... go ... don't let him, ahhh God, this freakin' hurts."

"He's not going anywhere. He's dead, Case. Hang on. Help is coming."

Mac tried to pull his hand free. "Let go, Casey. I've got to find Lenise. Where's Lenise?"

Casey wouldn't let go of Mac's hands. "Don't go..."

"Casey, where is my daughter? Where is she?"

Mac tried to shove away from the group and head to the opening of the mine. Brent reappeared at the mouth of the mine and intercepted him before he could duck through the low entrance.

"No, Mac. You don't want to go in there, man."

"Where is my daughter?" Mac's voice was whiskey rough and pain driven.

Casey seemed to struggle with his ability to speak.

His Adam's apple bounced against the weight of the words he couldn't form. His lips parted, but nothing came out.

"I tried to get to her, Mac," Casey whispered. He sounded as if he couldn't breathe, like his throat closed over the words. "I was too late. I'm sorry."

Mac tore himself loose from Casey's grip and rushed into the mine. In the next moment, a bellow made that much more ghostly by the tight walls of the mine ripped across the soft morning breeze.

Twenty-One

Kendra heaved a bale of hay from the loft onto the barn floor. She gritted her teeth against the pain in her leg. It wasn't anything serious, apparently. More like a graze than a gunshot. She'd hurt herself worse branding calves. If she could work through that, she could work through this. The horses didn't stop eating just because her family was dying.

She'd spent the last four days coming to terms with who she was; who she was supposed to be. She'd used her new computer to look up newspaper articles about Mason's family. His mother hadn't been able to handle the publicity surrounding the trial. Kendra had been too involved in her own life to notice, apparently. She remembered seeing the woman at the court appearances, but of course, had never spoken to her. She remembered seeing her son, as well. He'd only been a teenager then. For some reason, Kendra had always thought Mason was older than her, but he was younger by five years. Only seventeen at the time of the trial, he'd changed greatly over the intervening years. Hate and greed could do that to a person, she supposed.

Still, Kendra had been so wrapped up in pleasing the state, suing the charter company so she could keep the kids together – with her – she hadn't been more than passively concerned about the other family. If she'd only known...

Would she have done anything differently? Would she have stopped the lawsuit? Worked out a settlement that everyone could live with? She didn't know, she realized as she tossed another bale over the edge of the loft. And now, it was too late.

For all of them.

"Crap!" Michelle's voice rang from the lower level, ripping Kendra out of one nightmare and placing her foursquare into another.

Michelle.

Kendra closed her eyes, pulled off her work gloves and placed her hands on her hips. After a cleansing breath that didn't clean a damn thing, she looked over the edge. Michelle stood in the middle of the barn, almost exactly where Casey had built the water boarding contraption. She wore a pair of jeans that hugged every curve of her hips and thighs, a sleeveless, ribbed t-shirt and boots. Her hair was as wild as that first day she'd arrived, when she'd spend hours driving through the desert with the top down on her Mustang. Only now, the wildness was more natural, coming from the fact that she had grown to a part of this place. Almost a real cowgirl.

"You coming in for lunch, honey?" Michelle asked.

The diminutive sliced through Kendra's heart. She

gritted her teeth again. Pain was pain. Didn't matter it if was her leg or her heart. "No."

"You have to eat something."

"No, I don't. I'm fine. I have work to do."

"You've been out here for days, Kendra. How much work can there possibly be? You need to come inside and spend some time with your family. This isn't healthy, and you know it."

"Healthy?" Kendra asked, scoffing even as her heart was breaking. "Healthy? You think I give a shit if it's healthy?"

"You need to grieve, Kendra. We've suffered a huge loss, and—"

"We? We've suffered a loss?" Kendra threw her gloves onto the nearest bale and marched down the back stairs as quickly as she could. The pain in her leg shot through her entire side with each step but still didn't measure close to pain in her gut. "He was like a son to me, my brother. I was like his mother. Now, I've never had a kid of my own, so I can't be sure, but you can't tell me that losing a child could hurt any worse than this. So don't give me any crap about grieving and loss. Nothing will make this better. Nothing."

"I didn't mean..." Michelle's lip quivered. "I just meant that you might need some help getting through this. Counseling maybe, or at least let us help. Let your family help you heal."

"You're not my family. And I don't need any help. Not from them, and not from you."

How could she let them help her heal? How could ever allow herself to heal? How could she ever not hurt again when her brother, and his wife, and his baby were all dead; nearly buried? How could she go on loving Michelle, loving the Heartland, when she had failed all of them so miserably?

"Go away, Michelle. Go back to Las Vegas and your real life. There is nothing left for you here."

"You're here," she whispered, her voice trailing off into a future past that didn't exist anymore.

"No, I'm not. Not anymore."

Blue skies covered the world in a misleading canopy of pure light and joy. Birds danced about the sky as they raced from the branches of one Russian Olive tree to another. Somewhere in the distance, water sped over the rocks lining the Randall River. Michelle forced one foot in front of the other over the damp grass of the Randall City Cemetery.

It was done.

Kendra refused her offer to help her get back to the car. They hadn't shared more than three words since the fight. For three days, Kendra had been more than withdrawn; she'd been non-existent. At first, Michelle had assumed it had to do with her injuries, or with Casey's. Casey had been released from the hospital just this morning, while Kendra had never been admitted. Both of them would be fine with some rest. At least, physically.

Lacey attended the funeral in a wheelchair for no other reason than her doctor insisted. Even now, she fussed at the nurse Kendra had hired to help her for the day.

Michelle glanced back at the two graves flanked with matching mounds of dirt covered in cheap indoor-outdoor carpeting. The caskets, one gunmetal grey and the other a pink so soft that it looked white in sunlight, would soon be lowered into the ground and covered. It was so... final. Unchangeable.

Michelle stumbled over a broken branch. Kendra caught her arm before she fell. The touch of her hands on Michelle's arm burned her straight to the bottom of her lungs. "Thanks," she managed to whisper.

"Yeah."

They reached Kendra's new King-cab truck and settled Lacey and the nurse into the back seat. Brent collapsed the wheelchair and put it in the bed. Casey sat in the back while Brent slid behind the wheel. Michelle scooted to the center of the front seat while Kendra climbed in behind her.

Michelle closed her eyes. She'd finished packing this morning, before the service. All she had to do now was change into traveling clothes and she could be in Las Vegas by ten o'clock tonight.

She didn't want to leave. For the past days she'd prayed that Kendra would ask her to stay. Instead, she'd insisted she leave, right now. Right after the funeral.

"Let's go home."

Lacey interjected from the back seat. "I live in Las Vegas, in case you forgot. I want to go home, too."

"No," Kendra barked.

"Michelle, can I ride back with you? My car is apparently still on vacation at McCarran Airport."

Michelle glanced at Kendra. A single muscle in her strong jaw pulsed and her lips formed a solid line of determination and derision. But Lacey was a grown woman. And she was right. Their homes were in Las Vegas. "Sure, hon. No problem."

Brent sighed and pulled out of the parking lot. "When are you leaving?"

"As soon as we get back and Lacey packs."

"That soon?" Casey asked. "I figured you'd stay the night and get an early start in the morning."

Michelle shook her head. If she wasn't going to stay, if Kendra didn't want her to stay forever, then the sooner she left, the better for everyone. What good would another night do? What purpose would be served by torturing herself with glimpses of a life she could never have?

"No," she answered. "I've been here too long, already."

Two months later...

"I'd like to have the new campaign up and running no later than the thirtieth."

Michelle nodded her head and forced a smile. "No problem, Brandy. I'll set up the photo shoots for next week and take some prelim shots before I leave today."

"Are you alright? Ever since you got back, you've been distracted."

Brandy Kincaid, one of the wealthiest women in Las Vegas and Michelle's biggest client, tilted her head and leveled her with eyes so blue they seemed completely out of place surrounded by her sun-tanned skin and black hair. If those eyes were anything besides gorgeous, they were intuitive.

She was right. She'd been distracted. Even the simplest tasks seemed to make her weak and tired. If she didn't snap out of her funk soon, she would take her mother's advice and talk to someone. Still, she lied, "I'm alright, Bran. Really. It's just been a rough couple of months. That's all. But we'll be right on top of things for you, don't worry. The Touchdown Club is going to be the biggest party-spot on the strip and your holiday campaign will be up and running well before Christmas. I promise."

"I have no doubt."

An awkward silence filled the space separating them over a football shaped table on the third balcony of the nightclub. At only four in the afternoon, dozens of patrons sat at the football-shaped bar, two stories below. Michelle glanced over the railing to peer down to the main floor. She tried to think of a good angle for a picture, but instead, she heard the ghost of Kendra's voice telling her what a flamboyant and wasteful environment it was.

She swallowed and looked up at Bran. "So, how are things with you? We haven't talked in a while."

There. Small talk. She could manage small talk.

Bran folded her arms over her chest. "She's still sleeping around, if that's what you're asking."

"No," Michelle replied. Honestly, she hadn't even remembered the problems Brandy had been having with the wife she'd married in Canada several years earlier. Normally so in tune with her friends and what happened in their lives, it was another level of proof that she was losing it. "I really wasn't thinking about that, at all, Bran. Is it that bad?"

She snorted. "I don't care. There hasn't been any love there for a very long time. If it weren't for the pre-nup, I'd cut her loose."

"But, it's your money. And you have grounds, right?"

"Not really. For a divorce? Sure. But the pre-nup says she gets half of everything, no matter what."

"Why would you agree to that?" Michelle shook her head.

"Because I was a goddamn fool in love. And half of me thinks she's a witch. Have you ever felt like that, Michelle?" She leaned forward and placed her elbows on the edge of the table. "Have you ever felt that twitch in your gut, right here," she pointed to her solar plexus, "and it just twists you up until you can't breathe?"

Had she ever felt it? God, yes, she'd felt it. And she still experienced the impact every time she lay down at night, alone, and her dreams drifted back to a quiet woman on a horse, riding through the stars of the horizon like she owned them.

She felt it right then, as Kendra's face drifted in front of her closed eyes.

"Well, that's what it felt like. And I should have run like hell. You can believe me; the next time, if there is a next time, I will. Sometimes, I swear, I could just kill her."

"Probably not a good idea, Bran," she concluded. "But running away? That's got my vote."

Michelle took the brass and glass elevator to the ground floor of the club. She was supposed to meet Lacey for a drink at one of their favorite spots; a tiny theme bar in the casino where Lacey used to schlep drinks.

It wasn't late, but Michelle yawned. Her limbs felt heavy. No, that wasn't it. She felt old. And tired. And it had nothing to do with throwing herself into work she couldn't concentrate on and everything to do with the fact she hadn't had a decent night's sleep in weeks.

She'd call Lacey from her car and cancel. Maybe if she went straight home and crawled into bed, things would seem better in the morning. Of course, there was always that possibility that she would stay there forever.

The electronic buzz of her cell phone vibrated against her hip. She pulled it from her pocket and slid the icon to the edge of the screen. It was Lacey.

"You're still coming tonight, right?"

Michelle sighed. "I don't know. I'm really beat."

"You can't bail on me, now. You promised."

"What's the big deal. Can't we do this another night?"

"No. We have to do it tonight. I reserved a table. Come on. You know you need to get out."

"Okay. I'll be there in a few minutes. I'm at the other end of the strip. But I can't stay out all night, Lace. Seriously, I'm exhausted."

"We'll see." Lacey disconnected and Michelle pulled the phone away from her ear and stared at it for a moment.

What's up with her?

It had taken Michelle over a week to convince Lacey to come out of her apartment at all. She was recovering well physically, but the rest of her was taking a little longer. She was still embarrassed by the jagged, angry scar on her cheek, and she had been suffering from increasing anxiety attacks for the past few weeks.

Then, Lacey had called out of the blue, yesterday, insisting they meet at their old haunt. Michelle should be thankful she was making progress, not contemplating standing her up.

If Lacey could do it, so could she.

Almost a half-hour later, Michelle swerved her convertible into the valet parking lane at the hotel. George greeted her with the same wide smile that he always did. He pointed around the bend in the drive and she circled to the next available valet.

Nothing around here had changed. A sense of deja-vu overwhelmed her for a minute before she realized it wasn't deja-vu at all. This was how it all started. Six months earlier, she'd pulled into this driveway to meet with Lacey about her sister's ranch. She swallowed at the irony.

Yeah. Nothing had changed, except for *everything*. Michelle would never be the same. Nothing and nobody would ever be the same again.

From out of nowhere, something appeared in front of her car. Michelle closed her eyes, slammed on the brakes and grimaced as the tires made a short, loud squeal that echoed from the high ceilings of the elaborate hotel entrance. What the hell? Did she hit something?

She opened first one eye, and then the other. Someone stood in front of her car. A placard covered most of the person, from above their head to their waist.

Then her eyes fell on the poster. A string of letters jumped off the board, all lower case... all one word.

www.willyou.marryme

"Seriously, you asshole!? Risking your life to advertise a website? Are you insane?"

The poster lowered.

Michelle's heart leapt out of her chest. Her lungs emptied.

Kendra, complete with her cowboy hat set back just an inch or so off her forehead, smiled at her through the windshield.

Michelle couldn't breathe.

Kendra circled to Michelle's window and leaned inside. "Hey, Michelle? You're blocking traffic."

"Oh, my God, Kendra! What are you doing here?"

She lifted the sign several inches and laughed. "I thought that was pretty obvious."

"But, I thought you didn't want me." Damn it. She would *not* cry.

"Yeah, well, nobody has ever accused me of being smart."

Michelle opened the door and Kendra backed up a step to let her out. Then she set the poster in the backseat of the car and took Michelle into her arms. She smelled of open range and happiness with a hint of the spices she missed so much.

Kendra pulled back slightly and focused her attention on Michelle's face. "Listen, Michelle, I've had a lot of time to think. And I've come to a conclusion that I hope you'll agree with. The way I see it, Brad had it all." Her voice caught when she mentioned her brother's name and she cast her gaze to the high, decorated ceiling of the portico as though she were trying not to cry. When she looked back at Michelle, her green eyes bore directly into her soul. "Brad had it all, and he died fighting for what he loved. How do I honor his memory if I'm not willing to fight for us? If I have one shot at happiness, I think he'd want me to take it."

"Kendra," Michelle interrupted only to have one of Kendra's strong fingers settle over her lips.

"Let me finish. Please. I was a fool to let you go. I love you, Michelle. I've loved you from the first minute you walked into my house. I want to spend the rest of my life with you, starting right here, right now."

So much for not crying. Michelle pulled Kendra tight against her and sobbed. All of the pain, loneliness and fear of the past six months poured out and disintegrated in the warm, Las Vegas air. Michelle sniffled and squeezed Kendra until she thought she might lose feeling in her arms. "I love you, too, baby. I've been so lost ever since I left the Heartland. I want to go home, Kendra."

"Home?"

Michelle pulled away and looked up into the most beautiful green eyes she had ever seen. They looked like prairie grass in the sunlight. She wanted to lose herself in them again, and forever.

"Home, Kendra. Take me home."

The End

D<small>ID YOU ENJOY READING</small> *L<small>OVING THE</small> H<small>EARTLAND</small>*
<small>BY</small> M<small>ARJORIE</small> J<small>ONES</small>?

Please leave a short review on Amazon.com!
You can write to the author directly at her website:

www.marjoriejones.weebly.com

About the Author

Marjorie has been writing professionally for more than 10 years in various capacities and is an award-winning novelist. Nominated twice for the coveted Romantic Times Reviewers Choice Award for Best Romance from a Small Press, she currently resides in Utah with her wife and their shared eight natural, step, and elected children. She is the author of Marko Loves His Family, Hope, Hunting Camion and Dance in My Heart from Indie Artist Press as well as several full-length novels you can find listed in the front of this book.

LET INDIE ARTIST PRESS HELP
YOU PUBLISH YOUR NOVEL!

Are you a writer? Looking to become an author through the art of publishing your novel, poetry, how-to book or memoir? If you've written a book and would like to learn more about the immense benefits of self-publishing, we'd like to help.

Indie Artist Press is the first non-publisher publisher dedicated to helping YOU succeed.

What makes us different from a vanity press?

A vanity press charges you for the privilege of printing/publishing your book. They do not:

- Edit your book for grammar or typing errors
- Edit your book for continuity
- Edit your book for characterization or plot
- Care, one way or another, whether you succeed
- Care, one way or another, whether they are selling quality literature

They don't care because you have already paid them! But that won't stop them from keeping 80% or more of each retail sale price, paying you only about 20% in royalties. You've paid the costs of publishing, and they keep the lion's share of your money. Sound fair? We didn't think so, either.

Indie Artist Press will charge you less and do so much more! *We can* :

- Edit your book for grammar, typing errors
- Edit your book for continuity, characterization, plot
- Design a customized book cover
- Format your manuscript for print and digital distribution
- Help you set up your payee account through your bookseller of choice so that 100% of the proceeds of your book are delivered directly to you!
- Help you design your website and social marketing venues
- Create promotional materials to help you market your book
- Work with you to create a payment plan that fits your needs and overall goals for success

We have several plans to choose from, all for far less than you can expect to pay to a vanity press, or even a "traditional" publisher. When you "sell" your book to a publisher through a publishing contract, you are giving away up to 90% or more of your money for the rest of your life, and sometimes even longer. (When a publishing house contracts your book for the life of the copyright, that's your natural life, plus another 70 years.)

Why not invest in your own product by securing top-of-the-line editing and other services and then keep 100% of your earnings for the next several decades and beyond?

Please visit indieartistpress.com to learn more about how we can help you publish your first book, or your next book, with affordable, professional services.

Indie Artist Press

Written Tapestries
by Beckyjean G. Cooke
A Collection of Poetry
ISBN: 978-1625220134
Now Available!

www.ingramcontent.com/pod-product-compliance
Lightning Source LLC
Chambersburg PA
CBHW020501260626
47156CB00006B/1819